A Unique Space for Us

A Fated Mate Romantasy Thriller

A Trianah Metro Series
Book 1

Chantell Monique

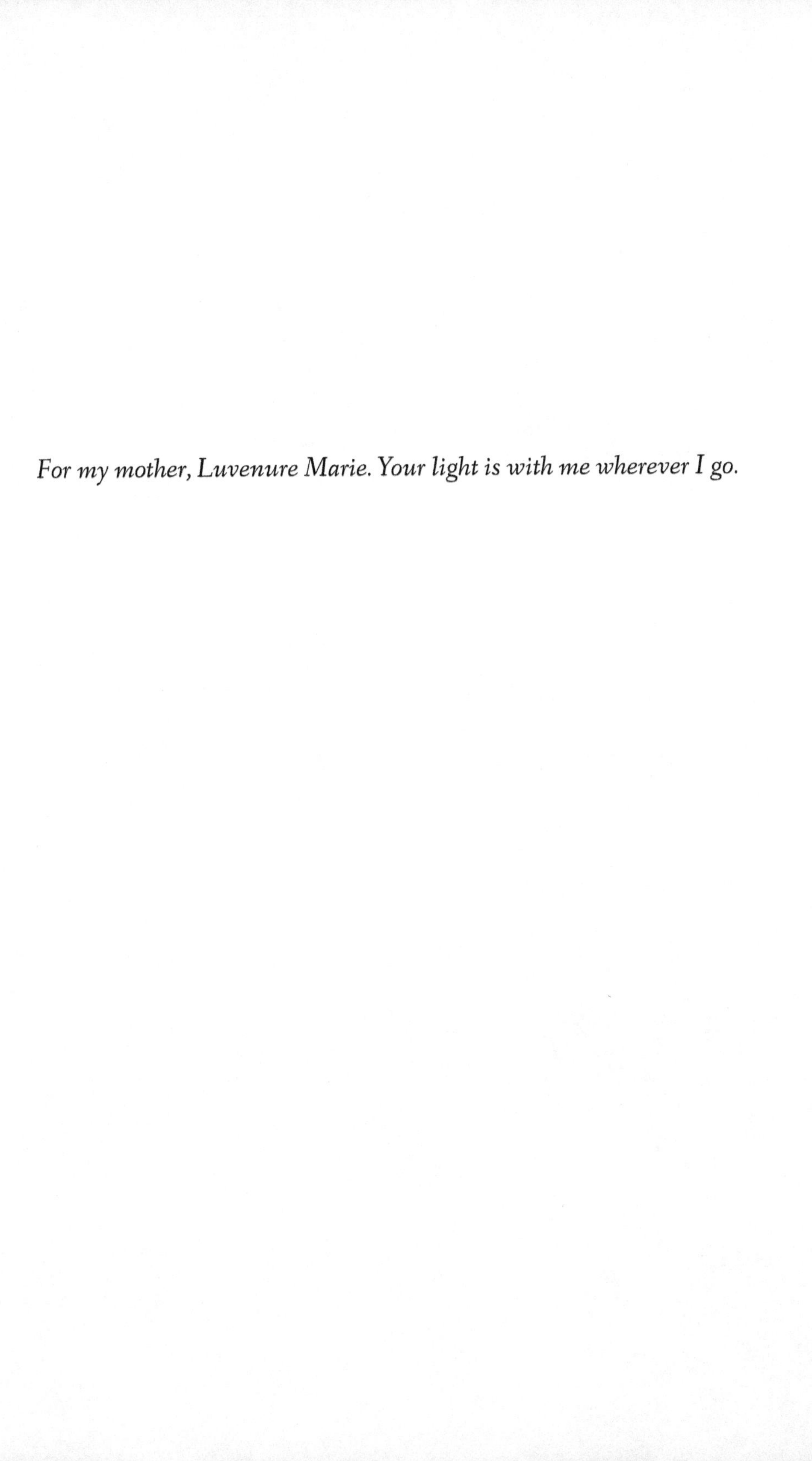

For my mother, Luvenure Marie. Your light is with me wherever I go.

Author's Note

Mental illness, Suicidal thoughts (ideation), Grief, Bullying (by parent), Suicide (off-page), Murder (descriptions of violent murders), Child loss (off-page).

If these topics are sensitive for you, please be mindful. Take great care of yourself.

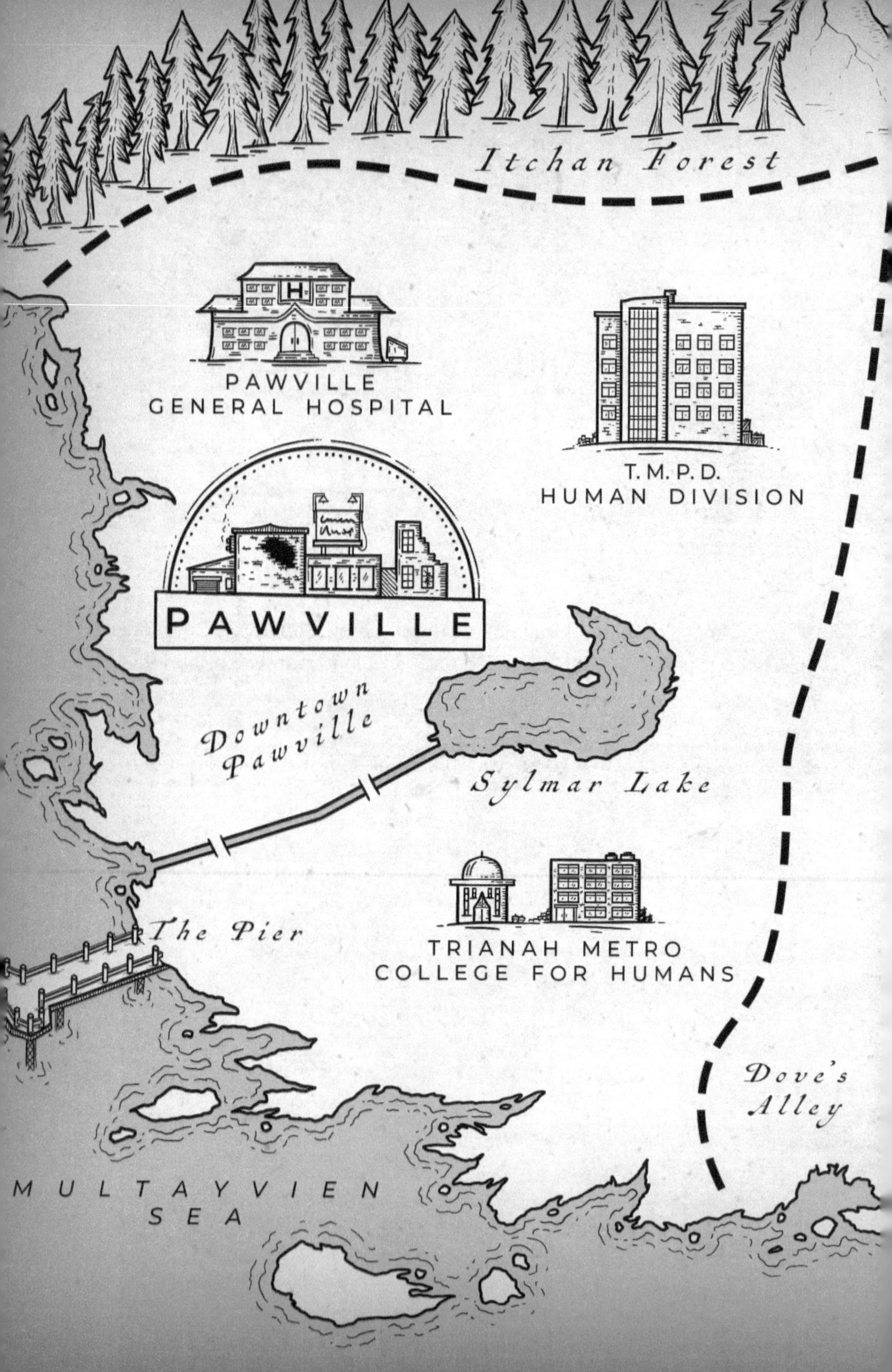

Itchan Forest
PAWVILLE GENERAL HOSPITAL
T.M.P.D. HUMAN DIVISION
PAWVILLE
Downtown Pawville
Sylmar Lake
The Pier
TRIANAH METRO COLLEGE FOR HUMANS
Dove's Alley
MULTAYVIEN SEA

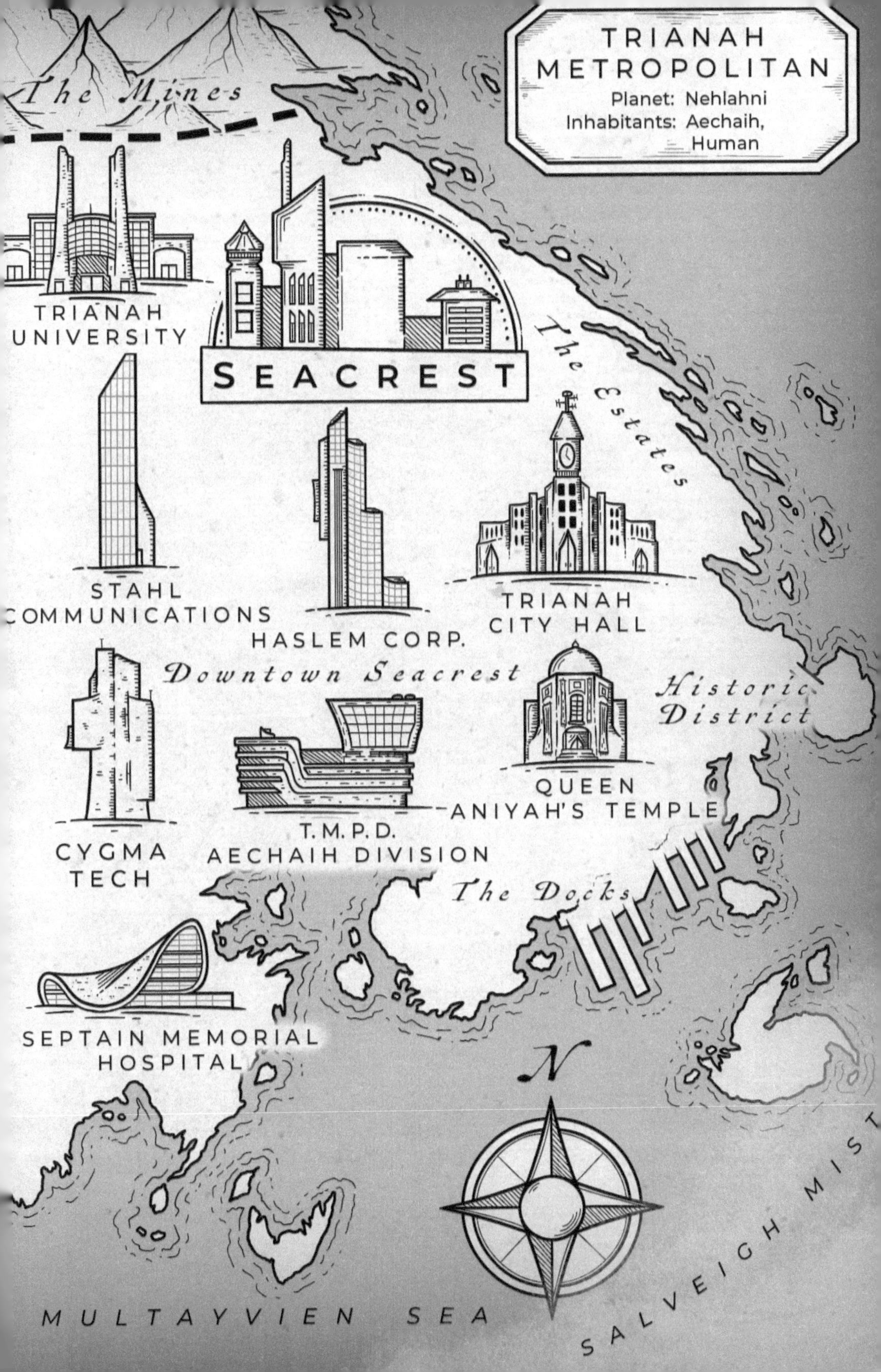

The Mines
TRIANAH
METROPOLITAN
Planet: Nehlahni
Inhabitants: Aechaih,
Human
TRIANAH
UNIVERSITY
SEACREST
The Estates
STAHL
COMMUNICATIONS
HASLEM CORP.
TRIANAH
CITY HALL
Downtown Seacrest
Historic
District
CYGMA
TECH
T. M. P. D.
AECHAIH DIVISION
QUEEN
ANIYAH'S TEMPLE
The Docks
SEPTAIN MEMORIAL
HOSPITAL
N
MULTAYVIEN SEA
SALVEIGH MIST

PRONUNCIATION GUIDE

Trianah — *tree - AH - nuh*
(ah = father, uh = puff)

Aniyah — *uh - ny - UH*
(uh = puff)

Nehlahni — *nuh - LAH - KNEE*
(ah = father)

Aechaih — *uh - SHY*
(uh = puff)

Seacrest — *SEE - CREST*

Multayvien Sea — *mul - TAY - VEE - n*

Itchan Forest — *ih - SHAUN*
(ih = pin)

Salveigh Mist — *sal - VAY*
(ay = fate)

Septain Memorial — *sep - TAYNE*
(ay = fate)

Chapter One

The girl's dead body is stuffed among piles of garbage in the grimy alley behind her apartment building. The smell is unbearable—trash mixed with decaying flesh—sharp, putrid. Her body, stiff from rigor mortis, is bluish-green like fading watercolors splotched over once-cocoa skin. It's twisted in unnatural angles. An ashen, abandoned shell, her brown eyes are empty and frozen in desperation, fear. The side of her round face and thick black hair is caked with dirt, and days-old blood. Letting out a breath to keep from passing out, Fellowship Dancy can't look away from her best friend and roommate, Daize. They were just together, joking and laughing—two brown, human, headstrong friends against the world. She still hears Daize's high-pitched, infectious cackle, and now she's gone. Fellowship stares and stares as darkness descends upon her; she can't breathe. Frantic words of distress and apology are trapped in her burning throat.

Daize's almond-shaped eyes blink once, then twice. She opens her once-perfect mouth now black with blood. "Why didn't you tell me?" she pleads, her voice distant and brittle. Fellowship wants to answer—to tell her everything. What she saw. Felt. Before Daize walked out of their apartment, for the last time. But she can't speak. Looking upon her beautiful, dead friend, she realizes she's alone—again.

A sweat-covered Fellowship bolted upright in bed. Tall windows glowed from the city lights, casting a blue hue across her bedroom. Head pounding, she rubbed her chest to feel something, anything besides heartbreak. Even though it was only a dream, its impact left her feeling cold and alone. Abandoned.

Daize.

Her light, her friend. Daize's natural, fearless charm coaxed Fellowship out of the darkness—the same darkness that taunted her almost every night. In Daize, Fellowship didn't just lose a friend, she lost a sister. Reaching for the bottle of water on her nightstand, she felt a body shift followed by a deep sigh. Looking to her left, she saw the muscled back of a man.

Who the fuck was that? Was she still dreaming? No. That's right, he was from Lonnie's, her favorite dark and dingy bar. They laughed over tumblers of warm Zion's Ink whiskey. Lazy glances and slurred speech. With a decent smile and large hands, he was everything she needed at the time. But that time had passed. Sitting up, she gave him a tentative poke. Nothing. A shake of the shoulder. Silence. She tried the sequence again.

Finally, a tired grumble. "Mmph?"

"You need to leave," she said around the frog in her throat. A beat, then nothing. *Fuuuuck.* "Hey," she barked.

"Whah?" he asked, rolling over to face her with his eyes still closed. A complete, albeit handsome, stranger was in her bed. *Again.* But that didn't bother her—what *bothered* her was that he wouldn't wake the fuck up.

"It's time to go," she ordered. Would probably help if she knew his name. Marque? Jeff? Nothing. Taking a healthy gulp of water, it hit her: *Roan. Yes!* Rocking him again, she insisted, "Roan, get up." A moan, then opened eyes followed, by a sleepy smile.

"Ready for another round?" he asked, charming and raspy.

"I'm ready for you to leave."

That woke him up. "What?" He rubbed his eyes like a baby as she rolled hers. "What time is it?" he asked, looking past her for a glimpse of the digital clock on her nightstand.

"Time. To. Go."

"It's two in the morning. Can I—"

"Sorry, I have to be up early." It was a half-truth: yes, she had to be up at 6:30, but no, she wasn't sorry. Roan sighed and then lifted his six-foot frame out of her bed. He was younger than her forty-two years; she wasn't sure by how much. It didn't matter. She took one last guilt-free look at his ass while he fumbled around for his clothes. Jumping on one foot, he slipped on his shoe before looking at her, pleading. Flashing him her thanks-for-the-good-time smile, his shoulders slumped as he pulled on his hoodie.

"Can I call you?" he asked from the bedroom door.

"Of course," she lied. She could make out a relieved smile and nod, then he was gone, using his phone to light the way out of her apartment. After a few beats, she heard the front door open and close with a soft clasp. If only he had her number. *Oh well.*

Pulling back her rose-colored duvet, she slipped out of bed, and shuffled to the bathroom. Flipping on the light, she squinted then beheld herself in the large mirror. She wore a ratty, gray TMPD t-shirt that hit the middle of her soft, heavy thighs. Dark circles from exhaustion and smudged mascara marred her eyes. Her short black hair was cut into a bald fade with low coils on top. Either the bathroom lights washed out her brown skin, or she looked like shit—maybe it was both. Turning on the water, she grabbed her turmeric and shea butter face soap and lathered up. There was something calming about making soapy circles around her eyes, on her forehead, and cheeks. The mirror fogged as steam rose from the running water. Splashing her face multiple times, she pretended like she was in a skin commercial. But unlike Fellowship, the girl in the commercial never got water all over her shirt and sink. Eyes closed, she waved her hand in the air just as she heard a melodic ringing emanate from her bedroom. *Shit.* Popping one eye open, she grabbed a face towel. Out of the bathroom, she dove across the bed and snapped up her phone. Recognizing the number, she slid the bar to accept the call.

"Hey, Miss Sylve. What's wrong?" she asked as she sat on the side of the bed, patting her face.

"Oh, Detective, I'm sorry to call so late," the older woman said.

"It's not a problem, what's up?"

"It's Kahleb. He hasn't been home tonight, Detective. Rey's been sniffing around, and I'm terrified he's mixed up with him," she said in a rush of air. That fucking kid was a pain in her ass which was precisely why his grandmother had her number. It wasn't the first time she had to hunt the teenager down in the middle of the night. Tossing the towel on the bed, she stood and looked for her jeans.

Sylve continued. "I know I shouldn't ask, but I don't have anyone else to call. I'm afraid that if one of your patrol cops pick him up, they'll throw him in Containment," she said.

"Of course, you did the right thing by calling. I'll find him."

A sniff and small whimper. "Thank you, Detective."

"My pleasure."

"He's a good kid. It's just that—"

"I know. Don't worry. In the meantime, I'll reach out to Brenda from Human Works—maybe she can help," Fellowship said, putting the phone on speaker while she shimmied into her jeans.

"Thank you, Detective."

"You're welcome, Miss Sylve," she said, ending the call and slipping the phone into her back pocket before peeling off her half-wet tee. Replacing it with a sports bra and black sweater, she shoved her feet into her trainers and stalked out of the bedroom. Moving around her apartment like a wraith, she shrugged on her holster and a black motorcycle jacket before putting her Trianah Metropolitan Police Department badge around her neck. The 9mm wasn't necessary, but she clicked it into her holster anyway. With keys in hand, she locked her apartment and set off to find a hardheaded teenager.

Trianah Metro was split into two districts: Pawville, the Human District, and Seacrest, the Aechaih District. Pawville was a poor, neglected version of Seacrest. Filthy and cramped with little real estate, buildings were pressed together to make room for corner markets, mobile phone repair, and check-cashing storefronts. With trash-cluttered gutters and shuttered businesses, one would be hard-pressed to remember the good old days when there were steady jobs and disposable income. But despite its hardships, the streets of Pawville were still alive at 2:30 AM. People meandered in and out of small, dank bars and sticky-floored clubs, or stood huddled in groups, shooting the shit. Neon lights reflecting off the slick streets made the district look like a shabby yet vibrant pinball machine.

Fellowship gunned her blacked-out muscle car down 10th Avenue in search of Sylve's grandson, who was surely mixed up with Rey, a two-bit hustler whose drug-dealing enterprise relied on young, dumb runners like Kahleb. Easing through the neighborhood made up of tall, worn-down tenements, rusted playgrounds, and net-less ball hoops, she spotted a cluster of teens on the corner; some were on their phones while others watched traffic for customers. From where she sat, she didn't see him, so she revved her V8, roaring her presence. Like a mob of meerkats, they looked in her direction. That's when she recognized a gangly teen with a mop of unkempt blonde curls—Kahleb. The meerkats scattered in multiple directions. Fellowship sped toward the teen as he dipped through the courtyard onto the next street. Throwing her car in park and jumping out, she locked it with a beep and took off after him.

"TMPD, stop!" she yelled to his back as her trainers slapped against the greased asphalt. She smelled wet garbage as she burst from a side street onto the jammed city sidewalk. Following the screams and shouts of pedestrians, she shot through the crowd. Pushing harder, she launched forward like a racehorse accessing its power reserve, brown eyes narrowed in determination. Swerving around citizens, she ignored her raw lungs and nagging left knee pain. Dodging an elderly woman, Kahleb attempted to jump a chain-link fence just as Fellowship caught him from behind.

"I said *stop*," she ground out, grabbing a handful of his sweat-soaked t-shirt. Yanking him from the fence, he landed with a thud as she wrestled him face down on the ground. Thighs screaming, she straddled him while he squirmed in protest. High off the chase, she paid no mind to her scorched lungs as the street melded into neon purples, pinks, and blues. No longer could she hear blaring horns or see gawking onlookers; it was just the sound of her breath as she stared at Kahleb's profile and tangle of dirty blonde curls. She took a moment to savor the feel of blood coursing through her veins; she was a live spark, frayed and popping with electricity. This was *definitely* better than sex with what's-his-face.

"I told you to stop, but did you listen? No." Annoyed and breathless, she pinned his arms behind his back but didn't cuff him.

"Get off me, lady," he said with face pressed against the concrete.

"It's *Detective Dancy* to you, Kahleb. Don't act brand new."

A grunt.

"What were you doing on the corner? You have no business being out this late. *Solneur*, you're a pain in the ass."

"I didn't do anything—"

"Working for Rey *is* doing something. He's gonna get you thrown in Containment and not think twice about it. I know it's shitty, but dealin' isn't the answer."

"What the fuck do you know about it, huh?" he spat.

What did *she* know? Oh, to be young and arrogant. "I know how it feels to be hungry, how to heat an apartment with the stove. I know how to dodge bill collectors, or how to pay a little here and there to keep the lights on. I was on these streets before you, Kahleb—I *know*."

He stopped struggling, closed his eyes and let out a resigned sigh. "It's fucked up," he admitted. There he was—the *real* Kahleb. Instead of the bony, disgruntled teen, she saw the cute, sticky-faced seven-year-old she had met on her first day on the job. Now here he was, older and angrier. Harder. Solneur-be-damned, she wasn't going to let him be devoured by Pawville's underbelly. Fewer jobs, leading to more financial constraints, hunger, and idle time, lured kids like Kahleb right into the hands of dealers like Rey. The promise of catching up on a bill or two was incentive enough for them to drop out of school, risking it all just to put food on the table.

"Find *me* if you need help, not Rey. I know it's easy money, but it's not worth the price. Okay?" she asked, grabbing her cell out of the back pocket of her jeans.

"Whatever," he mumbled.

"Good." Still sitting on him, she made a call. "Brenda, it's Fellowship Dancy. Sorry for the hour. How are you? I'm okay, thanks. Look, I've got a good kid here who needs help—it's just him and his grandmother. Think you can chat with them and see what you can do? Thanks, Bren... He'll be at the precinct. Thanks again." Fellowship pocketed her phone.

"Are you arresting me?"

"Did I cuff you and explain your rights?"

"No."

"Then no."

"Why'd you come looking for me?"

"Your grandmother called."

Kahleb groaned into the sidewalk, embarrassed.

Fellowship scoffed. "Boo-hoo, you've got someone worried about you. You're smart and capable. You have to finish school—"

"For what? It's not like you need an education to work the mines."

"You're right, but there aren't many mining jobs left for humans. That's why you have to get your diploma so you can do something else."

"Like what?"

"I'm not about to have a career counseling session with you right now. I know you're smart—you're gonna have to ignore the bullshit in order to better your situation. Okay?"

A grunt.

"*Okay?* I don't want to see you dead or in Containment, and at the rate you're going, those are your only two options. I'm not always going to be around to get you off the block."

"Rey's not gonna let me walk away," Kahleb said, after a thoughtful beat.

"Return the stash and cash. If he gives you shit, find me *immediately*."

A moment of consideration, then, "Fine."

"Fine," she repeated, finally clocking her surroundings. Most people had meandered away. There was nothing to see; arrests were normal in Pawville. The smell of warm, home-cooked food wafted from her favorite family-owned noodle shop a few doors down.

"Are you hungry?" she asked, stomach growling.

A muffled grunt.

"I'll take that as a yes. Have you ever had Santander's over there?" Kahleb shook his head. "Oh, you've gotta try it. It'll change your life. C'mon," she said, standing. "Let's get some food in you."

Taller than her five-seven, he gave her a faint nod, then shoved his hands in his pockets. Patting his back, she walked him to Santander's Noodles. Her heart ached—Pawville's streets were getting darker and more desperate. It was almost impossible not to lose someone to the ruthlessly violent culture that had clawed its way into the once-thriving community. With mining jobs dwindling, the lack of resources had carved a hole into her beloved district. But Pawville's decline wasn't by accident; it was the consequence of being human. Although the Aechaih had amassed wealth for centuries, they allowed humans to work in the mines for a livable wage. However, years ago, the mines started laying off workers until they were run by bare-bones crews. Kahleb's parents were lost to the streets eight years ago—another wave of folks who struggled to make ends meet. His grandmother did all she could to support them on her fixed income, but it was difficult.

Opening the door to the noodle shop, she let Kahleb in and followed behind. It might've cost her a night's sleep, but getting Sylve's grandson to safety was worth the inevitable grogginess she was sure to feel when she started her shift in a few hours.

Hyphen Haslem had a monster of a fucking headache and riding the vandalized elevator of a seedy Seacrest motel wasn't helping. As the piss-smelling tin can groaned in protest, he clocked the ceiling, noticing stray wires poking around misplaced panels. Great, he was in a death trap. Rubbing his neck in an attempt to release tension, he closed his eyes and sighed. New crime scenes used to pump him full of adrenaline, but after twenty-five years on the force, it was just another tedious night on the job.

Ding! A text alert interrupted the moment. He didn't have to look at the screen to know who it was. Hyphen pulled his phone out of his pants pocket before opening his eyes to see the text from his girlfriend. His initial response was to ignore it, but—*ding!* Exactly. When she wanted something, there was no stopping—*ding! Dammit.* He opened the text:

Bronwyn: Dinner at 7.

Bronwyn: Lilly's.

Bronwyn: Don't be late.

She was relentless and since he wasn't in the mood for one of her tantrums, he responded:

Hyphen: Okay.

It wasn't okay. Like his job, Bronwyn Phor had become a monotonous responsibility and reflection of his stagnant life. Like him, she was from an influential, well-connected family, attended the right schools, and socialized with the right people. They were both expertly bred to continue the Aechaih tradition of wealth and power, but unlike her, Hyphen could give a shit about the Seacrest elite and their overall snobbery-bullshit that did nothing to benefit Trianah as a whole. No plans for growth or helping the residents of Pawville, just social calendars and who's who lists. Dating her had become unbearable, so why was he still with her? He had no Solneur-damned idea and was too exhausted to find out.

The elevator doors opened to reveal a dreary hallway with graffiti-stained walls. Around the corner was the crime scene guarded by two Aechaih patrol cops stationed on either side of the open motel door.

Tall and built beyond the traditional Aechaih physique, their black uniforms looked painted over their muscled bodies. Pointed ears and eyes hidden by downward-tipped hats, their presence screamed *don't you fucking dare.* Techs and scene processors from TMPD's Aechaih Division bustled in and out the room, silver cases in hand. Hyphen nodded as he walked past.

"Detective Haslem," one of them mumbled. As his eyes adjusted to the dark room, he detected various types of Aechaih blood, which was to be expected in a Dove's Alley hotel. Old, heavy drapes covered a large window, casting a shadow over the stained sofa and scuffed table that made up the front room. He regretted not grabbing a pair of booties from a passing tech as his shoes sank into the filthy brown carpet.

"Where the fuck have you been?" Detective Gabe Monroe asked, emerging from the bathroom. He plucked a pair of black latex gloves out of his pocket and shoved them at Hyphen. While they weren't official partners, he preferred working with Monroe because they were the same: straightforward and work obsessed. Perhaps that came with being over two hundred years old, who knows. Monroe stood eye level to Hyphen's six-five. He was a rare, no-frills Aechaih, dressed in basic slacks, a collared shirt, and sport coat. Hyphen, on the other hand, had elevated taste, which was evident in his navy bespoke suit, white shirt, and silver tie.

"Hello to you, too." Taking the gloves, he slipped them on with a pop, then nodded to the room. "What's up?"

"A shit show, that's what's up," Monroe grumbled, before leading the way.

Monroe was right: it *was* a shit show. One bed, stripped with white sheets crumpled in the corner. On top of the beat-up nightstand sat a tarnished lamp with a lopsided, dirty shade. Clothes were strewn over the floor along with trash. In the center of the stained mattress lay the naked body of a dead female Aechaih. Her neck was broken, eyes open in fear, with auburn hair sprawled around her awkwardly-angled head. There was dried blood in her pointed ears and nasty bruises covering the right side of her body, including her face.

"We think she was thrown against the wall, here," Monroe said as Hyphen followed his eyeline to the body-sized dent in the drywall.

"Hey, guys, give us a minute," Hyphen said to the techs. Between his headache and the snap-snapping of pics, he felt crowded, making it difficult to process the scene. The techs immediately stopped and shuffled out.

"We got into her cellphone," Monroe said, nodding to the nightstand.

Hyphen picked up the phone and swiped through the homepage. He skimmed the apps before scrolling through her text messages. The vic's name was Lena and someone named Khaki was worried about her:

Khaki: How was it? *12:30 AM*

Khaki: That good? *12:58 AM*

Khaki: Lena? Seriously? *2:00 AM*

Khaki: You haven't been kidnapped, have you? Hahaha. *2:30 AM*

Khaki: Please hit me up, I'm worried... *2:47 AM*

"Got a worried friend here. Any family?"

"Still looking," Monroe answered, scribbling notes in a tiny black book.

Hyphen swiped through the homepage again, this time noticing a black square with a white 'F' in the middle. "You ever heard of *FBDn?*" he asked, opening the app.

Monroe pocketed his black book and walked over. "No. What is it?"

"Looks like a messaging app." There were multiple energetic message threads with various usernames. He opened the most recent thread:

Manic1009: u looked fuckin hot at SeVere last night.

LeeenAguRL9878: Aw. Thank u.

Manic1009: u gonna take me up on my offer?

LeeenAguRL9878: 2 meet?

Manic1009: yea

LeeenAguRL9878: Y would I do that?

Manic1009: y not

LeeenAguRL9878: I don't fuck wit humans like that.

Manic1009: bullshit. if you didn't then y go 2 SeVere?

LeeenAguRL9878: u got me.

Manic1009: ur so sexy

LeeenAguRL9878: How about Dove's Alley?

Manic1009: of course baby c u there

Manic1009: im here baby where r u

LeeenAguRL9878: The parking lot. Purple car.

Manic1009: i c u

No fucking way. Hyphen looked at Monroe. "You don't think—"

"A human did this?" Monroe finished. "Impossible. What the hell is *FBDn* anyway?" he asked, pulling out his phone and scrolling. After a minute, he looked up, his gray eyes stern and focused. "*Forbidden,* better known as *FBDn,* is a messaging app for those in search of particular pleasures and proclivities. How did I not know about this?" Monroe said, more to himself than Hyphen.

"You don't strike me as someone who uses hook-up apps," Hyphen replied.

"Did *you* know about it?"

"Do *I* look like I use hook-up apps?"

"Fair," Monroe conceded before he dialed, then pressed the phone to his ear. "Get back in here and get this shit bagged, *now.* Did you call the coroner? Well, get it done," he barked. He ended the call, then looked at Hyphen. "I'll get the phone to forensics. We have surveillance footage to watch as well."

Hyphen nodded as he continued staring at Lena. No matter what the evidence suggested, it was hard to fathom that a human could overpower and kill an Aechaih, female or not. Something about the scene felt off, like perhaps none of this was as clear-cut as it seemed.

Chapter Two

Fellowship walked through the brown double doors of the Criminal Investigation Unit with a large to-go cup of black coffee. It was a standard, rundown precinct: smudged, once-white walls plastered with faded posters, and clusters of desks with outdated computers under unforgiving fluorescent lights. She navigated through a sea of cluttered workstations occupied by detectives, nodding in acknowledgment as she walked by. In the far corner of the bullpen was a small glass office belonging to her lieutenant, Noon Ceager, who was meeting with the Human Division's captain, Myles Pope. The sight caused a hitch in her step; she hadn't seen Captain Pope on their floor in some time. The medium-height, ordinary man wore a plain black suit, white shirt, and black tie. Lieutenant Ceager, taller and broader with a perpetual scowl, looked more rumpled and exhausted than usual. Fellowship's stomach lurched at the sight of them, followed by a pressing need to know what they were discussing.

Unlike her co-workers', Fellowship's desk was organized with neat piles of papers and folders, along with a TMPD mug. She flopped down on her chair then powered up the computer. Eyes back to her lieutenant's office, she watched Ceager pace back and forth like a caged animal. Even though Pope wasn't moving, he looked just as concerned. She didn't hear anything out of the ordinary when falling asleep to the police scanner after dealing with Kahleb. Maybe it was more human-Aechaih political bullshit—either way, her curiosity was piqued.

"I heard you ran a perp down *on foot*," said an amused voice. Smiling, Fellowship looked up to see her co-worker, Detective Rayna Gilbert, easing onto the worse-for-wear chair next to her desk. Rayna and Fellowship attended academy together and immediately bonded over being the only female recruits—a bond solidified when they graduated top of their class. Crossing her long legs, she flipped her black box braids over her shoulder. A toasted amber with clusters of freckles sprinkled across her nose, she wore her usual: jeans, t-shirt, leather jacket, and boots. Fellowship's attire was no different.

"I ran *Kahleb* down on foot," she corrected. "His grandmother called afraid that he's mixed up with Rey."

"Is he?"

"Yeah, I found him on the block. When I pulled up, they scattered so I pursued on foot."

"Did he have anything on him?"

"No, thank Solneur. I gave him my standard get-your-shit-together lecture, fed him then connected him with Brenda."

"All of that in the middle of the night?"

"I was up anyway," Fellowship said, logging onto her computer.

"You were up, huh?" Rayna asked, her golden-brown eyes flickering with mischief.

"Yeah."

Rayna remained quiet. After Fellowship finished typing her credentials, she frowned. "What?"

"You know what, bitch. Who were you up *with*?"

She wasn't sure why, but her face prickled with embarrassment. "What makes you think I was with someone?"

"Because I know you."

The-fuck? She didn't like that shit at all. No one really knew her—she made sure of it. "Goes to show what you know, I was alone."

"Because you already kicked his ass out."

Busted. "Fuck you."

"Like I thought. What was his name?"

"You're a hateful bitch. You know that?"

"A hateful bitch who knows you don't remember his name."

"His name was Roan," Fellowship said, leaning back in her chair. Something about Rayna calling her on her shit was irksome. She craved anonymity in sex and work was no different. Yes, the shit-talking was fun but there was comfort in keeping people at bay. It made things less complicated.

"Poor Roan," Rayna joked.

Fellowship sucked her teeth. "You, of all people, can't talk with your revolving door of vapid-ass, opportunistic sex kittens in and out of your loft."

Rayna's face lit up. "I love that you know that about me," she squealed. "You wanna go to MoonLyte tonight?"

Fellowship frowned. "You know I don't like going to Seacrest; besides, I have class."

"I don't understand your beef with Seacrest aside from the obvious. The district is beautiful and everyone's fine as hell," Rayna said.

Fellowship turned up her nose. "That's a hard no."

"You mean to tell me you've never fucked one, or two, or three?"

Fellowship recoiled, outraged. "An Aechaih?"

"Yeah."

"First, it's illegal and second, no." She knew she sounded like a law-abiding nerd, but she never saw their allure. Tall. Built. Pointed ears. Elongated canines. Conceited. Entitled. No thanks.

Rayna waved her hand. "It's illegal to marry one, not fuck—there's a difference."

"If you say so."

"The sex is phenomenal," Rayna replied, licking her lips.

"Yulk."

"Speciesist."

Fellowship choked on her coffee. "What? No, I'm not." She may not have liked the Aechaih, but she wasn't *speciesist*, right? Had her distaste for them evolved beyond general disgust to something more sinister? Meh, she was justified in her opinion.

"Sure," Rayna said, unconvinced. "Either way, we're still cool. How's the semester going?"

"Good. *Actually*, you wanna join us for our field trip tomorrow?"

"Where?"

"Queen Aniyah's Temple."

Rayna scrunched her nose. "Queen Aniyah's *Temple?*"

Fellowship nodded, eyes flicking back to Ceager's office. Pope was finally gone.

Rayna turned to see what caught her attention. "He looks like shit."

"Pope was just in there."

"Ah, makes sense," she said, pulling out her phone. "Go see what they were talking about. He'll tell his favorite."

Fellowship whipped her head around. "I'm *not* his favorite."

Rayna looked up from her phone. "*Really?*"

Fair. Somehow, over the years she'd managed to build a decent work-relationship with her boss. She'd break rules. He'd yell but never discipline her. It was a match made in the Salveigh Mist. "You're right. I'll go see what's up, but for real, you should come tomorrow," she added with a charming smile.

Rayna looked up from her phone then rolled her eyes. "You need another chaperone, don't you?"

Busted again. "They're college students. I don't *need* one, but it'd be nice to have another body with us."

"Queen Aniyah's Temple," she scoffed. "Fine."

"You know," Fellowship added. "Trianah has a rich history. You can learn a lot from it," she said as Rayna pretended to nod off. "Bitch!" she hissed over Rayna's laugh and sly smile. Fellowship shook her head then smacked her on the knee. "I'll talk to you later."

"See, ya."

Fellowship stood and moved toward Ceager's office, coffee in hand. Snaking through the desks, she wondered what had her normally stoic lieutenant looking like he'd just seen a phantom. She slowly approached and leaned in the door frame.

"Hey, Lieutenant," she said as casually as she could without giving off a snooping vibe. Ceager looked up. Calling him exhausted was an understatement. The bags underneath his eyes looked like they held years of sleepless nights. "You look like shit," she blurted out.

"Thank you. Get in here and close the door," he barked. Doing as she was told, she eased onto one of the chairs across from his desk. Leaning back, Ceager let out an aggravated sigh and rubbed his bald, pink head.

"That bad?" Fellowship asked.

"Worse. There's been a human-Aechaih homicide."

Fellowship leaned forward; she must've misheard. "I'm sorry, I thought you said, *human* on Aechaih."

"I did."

"Bullshit. I mean *how?*"

"I have no Guardians-damned idea. To make matters worse, it happened in Seacrest."

That's why he looked sick. The thought of a human-on-Aechaih murder made her stomach roll, too. Magical abilities, enhanced strength, and long lifespans made Aechaih the dominant species. Killing one was impossible, or so she thought.

"What happened?" she asked.

Reading from the file on his desk, he said, "The body of a young Aechaih woman was found dead at a motel in Dove's Alley. Broken neck."

"A *human* broke an Aechaih's neck? I don't think so, sir. I know they'll stop at nothing to blame us for shit, but this is ridiculous."

He continued, ignoring her jab. "They found a conversation thread between the vic and perp on some app and tracked him here."

"Which app?"

Ceager squinted at the file. "*FBDn.*"

"Makes sense," she said with a nod. "Did they apprehend him without telling us?"

"They contacted Pope then moved in. He was dead when they found him in his apartment," Ceager said, rubbing his face.

"What?! What was the cause of death?"

"10-56."

"Suicide? What the fuck?!"

"I know."

"Did they take his body?"

"No, it's at our coroner's."

"I guess *that* was kind of them."

"Dancy..." Ceager warned.

Fellowship held her hands up in surrender. "Does the Council know because once they get wind—"

"I'm sure they do. Detective Haslem's running point."

"Rich Boy Playing Cop's gotta case? Nice," she snarked. Ceager let out an aggravated moan and rubbed his head again. "Sorry, sir." She wasn't sorry. The Haslems were one of the three families that made up Trianah's Tri-Family Council; they were well-connected, powerful, and disgustingly wealthy. No, she didn't know Detective Haslem *personally*, but he was Horace Haslem's only son and heir to the Haslem empire. With the amount of money his family had acquired over the past millennium, there was no reason for him to work, so like she said—Rich Boy *Playing* Cop.

Ceager continued. "Obviously, we're trying to keep a lid on this, especially with human tensions growing. Pope doesn't want to invite further restrictions on Pawville."

"Fair."

"With the perp dead, there's not much we can do, but I'd like you to take this. What's left of it, anyway."

A bubble of amusement floated up and out of her, popping into a confetti-storm of manic laughter. It wasn't until she laughed herself into a coughing fit that she noticed her boss hadn't joined in.

Oops. She cleared her throat. "I'm sorry. I—you're *serious?*" she asked, wiping an escaped tear from the corner of her eye.

"Yes."

"Sir, I'm the *last* person you want on this," she advised. Her armpits began to itch with sweat. While she wasn't pleased there was a dead woman, she didn't have the bandwidth to deal with arrogant Aechaih cops. Even though her detective brain wondered what went down in that motel room.

"I'm aware of your lack of patience and diplomacy when it comes to the Aechaih, but you shouldn't have to interact with them as the case is essentially closed," he said, snapping shut the black folder with the Aechaih Division sigil embossed on the front. "Look it over. Check out his apartment for anything that could help us figure out *how* he did it," Ceager said, handing her the file.

She took it, giving him a curt nod. "Yes, sir." Elitist pricks or not, she was happy to get the case. If something was going on with humans and the Aechaih Division was involved, then she was, too.

"How've you been? You have any time in your schedule for lunch or something? I know you're busy," Auten Dancy, Fellowship's grandfather, said as she sat in the parking lot of Trianah Metropolitan College for Humans.

Shoving books into her tote, she put the phone on speaker. "I don't know, I was just assigned a case," she said, as she applied her lipstick in the rearview mirror.

"I understand," Auten said, disappointed. "Maybe another time."

"I can't make any promises," she said, capping her lipstick and throwing it into her tote.

Auten sighed. "I'm trying here, Fell. Really trying. Why can't you?"

A call that she needed to take pushed through. "I'm sorry, I'm busy. Look, I have another call I must take."

"Fine. I love you, Fellowship."

"Same here," she said, ending the call to take the other. "Hey, Lemin, thanks for getting back to me."

"No problem, Dancy," he said, chipper as always. Lemin was their unofficial tech forensics lead. He was a sweet, young kid who had a knack for using ones and zeroes to find shit.

"Could you find anything?"

"Yeah. Like the Aechaih report stated, due to our shitty street department budget, the traffic camera on the perp's block is out of order. I was able to get into the pawn shop's security camera across from his building. I'm sending it now."

Fellowship clicked her work email app and opened the file. The CCTV footage was black and white and severely grainy, but it showed the perp walking to his building. Stout and solid, he looked disoriented. Then, after a beat, he stopped like someone had switched him off. Standing in place for an extended moment, he began to move again. As if coming out of shock, he seemed to recognize where he was. Checking to see if anyone was around, he pulled keys from his pocket and entered the building.

"What the fuck?" Fellowship asked.

"I know. Weird, right?"

It was time for class. "Thank you, Lemin. I appreciate you."

"No problem, Dancy. See you tomorrow."

Fellowship ended the call. Even though her mind was teeming with possibilities, she didn't have time to sort through any hunches. Exiting the car, she slung her tote over her shoulder and walked across the modest campus to her building.

Fellowship rounded the corner and entered her brightly lit, yet generic classroom. "Good evening, everyone," she chirped, putting her tote on the desk at the front of the room. Her class of twelve popped their heads up from either talking, reading, or texting, mumbling a general hello. Fellowship unpacked her things and got settled. After a beat, she looked up and smiled. "Let's get right into it; what were the social implications of Rhoman's Massacre?"

As an adjunct, she only taught one class a semester and this one happened to be her favorite: History 101: Aechaih-Human History from *Dawn of the Aechaih* to Present. Three hands shot in the air. She smiled and considered who to call. There was Llewyn, a bright young man, albeit flighty. Hard worker. There was Zaphine, quiet but coming out of her shell. Last, there was Nigh, her favorite, even though she wasn't supposed to have one. Nigh was tough, whip-smart, and struggling to survive the wicked streets of Pawville. Each night she arrived to class, Fellowship relaxed, relieved that she hadn't gotten herself into a bind. TMCH didn't have a flourishing endowment, but it did have hungry students desperate to better their situation—students who compelled Fellowship to continue teaching well after she joined the police force. No matter how shitty her shift was, the politics she had to navigate, or destitute humans she arrested, teaching was her saving grace.

"Nigh." Of course, she called on her—she couldn't help it.

"First and foremost, Rhoman's Massacre decimated the Aechaih-human relationship. As we all know, the Aechaih and humans lived in harmony for centuries, but that relationship was severed when Rhoman, the queen's human husband, and his followers slaughtered Aechaih at the sacred *Kumalada* ceremony in an attempted takeover."

Fellowship leaned on the desk, having changed from her work clothes into black leggings, booties, and a pale pink blouse. Her shimmering, caramelized skin caught the classroom lights, giving her an added glow. She had a plus-size frame with a smaller waist, rounded hips, and a soft tummy. Her thighs and ass were fat, and she had a medium bust that made work a lot easier when she had to slam someone's ass to the ground.

Fellowship nodded, as Llewyn raised his hand. "Llewyn."

"After the massacre, the three prominent families that served on Queen Aniyah's court created the Tri-Family Council," he said.

"I always thought it was impossible for humans to kill Aechaih," Zaphine said. Fellowship opened her mouth, but nothing came out. *Shit.* The last humans able to kill multiple Aechaih were Rhoman and his followers. And now centuries later, there was a human-Aechaih murder? Wait—

"It says here that he was jealous of the queen's power and got mixed up in dark magic which gave him superhuman strength," Nigh said, looking down at her book then to Fellowship who was still frozen in thought. Did the perp get his hands on dark magic? It seemed unlikely as magic was relatively contained in Seacrest. But he *was* in Seacrest—

"Professor," Zaphine said gently.

Fellowship's eyes snapped up. "What? Yes, you're right, Nigh. Jealousy clouded Rhoman's mind," she said. "Why didn't Trianah keep the monarchy?" Fellowship asked, trying to regain focus.

"During the massacre, Rhoman killed his wife and their unborn baby before being captured and executed," Zaphine said. "After that, they swept all of Trianah, searching for and exterminating any remaining human-Aechaih hybrids."

"Excellent, Zaphine. What happened to the remaining full-blood humans?"

"They were gathered up and subjugated. As centuries passed without incident, humans were able to make a life for themselves in the forest. Once Trianah Metropolitan was established, we were *allowed* to live here but with *conditions*," Llewyn answered.

"Great, what were those conditions?"

"HPC, or Human Population Control, was one of the biggest, most influential conditions," Zaphine said. "We can only have one child per family and Aechaih can breed as often as they want."

"As often as they can," Nigh interjected.

"What do you mean by that, Nigh?" Fellowship asked, walking to the board. She scribbled their comments, adding specific dates so they could add them to their notes.

"It's hard for them to get pregnant. When they do, they have difficult pregnancies. But it hasn't stopped them," Nigh replied.

"Yeah, even if it kills the mother," Llewyn added. "That's pretty messed up."

"How many children can humans have if they live in the Itchan Forest?"

"Two, but who wants to live in the forest? It's worse than here," Nigh said.

Fellowship nodded as she continued to write on the board. She grew up in the Itchan Forest, and while it was a rustic upbringing and her memories of that time were hazy, she still missed the quiet protection of the woods. "Why did they implement this condition on humans?"

"To prevent another uprising," Nigh answered.

"Excellent. Additionally, they also implemented the Aechaih-human Anti-Miscegenation Law, banning marriage or intimate relationships between the two species," Fellowship added. The law was archaic but remained in The Kingdom of Trianah Bylaws and was enforced by the Council if discovered.

"The Aechaih are speciesist," Cygar, a normally reticent student, said from the back of the class. Everyone turned to look at him. Leaning against the wall, hoodie up, all they could make out were his blue eyes and ruddy skin. "Yeah, they don't kill us like they did the hybrids back in the day but—"

"They oppress us to death," Nigh said with a sinister laugh as the class joined her.

Fellowship smiled and shook her head. She definitely preferred her students calling the Aechaih speciesist instead of her. "Name the three families of the Tri-Family Council."

Nigh's hand shot in the air. Fellowship nodded for her to speak. "Haslem, Syon, and Tarnicon."

"Very good." Fellowship walked back to her desk and sat on it, her booted feet dangling back and forth. "We can't forget where we've come from. If we want to implement change in Pawville or Trianah as a whole, we must know how we got here," she said.

Zaphine raised her hand and spoke. "To be honest, Professor, I didn't care about our history until this class." Most, if not all of her class, nodded in agreement. Fellowship smiled as Zaphine continued. "Now, because I understand why life seems extra hard for us, I feel like I want to make a difference. Like you being a cop or your grandfather being the Human Ambassador to the Tri-Family Council," she said, bright-eyed and hopeful.

Fellowship swallowed hard. She *hated* that her grandfather was Human Ambassador to *them*. She felt his social activism would've been put to better use in Pawville instead of Pawville *and* Seacrest. His position as Ambassador was the crux of their strained relationship, but she couldn't tell that to her students. Like them, she was once idealistic and confident that she could impact her community by becoming an activist. Her best friend, Daize, felt the same way. They were in the process of earning advanced degrees when Daize fell in love with an Aechaih and was suddenly gone. Fellowship's world was never the same. The passion that fueled her had been replaced with heartbreak. She was obsessed with solving Daize's murder. Disgusted by the Human Division's lackluster approach to the case, she knew that becoming a criminal investigator could make all the difference. If not for her, then hopefully for someone else. When she graduated, she enrolled in the academy that same day.

"I'm excited to go on this field trip to Queen Aniyah's Temple," Cygar grumbled from the back. "I skipped that shit when they took us as kids." The class laughed, except Nigh who was feverishly texting with a frown.

"I'm glad you brought that up, Cygar. Tomorrow, we'll meet here first, grab lunch then head to the Historic District to visit the temple. For the rest of our time, I want you to start drafting your essays on Rhoman's Massacre. Don't forget to unpack the social and cultural implications."

The class erupted in light chatter. She couldn't help but watch them; her own idealism might have been a distant memory, but that was why she taught. She wanted her students to be different from her, *better*.

Chapter Three

The Haslem estate was a waterfront compound sitting on sprawling acres of trees, ponds, and a boutique vineyard. Hyphen's tires crunched on the white gravel as he circled the drive. The mega-house represented quintessential Aechaih wealth: pristine, manicured, vast, and cold. Refusing to use his key, he pressed the doorbell. The heavy oak door opened to reveal his sisters, Haze and Harleigh, wide-eyed and ever excited to see him. The young Aechaih twins were both tall and thin, with long, dark chocolate hair and large, expressive blue eyes. Basically teenagers in Aechaih-years, they were astute, highly intelligent and dialed into more than just pop culture and fashion—although they were into that, too.

"Where have you been?" Haze asked, dragging him into the marble foyer. Harleigh closed the door behind them, then laced her arm through Hyphen's, Haze mimicking her on the other side. The girls were dressed in faded jeans and oversized sweaters. Haze's hair was piled on top of her head, while Harleigh wore hers in a braided crown.

"I've been working," he said, amused. They marched him past the double staircase to the family sitting room.

"The Gazette reported an uptick in crime, most notably in Dove's

Alley," Haze said. Thank Sylena he kept up with current events, most of which he listened to during his morning workouts. The last thing he wanted was to be uninformed in front of his sisters.

"There's nothing to worry about," he said, nodding hello to one of the many household staff as they entered the sitting room. Expertly decorated and dripping with his mother's style, the space was navy and gold. Floor-to-ceiling windows, plush double sofas in front of a massive fireplace, intricate handwoven rugs, chairs, gold tables, and various decorative items he rarely paid attention to adorned the room. The twins plopped him on the navy sofa between them. Haze tucked her feet under her while Harleigh grabbed his arm, snuggling in tight. The youngest in the family and the only girls, they were born well after Hyphen was out of the house. Because of this, he made a dedicated effort to be in their lives, taking great pride in big-brotherhood. Despite how much time he spent with them, it wasn't until they were old enough to develop unique personalities that he was able to tell them apart. Haze: introverted, bookish, thoughtful, and sensitive—like him. Harleigh: extroverted, charming, and outspoken—like Hudson, their older brother.

"Are you working a case?" Haze inquired.

"I'm always working a case."

"What is it?" Harleigh demanded.

"Classified," he said with a smirk. Normally, he'd share his work, skipping the gory details, but this most recent case was the highest level of classified with his captain adamant that details weren't leaked to the press.

Harleigh frowned. "What's the point of having a brother on the force if you're going to gatekeep?" she asked.

"I'm not gatekeeping, I'm being professional," he said, lifting a perfectly arched eyebrow.

"Fine. We'll figure it out, eventually," Haze said, twirling a piece of hair between her slender fingers.

Hyphen laughed. "I'm sure you will. What's up with you two?"

"Meh, the usual. We started our class project for Civics," Harleigh reported.

"We're responsible for analyzing a current social issue," Haze added.

"To what end?"

"She wants thoughtful solutions," Haze started.

"If not a solution, at least guidance for change," Harleigh finished.

"Which social issue did you choose?"

"We're examining the current human-Aechaih dynamic. How it got to its current state and whether or not there should be fundamental change in how we engage with the human population," Harleigh said.

"The situation in Pawville is cause for concern. A lot of our friends think so, too," Haze added.

"And what situation is that?" he asked, draping his free arm along the back of the sofa.

"The gutting of mining jobs leading to a rise in crime, violence, and drug use in the district," Haze explained. "There's no reason for humans to be practically walled off, struggling for basic necessities when Seacrest—*Trianah* has more than enough."

"The chance of another human uprising is slim. People are struggling in Pawville and we can help," Harleigh said.

"How would you help?" he asked.

Haze frowned. "We're not sure yet."

"There's a population of Aechaih who support human-Aechaih equality, then you have self-absorbed asshats who fear change," Harleigh said, rolling her eyes.

Hyphen laughed. "I know you'll come up with something," he offered.

"Of course, they will," Honey Haslem said from the door. "Even though I wish they would've chosen a different topic, or at least didn't discuss it at dinner. It agitates Horace," she added.

"He's always agitated," Harleigh mumbled under her breath. Hyphen nudged her with a wink.

"Hyphen, how are you, love?" she asked, walking across the room.

Honey wore heavy cream dress slacks and a fitted cream cashmere sweater with simple gold jewelry. Her shoulder-length, chocolate hair was cut into layers.

Hyphen peeled Harleigh off him and stood to hug his mother. "I'm doing well, how are you?" Honey sat across from them on the other sofa. As soon as Hyphen sat back down, both Haze and Harleigh attached themselves to him.

"Oh, I'm fine. Just returned from a planning committee meeting," she said, crossing her long legs.

"What are you planning now?"

"The Sylena Lunar Ball," Harleigh said. "I've already got my gown. Haze still needs to get hers."

"Yeah...about that. I don't want to wear a gown," Haze announced.

"What else would you wear?" Honey asked, perplexed.

Haze shrugged. "I want to wear a tailored tux," she answered.

Harleigh leaned in front of Hyphen to look at her sister. "You never told me that."

"We'll have to talk about that, Haze," Honey said, visibly uncomfortable.

"What's to talk about? I'll take her to Al's," Hyphen said as Haze beamed. Her smile made his heart expand in his chest. There was nothing that made him happier than making his sister's smile.

"Are you coming?" Harleigh asked him.

"Of course, he is. It's all Bronwyn can talk about," Honey answered.

"Ugh, Princess *Phor*," Haze groaned.

Hyphen turned to her. "What?"

"Don't be rude, Haze," Honey admonished.

"She's awful, Mom," Harleigh said, coming to her sister's defense.

"Wait, what? You've never mentioned this before," he said to them.

"She seems like she has an agenda," Haze said, resting her head on his shoulder. *An agenda?* What the fuck was going on?

"Bronwyn is lovely and a great match for your brother. You two are too young to understand," Honey said, waving off their comments.

Haze cut her eyes to Hyphen; they were full of skepticism. Something inside him sprang to attention—his sisters weren't capable of bullshit. Suddenly, he could see every strained, awkward interaction Bronwyn had with the girls. She had yet to truly embrace them or integrate them into their lives. In fact, whenever the twins visited him, they'd leave once Bronwyn arrived.

"We're young but we know Bronwyn Phor wants Hyphen because he's a Haslem. Have you seen her *Vizable* account? It's curated to death," Harleigh said. "And not in a good way."

Honey frowned. "*Vizable?*"

"It's a social media platform," Haze explained.

"You should see the pics she posts of her and Hyphen. You'd think they were running for king and queen of Trianah Metro."

Hyphen didn't have a *Vizable* account, so he had no idea how she presented them online. It was easier to let her do whatever she wanted in order to maintain the peace. But according to his sisters, she had packaged them as some kind of manufactured version of Seacrest royalty and he wasn't feeling that shit at all.

"Bronwyn is smart, beautiful, and from a lovely family," Honey said as if pedigree was enough to make a suitable match.

"She doesn't appreciate who he really is: a funny, thoughtful bookworm," Harleigh said.

"*Bookworm,*" Hyphen groaned.

"Yes," Haze said, looking at him. "How many books are on your nightstand?"

Fuck. His sister knew him better than he gave her credit for. "Five," he grumbled.

"And how many reading lists have you given us?" Harleigh followed up.

Damn, they were coming for his whole life. "Okay," he conceded. Bookworm label aside, he liked to read—it was an escape. It always had been. Despite that, the twins had a point. Bronwyn hadn't embraced that part of him either, always complaining that he'd rather spend time with a book than with her.

"Girls, please," Honey said. "I'm sure Bronwyn loves Hyphen as much as we do."

"I doubt it," Harleigh said under her breath. Honey shot her a look, causing her to curl tighter into Hyphen for protection.

"Mom, who's catering the Lunar Ball?" he asked, changing the subject.

Honey's eyes brightened. "Oh, we've secured Chef Tilly Fields of Rapture; she's outstanding. Have you been there yet? "

"Not yet," Hyphen said, thinking it was only a matter of time before Bronwyn dragged him to another fancy restaurant when he'd rather be at home. "Look, ladies, I can't stay long. I've got lunch with Soren. I just wanted to stop by and say hi," he said, squeezing the twins, who launched into whines about him leaving so soon and never being around. A sucker for their doe-eyed pouts, he stayed longer.

<hr>

Hyphen's hard-sole shoes echoed in the hallway as he made his way to the front door, which opened as soon as he hit the foyer's double staircase. Horace Haslem and his long-time advisor, Talon Seram, walked into the mansion, mid-conversation. Hyphen's stomach dropped. He'd timed his visit so that he wouldn't run into his father. Horace, blond and blue-eyed, wore a gray suit and teal tie. Ruthless, unforgiving, and calculating, nothing eclipsed his desire for power. Talon was the opposite. Always the diplomat, his white hair was parted on the side, and he wore dark round glasses. Always in a three-piece suit, Hyphen often thought Talon seemed frozen in time. As soon as Horace's eyes landed on him, his face iced over in disappointment.

"Hyphen, so good to see you," Talon said with a warm smile.

"Talon, same here. How are you?"

"I'm great," he said. Horace and Talon might've looked young, but they were part of the old guard rooted in tradition. As members of the dwindling group of Aechaih who were alive during Rhoman's

Massacre, they remained fixed in a way of thinking that didn't align with the shifting times.

"Father," Hyphen said as cold as Horace looked.

"Why didn't you tell me there was a human-Aechaih homicide? I had to hear it from your captain."

"I thought you weren't interested in anything I did unless it was at Haslem Corp.," he replied, sliding a hand into his pants pocket.

"Think you're funny, do you?" Horace asked. He was as tall as Hyphen with the same fair skin tone and granite jawline, but that's where the similarities ended between the two.

Uninterested in an argument, Hyphen walked toward the door. "I'm late for an appointment."

"There needs to be an arrest, now!" Horace barked, blocking Hyphen's path. His father's steely-blue eyes roamed over his son's face. Most cowered under Horace Haslem's stare—Hyphen wasn't most.

"If you've already talked to Weeden, then you know the perp's dead," he said flatly.

"That's not good enough. Pawville is full of *dogs*. Look at what they've done to that district. They've clearly developed some sort of drug or sinister method to take us on. This is just the beginning," he said. "You should be scouring the streets, looking for what that human took to make him strong enough to kill one of your own. Our survival depends on it."

"I take orders from my captain," Hyphen said, pushing past Horace to the door.

"You're just like your brother—how you two managed to be soft-hearted toward humans is beyond me. At least Hudson served on the Council *and* worked in the family business. You finally have a chance to make a difference with that ridiculous job of yours, and what do you do? *Nothing,* " Horace spat at Hyphen's back.

See, that was the shit that irked the fuck out of him, and his father knew it. Unable to ignore the dig, Hyphen turned around, his magic humming over his skin. Invisible, it billowed around him, pressing against Horace's magic. Hyphen ground his teeth so hard he was surprised they didn't turn to dust.

"Horace, *enough*," Honey said from the hall, her face a mix of worried and disappointed. Horace's magic receded, but Hyphen's didn't. He pushed it past his father, letting him know that he had no intention of backing down. "Hyphen, dear, don't keep Soren waiting," she continued. Hyphen's eyes slid from his father to his mother, then to Talon, who looked apologetic. He turned on his heel, opened the door and walked out.

Fellowship snapped on a pair of black latex gloves and eased into the perp's apartment, shutting the door behind her. Bathed in shadows, a stream of sunlight poked through the blinds, reflecting off the scuffed hardwood floors. Minimally furnished, the front room had a sofa, coffee table, chair, and a TV stand holding a modest-sized flat screen. Everything was orderly, clean. To the right was a kitchen with enough room for a small dining table and two chairs. Easing down the short hallway, she came upon the bathroom and bedroom. The bed was made; a chalk outline of the perp was by the window to her left. Walking the apartment again, she retraced her steps before carefully going through drawers and closets. Fellowship could discern a lot from how a person lived, and this perpetrator lived like a law-abiding citizen, which was affirmed in the police report. His name was Davis Manicow, no priors—he worked as a clerk at a nearby convenience store. Fellowship's phone buzzed.

"Hey, Ray," she said, putting the phone on speaker.

"Are you at Manicow's?"

"Yeah."

"I'm heading to campus but wanted to make sure you were on your way. I don't want to show up without you."

Fellowship rifled through Manicow's desk drawer: bills, pictures, old mail. Nothing. "Did you happen to watch the club footage?"

"Yep."

"See anything interesting?"

"Nah. Just Manicow chatting up an Aechaih way out of his league. She and a friend left after an hour."

"There's *nothing* here," Fellowship said, standing in the middle of the front room. "Unless I'm missing something, he was just a dude. We won't have the toxicology report back for at least three weeks and that's if they're not backed up."

"You know they're backed up."

"*Fuck.* Okay, I'm headed out. I'll see you on campus," she said, ending the call. Sweeping the apartment one last time, she stopped in the bedroom again, kneeling beside the chalk outline. What the fuck happened in Dove's Alley? Better yet, how in Solneur's name did Manicow kill an Aechaih? On her way to the front door, she stepped on a squeaky floor panel and stopped. Something told her to turn around, so she did. Fellowship stomped until the plank popped up. Heart pounding in her ears, she swiped on her phone's flashlight and looked. Lying on a pile of dust was a phone—*his* phone. Plucking it out of the hole, she pressed the button. As it powered on, she replaced the wood plank. A quick scroll revealed nothing. Searching his pictures, she saw a recording. She pressed play and held her breath. Appearing on the screen was Manicow, who looked frantic and disoriented.

"I—I don't know what happened," he said started. "I'm fucked," he continued, shaking his head in desperation. Returning to the camera, his eyes pleaded for help before he opened his mouth. "I'm innocent of whatever happened because I. Don't. Know. What. The. Fuck. Happened," he said, running his hands through his blonde hair. "I'm hiding my phone because I know if Aechaih cops find this—"

The video ended. *Shit.* No need to wonder how he killed the Aechaih girl—he didn't. Or if he did, he couldn't remember how. None of it clicked in a way that gave her confidence. Pulling an evidence pouch out of her pocket, she bagged the phone. If Manicow didn't know what happened, then the security footage explained his odd behavior. It also explained why he didn't turn himself in. He knew his story wouldn't hold. At the door, she texted Rayna to let her know she'd be on her way once she dropped the phone off to Lemin. Then, with one last look at the apartment, she left.

Chapter Four

Hyphen walked into MoonLyte, an exclusive restaurant in the Historic District. Upon entering, he was whisked away into a jewel-toned eatery with hand-painted walls depicting a romanticized version of the Itchan Forest. A long bar took up the far wall, manned by tall, attractive Aechaih dressed in deep purple dress shirts and slacks. Most of the dark mahogany tables were occupied by stylish customers conversing over high-priced meals. A hostess with a platinum bob and deep purple dress gave Hyphen a cheery smile upon his approach.

"Mr. Haslem, great to see you," she chirped. Hyphen gave her a nod as his eyes scanned the dining room for— "Mr. Syon has already been seated, if you'd like to follow me."

Hyphen, dressed in a black bespoke suit, shirt, and tie, gave her another nod as she led the way. Multiple pairs of eyes watched as he followed her through the dining room to a corner table. He hated the attention he garnered, which was why he didn't frequent popular Aechaih establishments like this one. At work, he was Detective Haslem; everywhere else, he was Hyphen Haslem, heir to the Haslem empire, non-voting member of the Tri-Family Council, and the youngest son of Horace and Honey Haslem. His left hand white-knuckled his phone as he slid his right into his pants pocket, flashing his expensive, custom watch. Like the twins, his hair was a glossy, dark chocolate, faded on the sides into a heavy top that lay in a perfect wave off his face. But unlike them, he was the only family member who had inherited his mother's seafoam green eyes. The hostess extended her hand for him to take a seat across from his childhood friend, Soren, who sat with his signature impish grin, holding a tumbler of whiskey.

"Thank you," Hyphen mumbled, taking his seat.

"Can I take your drink order while you wait?"

"Zion's Ink, neat."

"Coming right up."

"In a mood?" Soren asked. His ice-blue hair was cut into a shaggy style: cropped on the sides and heavy on top, causing most of it to fall over his right eye. He wore a tailored white shirt coupled with gray slacks. His pointed ears sparkled with two diamond studs. Tall and thin with effortless charm and a bountiful trust fund, Soren took no issue with living the Seacrest high life.

"I'm always in a mood," Hyphen replied, setting his phone on the table.

"Fair. What's going on?"

"I stopped by the estate to see my mom and sisters. Ended up running into Horace." Out of nowhere, the hostess appeared with his drink order, placing it gently in front of him. He nodded his thanks and grabbed it, taking a healthy sip.

"How are you not measuring up now?" Soren asked.

"Besides not being Hudson?" The whiskey eased its way down, immediately warming away his angst. He breathed deeply, finally able to settle from the surprise encounter with his father. "He had opinions on my case."

Soren frowned. "I thought he could care less about your job."

"Exactly." Hyphen took another sip. "I wanted to rip his head off. Literally."

"Messy but effective," Soren mused.

Hyphen couldn't help a smile. "Sometimes, I wonder how I'm related to him."

"To be fair, Hudson shielded you from Horace's *stellar* personality."

"Yeah." Hyphen let out an aggravated sigh, unbuttoned his collar, and loosened his tie. "Is your mom on the Sylena Lunar Ball planning committee?"

"*Is* she? It's all she can talk about," Soren said, rolling his eyes.

"That means you're going?"

"I was thinking about making an appearance. I'm sure Bronwyn's insisting you go."

"Yeah—"

"Gentlemen, can I take your order?" Like the rest of the staff, their waitress was tall, thin, and styled to perfection. Hyphen smelled Soren's attraction—his friend was fucking shameless.

"Yes, you can," Soren purred, leaning forward with his elbows on the table. "I'll have the olive wagyu, medium rare, baby potatoes, and your number."

The waitress hid a bashful smile, then turned to Hyphen. "And for you, sir?"

"The same, not your number, but everything else," he said, knocking back his drink. "And another one of these." She nodded and disappeared. "You're out of control," he said to Soren, who was engrossed in watching their waitress walk away.

"She's delicious," he said, practically salivating. Turning his attention back to Hyphen, he frowned. "What? Don't begrudge me a treat."

"When have I ever begrudged you anything?"

Soren gave a playful pout. "True. Speaking of treats, how's the girlfriend?"

"Funny you should ask. I found out the twins don't like her."

Soren's blue eyes widened. "Oh, really?"

"They said she's using me for my name and that she doesn't appreciate me for who I am."

Soren whistled. " Perceptive. Those two are poised to take over the world."

"So, you agree?"

"About Bronwyn? I thought you knew she was obnoxious," Soren said off Hyphen's nod.

"I did but—"

"Didn't think anyone noticed?"

Hyphen shrugged. "Pretty much." That and he couldn't be bothered giving Bronwyn a second thought. After three years of dating, she'd become as important to him as one of his mother's knickknacks.

"What did your mom say?"

Hyphen gave his best friend a look.

Soren nodded. "She loves her."

"She thinks she's a perfect match."

"Hmm. I'd say trust the twins."

"Fuck," Hyphen hissed.

"Sounds like you don't want to deal with Bronwyn *or* your mother's wrath," Soren said with a wink.

"I don't," he grumbled. The response slipped out before he could stop it. He didn't know if it was the Zion's Ink, but the truth of it smacked him in the face. Was he tolerating a shitty relationship to avoid the inevitable fit she and his mother would pitch if he ended it? Did he think she'd somehow turn into a woman he wanted to spend time with? It wasn't like she was his best friend, someone he could be comfortable with. Vulnerable even. Bronwyn had become part of the backdrop to his uneventful life.

"No bullshit: Bronwyn Phor is determined to capitalize on her looks and your family's status to run Seacrest high society. Nothing's wrong with that except you aren't about any of that shit," Soren explained. "So, if you want my advice, get off that ride before it's too late."

Hyphen sighed. He'd been sleepwalking through his own Solneur-damned life, accepting mediocrity over passion. If he didn't wake up, Bronwyn would turn him into a limp-dick asshole she could dress up and parade around like a Solneur-damned dog. She could forget that shit; Hyphen Haslem wasn't anyone's fucking pet.

"If you look over here, you'll see Queen Aniyah's dais and throne," Fellowship said to her students. Once Queen Aniyah's throne room, the ancient, marbled space was now considered a *temple*—a place of reverence. Standing in front of the cream velvet rope that separated visitors from the sacred area, her students crowded around the gold placard. Simple in its explanation, it mentioned the queen's reign without a word spared for her human husband. The tastefully opulent gold and white throne had sat untouched for centuries, save for the few responsible for its maintenance. "Although we've studied the devastating impact of Rhoman's Massacre, we must remember and honor our last Aechaih queen's gifts and love for all," Fellowship said, staring at the throne.

"I don't care what anyone says, she was a badass queen," Nigh said. "Anyone who could bring humans and Aechaih together had to be special."

"I think the Aechaih forget that she was *our* queen, too," Zaphine added. Fellowship couldn't stop her heart from expanding at the sight of her students taking in their history—their *legacy*. Even Cygar looked captivated by the glossy marble dais and shimmering throne. Yes, life was harder for them, but the temple was a gentle reminder of a time when humans were accepted and equal, despite not possessing magical abilities. It was something she felt they needed to experience.

As they descended the steps of the temple, they came to Queen Aniyah's fountain—a glorious marble statue of the Aechaih woman in the center of a lush, green courtyard. The students formed a circle around the base and stared up at the statue as the fountain water softly gurgled. Queen Aniyah, with long, tightly coiled locs and flowing marble robes, stared down at them.

"According to legend, if you throw in a coin and make a wish,

Queen Aniyah will hear and take it to our Guardians Solneur and Sylena," Fellowship said. She knew it was campy, but she couldn't help it. They all needed a little whimsey. She dug into her jacket pocket and produced a coin; looking at Queen Aniyah, she made a wish for a better Trianah. When she looked up, she noticed her class, including *Rayna,* followed suit.

"It's hard to believe you're a cop when I see you with them," Rayna said, as they took a chunk of stairs down to the main street.

"They're my saving grace after the shit we see at work," Fellowship said with a smile.

"They're lucky to have you."

Her faced warmed at the compliment. "Thank you for coming."

"Thanks for inviting me." Fellowship smiled as they descended the rest of the steps toward her class. Yes, she had invited Rayna as a chaperone and to show her a little history, but it was nice having someone next to her—a friend.

Chapter Five

The Historic District was a snapshot of cobblestone streets, and white shops with flowers and manicured greenery lining the sidewalks and hanging from black streetlamps. Not only was the district home to most of Trianah's historical sites, but it also had unique furniture shops and galleries, mixed with trendy restaurants and dark, classy bars. Full and satisfied, Hyphen walked out of Moon-Lyte into one of those perfect Trianah days where everything seemed freshly scrubbed, and vibrant. Leave it to his best friend to lift his spirits. By the time their steaks arrived, the run-in with Horace was a distant memory, and he finally realized he needed to end things with Bronwyn. Hyphen buttoned his collar and tightened his tie while crossing the street. Digging in his pocket for keys, he glanced across the main drag to Queen Aniyah's Temple. He loved that temple and everything about the queen and her time on the throne. As a kid, he couldn't read enough about Trianah's history. After he finished all the books in their family library, Hudson would sneak him volumes from The Archives. The more he read about Queen Aniyah's reign, the more he saw flaws in how Trianah treated its human citizens centuries after the massacre. Although it frustrated his father, he didn't hate them. In fact, after losing Hudson, he admired their ability to love and lose in such short lifespans.

Opening the door to his SUV, Hyphen clocked a group of humans standing in front of the grand staircase. He was about to look away when he saw a woman with short black hair and skin so shimmery brown, it looked like she'd been kissed by Solneur, the Sun God himself. The woman she was talking to must've said something funny because she smiled and he instantly felt sick.

Her. Fucking. Smile.

Hyphen stilled as his Aechaih senses brought her into hyper-focus. She was unlike anyone he'd ever seen and it had nothing to do with her attire, although she looked great in the black leggings, boots, a chunky cream sweater, and a motorcycle jacket. It wasn't the length of her elegant neck when she tipped her head back to laugh or her full, glossy lips. There was something else about her—something familiar. Like getting a shot of adrenaline, he felt like he was flying and grounded at the same time. To him she looked short, but she was probably average height for a human. She was curvy in places he didn't know he wanted soft and plush until now. Massive amounts of Aechaih heat pumped through his veins. He felt possessive. *Primal.* Rooted in place, his eyes lingered on her rounded thighs and ripe, succulent ass. *Oh,* to grab a handful of that ass. He felt sweat on his upper lip.

So, he was a creep, leering at a woman. *Great.*

Hyphen rubbed his clammy hands on his pants as he admired her face. It was open just enough to convince someone she wasn't guarded, but it was there—a protective wall. Even with that megawatt, knock-you-on-your-ass smile, shadows lurked beneath the surface, and sure as shit, he wanted to know why. In fact, he wanted to know *everything* about her. He wanted to hear her voice. He wanted her smile directed at him so he could bask in its glorious—what the *fuck*?!

Shaking his head in an effort to disengage from her magnetism, his Aechaih ears picked up an aggressive growl from a car in desperate need of a muffler. Turning, he saw two humans driving a small, rusted sedan, one holding a *semi-automatic shotgun* out the passenger side window. They didn't see it coming. *She* didn't see it coming. Before he could move, he heard a spray of bullets followed by shrieks and screams. Hyphen slammed his door shut and, without a second thought, sprinted to her.

***

Fellowship was dying.

Eyes on the Trianah-blue sky, she saw there wasn't a cloud in sight. It was perfect. So perfect that she regretted not enjoying it before. Tiny pebbles and minuscule grains of dirt dug into her head. It all happened so fast. She and Rayna were talking shit with Nigh and Zaphine. Shots were fired and, on instinct, she dove in front of her students, taking the bullets instead of them. As darkness ebbed its way into her consciousness, all she could hear was the muffled sound of Rayna calling for medics. Then, like Solneur at dawn, he was there. A violent pain exploded from where his large hand applied pressure to the wound, sending tears sliding from the corners of her eyes.

"Look at me. *Look at me*," he said, his low, smooth voice snagging her attention. Fellowship worked to focus on him—on the greenest eyes she'd ever seen. Green like the Multayvien Sea and just as dangerous. He had long, dark eyelashes and smooth fair skin. Her view zoomed out, revealing hard-angled eyebrows and a straight nose. Impossible cheekbones, a strong jawline, and glossy, dark chocolate hair that she would've loved to run her fingers through. His mouth was alarmingly seductive mouth with pouty, puff-of-pink lips that she wanted to nibble on. An intricate and surprisingly exquisite black tattoo inked its way down the left side of his neck, dipping into his black shirt. He was stunning. Not pretty. Refined. Then her eyes landed on his ears: flawlessly rounded to a point.

He was a Solneur-damned *Aechaih?*

She groaned in protest. Why the fuck was there an Aechaih hovered over her? Where was Rayna? The metallic taste of blood filled her mouth just as her eyelids grew impossibly heavy. She closed them, just for a second—she was so tired.

"What's her name?! Her NAME!" she heard the Aechaih yell.

"Fellowship. Fellowship Dancy."

"Dancy? As in Auten Dancy's *granddaughter*?"

"Yes!" Rayna screamed, returning to the medic call.

"Shit," she heard the Aechaih hiss before he whispered, "Fellowship, open your eyes."

The timbre of his voice crackled over her skin, causing her arms to prickle. Opening her eyes, she found his, and everything stopped. It was only them in a cocoon of safety. Taking a deep, satisfying, and oddly pain-free breath, Fellowship felt a tug at her consciousness. Like trying to remember something just out of reach, it scratched at her until his green eyes melded into the soft, watery green of the Itchan Forest. Suddenly, she was yanked back to her childhood. Like snapshots, she saw her small, brown hands sticky with sweet fruit. Saw herself chasing pixies and playing in the creek. Instead of blood in her mouth, she tasted her grandmother's sweet potato pie and heard her mother's bedtime stories. She felt her father's warm embrace and heard her grandfather's booming laugh. Her mind was overrun with images from a long-forgotten past. The forest, her heart, her home.

Then, in a flash, she was transported to another memory, but it wasn't her own. There were vast and cold marble hallways, banquet tables filled with luscious foods, a cozy bedroom with heavy drapes, and tons of old books. As the memory faded, the green of the forest returned only to reveal his eyes. His face. A cool ripple of energy trickled from the tips of her toes, up her legs, and continued until it felt like she was lying in cold water. Shivering, the cool sensation faded, leaving her suddenly warm, like being swaddled in a wool blanket. His face was so familiar, like a key to some locked part of her psyche. The sudden comfort she felt eased a tightness in her chest—a constant state of worry. Anxiety. Always present. Guilt. Shame. All stacked on top of each other. On top of her. But with him, she felt nothing in the best of ways. The kind of nothing where she could finally rest.

If this is death, dying in his eyes isn't so bad.

"You. Are. Not. Dying. You hear me, Fellowship? You are *not* fucking dying," the Aechaih commanded. He looked at Rayna. "I'm taking her to Septain Memorial," he snapped.

"*Septain?* She's human—"

"She's going to be a *dead* human if we have to wait for your medics to get their asses over here. Besides, she needs healers *now*."

Even as Fellowship admired the Aechaih's profile, she wanted his eyes. She wanted to dip back into their light green sea of safety. If she was going to die like her mother. Die like her grandmother. Die like her father. Die like Daize. She wanted to die in his eyes—float away in a pain-free state of nothingness.

The Aechaih snapped his head down like he'd heard her. Did she say that out loud? His face contorted in confusion, then understanding, and finally fear. True, unguarded fear. "Fuck this," he mumbled. He was gone one moment and back the next, *shirtless.* Lifting her off the sidewalk, she settled into his strong grip, his tattooed chest warm and solid against her face. "Stay with me, Fellowship," he whispered.

Where am I gonna go, Aechaih?

He smiled, his lips parting to reveal gleaming white teeth and slightly elongated canines. *My name's Hyphen.*

You shouldn't have heard me. I'm dead.

You're not dead, but I can hear you.

How?

I don't know. Look, Fellowship, I don't want you to freak out, but I'm going to fly you to the hospital, okay?

Fly? If you say so.

I say so, Fellowship.

Darkness.

A soft, yet powerful, flap of wings. She was flying. *They* were flying. *I'm dead. I'm dead and being carried to the Salveigh Mist.*

You're not dead, Fellowship. We're almost there.

And yet we're flying.

Yes.

And we're speaking telepathically.

Yes.

I'm dead.

You're not dead, I promise.

Darkness.

Fellowship, wake up.

Her eyes felt like lead, but she did as she was told. Focusing, she saw him. *Hyphen, I'm going to share something with you, but I don't want it to go to your head, okay?*

His brow furrowed, then he gave a small nod. *Okay.*

Your eyes are fucking beautiful.

He laughed. *Thank you.*

I normally don't compliment Aechaih because, well, that doesn't matter. But I thought I'd tell you since you've been so nice, and in case I don't make it.

You'll make it, Fellowship.

But just in case.

Okay.

Okay, good.

Smiling down at her, she noticed faint lines at the corners of his eyes. Eyes that looked like they'd seen their fair share of death. Eyes that were haunted, dark, and tired like hers.

"You're going to be okay, Fellowship," he said. For some strange reason, she believed him. After a beat, she heard the wheels of a stretcher draw near.

"What do we have, Detective?"

"GSW, no exit."

"Get her on the stretcher."

Fellowship felt herself being lowered down, but being out of his arms felt wrong. Unsteady. Unsafe. The nothingness ebbing at her consciousness suddenly felt frightening as the thought of dying lost its appeal. She didn't want to be alone. Didn't want to be out of his arms.

Hyphen, I'm scared. I used to think death was better than the darkness, but now I'm not sure. Don't leave me.

Blinking, he held her gaze as the muscle in his jaw feathered. *Never, Fellowship. I'll never leave you.*

Darkness.

Hyphen stood in his steaming shower and watched pink water swirl down the drain. Blood. *Her* blood. The human that stopped him in his tracks. The human who lay dying. The human he managed to men-com with. The human he *flew* to Septain Memorial.

He *flew*.

He hadn't flown in over twenty-five years and hadn't wanted to. Sometimes he forgot he was a winged Aechaih, seeing that he was the only one in modern Trianah. By the time he was born, there hadn't been winged Aechaih in centuries, which made him an outcast—a freak. Even his last name didn't protect him from the onslaught of torment. It was Hudson who made him feel special, who brought him history books on the ancient, winged Aechaih who fought to protect Trianah. Hudson who taught him to be proud of his gift. After some time, he listened and took pride in his wings, understanding that he was unique. But when Hudson died, his love for flight, for being different, died with him until he heard Fellowship Dancy resign to death. Suddenly, he was consumed with a vehement determination to save her. Who cared about the whispers or the stares. For her, he stretched his wings. For her, he soared.

Don't leave me.

Never, Fellowship. I'll never leave you.

He stayed with her until she was out of healing and safely tucked into a private hospital suite. The room, with its creamy white walls and heavy linens, still smelled like disinfectant. Without thinking, he grabbed her hand. She looked so small, so fragile in the oversized Aechaih bed. Her skin was as soft as Aechaih-spun silk as he tenderly rubbed the back of her hand with his thumb. Fellowship Dancy was an aberration, some glitch or test by the Guardians because nothing could be so Solneur-damned perfect. When her mind opened to him, and they dipped into conversation, he figured it was because she was in bad shape. And while he hated that she was in pain, he loved how she felt in his mind.

I'm here, Fellowship. Wake up.

No response.

She was healed, so maybe their connection was gone. The silence was overbearing and whether he wanted to admit it or not, it scared him. He felt the familiar, icy wind of abandonment slap him in the face. Hyphen stepped out of the shower, dried off, and slung the towel around his waist. His penthouse was an open concept with floor-to-ceiling windows, custom-made furniture, a crackling fireplace, and private elevator. His rooftop living space had a pool, outdoor furniture, and a fire pit. He padded to the kitchen, opened his subzero fridge, and grabbed a beer. Twisting off the cap, he tipped it up, letting the coolness chill his insides.

Hyphen, I'm scared. I used to think death was better than the darkness, but now I'm not sure. Don't leave me.

Her honesty tugged at an old wound. When Hudson died, he welcomed the darkness. Longed for it, confident that it would be better than his painful reality. Her truth made him feel seen, like shining a spotlight on his shadowed existence. His arms still tingled from carrying her, and his mind was raked raw from their mental telepathy. Realizing nothing good could come from whatever the fuck he was feeling, he tried to push the incident to the back of his mind and finish his beer. His phone rang; thankful for the distraction, he grabbed it and frowned. It was his father.

"Yes," he answered, unenthused.

"You *flew* a *human* to *our* hospital? Are you dense?" Horace spat.

Hyphen leaned against the counter and closed his eyes. Dealing with Horace twice in one day was too much for anyone to handle. "She was in trouble, so I helped. I'm a cop, remember," he said as calmly as he could.

"How could I forget? Reckless. That's what you are, a bleeding-heart, reckless *boy*," Horace said, his voice thin and cold.

"I wasn't going to let her die." What he should've told his father was that he was *physically incapable* of letting her die, but he had a feeling Horace wouldn't appreciate his candor.

"It's not our job to save them."

"It's my job to help whoever I can, especially another cop."

"A *human* cop."

"A human cop who also happens to be Ambassador Dancy's grand-daughter," Hyphen clipped out, running low on patience.

"Fine. If you *had* to help, you could've at least *driven* her to *their* hospital."

"She wouldn't have made it."

"How is that your problem?"

Hyphen gripped the beer bottle so tight, he almost shattered it.

Horace continued, "Why did Septain admit her? There's a strict Aechaih-only policy for a reason. They're to have *no* access to our healers."

"It might come as a surprise, but you're not the only Haslem in Trianah."

"And *that's* how you use our name? To help a human?"

"Is there anything else?" Hyphen asked his arrogant, piece-of-shit father. The phone beeped. Pulling it from his ear, he looked down—Horace was gone. Hyphen set the phone down and sighed. He may have won the battle, but the war would never be over.

The private elevator dinged then opened—Bronwyn. *Great.*

"You're here," she said, sauntering across the beige hardwood floor. All legs and blue eyes with thick, long blonde hair, she wore a blue sheath dress and heels, making her almost eye-level with him. Take a rich, mean girl with a bullshit job and a desire for prestige, and you'd have Bronwyn Phor.

"Where else would I be?"

"I don't know, out saving more humans, I guess," she said from the other side of the kitchen island. Face tight in annoyance, she set her designer bag on the counter. "So, it's true. You saved a human?"

Taking a pull from his bottle, he nodded. "Yes."

"And you *flew?*"

Of course, she'd zero in on *that*. Bronwyn had never seen his wings because, no matter how often she asked, the request always felt disingenuous. So around her, he kept them tucked behind his energetic field.

After a few scrolls on her phone, she looked up. "At least it's playing well over social media. It helps that she's the Human Ambassador's granddaughter."

Solneur help him. "I don't care."

"I know you don't, but *I* do. It's definitely not hurting our brand," she said, finally walking around the island and past him to grab a bottle of white wine. Her normally average scent had become foreign to him. It was repugnant, almost gagging him with its aggressive twang. She poured, recapped, and took a sip. "Did she live?" she asked, as an afterthought.

"Yes. Still unconscious," he said, finishing his beer. *Hyphen, I'm scared. I used to think death was better than the darkness, but now I'm not sure. Don't leave me.* Fellowship's smell was still with him—shea butter, a sweet perfume, and her humanness. And to his fucking surprise, it comforted him like a hushed library. Why was he so out of sorts? None of it made sense—unless it made so much sense that it scared the shit out of him. Freaked out, he decided bitch or not, Bronwyn was a much-needed distraction, even if she still hadn't asked how *he* was doing.

Returning to her side of the island, she slipped onto the barstool and scrolled through her phone again. Without looking up, she said, "Let's hope she wakes up or all of this drama was for nothing." Ignoring the dig, Hyphen put his beer bottle on the counter, walked over, and stood in front of her. She looked up, shocked. Taking a deep breath, he gave her his best I'm-going-to-fuck-the-shit-out-of-you look. She returned it immediately. Sex was the answer. It was all he needed to purge Fellowship Dancy from his system.

Chapter Six

The hushed city gleamed like polished onyx. Fellowship pounded the pavement, earphones blasting. She'd run the ten-mile stretch from her high-rise, through Pawville to the Multayvien Sea, and back *every* morning since she was discharged from the Aechaih hospital six weeks ago. Running turned out to be the only thing that cleared her head from disjointed memories, vivid nightmares, and increased restlessness.

Never, Fellowship. I'll never leave you.

Even though she couldn't remember much from the shooting, the phrase was on a constant loop in her head. That and soulful green eyes. After she woke, her grandfather told her that it was Hyphen Haslem who took her to the Aechaih hospital and ensured she received the best care. If it weren't for the fact that she woke up *in* Septain Memorial, she wouldn't have believed it. What were the chances of being saved by the very Aechaih she was convinced didn't take his job seriously? Although grateful for his help, she wasn't sure how she felt about being saved. Not because of him, but because healed or not, she still felt an inescapable darkness within. A darkness so violent, she'd started to wish that he hadn't saved her at all. But those were the feelings she kept to herself, tucked away in her heart while she pretended to be happy. Besides, being healed wasn't all bad—it happened to bring someone special back to her life.

When she woke up in Septain and saw her grandpa next to her, his eyes red from crying, her heart's protective shell cracked open, unleashing years of pent-up emotion. The release freed her from some of the darkness, or at least the cold, walled-off version of herself that had cut off her only remaining family. Unable to hold it back, she bawled. Auten rubbed her hand, his own tears flowing freely.

"Grandpa," she choked out. There was so much she wanted to say, so much she *needed* to say. Daize and her family, her safe spaces of love, had been taken from her, and the anger from that loss made her push people away, including her grandfather. It made her sick, the ignorance of it all. Auten shushed her as he lovingly stroked her cheek with the back of his hand. He was handsome with his creamy brown skin, neatly cut white hair, and beard. He was dashing. Her lovely, dashing grandpa.

"Fellowship, I love you so much. The thought of losing you was my nightmare come true," he whispered before he dropped his head, his shoulders trembling. Guilt and shame warmed her face.

"Grandpa," she said, her voice hoarse from not being used. "I'm sorry. Sorry for being a selfish asshole. Sorry for my hostility and lack of understanding. You've only wanted the best for me," she said through her tears. "Please, look at me," she whispered. Although her throat was dry and brittle and her tongue felt like sandpaper, she had to get him to understand how much she loved him. Missed him. Auten looked at her, his face red; she continued. "I don't care that you're the Human Ambassador for the Council. They need someone as wonderful as you. As smart and thoughtful. As conscientious and loyal. I've been so arrogant. Shortsighted..." It was all she could get out before she crumbled into another sob. Coughing over tears of guilt, shame, relief and exhaustion, she sank into his brown, loving eyes. Eyes that she loved in return. Although the memories of her childhood were faint, she still had access to her love for him. Her grandfather. Her person. The only one in all of

Trianah who knew and loved her no matter what. Auten grabbed tissues off her bedside table and dabbed her eyes before dabbing his own. She grabbed his hand.

"I fucked up," she said, closing her eyes.

"Fellowship, no. I've always understood your resentment," he said, offering her a way out.

Opening her eyes, she pinned him with her gaze. "No. I fucked up. Even if I didn't understand, I should've supported you like you've always supported me," she said. "I owe you everything and..." Pain and years of solitude surfed the wave of her tears. In that hospital room, she made the decision to grow the fuck up and mend their relationship. No more unsaid things. No more grudges or animosity. He was the one thing that held any value to her besides her job.

Fellowship continued running. With a sharp chill settling over Trianah, she was dressed in warm running gear and a TMPD hat pulled down low. She wasn't out of breath, nor did she have scorched lungs or nagging pain in her left knee. Call her crazy, but she felt *better* than ever. Fellowship had no idea what was going on, but she didn't complain. Since Ceager still had her on desk duty, petrified that letting her out of the precinct would lead to her imminent death, all she had was her new rhythm: a few hours of sleep and a lot of running.

"You've only been back a month, Dancy," Ceager told her the last time she badgered him about getting back on the Manicow case.

"That's fair, sir, but believe me when I tell you—I'm *fine*. I've passed my mental and physical evaluations, and it's not like I was shot in the line of duty," she pushed back.

Ceager rubbed his head. "You think you're fine, but that's because you don't feel as bad as you did. I won't let you overdo it."

"Sir, I've lost so much time. We still need to figure out what happened to Manicow."

Ceager sighed. "Dancy, the case is closed."

"But—"

"We told the Aechaih Division about the footage Lemin found, and they weren't interested. Take it as a sign to go easy."

Fellowship knew he meant well. He'd called multiple times while she was in the hospital, asking her grandfather for updates. And while she was grateful for the concern, it bordered on coddling, and she was sick of it. In fact, she was sick of everyone treating her like she was some fragile thing. To top it off, the college found a substitute for her class, which meant she had nothing but her day job to keep her sane, and it was failing miserably. If she didn't sink her teeth into another case, she was going to become a whole-ass menace.

Feet pounding the worn, brown pier, the sweat on her face made the wind feel even more icy on her skin. Stopping, she took in the Multayvien Sea. Taking a deep breath of salty air, she leaned on the wooden rails and stretched her muscles as the green, heavy water lapped against the pier. There was something familiar about it—the sea. It was one of the reasons she ran to it every morning. It temporarily warmed her from within, like sitting in front of a fire or slipping on wool mittens. The seafoam green had become her safe place, wrapping its arms around her, telling her everything would be okay. That the increasing hollowness she felt inside her chest would one day recede. After a few more stretches, Fellowship turned around and began the journey back to her apartment.

The studio apartment looked like a young woman lived there. It was colorful, slightly cluttered, and lived in. A cream screen separated the living area from the bedroom. From where Hyphen stood, he couldn't see past the screen but that didn't matter because whatever was behind it wasn't good if Monroe's face was any indication. Crossing the room in a few steps, Hyphen stood at the foot of the blood-soaked bed where the body of an Aechaih woman lay with multiple stab wounds. It was a violent kill by someone who didn't give a shit.

"We have a second set of prints all over the apartment," Monroe reported. "And the fucking murder weapon."

Hyphen nodded. The killer was either enraged, sloppy, or trying to be caught. The victim was still in her pajamas. Her short pink hair was disheveled, and her eyes were closed, indicating that she might have been killed in her sleep.

"Sir, we've got a human on CCTV," a patrol cop said, poking his head in the bedroom.

Hyphen looked at Monroe and sighed. "Another fucking human?"

Monroe shook his head. "Shit."

"We have a cellphone?"

"Yes."

"Let me guess, *FBDn?*"

Monroe nodded and flipped open his black book. "Yes, but she knew the person. Had a long thread with them. In between random conversations, there were short discussions about glower-weed deliveries," Monroe explained.

Hyphen nodded, his eyes still on the body. "Glower-weed doesn't give someone superhuman strength."

"No."

Hyphen felt a twinge of unease when it came to the two murders. Obviously, there was a connection. They needed a break in the case before more Aechaih ended up dead at the hands of *humans*, even if that shit sounded ridiculous.

———

The Human Division's Criminal Investigation Unit was deserted, save for Fellowship who sat at her computer, staring at nothing in particular. Thankfully, Ceager was out, so she didn't have to work hard at looking busy. Her desk had been cleaned and organized multiple times; files were rearranged, and cold cases sent down to the archives. With nothing left on her to-do list, she was close to cleaning her colleagues' desks when her cellphone buzzed.

She answered and leaned back in her chair. "Hey, Grandpa."

"How's my girl?"

"Meh," she said as she fiddled with a TMPD pen.

"Ceager still has you on the desk?"

"Yes," she said, looking around the empty office. "I might be going crazy."

"Want me to talk to him?" Auten asked with a mischievous note in his voice.

She smiled. "Absolutely not. No fighting my battles," she playfully reprimanded. "I'll figure something out."

"Because I can," he added.

"I know you can, but no," she said. "He can't maroon me on the desk forever. He knows what I bring to the table." At least she *hoped* he did. Her workdays now consisted of being left alone in the office under the watchful glare of her boss while Rayna and her colleagues worked various cases. Grateful that neither Rayna nor her students were injured, she couldn't face her friend beyond work pleasantries. Ray's compassionate stare and hushed tones grated on her nerves. The pity was too fucking much.

"You think you'll be back in the classroom next semester?"

"I hope so. I miss it," she said with a sigh. Everything was off. Different. It felt like she'd lost so much time while recovering, like her place in the world had been filled, leaving her an outsider.

"Have you been sleeping?"

She paused. "I'm getting a few hours."

"Nightmares?"

"They're manageable."

"The same ones as before?"

"Plus new ones," she said, not wanting to worry him.

"Anything you can talk about?"

Fellowship bit her lower lip. The nightmares were mostly fragments of images she didn't recognize, but it was the *fear* that woke her. The inevitable feeling that all was lost. Sometimes, she'd wake up crying, distraught over something she couldn't even remember.

"You don't have to," he added quickly.

Spinning her chair, she looked out the office windows. "It's mostly stuff I don't understand, places I've never been. The fear is unbearable. The loss, but not my personal loss; it's for someone I don't know."

"Oh," Auten whispered.

"But by the time I go running, it disappears."

"You think you should talk to someone about them?"

"I'm fine." The last thing she needed or wanted was some doctor poking around in her head.

"Okay, sweetheart. So, I've been meaning to ask, would you like to be my date for the Sylena Lunar Ball?"

"The Aechaih event?"

"Yes."

Seacrest. Ugh. Aechaih. Double ugh. Maybe going out with her grandfather and seeing him in action wouldn't be so bad. "Okay," she said, nodding even though he couldn't see her.

"Really?"

"Sure," she said. "I wouldn't mind getting dolled up and hanging out with you."

"I..." Auten paused.

She heard a sniff on his end. Solneur, he was crying *again*. Since her accident, he'd been extra emotional, crying at the drop of a hat. "Grandpa, what did I tell you about all this crying? Get it together, Mr. Waterworks," she teased.

Auten barked a laugh. "I didn't think you'd say yes," he admitted.

"I'm not going to pass up a chance to hit the town with my favorite guy," she said just as her line beeped. Not recognizing the number, she frowned. "Grandpa, it's my other line."

"Yes, yes of course," he said. "I'll talk to you later."

"I love you."

"I love you, too, so very much," he said, ending the call.

Fellowship answered the other line. "Detective Dancy."

"Professor Dancy, it's Zaphine."

Fellowship immediately picked up the distress in her voice. "What's wrong, Zaphine?" Her senses kicked into overdrive as hot adrenaline pumped through her veins.

"It's Nigh. She's in trouble, serious trouble, Professor."

"Tell me."

"She's been picked up by the police. They think she murdered an *Aechaih*."

"Was she arrested by the Human Division or Aechaih?" Fellowship asked as anxiety congealed in her stomach.

"The Human Division. She called me last night, saying she was in trouble. I told her to call you, then I tried to get her to meet somewhere or come to my house, but she refused. I didn't hear from her again. My cousin saw TMPD grab her early this morning. She was hiding in the alley behind the Save-Mart," Zaphine said through tears.

"And you're sure it was humans who arrested her?"

"Yes. I don't know if you can help, Professor, but I *had* to call. I'm sorry, I know you're still recovering from—"

"It's okay, Zaphine, you did the right thing. I'm going to find out what's going on. Don't worry," Fellowship said as she tried to tell herself the same thing.

"Okay. Thank you, Professor."

"Take care of yourself, Zaphine. I'll try to get you an update if I can."

"Okay."

Fellowship ended the call and let out a breath. Her head ached and her hands itched with heat as she tried to process the information. She needed facts, and calling Ceager or Rayna wasn't an option. If Nigh was just booked, there was a chance she hadn't been transferred to Seacrest yet. Standing, she shrugged on her blazer and stalked out of the unit.

In the basement of the precinct, Detainment was a long, washed-out hallway with plexiglass cells on either side. Fellowship approached the processing desk with a dazzling smile. The cop, a young man with hazel eyes, smiled back.

"Detective Dancy, good to see you," he said.

"Same here. How are you?"

"Oh, I'm okay," he said.

"Ceager sent me down to question Nigh Rygle since I'm still on desk duty and he's busy," she said.

"Yes, of course," he replied, eager to please. "She's in four."

"Thank you," she said, adding extra wattage to her smile.

"My pleasure, Detective," he said as he buzzed her in. The door clanked before she pulled it open and walked to cell four. The cell was bright, scrubbed, and small, with only a bed and toilet. Nigh sat curled in the corner, wearing an orange jumpsuit. She bit the inside of her jaw, then looked at the camera. The cop buzzed her in.

Nigh looked up, her face pale. As soon as her eyes landed on Fellowship, she started crying. "Professor, what are you *doing* here?" she asked, her voice hoarse and thin. It took Fellowship all her strength not to wrap the girl in her arms.

"What happened, Nigh? Tell me everything, now," Fellowship said, leaning against the cinderblock wall.

"You're not supposed to be here. You're recovering," she choked out.

"We don't have much time, Nigh."

"I fucked up," Nigh whispered.

"What happened?"

"I was in Seacrest with one of my regulars when I blacked out or something," she said, her voice wavering. "When I woke up, I was covered in blood. And there..." Her face turned red as she choked up. "There she was, throat slit with stabs everywhere. I freaked out and came home."

Fellowship's stomach rolled. Back against the wall, she sank down, squatting. "She was a regular?"

"Yes." Wiping her eyes, Nigh looked away.

Fellowship knew there was more to the story. "Nigh," she said softly. "I can't help you if you don't tell me the whole truth."

Tears fell as Nigh closed her eyes. "We were seeing each other," she whispered, head down. "We met on *FBDn*. She was a customer first, then we started talking."

"What did you sell her?"

"Just glower-weed," Nigh said.

"How long were you in her apartment?"

Face red, Nigh's shoulders trembled. "Half the night. When I woke up..." she choked off a sob.

Fuck. That meant her prints were all over the Solneur-damned apartment. "When you woke up, did you have the murder weapon?"

"No," she said, hiccupping through her tears.

"Were you blackout drunk?"

"*No*, Professor. I don't remember anything besides laughing and talking with her, then falling asleep. I wouldn't kill her, Professor. I mean, if I did, I don't remember. I wasn't drunk. I just...I don't know," she cried, shaking her head. "I don't know what happened."

Fellowship knew Nigh was telling the truth, but as it stood, there was too much evidence to prove otherwise. She felt herself unraveling at the sound of Nigh's sobs. What the fuck was going on? Two murders with two human suspects reporting memory loss. None of that shit sounded right.

"Nigh, I'm not going to shit you, it looks bad. I believe you, and I'm going to do everything in my power to delay your transfer to Seacrest and figure out what's going on. Keep telling the truth, no matter how they intimidate you. Can you remember anything before you blacked out? Anything at all?"

Nigh wiped her eyes and took a few calming breaths. She looked so young, so small. "While we were on the balcony, I didn't see Sylena or her sisters. It was so dark. I know it sounds weird, but that's what I remember thinking," she said.

Fellowship couldn't remember the last time she didn't see the Moon Goddess and her sisters in the Trianah night sky. "Okay. I've gotta get out of here," she said, standing. "Tell the truth and don't be afraid, okay?"

Nigh nodded, eyes still watering. "Thank you, Professor. Zaphine told me to call you, but I didn't want you to be disappointed in me."

The stone in Fellowship's throat refused to descend. She blinked back a tear, steadying herself. "Can I trust you, Nigh? From what I know, you're a capable young woman. Am I wrong?" Fellowship asked, pinning Nigh with her stare.

Nigh returned it. "No, you're not wrong, and yes, you can trust me, Professor. I promise."

"That's what I thought. Okay, I have to go."

"Thank you, Professor, and I'm sorry," Nigh said, her shoulders slumping even more.

"There's nothing to be sorry for, Nigh."

"Yes, there is. The shooting at the temple. Rey's got beef, and they retaliated. You jumped in front of me. Saved me. I should be dead. Maybe if I was, Sari would..." She crumbled into sobs. Fuck the cameras *or* her boss. Fellowship crossed the room, sat on the bed, and hugged Nigh, who cried into her shoulder. Rocking her back and forth, she shushed her as her student shook with tears.

"Everything's going to be okay," Fellowship said.

Nigh wiped her face and gave her a sad, bleary smile. "Thank you, Professor."

"Take care of yourself, Nigh. I'm working as hard as I can," she said. Nigh nodded as Fellowship stood and left.

Chapter Seven

The red carpet at the Sylena Lunar Ball fundraiser held a steady stream of prominent Aechaih inching toward the entrance. Hyphen frowned as camera flashes snapped and cracked practically blinding him. Annoyed, he stood with one hand in his pants pocket as Bronwyn slung herself on his arm, showcasing her figure with quick, choreographed poses.

"The least you can do is smile," she said through her teeth as photographers shouted their names, hungry for the perfect shot. Ignoring the spectacle, Hyphen stalked away, entering the building and walking directly into the grand ballroom.

Bronwyn quickly caught up to him. "Why are you behaving like a child?" she hissed.

"I came to be inside, not outside," he snapped. The glassy marble floor reflected the oversized chandeliers' warm glow. Tables drenched with opulent, fresh-flower centerpieces, lavish buffet tables, and multiple cascading champagne towers would've felt decadently festive had he not been in such a shitty mood. Finding the nearest server, he snatched a champagne flute off a silver tray and drained its contents.

"Fine. We're inside now, so behave," Bronwyn whispered in his ear.

Clutching his arm, they snaked through the dense crowd of smart tuxedos and glittering gowns. "Oh, there's Mr. and Mrs. Varan. I need their backing for the next fundraiser. He's clueless and she's a poser, but that doesn't stop them from writing fat checks."

"I'm not in the mood for small talk." He'd been nursing a sour, non-work-related mood for some time. With no idea why he felt so *meh*, all he wanted was to go home, get in bed, and stream a movie. *Alone.*

"You don't have to say anything," she said, approaching the couple whose eyes widened at the sight of them.

"Daphne, Larz, how wonderful to see you," Bronwyn said with a bright, calculating smile.

"The pleasure's ours, Miss Phor. Mr. Haslem, great to see you," Daphne Varan replied. Offering a curt nod, Hyphen checked out of the conversation. The event was packed with Seacrest elite, from business moguls and celebrities to members of the Tri-Family Council. The soothing string arrangements from the orchestra helped to ease his nagging discomfort. Placing his empty flute on a passing tray, he grabbed another, ignoring his date's disapproving side-eye.

Once his sisters admitted to not liking Bronwyn, he was prepared to end it, until getting spooked by his growing obsession with Fellowship Dancy. In an effort to distract himself from the human detective, he postponed the breakup, but sadly the effort didn't work. The vines of her allure infiltrated his subconscious to the point that she was everywhere: on his way to sleep, in the shower, during his morning commute, or in his meetings. As days turned into weeks, memories of her held him hostage until he finally admitted to himself that he had a crush on a woman he didn't know while still in a relationship with a woman he despised.

Needing to see a friendly face, he scanned the crowd for his sisters or Soren when a wisp of familiar energy floated through his mind, directing his eyes to a parting sea of attendees.

No. Fucking. Way.

Standing next to her grandfather was Fellowship Dancy. It looked like a falling star had landed in their midst. She wore a sheer, long-sleeved gown with hand-sewn crystals over the sweetheart neckline and bodice, spilling down the tea-length skirt. Unlike most women disguising themselves with long hair, Fellowship's short black hair allowed her face to shine. Plainly put, she was one of a kind—a Solneur-kissed goddess in a room of mass-produced Aechaih women.

Heart thudding, his hormones went ballistic, scattering his thoughts. Blinking rapidly, he knocked back his champagne without taking his eyes off her. Suddenly, he smelled hospital disinfectant and heard the rhythmic beeping of monitors. Even his hands twitched like they remembered holding hers. As the champagne zipped through his bloodstream, it vanquished the night's tension. Seeing her again lightened his mood. Instantly, everything around him sprang to life as the ballroom sparkled with magic. The music sounded sweeter, and the food smelled so good his stomach growled.

Then, like a string tugging her eyes, she looked directly at him. To his credit, he held her gaze, refusing to disengage. Something unknown flashed across her face before she looked away. What in Solneur's name was that? Did she recognize him? Crackling with energy, Hyphen felt buoyant, bordering on hysterical. Seeing her again was a clear sign from the Guardians that he *had* to talk to Fellowship Dancy—of that, he was sure.

Fellowship felt someone's eyes on her, pulling at her consciousness. It was like an open mental line that allowed her to perceive their energy vibrating along the connection—like a mental text message. As surprising and odd as the sensation was, something about it felt natural. Looking in the direction of the energetic pull, she saw two seafoam green eyes. Heart in her throat, she swallowed. She'd recognize those eyes anywhere. It was Hyphen Haslem, watching her from across the ballroom in an impeccable tux, holding an empty champagne flute. *Solneur*, she didn't remember him being that fine—

"Fellowship, we're so happy you're doing well. What you did for those students at the temple was nothing short of heroic," someone said. She looked away from Hyphen to the older Aechaih woman whose name she couldn't remember. "We need more humans like you and your grandfather. You're such a *credit* to your species," she gushed.

What the fuck did she just say? Fellowship felt her grandfather tense. Biting her tongue, she smiled at the overdressed woman, giving her an obligatory nod as if she agreed with the bullshit sentiment. A swell of indignation expanded in her chest as her hands itched with heat. She needed a moment. Being trapped in a ballroom full of Aechaih made her lightheaded and vengeful. They all drifted about in carefree ignorance while across town, a population of humans lived in poverty and perpetual hunger. As hard as she tried, it was difficult to ignore the ease of their world compared to hers and those she cared about.

"If you'll excuse me, I need to find the ladies' room," she said with her most diplomatic smile. Lack of diplomacy her ass, if only Ceager could see her now. Auten winked, acknowledging her need to get away.

"Oh, of course," the woman said. Fellowship turned and walked toward an exit—any exit. With no idea where the restroom was, she moved down a darkened hall, following it until approaching three arched windows. The hallway was quiet and cool, the only light coming from planet Nehlahni's three moons—the brightest being Sylena, the Moon Goddess, and her two sisters, Mylena and Uphraine. Standing at the window, she beheld their reflection on the sea; the choppy water looked resplendent under their light.

Fellowship hated small talk, especially with Aechaih. Watching her grandfather engage with them was like being in a master class; he was all smiles and charm, completely comfortable in their presence. Meanwhile, she felt out of place, lost and vulnerable. They were magical beings and being around them felt like a bolt of electricity being shoved up her ass. A *credit* to her species; it was shit like that that dug underneath her skin. She and her grandfather were seen as acceptable humans while the others were, what? Unacceptable? Expendable? Determined not to fall into a shitty mood, she chalked the comment up to Aechaih ignorance. Watching the waves crash onto shore, her mind drifted to Nigh.

I don't know what happened.

They were the same words used by Davis Manicow. Fellowship's gut told her that it wasn't a coincidence both of them lost a chunk of time and woke up to a crime scene they couldn't remember. Unfortunately, she didn't have much to go on but a hunch, and with the evidence stacked against Nigh, she'd need more than that. Fear had made Manicow find another way out, and she didn't want that for her student. Without intel on the crime scene, she'd have to talk to Ceager, who would give her shit, but—

"You look better than the last time I saw you."

Whipping around, there was Hyphen Haslem standing in Sylena's light. In the time it took her heart to nosedive to her stomach, she took him in and decided that no one should look *that* good in a tux.

She figured that being charmingly aloof would play better than how she really felt, so she went with, "It's Ampersand, right?"

By the time he lifted a perfectly arched eyebrow, she realized she'd made a mistake. For most, the gesture was innocuous, but on him it was so effortlessly confident, it temporarily stopped her heart. Most Aechaih men were boringly good-looking, but Hyphen had managed to corner the market on painfully handsome and disturbingly sexy. To make matters worse, underneath the sharp jawline and commercial-worthy hair wasn't a rich boy *playing* cop—Hyphen Haslem *was* a cop. Steady. Alert. Resigned. And to her dismay, he emanated an I-wish-a-motherfucker-would-vibe that fanned the tiny flickers dancing in her lower abdomen.

"It's Hyphen," he corrected, slipping a hand in his pants pocket while taking a step toward her.

"I guess I need to brush up on my punctuation marks," she replied.

"Actually, ampersand is a logogram, not a punctuation mark."

This fucking guy. "Thanks for the tip."

"It's a common mistake, but to be fair, you were half dead when we met. I wouldn't expect you to remember me, let alone my name," he said, taking yet another step toward her.

The closer he got, the more unsettled she felt, and why did it suddenly smell like lavender, warm sand, and saltwater? *Guardians*, it was *him*. Her mind opened to a series of memories from her time at Septain: hospital disinfectant, oversized beds, and soft gowns. But the most prominent memory was of seacoast and lavender. It reminded her that everything was going to be okay and smelling it again—better yet, smelling its owner—left her head spinning like she'd had too many glasses of champagne. Her eyes traced his pointed ears down to the tattoo on the left side of his neck. Swallowing, she wondered what it would feel like running her tongue along the black ink. Shutting down her thirsty-ass thoughts, she desperately tried to remain unbothered.

"Sorry, I don't remember much from that day."

"That's okay, you were in shock."

"I never thanked you for your help." A half-truth: she never thanked him because she hadn't tried. Every time her grandpa badgered her about it, she'd dig in her heels and refuse.

"You're welcome."

"Although, I would've never expected an Aechaih to save a human the way you did," she added, suddenly hot. His body heat *and* magic radiated off him like flames, licking at her skin. She detected his lean, muscular frame underneath his tailored tux—broad and solid, not bulky. At least six-five, he towered over her even in heels. And the more she wanted to disconnect from his eyes, the more she couldn't.

"Never occurred to me. I heard shots and ran over. Who were those other humans you were with?"

"My students. I adjunct at the college."

"What do you teach?"

"History."

"A cop *and* a teacher...I didn't take you for a history nerd," he said with a smile.

Fuck that lazy smile and the heat it sent to her core. Taking a step back in a feeble attempt to escape him, she bumped into the cool window. Great, she was trapped with the planet's sexiest Aechaih—just her fucking luck. Realizing she hadn't responded, she went off the cuff. "Actually, I prefer history *enthusiast*," she said, lifting her chin.

Another smile. "That's why you were at Queen Aniyah's Temple."

"It's one of my favorite places to visit," she let slip. What was happening? The room felt like it was beginning to tilt, if she didn't hold onto something, she'd slide into him, drape her arms around his neck, and kiss his perfect, pink mouth.

"It's my favorite as well," he admitted.

Narrowing her eyes, she tilted her head. "Weren't you there when it was built? I mean, you *look* young but what are you, seven hundred?" she flirted—*asked*—she asked.

His laugh skipped along her skin, leaving tingles everywhere it landed. With a smile lingering in his eyes, he shook his head. "I'm not *that* old." Smooth and commanding, his voice triggered something in her that wanted to obey his every word. Suddenly horny (because she hadn't had *company* since being shot), her cool, collected cop exterior trembled under his attentive gaze. Then the strangest, most unexpected thing happened. Time seemed to slow down as she felt air on her face and heard the powerful yet graceful flap of wings. Through the haze of trauma, the memory of him carrying her materialized.

"Hyphen?" she whispered.

"Yes?"

"You're a winged Aechaih?"

His eyes left hers for the briefest of moments before returning. "Yes."

"And you *flew* me to Septain?"

"Yes."

Shit. How did she not know there was a winged Aechaih in modern Trianah? She was standing in front of someone with a remarkable gift— a gift he used to save her life. Attraction aside, Hyphen was special. "Lazlo Lysine, captain of Queen Aniyah's Guard, was Trianah's last winged Aechaih, but I'm sure you already knew that."

"Uh—"

"*Guardians*, I wish I could've seen them. Your wings, I mean. I bet they're exquisite," she continued, wistfully.

Hyphen stilled like a predator catching wind of its prey. It was preternatural and dangerously beautiful, warming her from within. Coming out of whatever daze held her captive, she realized she had to get out of there before she embarrassed herself even more.

"I should get back. My grandfather's probably looking for me," she mumbled.

Of course, he didn't reply. What could the tall, gorgeous Aechaih say to the horny, tragic nerd? *Nothing*. Face hot, it took a shit-ton of strength to push off the window and step past without touching him. Once she was far enough to take a breath without inhaling his scent, she made a beeline for the ballroom and got as far away from Hyphen Haslem as possible.

When Hyphen followed Fellowship into the hall, his main goal was to see how she was doing and build a rapport that might lead to coffee or lunch down the road. What he didn't expect was for her to leave him staring out the window, wondering how he could be so fucked up over one woman. Calling her brilliant and beautiful was a gross understatement, but it would have to do for now because he was a tangled mess of confusion and disbelief that someone like her even existed. When he rounded the corner prepared to talk to her, he operated out of a healthy dose of male arrogance—the kind that deluded him into thinking all women were essentially the same and that his standard rules of engagement would suffice. The first of many unexpected turns was when her rich, shea butter scent made its way to his nose, causing his body to release an obscene amount of testosterone into his system. To put it bluntly, as soon as it hit, he wanted to press her against the window and take his time exploring her red-lipped mouth.

Once he made himself known and she turned around, the idea of talking to her seemed foolish. As soon as she scanned him and *purposely* called him by the wrong name, he knew he was in over his head. When she was injured and at death's door, Fellowship was vulnerable and surprisingly honest. But that version of her had been replaced by a healed, sagacious cop and sharp academic. His ass was ill-equipped to handle that caliber of elite, feminine power. How dare he show up, slip his hand in his pocket, and think she was going to instantly melt from his charm. A woman like that didn't melt unless she *wanted* to. Despite that, their conversation fell into a give-and-take rhythm that lured him into a false sense of security before she stripped him bare with one phrase:

Lazlo Lysine, captain of Queen Aniyah's Guard, was Trianah's last winged Aechaih. But I'm sure you already knew that.

Fuck, yeah, he knew that—Lazlo was his *favorite* winged Aechaih. No one ever talked about him; he'd been forgotten, lost among centuries of modernization. Yet, she mentioned him as casually as one would the weather. It made him feel like a kid again, tucked away in his room reading the heroic tales of an honorable warrior. The long-lost memory was so vivid that he could smell the book's stale, yellowed pages and feel the cracked leather binding. Had she stayed a minute longer, he would've gladly shown her his wings. *That's* how fucking gone he was. Rubbing his face, he let out a ragged breath before heading back.

Entering the ballroom felt like stepping into another world. The roar of jubilant conversation didn't match the hushed, private moment he'd just experienced. Everyone seemed light and carefree while he was on the verge of a breakdown. If he couldn't stop thinking about Fellowship before, there was no way he could stop now. While searching for a server, a six-foot-one baby sister barreled into him. Arms around his neck, Haze was just what he needed to escape Fellowship Dancy. Hugging her back, he let out a sigh of relief. After a second, another pair of arms wrapped around him—Harleigh.

"Where have you been?" Haze demanded. Drawing back, he took them in. Haze's tux fit her to perfection, which wasn't a surprise. With her hair down and in soft curls, her white shirt was opened at the collar, showcasing long, layered pearls and an air of self-assurance that seemed to have appeared overnight. Harleigh wore an off-the-shoulder, soft pink gown with layers of gauzy silk. Her hair was up in a classy topknot, making her look like an Aechaih princess. They were fresh and sophisticated, and he couldn't be prouder.

"I was out getting some air," he said. Taking a much-needed champagne flute, he looked around. "Where's Mom?"

"Over there, holding court," Harleigh said, pointing to the front of the ballroom. Sure enough, Honey Haslem was a vision in cream and gold. Hair swept into a loose bun, she smiled and conversed with a group of Aechaih high society. To his delight, there was no sign of Horace.

"Oh, my Guardians, I loooovvvee her dreeesssss," Harleigh squealed. Turning, Hyphen followed her eyeline to—*Solneur,* no. Please.

"She's beautiful," Haze breathed.

Hyphen downed his champagne and diverted his eyes.

"She's with Ambassador Dancy. Oh, is that his *granddaughter?*" Harleigh wondered.

"It has to be. Hyphen, is that the human you saved at Queen Aniyah's Temple?" Haze asked.

"Yes," he bit out with a tight smile. Where was Bronwyn? He'd gladly put up with her bullshit if it meant getting away from this conversation. Just when he thought he'd escaped Fellowship Dancy, there she was mystifying his sisters.

Haze narrowed her eyes in thought. "She's a criminal investigator for the Human Division." Then she turned to him. "Hyphen, introduce us. We need to interview her for our project."

"Yes!" Harleigh exclaimed, cheeks flushed.

"I—she doesn't remember me. She was in pretty bad shape," he lied. He would do anything for his sisters because he loved them, but introducing them to Fellowship wasn't an—

"Of course, she does. Don't be ridiculous," Harleigh said, grabbing his arm. Haze, on cue, grabbed the other one. Both, incredibly strong for their age by the way, pulled him toward Fellowship and Auten. He hastily placed his empty flute on a passing tray as the twins marched him to her. She must've sensed their approach because she looked away from the conversation and caught his eyes as if to say *what the hell is this?* He wanted so badly to communicate, *it wasn't my idea, believe me.*

The twins plopped him next to her. Looking from him to his beaming sisters, she raised an eyebrow. "Hi?" Of course, she was apprehensive. He would've been, too, if a set of twins and a reluctant older brother appeared in front of him out of nowhere.

"*Hyphen.*" Haze nudged him with her bony elbow.

"Um. Hi, yeah, these are my sisters, Haze and Harleigh."

"Your dress is stunning," Harleigh swooned.

"Thank you," Fellowship replied, still uncertain.

"Since you and Hyphen know each other, we asked him to introduce us," Haze said, clarifying their presence.

"Oh, okay," she said, eyeing Hyphen.

"We're doing a project for school on the human-Aechaih relationship and the ways in which it needs reformation. Since you're a criminal investigator, we figured you'd have insight and suggestions for change," Haze pitched with slick professionalism while Harleigh nodded along. Usually, Harleigh was the first to lead a conversation, but Haze had stepped up, and it looked damn good on her.

"Wouldn't it be better to speak with the Human Ambassador?" Fellowship asked, moving away from her grandfather who hadn't noticed that she was surrounded by three Haslems.

"While we appreciate Ambassador Dancy, he's a *politician.* We're interested in speaking with someone who can give us the every-person perspective of life in Pawville," Haze explained.

Unprompted and totally random, Hyphen blurted, "Detective Dancy's also a history professor at the college for humans."

"A cop *and* a professor? I knew you were giving off bad-bitch energy," Haze said, snapping her finger.

Fellowship's face lit up as she tipped her head back and laughed.

Looking as bright and magnetic as the first day he saw her, his mouth went dry.

"Can we please interview you? We promise it won't take long," Haze added. Fellowship smiled, her eyes flicking from a mortified, red-faced Hyphen to his cheery sisters.

"It would be an honor. Do you want my cell?"

"Your *cell*? Solneur, yes!" Haze said, fangirling over the human. She produced her phone out of her clutch and handed it over. In a matter of minutes, Fellowship had managed to bedazzle his sisters as much as she had him.

As she punched in her number, she looked at Haze. "I'm digging your tux, by the way. I hate I didn't think of that—talk about bad-bitch energy."

His sister beamed so brightly, he needed shades. "It's a gift from my wonderful brother. Took me to his tailor and everything."

"That was kind of him." Handing Haze her phone, her eyes snagged his, holding them long enough for him to forget how to breathe.

"Thank you so much, Detective Dancy. We can't wait to talk to you," Harleigh said.

"Call me Fellowship." She flashed her wide-open smile—the one where her full, red lips pulled back to reveal perfect white teeth. The one that made his body respond like she'd physically touched him. Yeah, that was the one, and since there was nothing *appropriate* about being horny in front of his sisters, it was time to go.

"We're so happy Hyphen saved you and that you're better," Harleigh said.

"I'm happy, too, and very grateful," she said, looking at him from underneath her thick, curly lashes. Lower abdomen on fire, Fellowship Dancy took him apart inch by inch and he was powerless to stop it.

"Thank you so much, Fellowship. I promise we'll be in touch soon," Haze said.

"My pleasure."

The girls kissed Hyphen on the cheek and abandoned him in front of her. Watching them disappear into the crowd, he returned to Fellowship who watched him.

"Well, they're quite the bundle of delightful energy," she said with a soft smile.

"They are. I appreciate your willingness to talk to them."

"Of course. I don't think I've met young Aechaih interested in the human-Aechaih dynamic."

"Neither have I." Although he was desperate to say more, she had his thoughts jumbled and unorganized, and he couldn't risk blurting out—

"Hyphen Haslem, great to see you!" Auten boomed from behind Fellowship. Giving a tiny jump, she made room for her grandfather to join.

"A pleasure as always, Ambassador," Hyphen said with a nod.

"How many times must I remind you to call me Auten? I'm indebted to you."

He wasn't sure why he blushed. "Nonsense. I'm happy I was at the right place at the right time." Although he kept his eyes on Auten, he felt her eyes on *him*.

"I'm glad you were there too, and for getting her admitted to Septain." Auten shook his head, tears in his eyes.

"Grandpa, what did I tell you about that?" Fellowship whispered.

Auten pulled a freshly pressed, white handkerchief from his pocket and dabbed his eyes. "I'm sorry, Hyphen. I've been so emotional since the accident. She calls me Mr. Waterworks."

Hyphen smiled. "Scary situations like that can put a lot into perspective," he offered.

"It does, doesn't it? See, Fell, Hyphen says it's normal to be emotional."

"That's not what he said, Grandpa."

Auten lifted his chin with a dramatic huff. "Well, it's what he inferred."

Delicate hand on her chest, she played along. "Oh, that's what he *inferred*, huh? Well, excuse me," she said, laughing. Her bright, infectious laugh ignited Auten *and* Hyphen's. Standing with Fellowship and her grandfather felt right. Like he belonged.

Looking at Hyphen, Auten smiled. "See what you gifted me by saving her?" he asked before his energy shifted, darkness shadowing his regal face. "They said when you arrived at the hospital, you were covered in her blood. They said you *demanded* that they take her. I mean, with the policy and you being on the Council..."

It wasn't technically a question, but Hyphen could see it in Auten's eyes. He wanted to know why Horace Haslem's son saved his human granddaughter, why he threatened the hospital staff within an inch of their lives, why he paced the floor and asked for updates every five minutes, and why he refused a shower and just threw on the scrubs they offered him. Auten wanted to know the truth. But before he could respond, he felt her ease into his mind. He slid his eyes to hers.

You. Are. Not. Dying. You said that to me.

He held her gaze. *Yes.*

Then she was gone. Stunned, his mind hummed. It liked having her there, liked feeling her so near. Not knowing what to make of *that*, he returned to Auten. "I wish I could say I was just doing my job, but it was more than that. Sometimes, we wonder why we're here on Nehlahni. But after that violent spray of bullets, I knew I was here for this particular person. And to be honest, Ambassador, once I understood the assignment, I *had* to take her to Septain because failure wasn't an option." *Where the fuck did* that *come from?* Face on fire, he didn't want to meet their eyes, but he had to. They both looked at him—not with hero worship but with respect. Auten held out his hand. Taking it, the older gentleman squeezed, tears returning to his eyes.

"You're a good man, Hyphen Haslem. I'm grateful to the Guardians for you." It had been a long time since someone spoke to him in such a considerate, paternal way—thirty years, to be exact. Swallowing down the unexpected lump in his throat, Hyphen could only smile and nod as he released Auten's hand.

"I'm going to grab some champagne. Grandpa, would you like one?" Fellowship asked, causing Auten to look at her and smile.

"Yes, honey. Thank you." Nodding, she vanished into the crowd without giving him a second glance.

"She's not demonstrative, but I know she's grateful for what you did for her," Auten said, wiping his eyes.

"She thanked me earlier." It was all he could say seeing that he was still rattled by the fact that they could men-com *and* that he'd just bared his fucking soul to them.

Auten raised his brows. "Oh, good. I've been getting after her about that. She has strong opinions about Aechaih. I wonder whether being helped by one will ease her stringent views. Fell is tenacious and it manifests either as stubbornness or ambition." Auten's candid response bypassed Hyphen's defenses. He found himself imagining what it would be like to see more of Auten if he had the chance to see more of Fellowship.

He smelled Bronwyn before she approached. "*There* you are!" she said, interrupting the moment as she threaded her arm through his. "I've been looking for you *everywhere*. Ambassador Dancy, how are you?"

"I'm doing well, Miss Phor. Don't let me keep you," he said with a small nod.

"Thank you, Ambassador. Enjoy your evening," she cooed. Directing Hyphen into the crowd, she hissed, "Where have you been?"

"Right here," he said, just as his shitty mood slid back into place. Walking away from the Dancys was like leaving Solneur's warmth for a dark, cold cave.

Chapter Eight

The wind nipped and bit at Fellowship's face as she took her morning run toward the pier. Another nightmare from unknown origins pulled her out of sleep, but as soon as she woke, all she could think about was Hyphen *fucking* Haslem and their encounter the other night. What she hated more than anything was feeling out of control—no handle on her thoughts or body—and that's how she felt around him. Untethered, floating out to sea with no shore in sight.

I wish I could've seen them. Your wings, I mean. I bet they're exquisite.

She'd pay an inordinate amount of money to someone if they could tell her where the fuck that line came from and why it tumbled from her mouth. The fact that he didn't respond only stoked her embarrassment. She didn't know Hyphen Haslem, let alone how he felt about being a winged Aechaih. For all she knew, he could've despised that aspect of himself and only flown her to Septain because he had no other choice. But what she said was true; regardless of how thoughtless the comment was, she *did* wish she could've seen them. Then again, maybe not. If her physical response was any indication, seeing him shirtless *and* winged didn't sound like a good idea. Either way, once she escaped his heat and returned to the ballroom, she figured she wouldn't see him again until he showed up with his lovely twin sisters.

Beautiful, engaged, and full of energy, Haze and Harleigh obliterated her assumption that young Aechaih could give a shit about Trianah's social justice issues. Not only were they doing a school project investigating the human-Aechaih relationship, but she was confident it was their idea because Seacrest schools didn't teach much on human equality. What also impressed her was that they weren't satisfied with regurgitating whatever they found online. It seemed important to them to get a firsthand account of life in Pawville. As much as it agitated her that Aechaih assumed humans were nothing but wild things running the streets, she was guilty of having her own assumptions about them as well.

If Haze and Harleigh Haslem were interested in equity and inclusion, what did that say about Hyphen? Because let's be clear, she knew they weren't getting their liberal political views from their father. It meant not only was Hyphen attractive, but he was also socially conscious enough to educate his baby sisters on the real human-Aechaih relationship. None of this helped her forget about him. Neither did the fact that they could men-com—Mental Communication was an Aechaih ability, and she had no Solneur-damned idea why she could do it.

When she felt someone's energy tug at her consciousness and turned to see Hyphen watching her, she figured it was nothing more than instinct. It wasn't until her grandfather asked him about taking her to the hospital that she heard his strong, commanding voice pull her from the darkness. *You. Are. Not. Dying. You hear me? Fellowship? You are* not *fucking dying.* Along with his words, she felt his fear and determination to save her—the feeling was so powerful that by the time he looked at her, she sent the words down the line and without hesitation, he answered. The whole thing should've felt weird. Wrong. But Solneur help her, it didn't.

Septain Memorial—that had to be it. She didn't know of anyone healed by the Aechaih, so she couldn't confirm her suspicions, but she was truly starting to believe that they had *altered* her in some way, causing her to become uncomfortably attracted to *and* able to men-com with Horace Haslem's son. Yep. That *had* to be—

The music in her earbuds faded as her phone rang; without looking at the screen, she answered.

"This is Dancy."

"You're a pain in the ass," Ceager barked.

"Good morning to you, too, Lieutenant. What's wrong?"

"How you convinced that idiot rookie to let you question Nigh Rygle is beyond me."

"To be fair, it didn't take much convincing."

"*Dancy*—"

"I'm not trying to disrespect you, sir. Nigh's a former student, the very one I took a bullet for. Holding her for murder, of an Aechaih no less, is absurd. I had to find out what happened," she said, stopping at her usual spot at the end of the pier. She rested her foot against the damp wooden rail, to stretch.

"Which is why you shouldn't have been down there, you're too close to the situation. It doesn't matter now. There's been another murder."

"*What?*" she asked, dropping her foot. "Seacrest?"

"About ten miles away from where the last body was found."

"Is there a suspect?"

"No, and it's hit the media—all three murders."

"But you said Pope—"

"He did."

"I haven't checked the news. I didn't see—"

"It broke about thirty minutes ago. You need to get in here, *now*," he ground out.

"Yes, sir. I'm on my way."

"Good. Meet me at headquarters."

"*Seacrest?* Why—"

"I don't have time to explain. You've got an hour, Dancy," he said, ending the call.

———

TMPD's headquarters slash Aechaih Division, located in downtown Seacrest, was a gleaming mammoth of an architectural wonder. Fellowship had to hand it to them—no sense in hoarding wealth if they weren't going to spend it, right? Downtown Seacrest was sleek and modern, evident in the number of buildings that resembled art installations. There were high-end restaurants and boutiques with luxury sedans and exotic sports cars lining the streets. Swallowing her disgust, she slung her black leather tote over her shoulder and headed to the entrance.

Fellowship tried not to roll her eyes at the vast expanse of glass, lush plants, light, and open space that made up the ostentatious precinct. Her black, purple-bottom pumps clacked on the glassy lobby floor as she made her way to the reception desk. Black, wide-leg slacks swished around her legs as she walked, and her silk, pearl blouse came up into a dainty ruffled neck with a gauzy bow elegantly tied to the side. As soon as she reached the white command center, Ceager appeared out of nowhere. Tall and exhausted, he wore a pressed black suit and gray tie, which was a clear indication that something was up. Next to him was Captain Pope in his usual black suit and tie. Diverting from the reception desk, she walked to them.

"Captain Pope, it's good to see you," she said as brightly as she could.

"Same here, Dancy. Glad to see you up and about," he said with a quick nod.

She looked at Ceager, giving him a sheepish smile. "Good morning, sir."

He shook his head in an annoyance that didn't reach his eyes. "Morning. C'mon, we're on eighteen," he grumbled, leading the way to a bank of elevators. They waited in silence. After an extended moment, the doors parted with a hiss. Fellowship stepped inside first, followed by Pope and Ceager. Even the Solneur-damned elevator looked like a high-end boutique with polished tile, a mirrored back, and recessed lighting. The doors closed with a whoosh as they began their ascent.

Unable to tolerate the silence, Fellowship looked at Ceager. "Why are we meeting here?" she whispered.

He looked down at her. "You'll see."

Her stomach dropped as the doors opened on the 18th floor. Of course, there was more glass and a birch wall with *Criminal Investigation* in large gold letters, glimmering under recessed lighting. It was hard to keep herself from snorting in judgment. She could only imagine what her precinct could do with the money they spent on interior design alone. Fellowship followed Pope and Ceager through a set of frosted glass doors and into an open-concept workspace occupied by lithe, fashionable cops, if that's what you wanted to call them. Truthfully, they looked like a bunch of socialites sitting at fancy glass desks with sleek computers. The Human Division's rundown bullpen was where technology went to die, while theirs looked like a tech-bro was about to round the corner to introduce a new fingernail-sized phone that could read your thoughts.

Clocking the eyes that clocked her, they walked down the carpeted hall, and came upon a bright conference room with over-sized leather chairs around a lustrous, oval table. Ceager opened the door, letting Fellowship in first as Pope followed. Before they could sit, two Aechaih men glided in and past them. The first one had black hair and a neat beard with close-set, beady blue eyes. His sharp features, including thin, tight lips, made him look like the kind of uptight person who normally found their way to the top of the food chain through shrewd maneuvers and an impeccable work ethic. Wearing a navy suit, white shirt, black tie and black sweater vest, if she were a betting woman, she'd say he was Captain Weeden. The other one was a clean-shaven ginger with gray eyes. With classic Aechaih good looks, he came off like the don't-rock-the-boat type that always managed to fail up. Wearing a gray, off-the-rack suit, his ordinary haircut and basic dress shoes screamed rule-follower and competent brown-noser.

Captain Pope offered his hand to the black-haired man. "Captain Weeden," Pope said. Captain Weeden took his hand, offering a tight grimace that he failed to pass off as a smile. Fellowship sensed his disdain, smelled it. "This is Lieutenant Ceager and Detective Dancy," Pope added. Weeden, releasing Pope's hand, gave Ceager and Fellowship a nod.

Captain Weeden motioned to the ginger. "This is Lieutenant Ified." Although Lieutenant Ified's smile was warmer than Weeden's, it was tentative as not to upstage his boss. "Please, take a seat so we can begin," Weeden said.

Pope, Fellowship, and Ceager eased onto the chairs; Weeden sat at the head of the table, and Ified to his left, across from Pope. She placed her tote on the floor when the glass door opened and shushed closed. Immediately, she smelled seacoast and lavender. Sitting up, she saw Hyphen Haslem walk past in a deep maroon suit with a black shirt and tie. Unbuttoning his suit jacket, he took a seat next to Ified, directly across from her. As soon as he sat, his eyes snapped up. She saw a flicker of something before he schooled his expression. Putting his phone on the table, she noticed a sliver of black ink peeking from his left cuff. Not only did he have a neck tattoo, but obviously it continued down his arm, creating a sleeve. She ground her teeth as her imagination took off, wondering what it looked like up close.

He looked at Weeden. "Excuse my tardiness."

Weeden nodded. "Not a problem, we were just about to begin. Now," he began, clasping his large hands on the table. "As of today, there have been three Aechaih murders at the hands of *humans*. The first suspect is deceased, the other is in Detainment at the Human Division, and we have no whereabouts of the third suspect."

"Is the third suspect human?" she asked. Weeden looked at her, taken aback. Well, she didn't give two fucks about how he looked. She didn't like his dismissive tone and the assumption that the third suspect was human, so she crossed her legs and leaned back in the chair, not breaking eye contact with the Aechaih captain.

"We *assume* it is," he bit out. "Now—"

"But you don't know for sure?" she followed up. Was she crazy, or did the temperature in the room rise a degree or two? Out the corner of her eye, she noticed Ceager clench the armrest of his chair. Oh well. She'd suffer his wrath later. Besides, any cop worth their salt would ask these questions.

"No. Like I said, it's *assumed,*" Weeden replied, flicking his eyes to Pope. Weeden could look at her boss's boss all he wanted. She wasn't backing down. Her body warmed as something stroked her mind. Sliding her eyes to Hyphen, she saw amusement dance across his face before she heard, *coming out guns blazing, I see.*

She didn't want to answer him because she shouldn't be able to men-com, but she couldn't help it. *We're not allowed to ask questions?*

He's not used to being questioned...

By anyone or a human?

Both.

An Aechaih with a superiority complex. How original.

Hyphen hid a smile before returning his eyes to Weeden.

"To complicate matters, it's gone public, so we must act fast before public concern turns into outrage," he said. "There's no clarity on how these humans were able to dispatch Aechaih," Weeden continued. Then he looked at Pope. "Did you drug test the female human?"

"Yes," Pope replied. "She was clean." Weeden pursed his lips like the answer wasn't good enough.

"We're under severe pressure to solve these murders. Unfortunately, tensions between humans and Aechaih have increased over the years, turning a horrific set of crimes into a public relations nightmare. Prominent Aechaih are on the verge of demanding that humans be contained, which would inevitably lead to human rebellion. Social chaos won't help us," Weeden said. "Therefore, we've decided that collaboration between the two divisions is necessary."

Collaboration? What was he talking about? Fellowship glanced at

Ceager, whose face remained blank. Weeden nodded to Lieutenant Ified who cleared his throat.

"By having a human *and* an Aechaih detective work the case together, we show a united front," Ified said. "The partnership helps both communities understand that we're taking the matter seriously."

Was this some kind of PR stunt? When had the Aechaih Division ever want to partner with humans? And what, she and green eyes over there were supposed to work the case *together?* Risking a glance at Hyphen, he looked as confused as she felt. At least she wasn't the only one trying to figure out what the fuck was going on.

Ified continued. "Haslem is our most capable detective, and since he worked the initial case, we'll keep him on."

"As you've just witnessed, Detective Dancy is astute, tenacious, and unwilling to back down. This, among other things, has allowed her to build a powerful relationship with the human community that can only help in a matter as delicate as this one," Ceager asserted.

"Great. Then it's settled. Detectives Haslem and Dancy will partner, showing a united front to Trianah. Of course, Captain Pope, your detective will have *full* access to our advanced technologies here at TMPD's headquarters," Weeden said in a way that made her want to choke the life out of him.

"Excellent," Pope said. "It's greatly appreciated."

"When will the human female be transferred to us?" Weeden asked. Ah, there it was—fuck all that collaboration bullshit; he wanted Nigh.

"When we're certain, beyond a shadow of a doubt, that she's the one who committed the crime," Fellowship answered. "And her *name* is Nigh Rygle." Weeden stiffened as she felt the temperature in the room increase.

"Her prints are on the murder weapon," he clipped out.

"She's also missing a chunk of her memory, so until we can account for *that*, she remains with us."

Weeden looked at Pope and Ceager, neither of whom stepped in to contradict her. After an arduous moment, he nodded. "Fine. For *now*."

And with that, he stood and exited the room, leaving Lieutenant Ified behind.

"Detective Dancy, Haslem will show you around our facilities. You're welcome to claim any empty office as your own."

"Thank you, Lieutenant," Pope said with a nod.

Ified nodded and stood, offering curt handshakes to Pope, Ceager, and Fellowship before leaving the room.

Ceager let out a breath, then turned to Fellowship. "Can't keep your mouth shut, can you?"

"If you wanted a mindless pet, you should've brought someone else," she said, snatching her tote off the ground to look for a bottle of water. She was so pissed her hands shook. Under no circumstances did the Human Division need Aechaih help, especially when the purpose of collaboration was to make them look better in the public eye.

"I didn't want a mindless pet; I wanted some diplomacy," Ceager said, leaning back in his chair and rubbing his face.

"Then you've got the wrong Dancy. My grandfather's the one adept at kissing their asses, not me," she said, taking a pull of water. Hyphen snorted back a laugh causing, everyone to look in his direction like they had forgotten he was there.

"Dancy, we're counting on you," Pope interjected. "Ceager said you were chomping at the bit to get back to work, and since you made headway on the Manicow case and already questioned Miss Rygle, albeit without permission, you're on this. Work with Detective Haslem or forfeit the case to someone else."

Fellowship let out a breath and leaned back in her chair. *Fine.* She'd told Nigh she'd do everything in her power to solve this thing and get her home. So, for *Nigh*, she'd fix her attitude.

"Thank you, sir. I'll do my best," she bit out with a tight smile.

"Haslem, Dancy is a pain in the ass, but she's good at her job," Ceager offered.

"Thanks, boss," she mumbled.

"He needs to know what he's getting into."

"Don't worry, sir. I'm sure Detective Dancy and I will be just fine," he said with a smile so bright it could've powered all of Trianah. The shock of it sent water down the wrong pipe, causing her to cough until her eyes watered.

"You two have a lot of work ahead of you," Pope said, standing. "Good luck."

Ceager followed his lead, then looked at Fellowship. "Behave."

"You know me, sir."

"Exactly. Call me if you need anything," he said as both he and Pope exited the conference room.

Hyphen cleared his throat after a beat of silence. "If you follow me, I can show you to my office," he said, standing. Walking past, he opened the door and waited for her. She knew he wasn't responsible for their *collaboration*, but he represented all that she loathed about the whole fucking situation. So, taking her sweet time, she finished her water, stood, and walked past him without saying a word.

Chapter Nine

Hyphen felt Fellowship's eyes on him as he led her to his office down the hall from the conference room. Opening the glass door, he motioned for her to enter, which she did without looking at him *again*. The office was large and bright with a wall of windows showcasing Trianah's skyline. On the far right, a packed built-in bookshelf framed the seating area with a plush leather sofa, a beautifully-stained wooden coffee table, and two sleek chairs. On the other side of the office was his desk, somewhat covered with files, a computer, and a phone. The rest of the office was decorated with paintings and shit his mom bought when he made detective.

Fellowship stood at the windows, looking out over the city. When he entered the conference room and smelled shea butter, he thought the Guardians were playing a trick on him, but no, there she was, as radiant as ever. Sitting on the sofa, he watched her. It was strange seeing her in his office—about as strange as it was seeing her at the gala fundraiser or standing in front of Queen Aniyah's Temple. Not because she was a human in Aechaih spaces, but because there was no one else like her.

"Are you okay?" he asked after an extended beat.

"Why wouldn't I be?" she asked, moving away from the windows. Setting her tote on one chair, she sat on the other.

"I was just asking. Seems like we were both ambushed."

"Yeah, I'm fine. I guess we should get to work," she said flatly. There was no heat or banter from the fundraiser—she was cold, pissed, and annoyed.

"Would you like a tour of the precinct?"

"No." Reaching for her tote, she dug around before producing a few files and a notebook.

"Would you like a drink?" he asked. That got her attention. Furrowing her brow, she looked at him like he was either nuts, an alcoholic, or both. "A small one, to take the edge off, maybe?"

Thoughtful consideration, then, "What do you have?"

"Zion's Ink." It was strong, maybe too strong for her, but it was all he had.

Biting her lower lip, she nodded. "Okay, I'll have one. Neat."

Hyphen stood and walked to the wet bar in the corner of his office. Pouring two Zion's Inks, neat, he considered this the first step of *Operation Thaw*. It was imperative that he got her on his side—not just for the case but for his own personal reasons, like getting to know her. Holding out the tumbler, she grabbed it, her fingers accidentally grazing his. Unable to move, he watched her take a sip, then another. Not only did she not frown or complain, but she closed her eyes as if savoring every drop.

"What?" she asked, looking up at him.

"Nothing," he mumbled. Embarrassed, he moved back to the sofa and sat down.

After several minutes, she held up her glass. "Thank you."

"You're welcome. Did it help?"

"Yes."

Knocking his back, he set the glass on the table and looked at her. "So, this has been a pretty fucked up couple of months—the murders, your accident, now this."

Holding his gaze, she set her glass on the table, sat back, then sighed. "I'm going to be honest, Hyphen—I appreciate you saving me and all, but as you can undoubtedly tell, I'm not eager to *collaborate* with the Aechaih Division. When have Aechaih *ever* wanted to work with us?"

Forget guns blazing. She was so no-bullshit that it made his balls ache. "You're not working with the Aechaih Division, you're working with me," he said, lifting an eyebrow.

"You *are* the Aechaih Division, *and* the Tri-Family Council, for that matter."

"A non-voting member."

"But a member nonetheless."

"Look, I was just as surprised as you were about this sudden collaboration. It reeks of performative allyship, and I don't buy it. But if we're gonna solve this, we might as well work together." It was clear she saw him as the enemy. To make matters worse, he was a *Haslem*—a name that represented a cunning, ruthless power, and no manner of saving her life could erase that perception. The best he could do was be himself, respect her brilliance, and recognize that it wasn't easy for her to be there.

Narrowing her eyes, she lifted her chin. "Do you really believe humans are capable of killing Aechaih?" It was the first test of *Operation Thaw*—fuck up and she'd be forever closed off, making the partnership unbearable. After considering a few responses, he settled on the truth, mainly because something told him that lying wouldn't work.

"It's difficult but not impossible."

"Not impossible for one human male maybe, but a human girl? I don't think so."

"Most here seem to think humans have manufactured a drug that grants them superhuman strength."

"And how could we do that with no money, resources, or magic? People aren't trying to become serial-killing wizards; they're trying to survive."

That shit was funny, but it didn't seem appropriate to laugh. "I said *most* here think that, not me."

"Then what do *you* think?" she pushed.

"I think humans are being targeted," he said. It was a hunch he had kept to himself, but his new partner wanted to know where he stood, so he shared it with her.

Quiet and contemplative, her eyes searched his face, probably assessing whether or not he was full of shit. After a beat, she nodded at some internal conclusion. "So do I. Humans murdering Aechaih will cause inevitable panic and, like your *charming* captain said, lead to increased oppression. Why would we volunteer for more of that?"

"You wouldn't."

"Exactly, but why target us? It's not like we're living large over in Pawville or plotting to overthrow the one percent."

"You mean what's the endgame?"

"Yes," she replied with more energy than he'd seen since sitting across from her. "Tell me this, is there some sort of magic that could, I don't know, influence a human to do something they wouldn't remember?"

"Maybe. We can check the A.A.R., but if someone's advanced enough to use that sort of magic, the A.A.R. couldn't track it."

"A.A.R.?"

"The Aechaih Ability Registry. It lists every Aechaih, their primary ability, and usage," he explained.

"There's a registry for that?"

"There's a registry for everything."

"I thought Aechaih only registered humans," she said, raising an eyebrow.

"Human Population Control, yeah, there's that, but we keep tabs on us, too. You'd be surprised."

"Truthfully, I'm surprised you suspect Aechaih involvement."

"Aechaih give other Aechaih the benefit of the doubt, I don't. If I'm wrong, fine, but as of right now, it's worth considering."

"I agree," she said, as her thick, heavy energy eased over his skin, causing his body to tingle like he'd been plugged into a power source. It was so intense, he almost short-circuited.

Mouth dry, he swallowed. "We can, uh, discuss the cases thoroughly, check the registry, and go from there." For Solneur's sake, he had to remain professional—personal feelings aside, this partnership was about solving murders, not getting to know her. Well, it wasn't *all* about getting to know her.

"Sounds like a plan, Haslem," she said, unleashing the full force of her smile. Fuck that bullshit about being professional or whatever—she was intelligent, determined, and sexy, and he was turned all the way on. Clearing his throat, he shifted in his seat. Mind wiped clean, all he could do was watch how her diamond studs twinkled, making her face shimmer like starlight. If he didn't say something soon, she'd think he was—

"Before we begin, we need to address something."

"What's that?"

Leaning forward, she frowned. "Why the fuck can we men-com?"

Choking on a laugh, he shook his head. "I have no idea. At first, I thought it was because you were dying when we met, but at the fundraiser—"

She looked confused. "We communicated after I was shot?"

He nodded. "A little."

"What did I say?"

"Nothing much," he said, flashing an innocent smile.

She didn't look convinced. "What did I say, Haslem?"

Knowing it would annoy her, he shrugged. "You might've mentioned my eyes."

"Oh, my Guardians," she moaned.

"I didn't let it go to my head, I promise."

"What exactly did I say about your eyes?"

"Meh, something about them being *fucking beautiful*," he said, enjoying the moment. Her brown face blushed the cutest hint of pink, making him want to run his thumb over her cheek to see if it was as soft as it looked. Oh, he was in a bad, *bad* way. Going down a slippery slope. Up shit's creek, and any other idiom to describe how fucked he was.

"*Solneur*," she hissed, shaking her head.

"What? You don't think they're beautiful?"

She narrowed her eyes. "That's beside the point."

"I disagree, I think it *is* the point."

She shook her head. "Seriously, why are we able to do this? I'm convinced something happened to me at Septain."

"Like what?"

"Who knows," she said, worry clouding her eyes.

"I was with you the whole time, nothing happened."

She looked at him, her mouth slightly open. "I—my grandfather. I thought he—"

"He arrived after you were out of healing and in your room."

"Why did you stay? I mean, you'd already done so much."

He hesitated, concerned that she'd be embarrassed by the fear she expressed at the time or upset that he had witnessed it. "You, um, you asked me not to leave you," he said, his voice dropping low. She didn't respond, just stared through him like she was searching for something, *anything,* to corroborate his story. After a beat, he added, "You were in bad shape, Fellowship. I wouldn't judge anything anyone said in that state." He watched her continue to search for the memory.

After a moment, she whispered, "Never, Fellowship. I'll never leave you." In a flash, they were transported back to the hospital with her on the stretcher, asking him to stay. When she finally focused on him, he felt the gravity of her emotions: the fear, heaviness, and acceptance that in her most vulnerable state, he was there. Afraid of being swept away, he stayed afloat by keeping his mouth shut instead of confessing every confused feeling that swirled through him. He nodded, giving her a small smile.

"Are you able to men-com with other humans?" she asked, her voice small and soft.

"No, neither with Aechaih nor humans. It's not my ability. If someone can men-com with a specific person and it's not their ability, it's because they're experiencing a different kind of connection," he explained. "I could only men-com with one other person, and haven't done so since he died."

"Who? If you don't mind me asking."

He didn't talk about his brother to anyone besides Soren and the twins. But sitting across from Fellowship, with her luminous smile and sweet scent, he felt safe to share. "My brother, Hudson."

"Oh," she breathed, going silent. That's when he felt her drift away. Staring at her hands folded in her lap, she sat for a moment before she looked up, open and unguarded. "Loss fucking sucks."

The truth and sincerity of those three words knocked the breath out of him. Without having to expound, she immediately understood and articulated how he felt. After a few moments, he replied, "It does."

"When did he die?"

"Thirty years ago."

"I'm sorry. That must've been difficult, especially since Aechaih have long lifespans. I couldn't imagine losing someone who I assumed would be with me for centuries."

Her words settled on him like a weighted blanket. How could he be physically attracted to her one moment and emotionally attracted to her the next? Although she was young, there was a gravitas to her—an undeniable lived experience that didn't rely on age or background. He felt like he could tell her anything.

"It *was* difficult," he said. "Very."

She nodded. "I'm also sorry about what I said the other night."

"What did you say?"

"About your wings. I shouldn't have mentioned them. It was rude," she said, looking down.

"It wasn't rude, Fellowship." Guardians, what possessed her to think her comment was rude when it was the most thoughtful and authentic thing he'd heard in some time?

"But for all I know, you could hate your wings and I was...I don't know...mentioning them all casual or whatever."

"I wasn't offended. To be honest, I was more shocked that you know Lazlo."

She perked up. "Of course, I do. He was an exceptionally powerful and intelligent warrior. He was pretty much the Queen's Hand. Loyal to her until the end, some say that although she loved her human husband, she and Lazlo had an unbreakable bond forged through centuries of companionship."

Solneur. Fucking. Help. Him—who *was* this woman? With words lodged in the back of his throat, he couldn't respond.

"See, there I go again, rambling away," she lamented.

"What? No. I'm sorry... It's just that you're...different."

She frowned. "Different like how? Weird?"

"No! Wait. I'm not saying this right," he said, blushing. "Not weird, unique—no, that's not right either. Well, it's right but..." he stammered, panicked like a fucking teenager.

"Why are you blushing?" she asked, her face melting into a smile.

He blushed even more. "I don't know...I—you make me..." he trailed off, running his hand through his hair. Guardians, was he *sweating?* Relaxing further into her chair, she laughed. It was throaty and melodic, tickling his Aechaih ears with each note.

"Are you nervous, Hyphen Haslem?" she asked, flashing him a side smile.

"Get the fuck out of here," he said, caught between flirty and mortified.

"Then what is it?" she asked, crossing her legs. This fucking woman—her confidence was intoxicating. Never in his two hundred and ten years had he felt so comfortable. It was easy to talk to her, to tell her things that had been trapped inside of him for decades. With her, he didn't have to pick and choose what to say for fear of being misunderstood. It was like talking to Soren but better.

Before he had time to stop his mouth, it shot off the truth. "I stood out with my wings, and not in a good way. I was so self-conscious about them when I was young that I rarely hung out with kids my own age. I either stayed in my room or spent time with my brother. That's why I'm into history and shit. I read a lot as a kid, still do. Then, you know, as I got older, I built up the strength to keep them hidden behind my energetic field, so I'd look like everyone else," he paused. "Lazlo is my favorite winged Aechaih. When you mentioned him, it made me think of my brother, Hudson. He saw my wings as special, and it feels like you do, too."

Nope, he did not expect to share that at all—his face warmed again. Finally, he had gotten her to relax and open up, and the first thing he did was blab about how fucking awkward he was as a kid. The moment swelled between them until he couldn't help risking a glance at her. She watched him intently—no smile, no judgment, just quiet consideration. Then he felt her tentatively tug at his mind:

Your wings are special, Hyphen. Not only did they save my life, but they're a gift from our Guardians.

Like lightning striking a rock, his protective wall cracked, allowing a thin beam of light into his darkness. Swallowing the lump in his throat, he responded, *If you want to see them, just say the word and I'll show you.* To ensure she felt his honesty, he held her gaze as intently as she held his. After a beat, she smiled—a wide, open smile that squeezed his heart until he could no longer breathe. As fast as it arrived, it vanished as she blinked away the moment.

Clearing her throat, she nodded. "If you don't mind, I'd like to visit the ladies' room before we get started."

"Of course, it's out and to your left. Can't miss it."

Standing, she grabbed her tote. Shoving her things back in, she slid it onto her shoulder and walked out, taking her shea butter scent with her. Letting out a sigh, he sat back. *Operation Thaw* was a success— maybe too much of a success because without barriers, her magnetic charm overwhelmed him to the point that he offered to show her his wings. His *wings*. Solneur, this woman had a gift for making him feel seen in a way he'd never experienced before, and as disorienting as it was, he wanted more.

———

The Aechaih precinct's restroom was well-lit with marble floors and dark accents. Fellowship stared at herself in the gold, circular mirror, hoping she could figure out how she went from pissed that she had to work with the Aechaih to having a heartfelt conversation with Hyphen Haslem about the shooting and his wings. Slowly, she washed her hands in the porcelain basin, dried them with a fluffy white towel and tossed it in the assigned basket. Opening her tote, she pulled out a small bottle of lotion and proceeded to moisturize her hands before throwing it back in the bag.

Never, Fellowship. I'll never leave you.

Those words had swirled in her head since she woke up in the hospital and now, she knew why. Somewhere between being shot and flown to Septain Memorial, she asked him to stay with her and he did. She couldn't imagine how she must've looked lying unconscious in an oversized Aechaih bed. A part of her was embarrassed because she had worked so hard to create a solid, capable presence in the world. The thought of being vulnerable in front of someone, let alone *him,* felt unsettling. Whether she wanted to admit it or not, Hyphen was different. More than the heir to the Haslem empire, he was complex with an intriguing depth that tugged at her inquisitive nature. Until him, no one captured her imagination beyond a night in bed. Calm, reticent with an erudite air, Hyphen's energy complemented her own—he flowed *with* her, not against. And despite her better judgment, that shit was attractive as hell.

You mentioned Lazlo, who happens to be my favorite winged Aechaih, and it reminded me of my brother, Hudson. He saw my wings as special, and it feels like you do, too.

Of course, she saw his wings as special because they were. Why would anyone shame an Aechaih child for possessing such a beautiful gift? She imagined him as a little boy, winged and bashful, huddled in a corner reading. Without much effort, she could even see Hudson enter his room with stacks of ancient, leather-bound volumes on Trianah's history. Hyphen, pale, green-eyed with a head full of shiny chocolate hair, and Hudson, regal, blond with kind blue eyes—not that she'd ever seen Hudson Haslem, but she just knew. She knew the image was real.

If you want to see them, just say the word and I'll show you.

Out of all of the surprises Hyphen threw at her, that was the biggest. Although they had just met, at least formally, he was willing to share the most hidden part of himself with her. Heart fluttering, she knew that if she saw his wings, her world would irrevocably change yet she was willing to risk it all for one glance. Fishing her lipstick out of her tote, she applied a fresh coat when her phone dinged. Capping the tube, she looked down; it was from Rayna.

Rayna: Social media's a shit-storm—Aechaih are already calling for us to be stoned and locked away in Pawville for good. Be glad you're not connected.

Fellowship grabbed her phone and replied.

Fellowship: I am—you should log off; no good can come from doom-scrolling.

Rayna: Too late. I'm addicted. Meanwhile, Davis Manicow's toxicology report is in.

Fellowship: What does it say?

Rayna: He was clean.

Fellowship: Just like Nigh. Damn.

Rayna: Ceager told us the news—working with the Aechaih, huh?

Fellowship: More like working with Hyphen Haslem.

Rayna: Fuck off!

Fellowship: I know.

Rayna: What's he like?

Fellowship: Nice. Professional. Not what I thought.

Rayna: That's all?

Fellowship: What else is there?

Rayna: Fuckability?

Fellowship laughed. Only Rayna could distract her from her muddled musings on Hyphen.

Fellowship: OMG. Bye!

Rayna: Wait! Tell me! Hyphen Haslem is fine as hell.

Fellowship: Bye!!

Rayna: I know you don't like hanging out after work, but I'm coming over tonight. I've given you all the space in the world after that fucked-up shooting. Don't freak out, but I miss you. Even if we're just work friends.

Fellowship paused. What could she say? How could she justify reuniting with her grandfather but leaving Rayna out in the cold? Even though it was dangerous to admit it, she missed her friend too. Smiling at her phone, she replied:

Fellowship: I'll grab Santander's.

Rayna: Yaaasss, bitch! I'll bring the Zion's Ink!

Fellowship laughed, then threw her phone and lipstick in her tote. Taking another look at herself in the mirror, she decided that aside from the case, none of what she felt about Hyphen mattered. Their priority was solving the murders. Slinging her tote over her shoulder, she left the restroom, taking the carpeted hallway back to his office. Both Manicow and Nigh were clean, which implied something else had caused their blackout. Mind focused on the case, she rounded the corner to see Hyphen standing with a tall, blonde Aechaih woman wearing an emerald sheath dress and a heavy camel overcoat. Upon first glance, she was a typical Aechaih: long hair with soft curls, a designer bag hanging from her arm, and a cellphone clutched in her hand.

They spoke in hushed tones, neither aware that she was at the end of the hall. Fellowship wasn't blind; it was obvious they were a couple. He was too handsome and personable to be single. A quick twinge of disappointment tightened in her chest before she dismissed it. It wasn't that she liked him like *that*. No, seeing him with an Aechaih woman reminded her that they were, in fact, from two different worlds. But none of that mattered. Like she told Rayna, she wasn't into Aechaih men—current partner included. Not wanting to interrupt their conversation, she turned to leave when Hyphen caught her eye. Interested in what pulled his attention, the woman followed suit. So much for going unnoticed; she steeled herself and walked to them with her most diplomatic smile.

"Hey," she said. Now that she was closer, not only could she tell they were in a relationship, but she could also sense something was off.

The woman's energy felt aggravated, and Hyphen's felt...actually, she couldn't detect his energy—his heat—something she'd inadvertently become accustomed to even though they hadn't spent that much time together.

"Fellowship, this is Bronwyn Phor. Bron, this is Fellowship Dancy," Hyphen said flatly. A different person, his easy grin was replaced with cold stoicism. Whatever was going on between them wasn't her business, so she directed her attention to the blonde and smiled.

"Pleasure to meet you, Bronwyn," Fellowship said, offering her hand.

The Aechaih woman looked her up and down like she was nothing more than an unwelcome distraction before she flashed a tight, forced smile. "Pleasure," she said before turning back to Hyphen. "I reserved us a table. I can't show up *alone*."

Woah, now. It was like that? With all the money flowing through Seacrest, they couldn't afford common decency? Fellowship stayed put because suddenly she was in the mood to play *Biggest Bitch*.

"I told you this morning that I'd be swamped," Hyphen said, his voice void of personality and inflection. "It's serious. I've been assigned a partner."

Bronwyn scoffed. "Monroe won't mind if you dash off. What could you possibly solve in the next two hours?" she asked with a wave of her manicured hand.

"Monroe's not my partner."

"Who is?"

Hyphen looked at Fellowship, his face unreadable. After a moment, Bronwyn did the same. Standing tall in her four-inch pumps, Fellowship held her gaze and lifted her chin.

Yes, bitch, *I'm* his partner.

Once Blondie understood, her eyes widened as she whipped back to Hyphen. "*She's* your partner? Why would Weeden assign you to work with a *human?*"

"Because this human is a criminal investigator," Fellowship clarified.

"No offense, but," she started, her nose upturned. Then, putting two and two together, she narrowed her eyes, finally focusing on Fellowship like she was a flesh and blood person instead of a *human*. "*Dancy*...you're Ambassador Dancy's granddaughter. *You're* the human he saved."

"Yes."

She turned back to Hyphen. "Oh, is this like a charity thing because you rescued her from a *drive-by* shooting?" she asked with an impressive amount of condescension.

"Bronwyn," Hyphen sighed.

"Fine. Whatever," she huffed. Turning her eyes to Fellowship, her vibe switched from ice-cold bitch to ice-cold, *self-serving* bitch. "You don't mind if I take him to lunch, do you? I'm sure you can manage a few hours without him," she said with more artificiality than her blonde hair.

Cocking her head to the side, Fellowship flashed her signature fuck-you smile. "Don't let me keep you. Schmoozing with Seacrest elite seems like a better use of his time than actual police work."

Something flashed across Hyphen's face before Bronwyn's blue eyes hardened, her mouth thinning to a straight line. Standing taller than Fellowship, she made a point of looking down. "I don't—"

"If you need me, Detective, I'll be in my office," Fellowship said before whatever self-important bullshit tumbled from his girlfriend's mouth. And with that, she walked away because when Fellowship played *Biggest Bitch*, she played to win.

Chapter Ten

Hyphen watched Fellowship disappear around the corner. Sure, he was six-five, but at the moment, he felt small and expertly put in place by the human he couldn't get off his mind. Fellowship had unexpectedly dropped into his life like a fucking bomb, and he was still struggling to pick up the pieces. He hummed with curiosity bordering on infatuation, and if that wasn't stressful enough, he was confident he'd lost all the gains he'd made with her earlier—gains that he wanted more than the woman standing in front of him.

Visibly rattled, with red splotches climbing up her neck, Bronwyn flipped her hair as she turned to him. "Who the fuck does she think she is?"

Hyphen shrugged. "My partner."

She drew back like she'd been slapped. "Are you—"

Holding up his hand, he sighed. "Stop. We can either do this right here, in my office, or wait until I'm off work."

"Do what?"

"End this shit," he said, slipping his hands in his pants pockets. He felt better already.

"What the fuck do you mean?"

"You know what I mean."

Narrowing her eyes, she stepped to him. "You think you can dump me," she spat, face almost touching his.

"I don't think. I know." Bronwyn was a force of privilege and snobbery. He knew that she intimidated a lot of folks in Seacrest, but he wasn't one of them, and to his delight, neither was Fellowship. As usual, when she didn't get her way, Bronwyn unleashed her searing, hot magic toward him. Scratching at his skin, he remained unmoved. Tantrum or not—it was over.

"You think you're better than me just because *Daddy's* rich? You're nothing but an old detective wasting a good family name," she sneered.

It was a decent burn if he gave a shit. On a beat, he took in her rage —distorted features and depthless eyes—eyes that suddenly realized it was over. She blinked rapidly. After a beat, he nodded at the feeling of closure. "I'll message over your keys. Now, if you'll excuse me," he said, turning. "I have work."

Instead of going to his office, he continued to the restroom, which was empty. He let the cold water run while staring at his reflection. He needed to find Fellowship and apologize for the Bronwyn drama while assessing the damage. She didn't like Aechaih, and people like Bronwyn were exactly why. Despite that, he was sure she wouldn't leave, especially after the run-in. More than likely, she'd snagged one of their empty offices, which meant she wouldn't be working in his. *Damn.* Splashing water on his face, he dried it with a white, fluffy towel and threw it in the bin. Then, straightening his tie, he set off to find her.

Like he thought, she was tucked away in a small, windowless office. He stopped at the door and watched as she bit her lip in concentration. There was a smattering of notes on the glass evidence board and her infamous tote on the chair next to her desk. She worked on her laptop, oblivious to his presence. Entering, he slid his hand in his pants pocket just as she looked up. Stopping, he nodded to the glass board. "I see you started without me," he said in a shameless attempt to gauge her temperature.

"Yeah, just a few notes. Keeps me organized," she said, returning to her computer. No smile. No light. Just focus. Blood pumping in his ears, he decided that she was a woman of principles and the only way this partnership would work was if he owned up to the shitty encounter she had with Bronwyn.

"You mind if I take a seat?"

No answer. Just a nod as she continued typing. Undeterred, Hyphen moved to the chair next to her desk. After a beat, she looked at him, then at her tote, before he watched her contemplate whether she'd make room for him or make his ass sit on the sofa. Thank the Guardians, she moved the tote and set it on the desk. He sat down just as she returned to her laptop. Yep, she was done with him. After a couple of clacks, she looked up. Note, she didn't turn toward him, she only *looked* at him as if to say: *What do you want?*

"I'm sorry for Bronwyn."

"Don't worry about it."

"I won't make excuses for her, but it won't happen again."

"I said don't worry about it," she reiterated, returning to her laptop. Hyphen rested his arm on the desk and watched her work while simultaneously cursing himself for enjoying her shea butter scent. The ease of their previous meeting had disappeared, so if he wanted back into her good graces, he was going to have to get it himself because she wasn't offering him shit.

"My lieutenant said you found some Manicow footage."

She took a beat but didn't look up. "Before the *drive-by*, I found a video on his cellphone and my colleague, Lemin, found footage of him entering his building. I have both here," she said, nodding to her computer. "I can send them to you."

Bypassing the drive-by comment, he pressed on. "I assume they're not long. Can I watch them now?"

He sensed her annoyance, but she didn't say anything. After a few clicks, she turned her laptop toward him so he could watch. He leaned in, putting his elbow on the desk for a closer view. She picked up her phone and began scrolling while he focused on the CCTV footage of Manicow stumbling to his apartment building.

Hyphen frowned. "What the fuck?"

Setting her phone down, she looked up. "I know."

"That looks weird as shit."

"Exactly. Watch this one," she said, leaning forward to click around and play the other clip. The video was of Manicow in his apartment. Distraught, he confessed to having no idea what happened to him, with nothing in his eyes but fear.

"Shit. I believe him," he said, nodding to the screen.

"So do I. I also received his toxicology report."

"What did it say?"

"Clean. Only a little alcohol in his system."

"Which makes that first clip interesting because he looks wasted."

"Yeah."

"And Rygle was clean, too."

"Yes."

"Were you the one who took her statement?" Without returning to her computer, she leaned back in the leather chair and crossed her legs. It was a sexy, boss-ass move that, under different circumstances, would've brought him to his knees.

"Yes, her unofficial statement."

"Unofficial? Oh, that's right, Pope said you questioned her without permission."

"I did."

"What did she say?"

"She went to Seacrest for a drug deal with a regular customer. She and the Aechaih girl were hooking up, had been for a while. After spending part of the night together, Nigh woke up covered in her blood."

"That's why her prints were all over the girl's apartment," Hyphen said, thinking back to the grisly crime scene.

"Yes."

"Why did you question Rygle without permission? Were you not assigned the case?"

"I was still on desk duty and the Manicow case was essentially closed. A former student called and told me what happened."

"Rygle's a former student?"

"Yes."

"I'm surprised Ceager kept you on."

"You say that like he had a choice," she said without a smile or glimmer of levity. *Damn.* That's why neither Ceager nor Pope intervened when she challenged Weeden; she was formidable as fuck, and he was, once again, turned on. *Solneur, Sylena...anyone, help.*

"So, you know Rygle on a personal level."

"Yes."

"You believe she's telling the truth?"

"I do. And she's very scared, which is why she should remain in human custody. I don't trust Weeden or Ified to ensure her safety in Aechaih Detainment. No offense."

"None taken," he replied, drumming his fingers on the desk. "Are these the same students that were with you at the temple? The ones you jumped in front of during the shooting?"

Eyebrows knitted together, she tilted her head. "How do you know I jumped in front of them?" Fuck his big fucking mouth. As far as she knew, he heard the shots and sprang into action—not that he *saw* her get shot because he was leering at her like an Aechaih creep.

"I—um." He had nothing—no words. *Great.* Sliding his eyes to hers, his face warmed.

"You're blushing, again," she said, arching her eyebrow. "What aren't you telling me, Haslem?"

And there it was—a tiny spark of playfulness. It offered him hope that she wasn't entirely closed off and that *Operation Thaw* was back on track. And while that was promising, he still didn't want to admit how he saw her, so he massaged the truth.

"I told you that I saw you all across the way," he answered, avoiding her eyes because the intensity of her stare was unbearable. On many levels.

She considered him, then, "Hey, Hyphen?"

The sound of her voice made every nerve in his body spring to attention. "Yes?"

"You know I'm a cop, right?"

"Yes, and?"

"And it means I know when someone's bullshitting me. Call it an occupational superpower."

Occupational superpower. He was beyond fucked—she disrupted every logical neural pathway he relied on to maintain composure. It would've been wise to surrender, but he couldn't. Instead, he arched his eyebrow. "And here I thought Ceager was exaggerating about you being a pain in the ass."

"Can't say you weren't warned," she said, thawing little more. "How'd you know I jumped in front of my students?"

Fine, lying wasn't an option, so he confessed. "I was getting in my SUV after lunch with my friend, Soren, and I saw you across the street. I...might've been watching you when the car came around the corner and sprayed you with bullets," he admitted.

"Why were you watching me?" she asked, trapping him underneath her unrelenting glare. Was this how she got confessions? Normally, his height, tatts, and resting-asshole-face made people fess up, but her *occupational superpower* had him squirming like the guilty motherfucker he was.

He cleared his throat. "Because you caught my attention."

"You mean, *we* caught your attention—the group of humans chatting in front of the temple's grand staircase, right?"

Let's see if she *really* wanted the truth. "At first yes, then I saw you. I noticed you," he said, maintaining eye contact. Not only did she not flinch, but she held his gaze. Suddenly, warmth slipped over his skin like silk as her face opened for him. The energy in the room shifted, the air turning thick and heavy. Powerless to disengage, his lower abdomen tightened as blood pumped to his dick. Tongue thick, he wet his lips just as her eyes dipped down to his mouth and back. Her dark pupils flicked then expanded. *Guardians*, he could barely breathe—*ding!* His text message alert snapped whatever the hell was going on. Patting his pockets, he looked for his phone.

"I think it's mine," she said, reaching for her cell. Picking it up, she looked at the screen, then him, her face impassive. "It's my grandfather."

Thank the Guardians! He had to get out of there. Nodding, he stood so fast his head spun. "I'll make an appointment at The Archives so we can research the A.A.R. I'll text you the time."

"Thank you," she said with a faint smile.

Nodding again, he left, entering the hallway, which was a few degrees cooler. Once around the corner, he stopped. Perhaps he'd imagined what just happened between them. She was human, but her presence, her energy almost felt *magical.* Like a palpable force had settled around her, and when she directed it toward him, he felt free, like when he used to take to the sky. There was nothing like it except when he was around her. Yes, he needed to call The Archives, but first, he needed a fucking drink.

Flustered, Fellowship slumped down in her chair, keeping an eye on the office's glass wall in case Hyphen returned. Picking up a black file folder, she fanned herself in an attempt to cool down. Just as she convinced herself that he was different, the encounter with his girl-friend proved otherwise because only an asshole would date someone as obnoxious as Bronwyn Phor. But would an asshole take ownership for said girlfriend and apologize for her shitty behavior? She wasn't sure. Two seconds after he entered her office, she felt his heat waft toward her. It wasn't until he sat beside her, his stretching across his strong thighs, and she inhaled his crisp seacoast and lavender scent that she started sweating like she was standing before the Council.

At first yes, then I saw you. I noticed you. Why would he notice a five-seven curvy, brown-skinned *human* when his girlfriend was the opposite of her in every way? Maybe it was because she and her students were happily chatting at the bottom of the grand staircase. Or like he told her grandfather, he was supposed to see her that day so he could help. Whatever the reason, the idea of catching his attention thrilled her more than it should've, which was why she fell into those damn green eyes, and was swept away in some heated moment of what-ever-the-fuck. Letting out a deep sigh, she called her grandpa.

"Hey, honey. How's work with Haslem?" Auten chirped.

"Hey," she said, continuing to fan herself. "How did you know I was working with him?"

"I know everything," he mused.

"Grandpa."

"It was my idea," he said proudly.

She stopped fanning. "I'm sorry, what?" she asked, putting the phone on speaker.

"There was an emergency Tri-Family Council meeting last night. Weeden and his lieutenant were there along with Ceager and Pope, and me of course. Obviously, Old Man Haslem wanted to close the borders between Pawville and Seacrest, but thankfully the other fami-lies were hesitant. That's when I took the opportunity to suggest that TMPD's divisions partner on the case. My argument was that it would demonstrate to the humans that the Aechaih were willing to explore all options before taking drastic measures. I also emphasized that collabo-ration presented an opportunity for unity," he said.

"Weeden made it seem like it was *his* idea."

"Of course, he did. Horace hated it and stormed off when he was outvoted," Auten said, chuckling.

"Grandpa, I could've solved this on my own," she said, throwing the folder on the desk and leaning back in her chair.

"I know, but you've been in a bubble over there in Pawville, Fell. The only way Trianah will heal is if it ends these petty squabbles," Auten said, sounding effortlessly diplomatic.

"Yeah, I mean…" she started. Her grandfather had a point, but damn, she didn't expect this collaboration bullshit to be his brainchild.

"How's Haslem?"

"Was pairing us together your idea as well?"

"No. Ceager advocated for you first. Part of me thinks Weeden chose Haslem to poke at Horace, but I'm not entirely sure," he said.

"I can't believe this PR stunt was your idea."

"It might be a PR stunt for *them,* but for you, it's a chance to help any humans who might be in trouble."

Naturally, he was right. She pursed her lips in defiance.

"Fell?"

"I'm here," she grumbled.

"How's working with Haslem?"

"Fine."

"Just fine? I assumed it'd be a perfect match."

Blushing, she frowned at the phone. "Why would you think that?"

Auten sighed. "Don't get defensive. I'm just saying."

Of course, she was defensive—just a second ago she was ready to risk it all for a pair of seafoam green eyes. "I'm sorry," she said on a sigh.

"Hyphen's a good man. I'm glad you're working with him."

"Meh, he's okay," she said, knowing she was full of shit.

"I know you're busy, but lunch or dinner soon?"

"Yes, of course."

"Fantastic. Okay, get back to work, honey."

"Talk soon," she said, ending the call. So, she had her grandfather to thank for working with Hyphen. How fitting. Ultimately, he was right; the collaboration could prove helpful if only to give them time to figure out what was really going on. With that being said, she had to make the case her top priority and not her high-maintenance pussy, which seemed to only have eyes for her new partner.

Chapter Eleven

yphen finished his last rep of bicep curls in his home gym. Adding extra sets was supposed to help exercise Fellowship from his system, but it failed. Not only was she still on his mind, but he was fixated on the moment they shared in her office. After a cold shower, he put on joggers and a soft white t-shirt before padding to his kitchen. He opened the refrigerator, grabbed one of his favorite post-workout smoothies, and cracked it open. Just as he tipped his head back for a healthy gulp, his phone rang. He glanced at the screen, hoping it wasn't Bronwyn or his mother. Thankfully, it was Soren.

He pressed the speaker. "Hey."

"Did you fucking change the code on me? What's going on?" Soren asked, frantic.

Hyphen smiled. "Sorry, I changed it after I got home. Broke up with Bronwyn," he said, texting Soren the new code. "There you go."

"Oh, shit," Soren said, ending the call.

Hyphen walked toward the elevator. After a moment, it opened, revealing his friend in a cream sweater, jeans, boots, and a black over-coat. His blue hair was slicked back, accentuating his elegant Aechaih features. Stepping off the elevator, he opened his arms wide and flashed an impish grin, brighter than his diamond studs. "You did it."

"It's done, my boy," Hyphen said, moving to his living area. He took a seat on his custom leather chair. After shrugging off his coat, Soren walked to the kitchen, took a beer from the refrigerator, then eased onto the sofa and crossed his long legs.

"What happened?" Soren asked.

"Done sleepwalking through life."

"Ah, shit! Guess who's back!" Soren said, raising his bottle.

Hyphen returned the gesture with a nod and smile. "Thank you."

"What woke you up?"

"It was time," Hyphen said, averting his gaze.

Soren narrowed his eyes. "It was time, huh. Just like that?"

"Yes."

Soren took another beat. "Funny, you look like you just spent the night fucking a baddie."

Hyphen choked, almost getting green smoothie on his t-shirt. "*What?*"

"Unless you changed your skincare routine, you're glowing," Soren said with an arched eyebrow.

"I just worked out."

Soren frowned. "I know workout glow. This is something else."

Hyphen shifted his gaze—he was fucked. His best friend knew him better than anyone else.

"What's going on at work?" Soren continued, sipping his beer.

"Nothing."

"I've gotta hand it to you, still lying even though you're bad at it. That's what I call dedication," Soren said, nodding.

Hyphen had always been a terrible liar. When he was a kid, his mom used to tell him it was because he was so pure of heart, but as he got older, he realized it was because he didn't have time for bullshit. The truth, when it didn't pertain to Fellowship Dancy, didn't scare him, so he didn't mind speaking it.

"*Fine.* We're partnering with the Human Division on the case so I'm working with Fellowship Dancy."

"So, *she's* why you're glowing," Soren said, eyes wide.

"I didn't say that," Hyphen clarified.

Soren looked at him like the delusional piece of shit that he was. "So, what are you saying?"

"I'm not saying anything. I have a new partner."

"A pretty human partner that you just so happened to fly to Septain Memorial."

"Yes."

"Hmm," Soren said on a nod. "What's she like? I've only seen her from a distance."

"She's fine."

"That's it?"

"Yes."

Soren raked him over with his ice-blue eyes. Looking beyond the bravado, his best friend saw the truth without him having to admit that his crush on Fellowship had taken on a life of its own. Instead of fighting the inevitable, he sighed, slumped down into his chair, and confessed.

"When we left lunch that day, I saw her in front of the grand staircase and knew, even from across the street, that she was different. During the drama, we could men-com, which I thought was because she was almost dead, but we've been able to do it again and again."

Soren uncrossed his legs and leaned forward. "You can *men-com?*"

Hyphen nodded.

"You haven't men-commed since—"

"I know," he said, rubbing his face. "What the fuck?"

"Meh, I say explore it," Soren suggested.

"She's off limits," Hyphen said, shaking his head. Crush or not, they worked together. There was no way he'd let himself act on his attraction.

"No one's off limits," Soren replied with a wave of his hand.

"If I want to remain professional, she is."

Soren crinkled his nose. "Who wants to be professional?"

"I do."

"Boring."

Hyphen laughed. "I'm not going to jeopardize a professional relationship because I like her and we can men-com. It's good to like who you work with, right?" he asked.

Soren shrugged. "I wouldn't know. I don't work."

Hyphen rolled his eyes. "You know what I mean."

"I got you. You wanna keep things easy."

"Exactly."

"No drama."

"Right."

"Who cares that after saving her you can now men-com or that you broke up with your girlfriend and look happier than I've seen you in years. Let's keep it light," Soren said, sitting back.

"I know what you're doing."

"What? I'm agreeing with you—keep it light with the human who caught your eye before anything else popped off that day."

"Syx."

"Has."

"I'm not acting on it. Crushes are fleeting, *and* we're partners. Whatever I feel stays with me," he said with a nod.

Soren held his gaze, then smiled. "I guess we'll see."

Hyphen knew what that meant but his friend was wrong. He was definitely capable of working with Fellowship without making it weird. So what if being with her felt different. Safe. Warm. Familiar. There was nothing he could do about it but solve the case and go from there.

The room is dark and abandoned. The marble floor is cold against her bare feet. Pushing the cracked door open, she enters. Grief snatches her breath. The loss doesn't seem real as her eyes roam over the bedroom—an unmade bed, papers neatly stacked on a desk by the window, a pair of shoes on the floor, a coat draped across the bed. He'll never be back; she'll never hear his voice again. Her person is gone—the only reason she made it through each day, the only reason she felt seen and heard. How was she supposed to go on? She's lost. The pain is so deep. Ragged. Unbearable. She can't survive the pain. She can't survive—

Fellowship woke to the sound of her own cries. Sitting up, it took her a moment to orient herself: she was home, safe in her bed. Wiping her tear-stained face, she sucked in air as fear lay like a stone in her heart. Her person was gone. She'd lost him. The pain and loss was so real. So devastating. Snatching her phone off the nightstand, she plucked out the charger and called her grandfather. After a few rings, he picked up.

"Fell, what's wrong?" he asked, his voice thick with sleep and worry.

Just the sound of his voice calmed her. "Grandpa," she breathed, clutching the phone to her ear. "You're okay..."

"I'm okay, sweetheart. It was just a nightmare," he said, steady and warm. A cry of relief escaped her mouth. "It's okay," he said, soothing her sobs.

Leaning against her headboard, she closed her eyes. The dream, the loss—it wasn't hers. "I'm sorry for calling so early," she whispered.

"There's nothing to be sorry for. I'm here," he said. "I love you."

"I love you, too," she said as the drumming in her chest began to subside. "I'm gonna go for a run. I'll check in later—get some sleep."

"I'm here if you need me."

"I know. I love you."

"I love you, Fell, so very much."

Somewhat relieved, she got out of bed and walked to the window. Wrapping her arms around herself, she watched Solneur's light creep upon a quiet Pawville. After a moment, her eyes drifted toward Seacrest and her thoughts to Hyphen. Like clockwork, her stomach split in two before reforming, or at least that's what it felt like. Having never felt this way at the thought of someone, she was a bit annoyed at the whole thing. Before she knew it, her thoughts wandered to what he looked like when he first woke up: did he sleep shirtless? What did his hair look like? Was it sexily mussed? Then she imagined waking up from a nightmare with him next to her. She even allowed herself to enjoy, if only for a moment, what it would feel like to have his solid arms around her, to hear him tell her that everything was okay. Thinking about him released a knot in her chest that she was too tired to question.

Ding!

Snapping out of her fantasy, she turned from the window to get her phone. It was probably her grandpa, still worried. Tapping the screen, she froze. It was Hyphen. All thumbs, she opened the text.

Haslem: Sorry if I'm texting too early. We have an appointment at The Archives today.

A smile tip-toed across her face as she climbed in bed, dipping under the duvet. She responded.

Dancy: I'm up. About to go running. What time?

Haslem: Running this early? Impressive. Our appointment is at 8:00 AM. Do you know where The Archives are?

Dancy: No.

Haslem: In the vault underneath Trianah City Hall.

Dancy: I'll be there.

She locked her screen. Obviously, it was a coincidence that he texted right—*ding!* She opened her phone and smiled *again*.

Haslem: Are you always up this early?

Dancy: Yes. I'm lucky if I can sleep all night. What about you?

Haslem: I normally sleep all night but last night was tough.

Dancy: Why?

Haslem: Would you judge me if I said I had a nightmare?

Dancy: Of course, I would.

Haslem: You're the worst.

Dancy: J/k-ing. Would you believe I had a nightmare, too? Actually, I always have them.

Haslem: Always? That sounds awful. Is that why you go running?

Dancy: That's exactly why I go. You should join me sometime.

As soon as she pressed send, she locked her phone and threw it across the bed before palming her face. What the hell was she thinking? She was so wrapped up in texting that she—*ding!* Scrambling across the bed, she dove on her stomach and grabbed the phone. Heart in her throat, she opened the message.

Haslem: I'd love to.

She smiled at the three words like a lovesick goober. Catching herself, she locked the phone. *Running.* She needed to go running *now*.

———

Trianah City Hall was located in the heart of the Historic District, about an eight-minute walk from Queen Aniyah's Temple. It was yet another chilly Trianah day—blue skies, not a cloud in sight. Hyphen leaned on his SUV, waiting for Fellowship. After she invited him to go *running sometime,* his morning seemed to have snapped in place, with all things falling his way. He'd be lying if he said he wasn't eager to see her or that he hadn't spent an extra ten minutes choosing something to wear and an extra five making sure his hair was perfect. He shoved one hand in his black overcoat and scrolled through his phone, ignoring distraught texts from his mom, who was upset that he'd ended things with Bronwyn.

At 8:00 AM, he heard a V-8 roar into the lot. It was probably a young Aechaih arriving to pay a speeding ticket because a car like that was built for speed and speed only. Black and gleaming, it backed into a parking space. The door opened, and out stepped Fellowship wearing large, dark sunglasses. Well, fuck. He'd never imagined what kind of car she drove, but it was safe to say, if he had, he wouldn't have guessed a blacked-out muscle car. Something about her driving all that power made his dick twitch. Wearing a camel monochrome outfit, a soft blouse with wide-leg pants and a long, luxurious duster that almost hit the ground, she slipped her tote over her shoulder and walked to him. She looked so fucking good. Nothing else. Her heels clicked on the asphalt, and her gold necklace twinkled on her brown skin, as did her gold bangles and diamond stud earrings—she was regal. Sophisticated. Her lips were painted a decadent red that made it difficult not to imagine kissing her hard enough to smear it all over her beautiful face—

"Hey," she said on a breath.

"Morning," he said, dragging his thoughts out of the gutter. "Nice car."

Smiling, she arched an eyebrow. "You didn't think I'd be getting out of it, did you? And remember, I know when you're lying."

He shook his head. "Pain in the ass."

"I'll take that as a yes," she said, walking toward the building.

Already half in love, he pushed off his SUV and caught up with her. They ascended the marble steps, the Trianah flag snapping in the wind as they passed.

"How was your run?"

"Good, thanks for asking."

"How far do you go?" he followed up while opening the door for her.

"I go to the pier and back. It's about ten miles," she said, removing her shades as she entered the building.

Trianah City Hall was white marble and stone, like most buildings in the Historic District. The lobby was spacious, with a round reception desk and a curving staircase to its left. In the middle of the lobby floor was the gold Trianah Metropolitan sigil. Aechaih from all backgrounds walked the halls to and from various offices located in the building. None seemed to notice them enter. Nodding to the security guard at the reception area, he guided her to a bank of gold elevators.

"Ten miles is no joke," he said, calling the elevator.

"Scared you'll run out of gas if we go running?"

"More like afraid of smoking your ass *when* we go running," he said as the doors opened.

"We'll see about that," she said, stepping into the elevator. Following her in, he pushed the button for The Archives.

Doors closed, the elevator hummed, making its descent. That's when it occurred to him that they should've taken the stairs because she was too close—her scent traveling to his brain, then down to his dick. Her heat was suffocating. All he wanted to do was press her against the wall and bite her right there. *What the fuck?* He'd never wanted to bite anyone *ever*. Biting was an old-school way of bonding, and because that shit meant forever, modern Aechaih rarely did it. So, why did he feel the urge to bury his face in her neck? His dick pounded at the thought of her soft body against his, hands on her ass, her eyelids heavy with want. He was drowning in a full-blown fantasy, gulping down images of his tongue running along her sweet skin. Sucking—

"Is running part of your workout routine?" she asked. Holy fucking shit! They were still talking; he needed to get his shit together immediately.

"Um," he croaked. Guardians, he even *sounded* horny. "I mainly lift," he said as the doors opened. He practically jumped out to get away from her.

The Archives, located in the subbasement, was all white with glossy floors. Behind the director's desk was a frosted glass wall, leading to a set of frosted glass doors. The director of The Archives was Nolan Osmark, a short, round Aechaih with wire-rim glasses and curly brown hair. His face turned to stone as they approached his desk.

Nolan's eyes narrowed on Fellowship. "No humans are allowed down here," he announced, flicking his eyes to Hyphen who felt her stiffen. It took all his power not to grab the small Aechaih by the collar and throw him against the wall for making her feel unwelcome.

"I called for an appointment," Hyphen said in his best diplomatic voice.

Nolan clicked on the computer, looking from it back to Fellowship. "Yes, Mr. Haslem. I have you right here," he said. "But—but she can't enter. The policy stipulates that—"

"Hey, Nolan?" Hyphen asked with a smile.

The man stopped blustering, his watery blue eyes dancing. "Yes?"

"This is Detective Dancy from the TMPD Human Division, and we're here on official business. She's going in with me, and we're going to check the A.A.R. and be out of here before you know it." He was calm mainly because he didn't want her to see him beat the director's ass.

"I...the policy clearly states that no humans are allowed in The Archives," he replied, face red.

Hyphen sighed. He hated to name-drop, but he had no other choice. "Nolan, it would mean a great deal to me *and* my family if you let us in to do our job. Not to mention, Captain Weeden would also be appreciative."

Nolan's eyes shone at the idea of *any* attention from the Tri-Families. "Yes, sir. I meant no disrespect," he sputtered.

"Of course not. Please, let us in."

"Yes, sir," Nolan said, pressing a button so that the frosted glass doors buzzed and clicked. Hyphen pulled open the door and motioned for her to enter. He was sure to give Nolan a wink of gratitude before following her in.

As soon as the doors closed, she gave him a side-eye. "Gotta love Aechaih hospitality," she said flatly.

"Sorry about that," he said, guiding her through the narrow hall.

"Is that the same charm you used to get me admitted into Septain?"

Stopping in the dark hallway, he looked at her. "No, I didn't have time for charm. I told them to admit you, give you the best care, and that you weren't to be discharged until you were fully healed," he said, remembering the look on the healers' faces when he demanded that they violate policy and admit her.

"Oh," she breathed, holding his gaze.

Even with her impossible heels, he was still taller than her and something about that shit made him harder than he already was. Turning away, he resumed walking because, had he not, he would've pushed her against the wall and kissed her until their lips were raw. She followed behind him, stopping when they came upon The Archives. The massive space had curved walls and thick taupe carpet. On the room's perimeter were reading sofas, tables, and computers. But the focal point was the rare books library, encased in an obscenely large glass structure—a library within a library. Fellowship's mouth dropped as she craned her neck upwards.

"That's..."

"The library," he finished.

"Oh, my Guardians," she whispered.

"Is it making your nerdy heart go pitter-pat?" he asked with a smile.

"It doesn't do the same for yours?"

"Not anymore, I've pretty much read everything up there."

Snapping her head down, she looked at him, hand on one hip. "Are you trying to make me jealous?"

"No, I'm trying to impress you. Is it working?"

She shrugged, then walked toward the structure. "Maybe, if you weren't nine hundred years old. What else did you have to do with your time but read?" she said, looking at him from over her shoulder. Damn, he wanted to fuck the shit out of that smart-ass mouth of hers. As she admired the structure, he guided her to a bank of computers on a long, shiny table.

"Over here," he said. She followed him, eyes still on the books. Hyphen sat on a chair and entered his credentials. While waiting for the system to load, he looked at her as she sat down next to him.

"Have you really read everything up there?" she asked.

He looked at the library, then back to her. "Yeah, I have."

"Did you have a favorite topic?"

"Anything from Queen Aniyah's era."

"My graduate school thesis was on her reign."

"History, right?"

She nodded. "Double degree—history and law."

"You have a law degree, too?" he asked, raising his eyebrows. Shit, there he was, trying to impress her with the number of books he'd read over his two hundred and ten years, and she'd already earned two advanced degrees.

"Yes, but as soon as I graduated, I joined the academy."

"So, what you're saying is that you're an overachiever."

"Most nerds are," she said with a wide, open smile.

Solneur, there it was. It was like seeing a falling star streaking across the inky sky. It was so radiant he temporarily forgot why they were in The Archives and not out about town getting to know each other. Then, remembering that they were, in fact, *not* dating but working together, he opened the registry.

"Any suggestions?"

She leaned forward, her arm brushing his as she rested her elbow on the table. "What's the search criteria?"

Could one's heart race at a gentle brush of an arm? Because his most certainly did. "Names, abilities, anything really," he said, trying to remain focused.

"Let's start with the ability to alter memory," she said, staring at the screen.

Typing it in, he clicked *search*. After a moment, the result yielded two phrases:

No matches meet criteria. Memory alteration is an illegal ability.

"That's what I figured," he said.

She frowned. "Does this thing actually work?" she asked, skeptical.

"Yes. My friend is an El-man. Watch," he said, typing *Soren Syon*. The result pinged back Soren's age, parents, and ability.

"Tri-Family Council, Syon?"

"Yes. He's my best friend."

"Which element can he manipulate?"

"Water. If I type *Element Manipulator*, I'll get every Aechaih with the ability," he said, typing. After a moment, the screen filled with a list of names that went on for pages.

"That's impressive. What's your ability?" she asked, looking at him.

Without returning her gaze, he typed his name and hit *search*. After a second, it pinged back the result.

Hyphen Honor Haslem

Age: 210

Parents: Horace and Honey Haslem

Ability: Energetic Manipulator
Birth Defect: Wings

He stared at the screen. For some reason, he didn't want to face her, but it didn't matter because he felt her energy shift.

"They classified your wings as a *birth defect?* Are you fucking kidding me?" she asked, looking at him while pointing at the screen.

Finally, he looked at her. She was pissed—the kind of pissed he didn't want to be on the receiving end of. "There hasn't been a winged—"

"That's bullshit, Hyphen. Oh, my Guardians," she said, her beautiful face turned up in offense on his behalf.

"I'm over it, I promise." Two hundred and ten years was more than enough time to bury his childhood humiliation.

She regarded him for a moment, then shook her head. "I guess if you're okay with it, but it's fucked up, I'll tell you that. Who in their right mind would shame a *baby* for having wings? Ugh, Aechaih and their pretentious bullshit. No offense."

"None taken," he said. How a human could be upset with how an Aechaih was treated in their childhood was beyond him. But there she was, indignant and annoyed.

"Explain energetic manipulation," she said, changing the subject.

"I can use energy to move shit," he said. "That's a basic definition."

"Do it," she demanded.

"What?"

"I want to see you move something," she said.

Of course, she did. Meanwhile, she could ask him for anything, and he'd oblige. Shaking his head, he turned and, with no effort, moved one of the sofas a few feet before returning it softly to the ground. Turning back to her, he was met with a soft smile.

"So, that's what I feel when I'm around you."

"What do you mean?"

"Like," she said, wiggling her fingers over her arm. "You know?"

"No, no I don't know," he said, half-confused, half-amused.

"It feels like warm wisps of smoke," she explained.

Oh, shit. He didn't realize she could feel his energy. "I'm sorry. I'll do a better job at containing—"

"What? No!" she said, catching herself. "I mean, it doesn't bother me. I'm—I'm used to it." She avoided his eyes. "So, people just go around using all sorts of magic throughout the day?" she continued.

"You don't hang out in Seacrest?"

"Not if I can help it."

That was fair. "Pretty much. People use their abilities, but usually to make their days more convenient. Some run ability-based businesses. Regardless, it's all tracked."

"Like usage, right?"

"Yes."

"Let's try looking at usage on the dates of the murders—see if anything interesting pops up." Digging in her tote, she fished out a notebook. Flipping through a few pages, she stopped and set it on the table so he could see the date. "Here you go."

"Got it," he said, typing it in the search box. After a moment it pinged results. It listed the Aechaih, ability, time, and duration of usage. He felt her lean in closer to see the screen. Struggling to not be a creep and inhale her scent, he attempted to focus on the search results, but it was nothing but a blur of letters.

"Nothing looks strange to me, what do you think?" she asked, looking at him.

He turned to her, his eyes dropping to her mouth, taking in her lips. He swallowed. "You're right, just regular usage: sights, empaths, intuits, manipulators, healers, and lusion, of course," he forced out.

"Lusion?"

"You really don't know much about us, huh?" he asked, not as an accusation, but as an observation.

Shaking her head, she shrugged. "I know the basics."

He knew what *that* meant: she knew the bad shit. "It's short for illusion—it's like a social media filter. Makes Aechaih look younger than they are."

"Are you using it now?" she asked, searching his face.

"You don't think I'm this handsome on my own?"

She rolled her eyes in playful exasperation. "You know what I mean."

"Yeah, you wanna know if my eyes are this green in real life," he said, lifting an eyebrow.

"Are they?"

"What do you think?"

She caught his eyes and held them. He immediately started sweating—why didn't he take off his coat before sitting down? There was something gentle and thoughtful about the way she regarded him. It made him feel like his sole purpose in life was for her to look into his eyes.

"They're real," she said with a curt nod.

He blinked in the hopes that she'd look away, but she didn't. "You're right," he said, his voice low. "I never use it."

"Makes sense," she said, nodding.

"What do you mean?"

She paused. "Uh, you know. Makes sense."

"*You're* not making sense."

She blushed, then looked at the screen. "Checking the A.A.R confirms there was no ability used to alter someone's memory," she said. "And if an Aechaih used some sort of dark, underground magic, this thing couldn't track them, right?"

"Nice try, Dancy. What do you mean by *makes sense?*"

"I meant it's obvious you don't have to use Illusion or whatever," she said, flustered.

He gave her a quizzical look to push her buttons. "What you're trying to say is that I don't *need* to use lusion because I'm already so good-looking? Is that it?"

She shook her head. "Sylena, help me."

"Is that what you meant?" Then he mimicked her. "Oh, makes sense because Hyphen's sexy as fuck."

"Hyphen's obnoxious as fuck, and I don't sound like that," she said, punching him in the arm.

Rubbing where her small fist struck him, he laughed. "Hey, don't get mad at me. You're the one who avoided the question."

"Do all Aechaih men think so highly of themselves, or is it just you?" she asked with a sassy smile he'd never seen before. It was a mix between sexy minx and playful best friend, and he fucking loved it.

"Some are worse than others," he said, leaning back.

"I assume you identify as worse?" Turning slightly toward him, her knee grazed the side of his thigh and remained pressed against it. He knew she clocked it—she clocked it and didn't move. He didn't move either because there was no way he'd move away from her.

"No, I was a late, *late* bloomer."

"Really? I figured all Aechaih bloomed at the same time."

"Not a tall, gangly Aechaih with wings." He didn't mean to confess that, but her eyes were soft and encouraging, searching his face without judgment.

"But you found your way..."

"With a lot of help from my brother and best friend."

"Your best friend, Soren."

"Talk about an Aechaih who thinks highly of himself," he said with a laugh. "But I'm grateful for him. I didn't have many friends growing up because of...you know. Soren was popular and liked me, so we started hanging out. One summer, he took me to every party and bonfire, even though I was hopelessly awkward. If anyone talked shit, he'd threaten to kick their ass until I filled out or whatever."

"What happened once you filled out or whatever?"

Both of her knees were pressed against him, but that wasn't what stole his breath. It was the way she made him feel like he was the only person in the world.

He blushed and shrugged. "They suddenly lost interest in being assholes."

She eyed him. "Lost interest, huh? Just like that."

"Yep," he said, avoiding eye contact.

She remained silent for a beat. Then another.

He slid his eyes to her. *Fuck.* Her *occupational superpower* was at work again. "What?"

"You know what, Haslem. What *really* happened?" she asked, amused.

"It was a long time ago," he said, desperate to change the subject.

"Like you told me, you're not *that* old," she said. Then after a beat. "I'm waiting."

He sighed. He had to work on his lying. "They suddenly lost interest in being assholes because, after I filled out, Soren and I spent a large portion of our time exacting revenge on those who bullied us."

"I thought you said he was popular?"

"He was, because he'd charmed half of them who gave him shit for being the 'blue-haired late born.' But once we became friends, he stopped being charming."

"How bad did it get?" she asked, her eyes dancing with delight.

He shook his head, embarrassed. "Parents were complaining. Everyone was scared of us. My brother had to sit us down and threaten us within an inch of our lives. We were basically a two-man gang."

She tipped her head back and laughed. "So, you beat their asses."

"Every single one of them," he said over her laughter.

"Is that when you started getting tattoos? To help with your gang-affiliated-rep?"

He smiled. "Yes."

"When'd you get your first one?"

"Soren and I went after our first conquest. After that, I was hooked."

"To the pain? To the fighting?" she asked with a contemplative frown.

"Truthfully, both."

She held his gaze with compassion and understanding. Although she didn't respond, he could see the acceptance in her eyes. If only he had the guts to lean forward and brush his lips against hers. Then with a blink, the spell was broken.

She cleared her throat. "I, um," she looked at her watch. "Need to get back to Pawville," she said, standing. She took a step back, almost tripping over the chair. Shaking her head, she pushed it under the table. "So, we'll be in touch, right?" she asked, shouldering her tote. Before he could respond, she nodded. "Yeah, of course we'll be in touch. Thanks for making the appointment," she said with a forced smile. "I'll see ya."

Before Hyphen could find his fucking voice and stop her, she was gone.

Chapter Twelve

Fellowship sat at the end of the bar in Lonnie's. Cramped, dark, and smoky, it had been her favorite place to think since college. Zig, the burly yet lovable barkeep, had the gift of discerning when customers wanted company or to be left alone. As soon as she asked for a Zion's Ink, he knew she was having one of those days. With a slight nod, he placed the tumbler in front of her, filled it with her favorite amber whiskey, and kept his distance, chatting softly with other customers.

She nursed her drink, lost in thought. On her way to The Archives, she'd told herself to remain professional with Hyphen. And it was a solid plan until she found herself drawn in by his ease and confidence—from getting them past that gnome of a director to seeing how his own people classified his wings. Even a sweet story about meeting his best friend shaded in details and nuance that made him even more likable. The more he talked, the more she wanted to know. The more she asked, the more he told. On the outside, Hyphen was intimidating with his hard-angled eyebrows that gave off a *try me* vibe, but it didn't take much to see the sensitive man beyond his tough exterior.

After literally fleeing The Archives, she drove around before going back to her apartment to half-work and half-brood over her feelings. After hours of notes and phone calls, she changed clothes and left again, finally ending up at Lonnie's. A sliver of light shone across the dark carpet, revealing Rayna, who walked in and made a beeline for her while nodding to Zig for her usual: Zion's Ink on the rocks. Sliding onto the stool next to her, she bumped Fellowship then smiled.

"Can't believe you started without me," she said, shrugging off her jacket and hooking it under the bar's ledge. Rayna's braids were swept into a high bun. Her soft, black V-neck t-shirt dipped, showing a swatch of her tawny skin.

"Couldn't wait," Fellowship replied.

"I understand. My girl's struggling," Rayna said, nodding to Zig who placed a drink in front of her.

"I'm not struggling," Fellowship said into her tumbler.

Rayna sucked her teeth before pulling her phone out of her back pocket. Scrolling, she looked up at Fellowship. "Help. I think I like Hyphen," she said, reading from her phone. "I just abandoned him at The Archives. Why am I like this?" Rayna scrolled some more. "At Lonnie's drowning my—"

"*Okay*, you got me," she moaned.

"What happened?"

"Nothing."

"Then why'd you ditch him?"

Fellowship bit her lip. It was a great question: why *did* she ditch him and his heat and overall sexiness? "I dunno," she shrugged. It was as good as any answer, and it was the truth, sort of.

"I *dunno*," Rayna repeated, frowning. After a beat, she looked at the barkeep. "Ziggy! I need a Zion's Ink *neat*—I can't have my shit watered down when my girl's over here trippin'. I need all the help I can get!" she yelled.

"Ray!" Fellowship exclaimed, half-embarrassed, half-amused.

"Stop fucking around and tell me the truth."

"I ditched him because I like him," she admitted.

"Okay...what's wrong with that?"

"I'm not supposed to like him."

Rayna nodded in understanding. "So, what actually happened at The Archives?"

Sighing, Fellowship knocked back her drink. She figured she was just drunk enough to admit to Rayna *and* herself what was going on.

"When we first got there this morning, the director wouldn't let us in because I'm human. Without missing a step, Haslem finessed him so fast the man didn't know what hit him. Then he showed me his entry in their registry, where his wings are classified as a birth defect—"

"What?" Rayna asked, horrified.

"I know," Fellowship said. "I couldn't help but think: this man risked flying me to Septain, showing his wings to people who see them as a defect. On top of that, he gets me admitted even though we all know there's a no-human-healing policy," she said, shaking her head. "I asked—well, *told* him to show me his magic, and the warm, off-centered feeling I already have when I'm around him was magnified to the point that *I* felt like magic. He's just—he's a surprise, and I don't like fucking surprises," she said, motioning for another drink.

"*Fuck*," Rayna breathed into her glass. "Fell, this is real."

"What? No, I'm just—"

"You said you feel his magic? Fellowship, that's something," Rayna insisted.

"What do you mean, that's something? You're always in Seacrest. I'm sure you feel their magic, too."

Rayna shook her head. "This is why you need to go there more often. People barely, if ever, feel their magic. I mean, yeah, it's different being around them, but their energy is mostly contained, flowing on its own power grid. So, feeling his magic *is* something."

Was Ray right? She assumed all humans felt some kind of buzz around Aechaih. First men-com, and now this? All signs were pointing to the inevitable conclusion that Hyphen was more than just a partner or a guy who saved her. And that realization made her stomach feel funny.

"He was there when I was shot. Maybe there's been some sort of transference of energy or something."

"Yeah, no," Rayna said, shaking her head.

"Or—"

"No, Fell. You can't nerd your way out of this. You know it's something—that's why you ditched him."

Zig placed Fellowship's drink in front of her. She picked it up and stared into it for a beat or two. "We can men-com," she admitted.

"What?!" Rayna shrieked, causing everyone to look in their direction.

"Shhh," Fellowship hissed, slinking further into the shadowed corner.

"What?!" Rayna whispered. "How? Why didn't you tell me? Oh, my Guardians, how does it feel?"

"I didn't say anything because it's fucking weird. It feels like he's caressing my mind, coaxing it to relax and open," she said, shivering at the thought.

"Biiiiitch! Can you men-com with anyone else?"

"I don't think so," she said, somewhat relieved at Ray's positive, albeit dramatic, response to her news.

"What does he say about it?"

"He doesn't know why either. Otherwise, he seems cool about it."

"Mmm hmm, because he knows."

"Ray."

"What? Are you resisting this because he's Aechaih?"

"No..."

Rayna didn't respond—just stared at her like the conflict-avoidant coward that she was. The silence did nothing but amplify how ridiculous she sounded.

"*Fine.* I like him, but it's too risky," she admitted. "I don't know the last time I felt so fucking drawn to someone. Liking him puts me in danger."

"In danger of what?"

"Getting hurt."

"So?"

Fellowship drew back so fast the room began to tilt. "*So?* So, who wants to get fucking hurt?"

"No one, but that doesn't mean the shit's not going to happen. If you're gonna get hurt, might as well get hurt falling for Hyphen fucking Haslem," Rayna said with a confident nod.

Drink in mid-air, Fellowship's mouth dropped open. It was a valid point. "No," she said, coming to her senses.

Rayna sighed. "When we first met, you barely talked about your grandfather. He'd call and text, and I'd watch you ignore him. Then you got shot, almost died, and before I knew it, you and Ambassador Dancy were different. What changed? Why'd you let him back into your life?"

She knew where Rayna was headed. Shoulders slumped in defeat, she answered. "All of it seemed so stupid."

"Exactly. You opened yourself up to your grandfather's love because it was natural. Part of me thinks that's why you've let me in more," Rayna added.

"Yes," she admitted.

"I think your attraction to Haslem is beyond hormones. It's deeper. Natural. Just consider it."

"Consider liking him?"

"Yeah."

Fellowship had to admit Rayna made sense. "He *is* sexy as fuck," she said. "I mean, *really?*"

"It's obnoxious," Rayna said, knocking back her drink. "I'd risk it all for someone that Solneur-damned fine. Guardians."

Fellowship laughed because she felt better and she was a little tipsy. Then it hit her. "Girl, I'm sitting here thinking about this man, and he has a full-on girlfriend," Fellowship said, smacking her forehead.

"Who?"

"Bronwyn Phor."

Rayna grabbed her phone and began scrolling. Frowning, she held up a picture. "He's dating *her?*"

Fellowship squinted to see Bronwyn's *Vizable* profile. Her stomach rolled at the sight of Blondie. "Yeah," she mumbled. Suddenly, she had a headache.

"Are they even together? He's nowhere on her profile," Rayna said, scrolling.

"She was just at the precinct."

"She was at the precinct as in you met her?"

Fellowship nodded then rolled her eyes.

"Hmph. How'd *that* go?"

"She wanted to play *Biggest Bitch,* so I matched her energy."

"And what did *he* say?"

"He apologized. We started working, and he mentioned that he saw me jump in front of Nigh and Zaphine at the temple."

"He *saw* you? I thought he heard shots and ran over to help."

"Turns out, he was getting into his SUV and saw me," she said. "I caught his attention," she drawled. Okay, maybe she was more drunk than tipsy.

"Hyphen Haslem said that you caught his attention, which means he was watching you and *happened* to see you get shot, right?"

Fellowship rested her head on her palm and nodded. "Yep."

"Girl, please! There's something *there.* But I get it—you're freaked out, so just work with him and be open to what the Guardians have."

Fellowship laughed. "That's it, huh?"

"Hell, yeah."

Fellowship smiled, then leaned over, resting her head on Rayna's shoulder. "You're a good friend," she said, closing her eyes.

"If we don't have each other's back, who will?"

"No one," Fellowship mumbled.

"Exactly. Are you ready to go home, or do you want another one?"

Fellowship opened one eye and smiled.

"No, let's get your drunk ass home."

Fellowship giggled. Rayna wasn't Daize—she didn't have to be. No, she was her friend. A friend she fucking loved.

"I don't understand why you'd end a three-year relationship out of nowhere," Honey complained.

Hyphen pressed his whiskey glass against his temple and let out a deep, annoyed sigh as she continued.

"Bronwyn is beautiful, compelling, and smart, Hyphen. You're two hundred and ten years old. What are you waiting for?" she asked, her voice close to a shriek.

"I'm waiting for someone I like," he groaned, suddenly feeling like a kid again. Sitting on the side of his bed, wearing gym shorts and a t-shirt, he cursed himself for picking up her call.

"What? You *do* like her."

"No, I don't," he said, knocking back his drink. Already on edge, he set the glass on the nightstand and got into bed, leaning against the charcoal gray, upholstered headboard. All day, he replayed The Archives moment with Fellowship. One minute she was completely present, dialed in, and the next she was gone. He couldn't figure out what went wrong. Did he say something? Miss something—

"What changed?" Honey interrupted. "What changed that caused you to walk away from a woman like that?"

"I changed. I don't want to be with a woman who's disrespectful and single-minded in her ambition to acquire social status off our name," he explained.

Somehow, that stopped Honey's rant. "Oh," she breathed. "*Disrespectful?* Did something happen?"

"Yes, she was rude to a co-worker of mine."

"Who?"

"Fellowship Dancy."

"Auten's granddaughter? She was rude to *Fellowship?*" Honey asked in horror.

"Yes."

"After all that poor girl's been through? Why would Bronwyn be so nasty?"

"Because that's how she is."

Honey took a long beat. "I've been blind, haven't I?" she finally asked, her voice small and remorseful.

"Don't worry about it."

"There was a part of me that *sensed* she was insincere, but I ignored it."

"So did I."

"The girls were right."

"Of course, they were."

He heard his mother sigh. She didn't speak for an extended moment—so extended, he thought she'd hung up. Then she began. "After Hudson, you were so lost, and yes, you found a great job and made your way back, but I wanted you to have someone of your own," she admitted. "I wanted you to find your *person*."

Maybe he should be honest with his mother more often. It never occurred to him that she wanted him to be happy. He assumed she wanted him married off so she could brag to her social circle.

"You always told me to find a woman who added color and richness to my life," he said, thinking about a certain human cop.

"I said that?" she asked softly.

"Yes," he said on a chuckle.

"That's good advice, son."

"I know which is why I'm going to follow it this time."

"I just want you to be happy, Hyphen. I really do." Honey's honesty plucked at his heart, making him realize he'd spent so much time focused on his own life that he hadn't tended to his relationship with his mother. If breaking up with Bronwyn created an opportunity to find common ground with the woman who birthed him, then it was worth it.

"I love you."

"I love you, too, Mom."

"Oh, if you're not too busy, maybe you can be my date for our Casino Night? We're raising money for the children's wing at Septain."

"Of course."

"Oh, good. Your father's busy, and I don't want to go alone."

"I'll be there."

"My sweet boy," she whispered. "Don't work too hard, okay?"

"I won't. Night." He ended the call and tossed his phone on the bed.

What a difference a little communication made. The lump of dread in the pit of his stomach dissolved, knowing his mother was on his side. As he grabbed his current read off the nightstand, his phone buzzed. Resting the book on his chest, he picked it up. It was Fellowship. Heart in his throat, he sat up, sending the book flying to the floor.

Dancy: Hey, hope I'm not texting too late. We need to canvas Pawville for the third suspect.

Hyphen stared at the phone like it had grown a head and started talking.

Haslem: You want me to canvas with you?

Dancy: You don't want to come?

Haslem: Yeah. I didn't know if you wanted an Aechaih with you while you canvassed Pawville.

Dancy: You're Aechaih?! WTF??!!

He laughed. **Haslem:** You know what I mean.

Dancy: Meh. You look more intimidating than you are.

Haslem: I look intimidating?!

Dancy: Hyphen, you're six-five with a neck tattoo. You don't look like you're about to gab with someone over tea.

Haslem: I love a good gab over tea, thank you very much.

Dancy: Big on tea-time, are you?

Haslem: Absolutely. I have a standing reservation at Klaire's.

Dancy: Lol, the tearoom?

Haslem: Yes. I used to take the twins when they were little.

Dancy: Aw. They grow so fast don't they?

Haslem: They do.

Dancy: I'll go with you. I'm always down for tea-time.

Haslem: Sounds good, Dancy.

Dancy: Good. I'll see you tomorrow?

Haslem: Of course. I'm glad you asked.

Dancy: Of course, I asked. We're partners.

Grinning at the phone like an idiot, he nodded even though she couldn't see him. Locking it, he stared at it before setting it on his night-stand. Reaching down, he picked up his book and found where he left off. He tried to read, but the words jumbled as his mind drifted to her. There was something about the woman, about the way she made him feel that had him off balance. But none of that mattered. Like she said, they were partners.

Partners.

Work partners.

Professional partners.

Partners. Partners. Partners.

Chapter Thirteen

Pawville, in all its impoverished charm, buzzed as folks went about their day. Trianah was cool and clear—Fellowship's favorite kind of weather. She caught her reflection in the rearview mirror. With a quick swipe, she fixed her red lipstick, then turned her head to admire her fresh fade. Hyphen pulled up, snagging her attention. He stepped out of his SUV wearing a black sweater, flat-front pants with dress boots and a camel, single-breast coat. She hadn't realized her mouth had gone dry until his watch caught the light as he locked his vehicle, slipping his keys into his coat pocket. Grinding her teeth, she tried to center in the seconds before he got in her car but was unsuccessful. As soon as he opened the door, she smelled the sea. Dropping into the passenger's side, he closed the door, then reached down to the lower right, adjusting the seat for more leg room. Still not breathing, her eyes traced his pointed ears to his profile. After he was settled and buckled in, he looked at her.

"Hey," he smiled.

"Comfortable?" she asked, eyeing the seat.

"Yes, thank you. So, that's your precinct?" he asked, nodding to the rundown building.

"You've never been in there?" she asked. "Not even when you first joined the force?"

"Sad to say, I haven't. You know the culture—live and let live. Aechaih Division doesn't engage with humans, and vice versa."

"Even though we're all TMPD."

"When you put it like that, it sounds shitty."

"Hey, I'm not one to complain. I enjoy the autonomy. Although my grandfather said I've been in a bubble over here which, is one of the reasons he suggested to the Council that the divisions collaborate."

His perfectly arched eyebrows knitted together. "This was Auten's idea?"

"You didn't know?"

"I don't receive Council meeting minutes."

"Not even a newsletter?"

He shook his head, amused. "No."

"That's fair. Well, we're working together because your father was outvoted two to one."

"On what?"

"Rounding up the humans and throwing us into the sea, I assume," she said flatly. "But I think closing Pawville's borders until things get sorted out."

"Of course," he said.

"Grandpa saw it as an opportunity to try something new, so you can thank him for having to work with me."

"I will," he said so low she could barely hear. She fought the urge to reach out and run her hand through his hair, down to his faded sides.

"Where are we headed?" he asked, bringing her back to reality. Truth be told, she hadn't thought about it, but now that she needed to, it seemed obvious.

"Let's hit 10th and 11th Ave, see what's going on over there," she said, pulling into traffic. Out the corner of her eye, she watched him watch Pawville. "You've never been over here ever?" she asked.

"No, Hudson used to bring me when I was young," he said, staring out the window. "He was adamant that we spent time with humans.

He didn't want me growing up thinking Seacrest was better than Pawville—that *we* were better."

"Sounds like his views on humans differed from your father's."

"Greatly," he paused like he was choosing his words carefully. "Hudson raised me," he said after a moment.

She eased to a stoplight and looked at him. She expected him to have been raised by a nanny or something, but not his older brother. Before she could respond, he continued.

"My mom got sick with each pregnancy, but my birth was the hardest, almost killing her," he said. "When I was born, my father was consumed with nursing her back to health, so Hudson took the job, no questions asked."

"How long was she sick?"

"She was in the hospital for months and on bed rest until I was a little over one."

"Oh," she breathed.

He looked at her. "Horace resented me. Hudson was my primary caregiver."

"That's why you were so close," she said with a nod. He smiled and returned to the window. Solneur, she was a prejudiced dick. How long had she scoffed at the Haslem name? Scoffed at him, thinking he was just another privileged Aechaih. Hyphen's story was real. His tenderness and honesty, even his willingness to share, made her think about her own upbringing—something she buried so deep it was unreachable. "Not that you need my sympathy, but I'm sorry. I'm glad you had Hudson, though. Sounds like he was an amazing person."

"He was," he said before returning to her, green eyes dimmed with pain. The pain—*his* pain—slammed into her. She *knew* that feeling of loss, of hopelessness. Of a world being shattered. She recognized Hyphen's hurt; felt it deep in her bones. Could it be possible that she'd somehow *dreamt* of Hyphen's pain? The fuck? *How?* Dismissing the questions, she swallowed the lump in her throat, then turned onto 10th Avenue, easing down the street.

The neighborhood was alive with people either huddled in groups, walking around or kids playing as best as they could with whatever they had.

"I could do with some fresh air. How about you?"

"Absolutely," he said, unbuckling his seatbelt. By the time she was out and on his side, he was already out and closing the door. Locking her car with a *beep*, they started toward the apartments.

"Hi, Officer Dancy!" a tiny voice squeaked from the bare playground. Fellowship looked over to see the chubby, brown face of a little girl. She waved and smiled as they continued to the buildings.

"How long were you a patrol cop?" he asked.

"About eight years. The goal was always to be a detective. Once I was in, I put my head down and worked my way up."

"You mean you continued to overachieve?" he asked with a smile.

"Yes," she said, returning it. She liked that he recognized and accepted her persistence instead of taking it as a personal affront.

"Oh, my Guardians, Detective Dancy!" she heard someone cry. Turning, she saw Sylve and Kahleb. Sylve, short with thin blonde hair curled into a fluffy puff, beamed. Kahleb, carrying two bags of groceries, offered a shy smile. With some meat on his bones, he had transformed from a street menace back to a sixteen-year-old kid. His curly blonde hair was clean as were his jeans and silver puffer coat. Fellowship and Hyphen slowed to a stop as they walked over.

"Miss Sylve, Kahleb, how are you?" she asked.

Sylve stopped and opened her arms. Fellowship smiled as she leaned down into the woman's soft embrace. "I'm so happy to see you! We heard what happened and, oh, I prayed and prayed to the Guardians to spare your beautiful life, and here you are," she said, pulling away to look at Fellowship's face.

"Thank you, Miss Sylve. I'm sorry I didn't check in on you guys earlier—"

"Don't you *dare* apologize. After what you did for us," Sylve said, shaking her head. "Brenda helped us get on our feet, Detective. Had it not been for you, Guardians, I don't know where we'd be, where *Kahleb* would be," she said. After a moment, her eyes drifted to

Hyphen; she raised her eyebrows, then looked at Fellowship. "Who is *this?*"

"This is Detective Haslem from the Aechaih Division."

"Pleasure to meet you," he said with a smile.

"My, you are *beautiful,*" Sylve breathed. Kahleb groaned, shaking his head as Hyphen blushed. "I thought he was your fella," she said, looking at Fellowship. "You need someone like him. I don't like you patrolling these streets by yourself," she said, matter-of-factly. Then she returned to Hyphen. "Are you single, Detective Haslem?" she asked, her blue eyes bright with curiosity.

"*Granny,*" Kahleb moaned.

Hyphen only smiled. "Yes, ma'am, I am."

Wait, what? Fellowship whipped her head so fast she almost pulled a muscle. Before she could rein herself in, her body exploded with what could only be described as gleeful delight.

"That's good," Sylve said, nodding. "Detective Dancy needs someone by her side. She's given so much of herself to this community. Did she tell you? I called her in the middle of the night some time ago, worried about my grandson. Not only did she pick up the phone, but she patrolled the streets until she found him."

"Miss Sylve," Fellowship protested, but Sylve held up her hand.

"*Then* she connected us with an agency that's been more help than we could've ever expected. And she didn't have to do it. She's an officer, not a social worker. But she saved us, Detective Haslem. *Haslem?* Are you related to the Haslems of the Tri-Family Council?"

Shit. Fellowship wanted to step in, but Hyphen answered before she could intervene.

"Yes, ma'am, I am, but I don't serve on the Council. I just work in law enforcement."

Sylve nodded, then looked at Fellowship. "I like that you have him. Are you two working on those cases I heard about on the news?"

"We are. I don't know if you heard about Nigh Rygle," Fellowship said.

Sylve's face dropped, as did her voice. "Oh, that poor girl. Accused of *murder*. What a shame," Sylve said. "She worked for Rey, you know. That boy's a menace," she said, sniffing indignantly. "I'm so happy you intervened with Kahleb. That could've been *him*."

Fellowship looked at Kahleb. Though clean, he still looked anxious, eyes darting back and forth. "I'm glad I could help when I did. We're looking for the suspect. We hope the perp isn't human, but if they are, we need to find them," she said.

"Guardians. No, I haven't heard a thing," Sylve said.

"If you do, you have my number."

"Yes, yes of course, Detective." She looked at Hyphen with big expectant eyes. "It was nice to meet you, Detective Haslem," she sang, giving him a big smile.

He smiled back. "Same here, ma'am."

Sylve patted Fellowship and inched toward the apartment building. Kahleb followed her, then he stopped and turned around.

"What's up, Kahleb?" she asked.

"Um, so..." he looked around. "I, um, heard something."

"About Nigh?"

He shook his head.

"About the murder?" she asked.

He nodded, eyes wide. "One of my boys said that Rey was in Seacrest for a deal when some shit went down. He's stressing—been holed up in his house for days," Kahleb reported.

"Kahleb, this is huge. Do you know where he's staying?"

He nodded. "It's a trap house, Detective."

"That's okay. Here, put it in my phone," she said, handing him her cell. Kahleb looked at the cell, then down at the grocery bags he was holding.

"I'll take those," Hyphen said, holding out his hand. Kahleb handed him the bags, then took Fellowship's phone. After punching in the address, he handed the phone to Fellowship as Hyphen returned the bags.

"Thank you, Kahleb."

Kahleb nodded. "What's crazy is that I was about to ask Granny for your phone number. I thought by telling you he was in trouble, maybe you could help him. Which sounds stupid, but I heard you're trying to help Nigh and stuff..." he trailed off, his eyes cast downward.

"There's nothing wrong with helping someone in our community—that's what we do," she affirmed.

He blushed. "Thank you, Detective. Oh, and I'm glad you're okay, too—from the shooting," he said.

"I appreciate that, Kahleb, *and* your help. You know, had it not been for Detective Haslem, I wouldn't have made it that day."

Kahleb's eyes slid up to Hyphen, his brow furrowed in consideration. "So, you're a *cool* Aechaih," he said, giving him that slight teenagery nod thing.

Hyphen looked at her, then back to Kahleb. "I hope so."

"Trust me, he is. Now, get in there and make your granny some dinner," she said. "Thanks again."

Kahleb gave them both a smile and turned to walk into the apartment building. Once he was inside, she turned to Hyphen, whose eyes were already on her.

"What?" she asked.

"Nothing," he replied, holding her gaze like it was definitely something.

"Okayyyy," she said, narrowing her eyes. "Let's go see what's up with Rey."

Once they were clicked into their seatbelts, he looked at her again. She started the car and faced him. "What, Haslem? Out with it."

"How did you know you'd see Miss Sylve and Kahleb?"

"I didn't," she said. "I just knew we needed to come over here."

"Just knew?"

"Yes, Haslem, I just knew. Haven't you ever just known something?"

He didn't respond. Instead, his eyes searched her face for what seemed like an eternity. Fellowship felt lightheaded, like she had one too many Zions.

"Yeah, I've just known," he said with enough intensity to reverberate up her fucking spine.

"See," she finally choked out before pulling into traffic.

Fellowship parked a block away from Rey's home. He lived in yet another dilapidated pocket of Pawville, but instead of apartments, they were small, worse-for-wear homes.

Turning off the car, she looked at Hyphen. "What do you think?"

"I think if he's in trouble, he needs to be brought in. He'd be safer in your Detainment than in ours or on the street."

"You took the words right out of my mouth." She knew Haslem was different, but seeing how his general care extended beyond her to a young human in trouble fucked with her insides.

"You're staring at me," he said.

She blinked the world into focus. "You wish."

He snorted a laugh. "So, who's this guy?"

"Your average hustler; recruits kids like Nigh and Kahleb, promising financial relief in exchange for their time and possible freedom."

"You wanna play good cop, bad cop?" he asked, raising an eyebrow.

She nodded. "Yeah, I can play good cop—"

"I wasn't talking about *you* as good cop," he said with a smirk.

"I'm the *bad* cop?" she asked, eyes wide.

"I might look intimidating, but you *are* intimidating," he said, matter-of-factly.

"Whatever, Haslem," she said, smiling at how easy it was for them to tease each other. "Let's go."

Fellowship and Hyphen took the rickety steps to Rey's front door. The once-white home had chipped paint and a boarded-up window. Fellowship knocked on the squeaky screen door, then stood back.

"I didn't bring my gun," Hyphen said on a side-eye.

She frowned. "You all carry guns?"

"We don't shoot bullets out our asses, Dancy."

"Oh, and he's funny, too," she mocked. "It's okay, I have mine."

"Always prepared."

"Always, but if things get dicey, we'll just have to rely on your *energetic manipulation*," she said with a smile.

Hyphen shook his head. "Pain in the ass."

He might've thought she was a pain, but she immediately felt his heat float around her like a shield of warmth. The door opened and a teenager's pale face appeared.

"Who the fuck are you?" he spat.

Hyphen stilled, but she remained unbothered. "I'm Detective Dancy. This is Detective Haslem. Is Rey around?"

The teenager squinted. "He's not here." He looked sleep-deprived and anxious; not only was she confident Rey was in there, but that he needed help.

"Look, we know he's here and that he's in trouble. Tell him that we know what happened in Seacrest, and we're here to help," she said, lifting her chin.

"Wait here," he barked.

"He's stressed the fuck out," Hyphen said quietly.

"Right? Rey's gotta be worse."

The teenager returned and pushed open the screen door. "C'mon," he mumbled. Dressed in the standard teen uniform, he wore a white tee and baggy jeans. His brown hair was buzzed, and he had a massive amount of ink.

She stepped in first, and Hyphen was close behind. The dark, musty house smelled like mold, glower-weed, and body odor. It took all her willpower not to pinch her nose. The front room had a stained mattress on the scuffed hardwood floor along, with trash, empty cups, and two cellphones. The teen led them through a filthy kitchen to a small bedroom in the back of the house. The closed door was badly chipped. The teen knocked and pushed it open before he stepped aside, letting them in. Rey, no older than twenty-one, sat on a bare mattress. There was a handgun on his left and three cellphones on his right. He wore a white tee with baggy jeans and brown boots. His black hair was slicked back, arms covered with ink as well. There was one cloudy, curtain-less window, a small closet, and a flat-screen sitting on top of a crate. He held his head in his hands.

"Rey?"

He looked up with blue, albeit bloodshot, eyes. "You're Detective Dancy? Nigh's teacher?" he asked. Top dealer aside, he was a kid—a scared, vulnerable kid.

"Yes, I am."

Rey nodded. "Yeah. She always talks about you. Your class and shit," he said. "Had I known Seacrest was this fucked up, I wouldn't have gone—wouldn't have sent her."

"Rey, Nigh's safe in Detainment. She told me that after hanging with her Aechaih friend, she woke up covered in her blood," she said. "Did the same thing happen to you?"

He nodded, lowering his head. "He was a familiar—always hit me up twice a week. I had Nigh service the women and I always worked with the guys. Didn't want her getting caught up," he said, shaking his head. "As soon as we exchanged goods for money, everything went dark. Next thing I know, I wake up in his living room, covered in blood with a fucking knife in my hand. Obviously, I don't fuck with knives," Rey said, eyeing his gun. "The motherfucker's neck was slit ear to ear. It was gruesome."

"What'd you do next?" she asked.

"I took off. Been hiding ever since."

"Do you still have the knife?" she asked.

Rey looked up. "I tossed it in the sea," he said. "I—I don't know what happened. Shit doesn't scare me, you know? But this shit's fucked up."

"A couple more questions, Rey. Had you drank or consumed drugs before going to Seacrest?"

"You don't get high off your own supply," he said, dropping his head in his hands.

Fellowship nodded. "Right. How do you normally contact your customers? Through text on your burner?"

"We message."

"*FBDn*?"

He looked up. "Yeah."

"Lastly, can you remember anything else—anything that might help us figure out what happened to you?"

Rey took a moment to consider. "No. Except when I was at the pier, it was dark as fuck. Like no moons at all, which was weird, but I don't know. I was so fucked up, maybe I was imagining shit," he said.

Again, Sylena and her sisters were missing. She may not have known what it meant, but clearly it was something. "Rey, so here's the thing—I think someone's targeting humans, and I don't know how. I know you're not going to want to hear this, but you'd be a lot safer if you came with us, gave your official statement, and remained in custody."

"Fucking Detainment? Are you crazy?" he asked, irate.

Fellowship felt more of Hyphen's heat, which strangely enough, emboldened her. "Like Nigh, I won't turn you over to the Aechaih," she promised.

"What do you mean not turn me over to the Aechaih? There's a fucking Aechaih right there," he said, pointing to Hyphen.

"Detective Haslem's different," she said, turning to her partner. He was against the wall, his green eyes on her. She returned to Rey whose face was twisted in disgust.

"All fucking Aechaih are the same," he spat.

"Look, you're talking to someone who couldn't stand Aechaih. Didn't want to step foot in Seacrest if I didn't have to. Detective Haslem saved my life when I was shot at the temple," she said.

Rey's eyes flicked to Hyphen then back to her.

"A normal Aechaih would've let me die on the street, but he didn't. I'm not saying all Aechaih are like him, but trust me when I say you can trust Detective Haslem."

Rey considered her, then dropped his head. "Fuck," he hissed.

"Tell me this, what does Nigh say about me?" she asked. It was her last hope.

"She says you're legit. One of the few cops that's not full of shit. She told me that she needed to get out of the game because she was doing well in school and shit. I was down with that, you know? School ain't for me, but Nigh's smart," he said, dejected.

Fellowship eased to him and squatted down, gently putting her hand on his knee. "Rey, I'm working hard to figure out what happened. If someone's coming after us, we gotta look out for each other," she said. "I'm not worried about how you make your money; I'm worried about stopping this before another human gets caught up."

He took a deep, ragged breath and looked at her. His eyes were pained, sad. She immediately felt his anguish. Rey might've been a drug dealer, but he wasn't a murderer.

"Okay," he whispered.

On the sofa in her office at the Aechaih precinct, Fellowship stared at the glass writing board, studying everything they knew about the case, save their hunch. The last thing she needed was for someone to walk by and see that they theorized Aechaih involvement. Currently, there were three known victims and three suspects: two in custody, one deceased. The murders occurred in Seacrest; all three reported memory loss and not seeing Sylena or her sisters. Nigh and Rey both had a legal amount of alcohol in their systems and tested clean for illicit substances.

After getting Rey settled in Detainment, they stopped by Ceager's office where Hyphen had the brilliant idea to ask him for a search warrant for Cygma Tech, the creators of *FBDn*. Because it was an Aechaih company, there was no way Weeden would push for a warrant. Having Ceager do it would force Weeden to back the Human Division if and when Cygma Tech balked.

Meanwhile, Fellowship had to admit that working with Haslem

went better than expected. She was so used to working the streets alone that having someone watch her back felt good. Maybe Miss Sylve was right about needing someone by her side. Her phone buzzed. Picking it up, she smiled before accepting a video call from the twins. They appeared on the screen, all smiles and blue eyes, with a beautiful landscape of manicured trees against a Trianah blue sky serving as their backdrop.

"Hi, Fellowship," they said in unison.

"Hey, there. How are you?"

"Fantastic," Haze answered.

"Do you have time to meet with us tomorrow?" Harleigh asked. "We know it's the weekend."

"I read that the Aechaih and Human Divisions are partnering on these murders," Haze added.

Fellowship nodded. "Yes, we are. Hyphen and I are partners, did he tell you?"

Their eyes widened as their mouths dropped open. "What?! OMG, no! He didn't say *anything*," Harleigh said. "You two are the detectives they're referring to in these stories?!"

"Yep. I'm at the Aechaih precinct now."

"Where's Hyphen?" Haze asked.

"In a meeting. He should be back soon," Fellowship reported. "We'll more than likely be working tomorrow, so I'll be in Seacrest. Would you like to meet at your brother's?"

"Yes!" they exclaimed in unison. Fellowship laughed. They were so beautiful and bright; she couldn't help thinking about the days of old when she and Daize were that young and dazzling.

"Sounds good."

"How is it working with Big Brother?" Haze asked. "Is he all brooding and intense?"

She liked Haze—she liked both of them, but in Haze, she sensed a kindred spirit. "Not at all. It's been great, and to my surprise, Hyphen's a little bit of a history nerd," she said.

The twins looked at each other, then back to her. Their smiles were different, more open—if that were possible. "He's a *total* nerd," Harleigh agreed. "One of the many things we love about him."

"He tries to hide it, but those who know, know," Haze added.

"I have a nerdy side, too. Maybe that's why I noticed."

"Same," Haze said. "I'm trying to get through my schoolwork *and* a stack of books he suggested I read."

"Me, too," Harleigh said. "But I'm skipping a few of them; I have a social life to maintain."

"Of course, you do. Enjoy it. How about you, Haze?"

"Meh. Social lives are overrated," she said, shrugging. Yep, she was a kindred spirit all right.

"She's more like Hyphen," Harleigh said as Haze nudged her with a frown.

"How's *your* social life, Fellowship?" Haze asked.

"Nonexistent," Fellowship admitted, shaking her head.

"See," Haze said, turning to her sister. "Fellowship doesn't have a social life either, and she's super successful."

"Speaking of social lives, I've gotta go," Harleigh announced.

"See you tomorrow, Fellowship," Haze said. "Tell Hyphen we said hi and that he owes us lunch for not telling us you're his partner."

"I will."

The girls ended the call, leaving a grin on her face. She started to text Hyphen but stopped. She should wait until he returned, or better yet, she could try to men-com. Taking a deep breath, she felt around for his warm, steady energy.

Hope I'm not interrupting. Spoke to the twins; they want to chat with me tomorrow. I suggested that we meet at your place. Is that okay? After a beat, her body warmed.

You're never interrupting me. Is this an excuse for you to see my place?

Obviously. I'm dying to see how the uber-rich live.

Jealousy isn't a good look on you.

She laughed. *Whatever. Meanwhile, I might be obsessed with them.*

Trust me, they're obsessed with you, too.

You didn't tell them we're partners. Trying to keep me a secret?

Never. I hadn't gotten around to it. What else did you all talk about?

Nothing much. Discussed your nerd-like tendencies and how adorable it is that you give them reading lists.

I'm surprised they called it adorable. They usually whine and cry about them. Harleigh more than Haze.

They didn't call it adorable, I did. She felt his bashfulness travel along their line. *Are you blushing, Haslem?*

You can't possibly know that.

So, that's a yes.

Whatever. Did you tell them that your nerdiness supersedes mine by two advanced degrees?

She laughed out loud. *In a way. I'm sure Haze and I bonded a little. I don't want to pick favorites because they're both wonderful, but I like her.*

She's amazing, isn't she?

Yes. I wish I was that confident at her age—well, not exactly her age because I'm sure she's chronologically older than me.

His amusement sent tickles across her mind where they settled in her stomach. *Yeah, she is, or rather, they are.*

How's the meeting?

Awful. What are you doing?

Meh, the usual. Curled up on the sofa, watching a movie on my computer.

Stop. I don't think Weeden would appreciate if I laughed out loud in the middle of his meeting.

Yulk. That man. He wouldn't appreciate a good laugh if it bit him on his flat, uptight ass. She felt his laughter explode down their connection.

You're nothing but trouble. I had to disguise that shit as a cough.

Oh, Haze and Harleigh said you owe them lunch for not telling them that we're partners.

We'll take them to lunch tomorrow after the interview.

That means it's okay to meet at your place?

Of course, it is.

When's your meeting over?

Miss me?

Wait. Can you feel me rolling my eyes?

Funny. I'll be up soon.

Okay.

His heat receded, leaving traces of his smile lingering in her consciousness. She sighed. Rayna said to be open to what the Guardians had planned, and while it sounded prudent, in reality, she was too much of a control freak for that shit. Leaving it up to the Guardians meant anything could happen, and she wasn't ready for that, especially with Hyphen. But it was impossible not to think about their bond, the ability to men-com, and what Rayna said about feeling his magic and what it could mean. Ready or not, she was fucked. Swept out to sea, drowning in her attraction, better yet, *connection* to him. She grabbed her cup and shook it—empty. Needing water, she left her office in search of a break room. The carpeted hallways were hushed as she strolled past a few empty offices. Coming to a fork, she turned left and clocked a break room on her right. Well, make that a full-ass cafe.

Stepping in, she stopped. A wall of windows looked out onto the city. Plush, luxurious sofas sat on large cream and sage area rugs that looked intricately hand-woven. Plants everywhere. Pub tables. Recessed lighting. A marble countertop with every kitchen appliance one could dream of, not to mention the subzero refrigerator with glass doors that allowed her to drool over rows and rows of snacks. On the far wall were shelves, *shelves* lined with food. Boxes and boxes of shit. She rinsed out her cup and refilled it with ice water. Eyes snagging on a basket of granola bars and other snacks, she went over just as she felt Hyphen. Stopping, she took a shallow breath as her body warmed and vibrated with *him.*

Where are you? he asked.

What's the point of being able to men-com if you can't find me? she asked, finally able to move.

It's not a GPS, Dancy.

Smiling, she picked up two granola bars. *I'm shopping.*

What—where?

The artisan grocery store down the hall from my office.

What are you talking about, Dancy?

I'm sure you call it a break room, but that would be crazy because break rooms aren't the size of one-bedroom apartments.

Solneur. I can't with you.

Exiting, she rounded the corner, colliding into his very broad, very solid chest. Looking up, she smiled. "Oh, there you are. Hi," she said, taking a step back.

Looking down, he smiled. The corners of his eyes faintly crinkled. Without his overcoat, she was able to appreciate his body—*outfit* more. Especially his pushed-up sleeves, revealing that tatted left arm.

"Get everything you need?" he asked, arching an eyebrow.

Sidestepping him, she strolled back to the office. "Yes, but now I need to see your cafeteria. I bet it has its own zip code," she said as he settled in stride next to her.

Opening the office door for her, he shook his head. "Smart-ass."

Sauntering past, she shrugged. "Would a smart-ass grab a snack for you, too?" she asked as he followed her in. Turning to face him, she extended the granola bar.

"Thank you."

"See, that's what you get for making fun. Where would you be without a partner like me?"

"Hungry, obviously," he deadpanned. Opening the package, he took a huge bite, then looked at the glass writing board. Frowning, he pointed. "Nigh mentioned a moonless night, too?" he asked around a mouthful of granola.

"Yeah. I've been trying to think of what it could possibly mean. It's not like Trianah has a lot of cloud cover right?" she asked, opening her own bar and taking a bite.

"Right," he said, sitting next to her on the small sofa. "I've never heard of that and strangely enough, never noticed."

"Maybe that beautiful library at The Archives has something on

Sylena and her sisters' movements throughout the sky," she suggested with a twinkle in her eye. The internet probably had answers, but who wanted that when she could be surrounded by books.

"You're just trying to get in there so you can go all history-nerd in the rare books section," he said playfully.

"Don't act like you don't wanna join me," she said, equally playful. He smiled broadly, his eyes sparkling like two gemstones. It felt like someone dumped hot broth inside her chest, melting her defenses into warm cream. Crossing her legs to clamp down on the heat, she hoped he couldn't tell what was going on. As a matter of fact, what *was* going on? Okay, she knew what was going on, but she was just so thrown by it all.

His magic buzzed around her. His distinctive smell had turned into a Solneur-damned aphrodisiac. She wanted to fuck and cuddle him at the same time. She wanted to spend all of her time with him because being away from him was beginning to feel weird. Wrong. But as soon as she felt his slow, assured energy, usually well before he appeared, all that was wrong felt right. As much as she wanted to deny the connection, she couldn't. Not when he looked the way he did—as still as death with stormy, olive-green eyes. The playful spark snuffed out, jaw tight, the energy in the room shifted from playful to hot so fast her breathing became shallow. As if realizing how he looked, he blinked rapidly, finishing his granola bar in one bite. Chewing, he was flush, his fair complexion tinted with a hint of pink. If she hadn't known better, she'd think he was turned on, too. Was he? No—no, he wasn't turned on. She figured she was the only one behaving like a teenager in heat until she caught a whiff of something else riding his normal seacoast and lavender scent. Its sharp sweetness stirred something within her, something desperate to get out. It rumbled around her core before exploding, making her pussy clench around a phantom dick. The muscle in his defined jaw feathered, inviting her to run her tongue along the edge, then down his neck.

"So..." he said, his voice low.

Granola bar on its way to her mouth for another bite, she lifted her eyes to his. The arm nearest her was draped along the back of the sofa—the tips of his fingers ominously close. He arched an eyebrow.

She frowned. "What?"

"What are you thinking about?"

She paused. He couldn't tell. No, of course not. "The case," she lied, taking another bite.

His eyes searched her face for a thoughtful beat before he gave her a half smile so hot it almost singed off her eyebrows. "I didn't realize work turned you on," he said, his eyes daring her to contradict him.

Her thirsty bitch of a pussy throbbed like she hadn't had sex in *years*. Fellowship shoved the rest of the bar into her mouth, then shrugged. "I-don-kno-wut-yur-talkin-about," she mumbled.

Hyphen's eyes danced with amusement. "You don't?"

"Nope," she said, reaching for her cup of water to take a long pull.

"You don't have to admit it, I already know," he said with a casual shrug.

"What the fuck does that mean?" she snapped, setting her cup down and crossing her arms.

"It means, I *know*."

"You don't know shit," she said, cocky as ever. The audacity of men, *Aechaih* men at that.

"Alright, *Professor Dancy*—let me give you a short lesson on Aechaih physiology since we've established that you don't spend much time in Seacrest."

"Fine."

Before she could process the moment, he leaned in closer—too close. "You know when you're attracted to someone, your body warms or hardens," he said, his voice low and intimate.

Facing him, she inched closer, holding his green eyes in defiance. "Yes, I'm aware of that."

"Aechaih have heightened senses, so we can tell when someone's physically attracted to us," he explained. "Even if they try to hide it."

Oh, shit. Of course, he knew she was wet. Fuck! "You mean..." she said as her bravado melted, pooling at her feet.

"Yeah," he said, swallowing. And Guardians help her, even the bobble of his throat turned her on.

Was there a word for beyond embarrassed? Yes, mortified. She was fucking mortified. There she was, thinking she could hide her physical attraction to him when all along, he could sense it. He smiled in satisfaction, crossing his long legs. Then the motherfucker arched an eyebrow and eased into her mind: *Yep, I can smell all of that.*

Face on fire, she couldn't help but smile. Had any other Aechaih pulled that shit, she would've cussed him out, but Hyphen? His swag was undeniable. Only a man settled in his own skin could have her grinning like a fool. Then a thought popped into her head—*smell*. Since the shooting, her smell had changed. Like her overall stamina, it just got better. Perhaps the sharp sweetness entangled with his signature scent meant that he was just as horny as she was.

"That's what I smell on you," she announced.

He frowned. "Humans can't detect that sort of thing," he said, shaking his head.

"Well, we shouldn't be able to men-com, either, but—"

"Yes, but that's different," he said confidently.

It was that confidence that spurred her to turn toward him, sliding her right hand along the back of the sofa where his left arm rested. Inching closer, she lightly brushed the back of his hand with her fingertips.

He stilled. "Dancy," he warned.

"Just think of it as an experiment," she purred, gazing at him from underneath her lashes. "If I don't *smell* anything, then you're right—"

He shook his head. "Wait, I just meant—"

"Don't backpedal now." Her eyes landed on his left arm. "I love your tattoos, by the way," she looked up at him. If she had any compassion, she'd knock it off. He looked trapped, his green eyes wide and desperate. She ran her fingers along his forearm. "Such intricate work," she added, admiring the soft, slightly raised skin where the needle left its mark. She did the best she could to wrap her small hand around his not-so-small, veiny forearm, then looked at him. She stopped—he looked fucking feral, like they had been transported back to a less civilized time where primal instincts were all people had to survive. Whatever defenses kept her from tipping over into him crumbled, flooding her pussy with heat. Instinctively, her hand squeezed his forearm. "You smell like seacoast, lavender, and sex," she whispered, licking her lips.

"Who *are* you?" he whispered back.

She ran her tongue along the bottom of her teeth, then bit her lower lip. Truthfully, she didn't know *who* she was. While she could always pick up a guy at Lonnie's, what she was doing with Hyphen was different—worlds different. She gently took his sizable hand in hers—his palm wasn't too smooth nor was it too rough. It was perfect. Lifting it to her lips, she placed a soft kiss on his warm knuckles, making sure not to break eye contact.

"*Fellowship,*" he breathed.

He had unleashed something within her that couldn't be tamed. She barely recognized herself, but in a good way—a *liberated* way. Just to make sure he understood the lesson, she kissed his knuckles again, but this time, she was sure to use her tongue, for good measure, of course. He furrowed his brow and bit his bottom lip so hard she thought he'd bleed. She released his hand, then sat back, satisfied. They stared at each other—a showdown of wills and silent acknowledgment that their *mutual* attraction was very real.

"What?" she asked innocently.

"You know what," he said, his voice dipped in authority.

"Am I'm wrong?"

"No."

"I didn't think so."

He shook his head and stood. "I left my water bottle downstairs," he mumbled.

Watching him leave, she finally accepted that she liked Hyphen Haslem. *A lot.* She could give a fuck about the law or being professional. Hyphen was a once-in-a-lifetime connection that was powerful enough to make even someone like her take notice.

Chapter Fourteen

A nervous Hyphen stood in his kitchen looking at his phone for the hundredth time before setting it on the marble counter. Fellowship was on her way to be interviewed by the twins, and he couldn't sit still. Canvassing with her in Pawville did nothing but make him like her more. She was warm and open with Miss Sylve, honest and caring with Rey, and sassy with her lieutenant. There was something about seeing her in her natural habitat that seduced him. She was all charm and smarts—sexiness and power. He loved when she slid into his mind during his meeting. He didn't care how it made him sound—he *loved* it. After that, things were perfect, until he opened his big, arrogant mouth, arguing that she couldn't smell that he was so horny he could've fucked her on the sofa. With all the confidence of a woman comfortable in her own skin, she proved him so wrong that he escaped her office, tail between his legs.

Instead of going downstairs for a *non-existent* water bottle, he went to the restroom to pull himself together. The problem was, he couldn't escape the look in her eyes—a poised self-assurance that triggered a hidden nuance of his desire. By the time he got home that night, he worked out so hard he almost passed out. Then, in the shower, he succumbed to stroking his dick with a warm, soapy hand, thinking only of her. After that, he had a Zion's Ink and got in bed, sleeping until Soren showed up the next morning to use his gym.

After Soren left, he showered, dressed, and was now pacing in the kitchen. Determined not to work himself into a frenzy, he got out a tumbler and poured himself a small drink. Knocking back a shot, he took a deep breath as it warmed his chest. Fellowship had hijacked his thoughts. All he could think about was her smell, her smile and the way she looked when she kissed his knuckles. His *knuckles?* How the fuck could something so innocuous be so Solneur-damned erotic? Without knowing, she had him twisted up in desire, anxiety, *and* excitement—a foreign combination that left him feeling exposed and at her mercy. Worried that he was in over his head, he poured another—*ding!*

Fuck, it was her. Setting down the bottle, he rounded the corner just as the doors opened. She was casually dressed in black leather-looking leggings, a soft black hoodie, white trainers, and her black motorcycle jacket. Sylena, she looked so fucking good.

"Hey," she said, entering his place with an easy smile.

Approaching, he stopped short, keeping his distance. "You found me," he said, shoving his hands into his jogger pockets.

"Looks like it."

Clearing his throat, he worked to lock away every errant thought flying around his depraved mind. "Can I take that?" he asked, walking to her.

Shrugging out of her jacket, she handed it to him. "Are you serious with this penthouse?" she asked, one eyebrow cocked. He worried that she'd be put off by his money—something that had to look absurd to someone from Pawville, but she didn't seem to be. More than anything, she looked amused.

Heart on fire, he smiled. "If it's not the best, I don't want it," he said, taking her jacket and hanging it on a hook. By the time he turned around, she'd moved through his living space to the windows. Her leggings clung to her curves, the hoodie stopping above her ass. Mouth watering and canines itching, he closed his eyes. *Shit. Shit Shiiiitttt.*

Eyes snapping open, he made a beeline to the kitchen to finish pouring his drink.

Knocking back his second shot, he asked, "Would you like a drink?"

"Yes, please."

Taking a deep breath, he poured two double shots while stealing glances at her as she looked out his wall of windows. If someone had told him that the woman he saw laughing in front of Queen Aniyah's Temple would be in his home, he would've told them to fuck off. Yet, there she was—all soft and thick and captivating. Grabbing their glasses, he tried to calm his nerves before reaching her.

"Here you are."

Turning around, she took the tumbler. "Thanks."

"Don't mention it," he said. He held her gaze before they returned to the window and sipped in silence.

"It really is a beautiful place," she said without looking at him.

"Thank you."

"How long have you been here?"

"Years. I bought it after I made detective."

"A celebratory gift?"

"Something like that, yeah."

"Did you decorate it yourself?"

"If you count paying someone to do it."

"Did you offer input?" she asked, looking at him.

He did the same, but only for a second. "Yeah, a little."

"Then you decorated."

"You're being kind."

They returned to silence and sipped while watching life in Trianah play out below them. The moment lingered until his nerves settled, and suddenly standing next to her watching the city seemed normal.

"Can I ask you something?" she asked after a few comfortable beats.

"Of course."

"What happened between you and Bronwyn?"

Ah, yes. That. He shrugged. "We weren't compatible."

"Were you ever?"

It was a good question. Still looking out the window, he watched Seacrest traffic inch by, taillights blinking in a stop-start rhythm. "Truthfully, I don't think so. I'm not even sure why we dated. Maybe I thought it was the right thing to do," he said. "I know I'm older, but I haven't had many long-term relationships."

"Why do you think that is?" she asked, turning to him.

"Like I said before, I was an awkward, late bloomer."

"But eventually, you bloomed."

"True."

"I haven't had many long-term relationships either," she said, returning to the window.

With all the guts he could muster, he looked at her. Fellowship was different; her energy had shifted again, leaving him unsettled. Enjoying her profile, he cocked his head to the side. "Really? I find that hard to believe."

"You find it hard to believe that an overachieving female cop hasn't had many long-term relationships?" Turning to him, she leaned against the window and took him in from dick to face. Solneur, his balls were so tight he saw stars.

"What does being a cop have to do with it?"

"We're the job. You know that."

"Yeah, but..." *Nope. Nope. Nopitty. Nope.* He would *not* say what was on his mind. Shutting his mouth, he nodded.

She narrowed her eyes. "Yeah, but what?"

"Nothing."

Taking a beat, she searched his face. "I think it's cute that you can't lie," she said, taking a step toward him.

Every one of his Aechaih senses exploded as he shook his head. "Soren says the same thing."

"He also thinks it's cute that you can't lie?"

Holy-fucking-shit. She was as smooth as the whiskey they were drinking and just as intoxicating. "No, he just gives me shit about it."

She nodded, then returned to her whiskey. "Are you going to tell me what you thought but didn't say?"

"I was going to say, we're all the job in some way or another. But that shouldn't stop a man from wanting to get to know you." Yes, she made him self-conscious, but at the same time, she encouraged him to be open whether he wanted to or not.

Still leaning against the window, she turned and looked back over Trianah. "To be fair, they wanted to get to know me, but once they did..." Shrugging, she fell silent.

"What?"

Looking at him, she offered a faint, sincere smile. "Once they did, I wasn't who they wanted."

"Are human men stupid?"

"What?" she asked on a breath.

"I'm just wondering. Is it a *thing?*"

"Hyphen," she said, laughing. Damn, her laugh sounded so good in his place—like his house wasn't a home until that very moment.

"They must be stupid. *Have* to be," he said. "Because a chance with you, *any* chance, is worth taking."

She didn't respond. He wanted to touch her, to gather her in his arms and take her to the sofa, but instead, he savored her nearness. Her scent. Her soft, brown hands, nails manicured and painted a nude mocha color. And her eyes that invited him in past her wall of protection. She was opening to him, her heat cocooning itself around them, creating a blanket of closeness—a private space just for them. The whole thing was so fucking special that he didn't have time to be afraid. Instead, he clutched his glass and held her gaze as blood pumped wildly in his ears, all the way to his dick. The last thing he wanted was to get a massive hard-on while standing in front of the woman he liked, but he couldn't stop his physical reaction to her. Between her warm, shea butter smell and heavy heat, he was rendered useless. A useless, infatuated lump.

With cool assurance, she pushed off the window and stepped even closer, eyes unwavering as they dipped to his mouth and back. It wasn't a predator stalking prey as much as it was a woman acting on desire. Fellowship's face was free from the controlled effort of self-protection; she was vulnerable yet focused. Determined. She rose on her tiptoes, gently resting her left hand on his chest for balance. Frozen in place but body ablaze, his shoulder blades itched with heat as he restrained his wings. There she was, as face-to-face as she could get, with blown pupils and slightly parted lips. Exposed. Beautiful. Ready.

That's when he realized Fellowship transcended beauty. Trianah's skyline was beautiful, as were its monuments and landscapes, but the woman standing in front of him was more than a word; she was a movement. An ideal. A religion, and he was her most devout follower. He traced her jawline with his right finger before leaning down and brushing his lips against hers. Guardians, they were everything he thought they'd be—full, soft, and warm. He heard her breath hitch. It was barely audible, but he picked it up because, when it came to her, he didn't miss a thing. He kissed her—hard. Moaning, she opened just as his tongue slipped in to find hers. His insides detonated as she grabbed a handful of his shirt. The heat of her mouth and the feel of her tongue sent him tumbling over the edge. Breathless, he tore himself away, taking her glass and setting it on the coffee table along with his. When he turned around, her arms were up—a silent declaration that she wanted him. Without equivocation, he stepped into her as she slid them around his neck.

Hands on her hips, he pulled her to him, then pinched her chin before running his thumb along her plump bottom lip. Unexpected and utterly sinful, she took it into her mouth and *sucked*, swirling her tongue around it, her eyes never leaving his. And that's when he died— at least the Hyphen he'd been up until that point in his life. Legs weak, dick about to snap in two, he let out a guttural groan. She continued sucking. She was bold and sensuous, with a hint of daring. She was decisively sexy, unafraid of her sexual expression, and he was bewitched. Disrupted. Utterly absorbed by her essence.

Popping his thumb out of her mouth, he held her face with both hands and kissed her—uninhibited and demanding. Their lips melded into one rhythmic motion of perfect synchronization. Where she nipped, he licked; where he licked, she bit. She tasted like sweet whiskey with a hint of cinnamon and he was fucking addicted. Her hands traveled from his neck to the back of his head, then through his hair. *Fuck.* This woman would be his undoing.

Pulling away, she walked backwards, hands on his chest, taking him with her. Head empty, he followed. Then, before he realized, she turned him around and pushed. Falling back, he landed on the sofa with a bounce. Standing before him like the fucking goddess she was, she took him in, biting her lower lip. She settled between his legs as he sat up, inching to the sofa's edge. His hands slid to her lush hips, then around to her soft, *soft* ass.

Squeezing, he closed his eyes. "*Guardians,*" he hissed. He'd never felt anything so good in his fucking *life*. "Fell."

"Yes, Hyphen?" she whispered. Hearing his name on her lips sent another wave of blood to his obscenely hard dick.

"Fuck," he breathed because she had reduced him to one-word responses.

"I know. Who knew?" she asked, running her fingers through his hair, sending tingles throughout his body.

"I knew the first time I saw you," he confessed, opening his eyes and looking up. "I don't know how, but I knew."

She smiled. "That's shit people say in the movies."

"Was it cheesy? It was cheesy, wasn't it?" he asked, frowning. He was such a fucking nerd.

"It wasn't cheesy, it was perfect," she said with a throaty laugh. She put her hands on his shoulders and gently pushed. Unable to let go, he palmed her ass while she straddled him, easing down onto his lap. Her arousal invaded his system with impeccable precision, devastating him as she slowly and methodically ground into his now painfully hard erection.

"Fellowship," he choked out. His dick was so hard, he was losing his sight. Yes, he was going blind; he was sure of it. He cupped her face and kissed her again, taking her mouth hostage. Unbridled, their lips and tongues danced around each other. Hands in his hair, she gave a slight tug, sending a shockwave of lust shooting through him. Ready to drag her to his bedroom, he remembered why she was there in the first place. "My sisters," he said, half-dazed.

Resting her hands on his shoulders, she nodded. "You're right. They'll be here soon."

"What? *Who?*" he asked, enthralled by her mouth.

"Your sisters."

"Right," he said, nodding like his neck had no tendons or muscles to hold it up.

"Should we have our drinks in the kitchen? You know, so we look like responsible adults?" she asked, moving off him but not away.

"Yes," he said as he slid his hands from her hips back to her ass.

"You like that?"

Resting his chin on her stomach, he looked up. "It's perfection."

Her smiled turned into a smolder as she tilted her head. "Keep talking like that and I'll let you peel me out these leggings to see the panties I wore just for you." Her voice was low and raspy. None of that high-pitched baby talk; Fellowship's voice had resonance. So much so that it struck a primitive chord inside him, unearthing a primal instinct to claim her as his own.

He stilled. "You better watch it," he ordered. He squeezed her ass again, then moved down to rub her glorious thighs—thighs he wanted to set up camp between as soon as fucking possible.

"Or what?" she asked, arching an eyebrow.

"Or I'm going to throw you over my shoulder and carry your ass to my room."

"What about your sisters?" she asked, laughing.

Moving to her ass again, he squeezed, his hands sinking into her fleshy goodness. "Fuck 'em," he whispered, shaking his head.

"Hyphen!"

"I'm serious." Everything about this woman was exceptional. He never thought he'd find someone like her: a beautifully complex, intelligent woman with values and determination inside of a knockout body with, and he meant this, a flawless ass that he was prepared to worship for all of his days.

"Let's go to the kitchen," she suggested, combing his hair with her fingers.

No! This was the shit he'd been missing all his Solneur-damned life. An undeniable chemistry with a phenomenal woman was a rare occurrence, and he didn't want to take his hands off her.

But instead of saying that, he said, "Okay."

As soon as he stood, he grabbed her face, kissing her again. Sighing into his mouth, she took her time sliding her hands up his back, pressing her soft body into him before pulling away. Then, on her tiptoes, she pressed a sweet kiss on his cheek before coming down, as if she hadn't just had him begging like a dog. The way she expertly managed the tension between good girl and bad woman left his head cluttered. Flashing him a knowing smile, she grabbed their glasses, handing him his. Laughing as he knocked it back, she walked to the kitchen with him following behind in a trance. Sitting on a barstool, he nudged his glass toward her.

She refilled it, then slid it back. "Looks like you need this," she said with a wink.

"Funny," he replied, taking a healthy sip. "By the way, what's your middle name?"

"That's a random question."

He shrugged. "Gotta cool down somehow."

"Daelyn," she answered, amused.

"Fellowship *Daelyn* Dancy. That's beautiful." It rolled off his tongue with an elegant uniqueness. It felt priceless. Distinct.

"Thank you, Hyphen *Honor* Haslem."

"How'd you know that?" When he was younger, he didn't like his middle name, but like most things, he grew to accept it.

"The A.A.R."

"Ah, that's right. Perceptive."

"I like to think that I am," she replied, leaning across the counter.

He leaned forward, meeting her halfway. "It's sexy."

"Being perceptive?"

"Yes, everything about you is sexy," he admitted. They were so close; he could feel her breath against his face. Elbows on the counter, she tilted her head before she crooked her finger, beckoning him closer. Spellbound, he stretched forward, his forehead almost touching hers.

"Everything about you is sexy, too," she whispered before planting another kiss on his lips.

Guardians, he was so gone for her. Whatever composure he had left was thrown out the window as he grabbed her chin and pulled her in for a thorough exploration of her hot mouth. Lazy and intimate, there was a familiarity to it, like kissing her was something he'd done his whole life. A new and unexpected rush of emotion flooded his senses, threatening to spill out onto the kitchen counter. Thankfully, his elevator dinged before he confessed some ill-timed, super-emo shit. Pulling away, her eyes were still closed, but once they opened and landed on his, he realized he was incapable of questioning, doubting, or running from whatever the fuck was happening between them.

After a moment, he heard Haze yell, "We're here!"

Fellowship gave him a wink and grabbed her drink before she rounded the corner toward the twins. Taking a healthy sip of his Zion's Ink, he stood and followed her.

"Fellowship!" Harleigh called, running to her. Fellowship froze as Harleigh *and* Haze descended upon her with thin-armed hugs. Their instant affection solidified what he had suspected for some time: Fellowship was a gift to them all. A dazzling star in their midst, she drew out their excitement and curiosity. Plainly put, she fit him and his sisters like she'd always been in their lives.

Then they grabbed him, both landing kisses on his cheeks before Harleigh moved to the living area and Haze to his refrigerator. Fellowship followed Harleigh, joining her on the sofa. Wearing jeans, a sweater, and boots, Harleigh's shiny, heavy hair spilled over her shoulders and down her back. Haze rounded the corner with two sodas; her hair was in a soft ponytail. She wore leggings, a tee, a denim jacket, and trainers.

Handing her twin a soda, she sat on the other side of Fellowship and pulled out her phone. "Do you mind if we record?"

"Not at all," she said, sitting back.

"Fellowship, we're so grateful for this," Harleigh said, fishing a notebook out of her tote bag.

"My pleasure."

"What about me?" Hyphen asked in mock hurt. All three women looked at him, confused. "I mean, you're using my place, *and* I'm the one who introduced you to her," he said playfully.

"Awww. Thank you, brother," Harleigh cooed.

"Yes. Thank you, brother. You're the best," Haze added.

"You're welcome," he said with a sniff.

Harleigh leaned over. "Word to the wise, Fellowship. Always be mindful of the male Aechaih's ego as it must be handled with care," she whispered with a flicker of mischief.

Fellowship laughed over her tumbler of whiskey, eyes on him. Returning the gaze, he gave her a wink, then slid into her mind: *Watch it. Siding with the girls could get you into trouble later.*

Arching an eyebrow, she responded: *I hope so.* It was laced with so much heat that his dick pressed against his boxer briefs.

"Okay, let's get started," Haze proclaimed. "Fellowship Dancy, you grew up in Pawville, correct?"

"Guardians. You sound like you're cross-examining her," Hyphen interjected.

Haze turned to him, frowning. "Do you plan on being an interruption? If so, you can wait in your room."

He held up his hand in surrender. "Okay, okay, go ahead."

She turned back to Fellowship. "I'm sorry about that."

Fellowship smiled. "Yes, I grew up in Pawville. Moved there when I was ten."

"Oh, from where?" Harleigh asked.

"The Itchan Forest," she said.

Hyphen paused mid-whiskey-sip. It was the first he'd heard of her growing up in the forest, yet it felt like something he already knew. If he tried, he felt like he could see her as a child, playing by a creek surrounded by lush forest with a younger Auten looking on. The memories were so vivid he couldn't tell them apart from his own.

"What was it like living in the forest?" Harleigh asked.

Fellowship shrugged. "To be honest, I don't remember much of it, which is odd because I was ten when we left, but everything from that point back is fuzzy."

"Do you remember growing up in Pawville?" Haze asked.

"Yes."

"What was that like?" Harleigh asked.

"When we moved, Pawville was robust and full of life. Most humans worked in the mines, and although the work was grueling, it still provided for their families. My grandfather and I lived in an apartment for some time before we moved to a small house. Both experiences were full of memories: making friends, playing until dark, spending our allowances on candy. The families during that time looked out for each other. If I got into trouble, it wouldn't have been out of line for another adult to discipline me. It was a village," she said, smiling.

Hyphen watched her. Well, it was hard not to. But he couldn't help wondering how it had ended up being just her and Auten. Where was the rest of her family?

"I assume things changed once the mines began laying off workers," Haze said.

"Absolutely. My grandfather was laid off but, thankfully, he had made enough connections during his time in the mines that he was able to find work in Seacrest. He cleaned offices for little pay, working his way up, but everyone wasn't as lucky."

Harleigh shook her head. "With it being difficult to maintain a standard of living, humans did what they could to survive, right?"

Fellowship looked at her. "Yes, exactly. Even though my grandfather and I were better off than most, it still wasn't the same as when the mines were fully staffed. We tried as hard as we could to keep that semblance of togetherness, but as the economic atmosphere changed, so did the community."

Hyphen had abandoned his drink, engrossed in her story.

"Is that why you became a criminal investigator?" Haze asked.

Hyphen felt her pull back for the briefest of moments; he felt a pain, distant but acute, and then he felt her weigh the options of being honest or skirting the question.

Fellowship knocked back her drink and looked at the girls. "That's part of the reason. By the time I got to college, Pawville had drastically changed. Stores were closed, families shattered. There was more anger and frustration. My childhood friend Daize and I realized that if we wanted to help our community, we would have to do it through education. Our goal was to learn as much as we could, then figure out how to organize so that we could shrink the wealth disparity between Pawville and Seacrest. We were roommates in undergrad and grad school—we did everything together. Then Daize fell in love with an Aechaih and got swept up in a whirlwind romance. They dated for months—I kept asking to meet him, but she kept putting it off. Then one night she left and never came back," Fellowship said.

"What do you mean she never came back?" Haze whispered.

Fellowship kept her eyes on the empty tumbler clutched in her hands. "She went missing. We searched for days before finding her stuffed into a garbage bag behind our apartment building."

"*Guardians*, no," Harleigh breathed. Haze covered her mouth, eyes wide. Hyphen leaned forward, forearms resting on his thighs.

Without looking at them, she continued. "I was obsessed with finding out what happened, but it seemed like I was the only one who cared. The Human Division didn't have the time, personnel, or resources to perform a thorough forensic analysis, and the Aechaih Division—they weren't any help either. After I graduated law school, I enrolled in the academy. So, yes, I joined because I wanted to help the residents of Pawville, but at first, it was because of Daize."

"Did you ever find her killer?" Haze asked.

"No."

It was quiet. The twins' eyes sparkled with tears before they reached over and hugged her. Hyphen's chest hurt; her pain mirrored his own. Loss and hopelessness. Finding a way out through law enforcement. After an extended beat, the girls pulled away, both wiping their eyes.

Fellowship opened her eyes, then gave a faint smile. "I didn't mean to be a downer."

"Oh, my Guardians, *no*," the girls said in unison.

Fellowship's eyes slid to Hyphen's—she didn't have to say anything. He felt their loss, pain, and life in the shadows. Looking at her was like looking at himself.

"How did your grandpa become Human Ambassador?" Harleigh asked.

Fellowship pulled her eyes away from his, turning to his sisters. "After working his way up as a custodian, he built strong relationships with some Aechaih who thought he'd be a good liaison and offered him the role."

"Were you okay with that?" Haze asked.

"No," she said through a faint laugh. "I saw it as traitorous and stopped talking to him for a long time. It wasn't until my accident that we mended our relationship. After facing death, none of it seemed to matter."

"What would it take to mend the relationship between humans and Aechaih?" Harleigh asked.

Hyphen watched her face brighten as Professor Dancy emerged. "Excellent question. You know, humans don't want much but to be able to take care of ourselves and those we love. We need to figure out a way to increase opportunities for growth and redistribute wealth. Somehow, we must erase the invisible line that separates Pawville from Seacrest."

"Like when humans and Aechaih co-existed, equally," Harleigh offered.

"Exactly. The barriers that restrict humans must be removed. But that kind of change is difficult."

"Difficult but not impossible," Haze corrected. "It takes one policy at a time."

She nodded with an impressed smile. "That's true. What do you think can be done?"

Harleigh scrunched her nose. "Like you said, more opportunity."

"Strategic development," Haze added.

"Reimagined policies," Harleigh continued.

"And above all, taking ownership for the shitty treatment of humans since Rhoman's Massacre. If we don't face what we've done, then nothing will change," Haze said, lifting her chin.

Watching Haze seemingly bloom overnight gave Hyphen chills. He could already see the impact Fellowship had on her. Without realizing, Fellowship gave his baby sister permission to be her fiercest self.

"Those are exceptionally sophisticated ideas."

"I bet this is what it feels like being in your class," Haze said, eyes sparkling.

Fellowship laughed. "Pretty much."

"The next class you teach, we're coming," Haze announced.

"Ooh, yes!" Harleigh added.

"I'd be honored to have you."

As the girls continued to chatter, Fellowship slipped him a glance. He felt her warmth and gratitude for the twins and for him. The feeling filled his heart beyond anything he had ever imagined.

Fellowship stared at herself in Hyphen's guest bathroom mirror. The twins' interview had been the first time she'd shared her story in full. She hadn't planned on mentioning Daize or her reasons for joining the force, but when asked, she thought about how open Hyphen had been about his brother. He trusted her enough to reveal his pain and truth, so she felt a space had opened for her to do the same. Instead of feeling cold and alone after disclosing her painful past, she was surrounded by warmth and understanding. Harleigh and Haze's heartfelt hugs made her feel embraced. Being with them was normal, free of awkwardness or tension. It was one of the most perfect days she'd had in a while, and Hyphen was undoubtedly the reason. Spending time with him rekindled forgotten desires. Every time he caught her eye, often while the twins chatted away, another protective layer of her heart melted. She remembered Miss Sylve's prayers in Septain—could the sincere prayers of an old woman not only bring her back to life but transform it as well?

Washing her hands, she dried them, then smoothed down her hoodie before stepping into the hall. Approaching the living area, she heard water running in the kitchen. Rounding the corner, she saw Hyphen cleaning up from dinner. With his back to her, she stopped short to enjoy the view. Wearing a V-neck t-shirt, she could make out the twisted definition of his biceps. He also wore, and she had only Sylena to thank for this, gray joggers that were slim enough to show his muscled, round ass, lean thighs, and dick print.

She slid onto the barstool. "Hi."

He turned around and smiled. "Hey."

"Thank you for a good day."

"Thank *you* for a good day. I haven't had that much fun in a while," he said, wiping down the counter.

"Neither have I. Tell me, how did Horace Haslem's kids end up so grounded?"

He laughed. "Honestly, I have no idea. By all accounts, we should be assholes." Folding the towel, he hung it up before leaning against the sink. "But Hudson grew up in a time when the Kingdom of Trianah was focused on developing into a modernized metropolis. While serving on the Tri-Family Council, he was privy to behind-the-scenes political and economic maneuverings that didn't align with his core values. When raising me, he instilled a different perspective, and I tried to do the same with the girls, even though I was out of the house by the time they were born."

"How did he end up so different from your father?"

"I think my mom had a lot to do with it, but you'd never get her to admit it," Hyphen shrugged. "He was one-seventy-five when I was born and had amassed some life experience. He never went into detail about his life before me, but he always said that the Aechaih had it wrong when it came to our relationship with humans. I tried to do my best passing that down to the girls."

"You've done a great job with them."

His smile was the brightest she'd ever seen it. "I appreciate you saying that. Sometimes, I worry I haven't done enough," he said as the light in his eyes dimmed.

"They're great, Hyphen. And Haze, I know I don't know her well, but she's turning into a little powerhouse."

Light back in his eyes, he nodded. "She's finding her way. I think meeting you has encouraged her to become more of herself."

Her faced warmed. "That's kind of you to say."

"I mean it."

She had no words because her thoughts had evaporated with his eyes on hers. She thought she could actually hear his magic pop along her skin.

Clearing his throat, he broke eye contact. "Soren says they're poised to take over the world."

"For sure, and Trianah would be better for it. They remind me of Daize and myself—passionate, determined, and hopeful."

His face grew solemn. "I'm sorry you lost your friend, especially to an Aechaih. I understand why you hold such stringent views about us. It's not just the social aspect; there's personal pain involved as well."

She blushed. "Stringent views is a nice way of putting it."

He smiled. "I can't take credit. I got it from Auten."

Her face lit up. "What?"

"He and I chatted about you at the fundraiser."

"He didn't tell me that."

He smiled. "Of course, not. It was our private conversation."

"Oh, excuse me," she said with a laugh.

"After hearing your story, I understand why you freaked out when I showed up to help at the temple."

She frowned. "What do you mean?"

"You never said anything, but once you realized what I was, you started squirming in protest."

Her faced warmed. "Oh, I'm sorry."

"What? No." He crossed the kitchen, standing on the other side of the counter. "I didn't say that for you to be sorry. I said it because I understand why you reacted that way."

"Yeah, but I'm sorry." Eyes downcast, she focused on her hands. It was painfully embarrassing to think about how she'd reacted to him—his help, especially now that she knew and liked him so much.

"Fellowship, look at me," he whispered, leaning across the counter.

Lifting her eyes to his, she instantly connected to his warmth and the otherworldly way he grounded her.

"I don't blame you for a split-second reaction," he said.

His beautiful face was focused and determined, exactly how she remembered it from that day. The thread that linked them felt tighter, more secure. A security that encouraged her to be vulnerable even if her heart pounded in protest.

"Hyphen, I was slowly disappearing, then you were there. Your voice dragged me from the darkness. In your eyes, I felt safe, like it was okay to let go and float away. But you were so adamant that I stay, it started to override what I thought I wanted."

Face red, the muscle in his jaw flicked as he looked down. After a moment, his eyes met hers. "I couldn't let you die. I'd just found you and...I couldn't."

Swallowing the lump in her throat, she had to tell him the truth. The truth of what she'd been feeling for some time. Resting her hands on the counter, they inched closer to his.

"But I *did* die. The version of me that existed before you died to make room for the version of me here with you now." Pursing her lips, she held his eyes.

Inching closer, his fingertips grazed hers, causing her stomach to flutter. "Fell, I like you, very much. I know people go on about having never felt a certain way about someone, but I can honestly say that you've upended my world."

Oof. As much as she didn't want to admit it, it was the first time someone was so forthright about their feelings for her. When she told him that she hadn't had many relationships, she failed to mention it was because she didn't trust motherfuckers with her heart. At first, the self-isolation was difficult, but after a while, she grew accustomed to being alone. Closed-off. Safe. But clearly that was changing.

"I like you, too."

"Oh, yeah?"

"I mean, you a'ight," she shrugged playfully.

Tipping his head back, he laughed. The kind of open laughter you have with someone you like. Someone you trust. Aside from the ease of being alone, another drawback to hook-up culture was that she'd meet guys at Lonnie's, get drunk, talk, fuck, then send their asses home. No intimacy. No connection. She didn't care about who they were, where they worked, or which shows they streamed. Using booze and glower-weed to minimize anxious thoughts, her mind would relax while her body was pleasured. After it wore off, the thoughts, dreams, and worries returned as she went about business as usual. But business as usual meant she hadn't had sober sex with a man she liked in a long-ass time. Sure, it was easy to make the first move with Hyphen when it was a little make-out sesh before the twins arrived, but as much as her body rumbled like her car's V-8 engine, she was terrified at the thought of taking the next step with him—a step she very much wanted.

Hyphen's laughter died down probably because she was staring at him like a fucking psycho. Diverting her gaze, she glanced at the blue abstract painting on his kitchen wall before looking back at him. She shouldn't have looked back. Eyes dark, his smile had been replaced with so much heat that her desperately wet pussy spasmed in shock.

"What are you thinking?" he asked, standing straight.

Eyes on his face, *not* his dick print, she smiled. "Nothing."

"Oh, it's something."

She narrowed her eyes. "Is it, though?"

The muscle in his jaw clenched again as he rounded the corner. He stood in front of her so that her back was against the counter while still seated. All six-foot-five of his lean, Aechaih muscle was within reach, but she didn't touch him. Instead, she sat there as her heart shot out of the stable and surged around the track. With hook-up sex, Fellowship had manufactured control with substances so that it was easy to take what she wanted without worrying about shit. Everything was different with Hyphen. Being sober made her nervous and uncertain of whether she was capable of intimacy. Connection. And because of that, all she had to offer him was her submission.

Licking his lips, he arched an eyebrow. "What's on your mind, Fellowship?"

"Just thinking about my stock portfolio. Trying to decide whether I should diversify or whatever."

Face melting into his patented half smile, he stepped to her, settling between her open legs. His lethal, unassuming authority and sharp lavender scent made her lower abdomen clench, sending liquid heat to her pussy. She knew the moment he smelled her sex because his eyes turned dangerously dark and seductive.

"I'm glad you're taking an active role in your finances," he said, his voice low and hoarse. Leaning forward, he rested his hands on the counter, trapping her between them. Mere inches away, he looked down, holding her gaze with those fucking eyes.

"Hyphen," she breathed. The best she could do was to infuse his name with all her need and desire, hoping he would understand how much she wanted him, even though she was too afraid to act on it.

"Yes, baby?" His left hand cradled her neck as his thumb rubbed her bottom lip.

She closed her eyes as his touch sent heat rolling along her skin in energetic waves.

"Look at me," he commanded.

Obeying, she latched onto his eyes, holding on for dear life.

"Take off your hoodie."

The four words were so simple and diabolically sexy that she could barely breathe. Eyes never leaving his, she crossed her arms and removed her hoodie, tossing it on the floor. Standing straight, he appraised her without a word. She remained still—her eyes begging for more instruction.

"Stand up," he ordered.

She slid from the stool and he stepped to her. In one swift, surprising move, his hands went up her hamstrings and lifted her onto the counter.

Solneur.

Until that very moment, she'd never had the privilege of being handled like she weighed nothing. Moreover, she never let herself dream of a man strong enough to pick her up, allowing her to enjoy the feeling of letting go—of true surrender. It's a wonder she didn't come right there. Standing between her legs, his sizable hands rubbed her thighs; instinctively, hers rested on his veined forearms. Enjoying the feel of his warm skin, her eyes dipped to the ink spilling out the V of his t-shirt before returning to his face. He was virtually unrecognizable with sharp lines and dark eyes; his crackling energy tugged on her clit.

Left hand back to the side of her neck, his thumb returned to her bottom lip, gently pulling it down. Before she could do anything, he pressed his plush lips to hers with enough pressure to pry her mouth open, slipping his tongue inside. She patiently tasted him: vanilla with a hint of ginger. Knowing he had neither for dinner, she realized the taste was *him.* Sweet and spicy. Distinct. Delicious. Moaning, each pull of his lips and strong swipe of his tongue tweaked her pussy as the kiss heated, turning rough and desperate. Drawing back, he tilted her head to the left so he could drag his tongue along her shoulder, stopping in the nook to suck and lick as she rocked on the counter. He looked at her. Hyphen was all alpha—dominant, focused, and assured.

"Tell me what you want," he said.

Swallowing, she tried to catch a coherent thought as it dipped and dodged her like a firefly. Running her fingers through his hair, she realized she wanted, *needed,* to see more of him.

"Take off your shirt," she ordered, her voice raspy.

Pupils dilated, Hyphen obeyed. As he pulled it over his head, her eyes landed on his chest. In an instant, she saw the same chest and ink as on the day they met. The image cracked open the memory like a piece of ciambe fruit.

"Fellowship," Hyphen's voice gently lifted her out the memory. "What's wrong?"

"You risked everything for me that day," she said, her eyes on his. "Your wings are classified as a *birth defect*, yet you stripped off your shirt and reminded the world why you're so special."

"Fell..." he whispered, his face tight with emotion.

"You're beautiful, Hyphen," she said, running her fingers down his torso. Etched with precision, his pecs looked like they'd been chiseled by a master craftsman. Lightly dusted with dark hair, his mauve nipples begged to be nibbled. His creamy, pale skin had a slight golden tinge, and his abs were a masterpiece—each of the six muscles shaped and molded to create a valley that smoothed down into the V where his joggers sat on his narrow hips.

Eyes back up, she admired his ink—splashed on the left side of his neck, it covered his left pec, shoulder, and arm. Luxurious and expertly designed, it featured wisps, flowers, and wings, culminating in a unique, decadent collage. Hyphen was exquisite, and he was all hers. With less worry and more assurance, her eyes slid to his. Leaning back, she rested her hands on the counter and spread her legs—an invitation. Just as his hands rounded to her ass, hers slid up his ribcage, then down his tight abs. Fucking. Perfection.

Eyebrow arched, he bit his lip before running his tongue along his teeth. "Take that shit off and rub those perfect breasts for me."

Fuuuuuccckk. Eyes on his, she peeled off her tank and threw it somewhere—who knows. Keeping his hands on her ass, he nestled his fingers underneath so that he could grab more of her. Hands behind her back, she unclasped her bra, then took her sweet-ass time sliding it down one arm, then the other. His eyes left hers and dipped to her teardrop breasts, dark nipples, and round stomach. She cupped and squeezed them together while rubbing her nipples with her thumbs. Legs wide, she rocked back and forth on the counter as she massaged. Bottom lip snagged with a sharp canine, he devoured her as she tweaked her left nipple, rubbing it between her thumb and forefinger, causing her own damn pussy to purr in delight. Hyphen's face was flush as his eyes made their way back to hers.

"Yes, baby," he whispered.

His hands moved from under her ass back to her thighs before his left hand settled on her lower back, jerking her to him. Immediately, her arms were around his neck. Her mouth smashed against his. He pulled her close as she squeezed her thighs, trapping him between her legs—where he fucking *belonged*. Wild and reckless with need, she grabbed a handful of his hair and tugged, pulling a *growl* from him as his fingers dug into her back. Pulling away, he stayed close to her face, eyes dark with want.

His hand ease between her legs. "Spread."

She obeyed. Looking down, he clenched his jaw as his long finger stroked her. It was so soft, she could barely feel it, which only stoked her frustration. Inching forward for more pressure, his right hand held her in place.

"Did I tell you to move?" he asked.

Eyes snapping up, Fellowship's mind glitched because it took a beat for her to realize she was his. Forever. After a moment, she shook her head. "No."

"Don't worry. I got you," he said, still stroking.

Sylena help her. Hyphen Haslem and all of his two hundred and ten years moved in an effortless alpha-maleness that didn't abuse or torment. It didn't punish or manipulate. No, his masculinity was rooted in lived experience. It had been tried and tested, forged in fire, and refined. His masculinity didn't demand submission. It encouraged it. And Fellowship was ready and willing to do as she was told.

His thumb stroked her pussy, before settling on her clit. Soaked through her panties *and* leggings, he rubbed her nub with small, efficient circles, applying the perfect pressure. Her head fell back on a whimper. She rubbed her breasts, while rocking on his thumb. Feeling her ecstasy build, she pinched her nipples, grinding faster. As she moaned, he pressed harder. Everything within her ignited as she lifted her head, connecting with his eyes.

"I want you to come on my fingers," he said.

"Okay," she whispered.

With a smile, Hyphen dipped his hand under the waistband of her leggings and panties. Spreading her lips, he slid his thumb along her wetness until he re-settled on her fireball of a clit. His circles moved faster, building heat between her legs that traveled down her thighs. On impulse, she wrapped her arms around him, burying her face in his neck. Still grinding on his hand, she dug her fingers into his shoulders while his other hand pulled her closer, holding her in place.

Before she knew it, he slipped two fingers in her pussy, snatching a yelp from her mouth. Ragged and helpless, she rode his fingers almost in tears.

"You're so fucking *sexy*," he groaned. He rested his forehead on her shoulder while his extraordinary hand coaxed her free from the captivity of overthinking—from doubt and anxiety. Finding a quick rhythm, his thumb and fingers worked in expert tandem as she felt her climax gain momentum, forcing its way through her bullshit sexual past. Holding tightly, she heard him moan. The very thought, the very *sound* of him was her breaking point. Clasping her thighs around his waist, she exploded before she knew what happened.

"Hy-phe-n," she choked out.

Scraping his shoulder with her teeth, her body trembled as the orgasm tore from her pussy, flooding every nook and cranny of her body. He slowed until she was nothing but a limp, heavily breathing servant to his every fucking need. She clung to his broad shoulders as he removed his fingers and wrapped her in his arms. Lifting her head, she looked at him—heavy-lidded and satiated.

Clasping her chin, he pulled her to him and placed a gentle kiss on her lips. "You're beautiful."

Smiling into his mouth, she kissed him again as he rubbed her back with the flat of his hands. Body still shaking with aftershocks, she rested her head on his shoulder.

"Let's go to bed," he whispered, his breath tickling her ear.

With a shiver, she nodded because she had yet to find words. Picking her up, he headed toward his bedroom. Yet again, she was in his arms—safe and protected. But this time, there was no hospital because being with him was a different type of healing. Hyphen placed her on his bed. Where he slid in beside her and wrapped her in his arms. This time was different. Special. Sacred. This time, when she woke, she'd remember who saved her. Who pulled her from the darkness. Who commanded her not to die. This time, she wouldn't forget the man to whom she'd given her heart.

Chapter Fifteen

Hyphen stared at the city lights dancing across his ceiling. Fellowship was curled into him, her head and arm on his chest, sleeping off her orgasm. Still shirtless, they were tucked underneath his duvet where he enjoyed the feel of her warm, satiny skin on his. Auten was right; she *was* a gift, and he was all in. At one point during their time with the twins, he saw the three of them chatting—all smiles, the twins totally enamored with her, and her with them. In that moment, he saw himself with her for the rest of his days. Such certainty seemed absurd, seeing that they hadn't spent much time together, but a knowing clicked inside him—there was no version of his life where she wasn't present. Although he'd worked to see himself as worthy, having Fellowship come along and mirror it was powerfully unexpected. She saw past his heritage. Past his suits and family name. She saw the shy kid who preferred being with his books rather than with people. She saw him just as he was. Her presence expanded the safe space he'd already established within himself, reminding him that he wasn't alone. This culmination of things attracted him to her, but what tipped the scales was their encounter in the kitchen.

It was clear she wanted him, but her desire was trapped behind trepidation. He wasn't sure why she was hesitant, but it was there: unmistakable worry. Instead of articulating what had her spooked, she offered him her trust—trust that he would take command, that he would take care of her. With bright, obedient eyes, she put her pleasure in his hands. That's what made him fall *hard*—as capable and brilliant as she was, she surrendered to him, trusting that he would lead the way. The more comfortable she felt, the more she blossomed. Massaging her decadent breasts with her eyes on him, he witnessed her seductive confidence and intoxicating power. As he felt her hot cream on his fingers, her sexual energy was so electric, he almost came, dick untouched. The woman was singular in her existence, and she was all his.

On a deep breath, she stirred. "Everything okay?"

Looking at her, his heart lodged itself in his throat. "Yes."

Smiling, her small hand slid up his chest. "Can I ask you something?"

"You can ask me anything."

"Can I spend the night?"

This was the shit that made him crazy about her. Why in Guardians' name did she think she had to ask to stay with him? Easing down, he faced her.

"Fellowship Daelyn Dancy, you never have to ask whether you can stay the night. I'll always want you here."

"Always?"

"Always, Fell."

"Even when I'm in a bad mood?"

"Yes."

"Or when I hog the bed?"

"How can someone so short hog the bed?"

"Hyphen, I'm not short."

"What are you? Five-seven?"

"Yes."

"Short," he said, arching an eyebrow.

She rolled her eyes. "*Fine.* I can stay then, too?"

"Yes."

"What about when I have a nightmare and I can't go back to sleep?"

Her playful grin faded into concern. When he texted her about visiting The Archives, she had mentioned struggling to sleep through the night. While he didn't know what frightened her awake, he was determined that, in his bed, she would never face that fear alone.

Smoothing his thumb over her cheek, he kissed her nose. "Yes, and I'll hold you and tell you that everything'll be okay," he confessed.

Instead of a response, she leaned forward and touched her lips to his. No hard press, no tongue, no hands in his hair—just tenderness and gratitude.

"There's something special about you, Hyphen Haslem," she whispered, her eyes narrowed in curiosity.

"What's that?"

"I haven't figured it out yet."

He kissed her, his hand going to her ass. She ignited, swaddling them in her heat. His dick hardened as their tongues twisted around each other. She moaned in his mouth.

Pulling away, he frowned. "Why are you wearing pants?"

"Why are *you* wearing pants?"

"I asked you first," he said, squeezing her ass.

"You haven't taken them off yet."

"Excellent point, Detective," he said before throwing the covers over his head and inching down over her giggles. Aechaih eyes adjusting to the dark, he slid his hand up her thigh before hooking his finger in the waistband of her leggings. About to tug, he buried his face in her pussy as she *eeked*.

"*Hy-phen*," she said over a giggle. He loved hearing her voice, feeling her skin, and smelling her smell. Kissing her cloth-covered sex made her body stiffen before melting into the mattress. He tugged on her leggings as she lifted her glorious ass to help him peel them off. Pressing his face to her pussy again, he inhaled her sweet, pungent scent that was just for him. His tongue swiped her bikini line as she whimpered, then opened her legs. With no desire to fuck around with her underwear, he snatched it off. Then, situating himself between her legs, he opened her lips and tasted her with the width of his tongue, stopping at her clit. Instantly, it was brighter. Looking up, he saw her eyes on his.

"I wanna see you," she demanded.

He was happy she removed the duvet, so he could see all of *her*. She had voluminous thighs that were creamy and textured like chocolate cake batter, leading to a swath of black, coarse hair across her perfect pussy. Hissing, he gave her one last look before opening her dark lips, exposing her vibrant pinkness already slick for him. A low, gravelly groan rattled in his core, then out his mouth. Dipping down, his tongue explored her sweet creaminess, slowly moving up to her clit. Wrapping his lips around it, he gently pulled on the sensitive mound. Saying his name on a breath, she entangled her fingers in his hair. Lapping up her juices, his tongue pressed and swirled as she arched her back.

Eyes flicking up, he watched her enjoy his mouth. Head tipped back, biting her lower lip, her eyes were closed before she opened them and looked down. He pulled at her clit, releasing her sweet nectar. Body convulsing, her thick thighs closed on his head as she slowly rode his face. Sucking harder, he slipped two fingers in her hot canal, hooking to hit—

"*Fuck, Hyphen!*" Yep—that was the spot he was looking for. Diligently, he eased his fingers in and out, growing hotter and hotter each time. Pulling his fingers out, he slurped before returning to nibble on her clit. Sitting up, he took her in. *Solneur*, there she was—hot, soft, and ready. He shoved his joggers and boxer briefs off as her eyes took him in. She bit her lower lip and moaned. *Fuck*—he felt claimed and owned. No one had ever looked at him like that.

"Hi," he whispered, crawling over her.

"Hey, handsome."

Hovering over her, he kissed her hard, tearing at her lips. Cupping his face, her fingers went through his hair before she pushed him over and down. Shocked by how fast she moved, she straddled him, sitting just above his dick.

"Look at you," she whispered, sliding her hands over his torso.

"Look at *you*," he groaned.

Hands on her ass, he dug his fingers into her flesh as she moved to kiss him but dodged it, going to his nipple instead. With tiny, gentle licks, she tasted him, sending heat everywhere. His hands roamed over her back while she grazed his nipple with her teeth. Empty-minded and hard as granite, he grunted at the sweet pain. She pressed her lips to his, her tongue invading his mouth. Clutching her ass, their wide-mouthed kiss unhinged something within. A rush of need surged through him—primal, ancient, and possessive. *Fuuuck.* He needed to sink his teeth into her. *Needed it* like his next breath. At two hundred and ten years old, Hyphen had had plenty of women, but whatever was happening with Fellowship wasn't just sex. It wasn't even making love. It fell somewhere between death and rebirth—a place of unending stillness. Biting her would solidify their connection before the Guardians. Biting her meant that he'd love her for all of his fucking days. Unable to contend with *that* shit, he tore his mouth away.

"Put me inside of you," he demanded.

Without hesitation, she sat up. As soon as her hand wrapped around his dick, he clenched his jaw to keep from coming. Leaning forward, she adjusted his cock directly below her pussy.

"Like this?" she asked with a delicate innocence that split him in two.

"Just like that, baby."

With all the patience in the world, she eased her hot pussy onto his dick. He moaned as his hands gripped her ample waist. Resting in her, he took a moment to savor her hot, feminine decadence. As soon as he opened his eyes, they connected with hers.

"Tell me what you want," she whispered.

Hands on her hips, he moved them, silently indicating what he wanted. As she rotated, he realized he wasn't going to last much longer.

Squeezing her thighs, she moved with precision—rocking on his cock like some sort of celestial being sent to him from the Guardians.

"You feel so good, Hyphen," she cooed as her pussy stretched to fit his substantial girth.

Together, they established a rhythm that kept her wet and him on the brink. He cupped her perfect tits, grazing her nipples with his thumbs. It made no sense how soft she was. Rocking faster, she kept her dark eyes on his, biting her lip. Toes almost curled, his hands returned to her waist. She whimpered as she gyrated faster, harder. She was so beautiful. He couldn't—he couldn't let her go. Couldn't be without her. There was no life without her smile. Her laugh. He'd been alone for so long. With people, but not really. And now he'd found himself with a woman who made him believe in the impossible—in *miracles*. Spinning with shit he'd never felt before, he switched positions, flipping her over, face up.

Solneur help him. Please. He couldn't bite her. *Couldn't.* Not only was it illegal, but it was too much too soon. Just because he wanted forever with her didn't mean she wanted the same. But a swell of emotion challenged him, demanding that he claim her. It assured him that there was no one else *but* her. Hand on his cock, he spread her legs and quickly entered.

"*Hyphen!*" she choked out.

Pumping like a wild man, he closed his eyes. If he couldn't see her, then he wouldn't be tempted. Without seeing her lovely face and dark, trusting eyes, he wouldn't do the unthinkable. Just when he thought he had it figured out, she slid her hands along his biceps, then to his face. Caressing him, her thumb softly grazed his bottom lip. Like a goddess, she quelled his anguish, getting him to simmer just for her. Slowing down, he eased in and out, accessing a new level of pleasure. Hot, yet cool, it soothed his distress, encouraging him to open his eyes. As soon as he did, his body pulsed—yes, to come, but more than that, it pulsed for *her*.

"Hyphen?" she whispered. With one word, she asked what was going on. What was wrong with him. Where was he because he most certainly wasn't with her. He lowered himself onto her. Hands in his hair, she smiled with concern.

"Fell, I…"

What could he say? That he was prepared to risk it all for her? That he was confident she was his person? His *mate?* Thankfully, Fellowship seemed to understand that he was trapped in his mind because she pulled him in for a kiss. Instinct told him to surrender to the raw, physical expression of what he felt for her. Told him to accept the inevitable. Her pulse quickened as he increased speed, slipping in and out of her satin furnace. Pulling away, she draped both arms around his neck and waited for him to say the thing he didn't want to say.

"Baby…" he whispered.

"Yes."

"I want to…I *need* to bite you."

"Okay…"

"But if I do, you're mine."

"Okay," she said, cradling his face.

"I mean, *mine,* Fell. When we bite, we brand—we *claim,*" he said, continuing to ease in and out of her.

"Do you want me, Hyphen?"

Did he want her? Fuck want, he *needed* her. She'd become integral to his existence.

"More than anything," he clipped out.

"I want you, too," she said, voice hoarse.

Licking her lower lip, she turned her head, exposing her neck. Fuuuuccckkk, she was *everything*. Her blind trust made him pump faster. As much as he shouldn't, he *had* to. Had to because she was brilliant and compelling. Sexy and thoughtful. Compassionate and funny. Sweet and tender. She was what he'd been looking for his whole life. Heart overriding his mind, he sped up as she grabbed a handful of his hair. Canines pulsating to the point of painful, he lightly wrapped his hand around her neck.

"Are you sure?" he asked, hanging on by sheer grace.

"Yes, Hyphen," she said—so confident, so steady.

Fuck it. Fuck the law. His family. Their backgrounds. He'd never wanted anything this much in his life. He pressed his mouth to her neck, as she wrapped her arms around him. Swirling his tongue, he searched for the perfect spot. He loved her. He loved her so fucking much. He couldn't explain it away or dismiss it as lust because it wasn't. No one else but her had managed to get around his protective wall. And once she did, once she saw him, she wasn't afraid.

Sucking the tender softness where her neck dipped to her shoulder, he sank his teeth in. Like a crack of lightning striking his heart, his insides burst into flames. *Guardians*, she tasted like what he imagined to be pure starlight as her essence shot to his brain. Digging her nails into his back, she screamed, coming on his dick just as he erupted, coming hard, hot, and wild. White heat surged through his veins as her pussy contracted, siphoning his come, mixing it with her own. Chemically reacting to each other, their activation combined to create a new and powerful element. With no idea how his wings didn't explode from his back, he pumped until he was empty. Pumped until his body could no longer move. Head spinning, he gasped for air. Although he couldn't pinpoint what exactly had shifted, he was different; biting her had changed him from the inside out. Licking away tiny droplets of her blood, she shivered on a soft cry.

As their breathing slowed, he needed to see her face, but as he lifted his head, he panicked. What if she'd changed her mind and didn't want to be with him? Did he move too fast? Why couldn't he wait? But when her brown eyes locked with his, there was no regret, just satisfaction.

He rubbed her cheek with the back of his hand. *Hi.*

Hey.

I should probably move but—

Neither do I.

I could stay here forever.

And I'd let you.

He smiled, then rolled over. On their side, he pulled out of her before kissing her nose.

"I feel different," she whispered.

Shit, her, too? "In a bad way?"

She chuckled on a breath. "No, baby. Just different."

"I shouldn't have done that."

"Done what?"

"Bite you," he said as a bubble of regret floated around his chest.

"Hyphen, I'm yours."

And like that, it popped. They exchanged delicate, tender kisses as he rubbed circles on the small of her back. Raking her hands through his hair, she maintained eye contact, soothing his doubts, assuring him that she was exactly where she wanted to be. Letting out a sigh, he closed his eyes.

"There you go," she whispered, kissing his eyelids.

Until her, the thought of laying himself bare in front of someone wasn't an option. And the idea of *claiming* someone was unfathomable. Although the shit was unexpected, surrendering to her was more than worth it. In her arms, he was safe. Fellowship didn't require him to be strong. Stoic. Solid. That kind of liberated satisfaction was priceless. Opening his eyes, he searched her face before leaning in for a kiss, holding her tightly.

She eased back and raised an eyebrow. "So, you biting me...does this mean we're going steady?"

She was so fucking amazing, no wonder he didn't confess everything to her right there. "If you want to call it that."

"What would *you* call it?"

Shrugging away the truth of *I've bonded myself to you for eternity*, he settled for something less fucking intense. "I'd call you my girlfriend."

"Your *human* girlfriend."

"Yes."

"The human girlfriend you're not supposed to have," she added with a smile.

"Yes. And I'm the Aechaih boyfriend *you're* not supposed to have." He turned on his back so that she could properly latch onto him. Resting her head on his chest, she draped one of her luscious thighs over his before giving him a very slow, very hot kiss.

Pulling away, her eyes settled on his. "I've figured out what's special about you."

"What's that?" The pause she took before answering scared him because, in that brief moment, he realized that there was nothing protecting his heart from her words.

"Being our only winged Aechaih isolated you from the herd, and losing your brother shattered your heart. Despite the incredible diffi-culty of being different and alone, it shaped you into an exceptional man. There's no one like you."

Hyphen clenched his jaw *hard,* because if he hadn't, he would've fucking cried. It felt like the Guardians offered him a sign as to why he loved her. Why he bonded himself to her. Without him having to ask, they affirmed his choice. He wanted to respond, but the only words that would've tumbled from his lips were *I love you,* so he remained silent. Remarkably, his silence didn't scare her. Instead, she caressed his face, a faint smile in her eyes. After a moment, she kissed him and then nestled into him with a deep, contented sigh. Holding her close, he silently thanked the Guardians for his person. For his mate. He thanked them for everything that had happened before he met her—the hurt, the loss, the pain. Because without going through that fire, he wouldn't have been rewarded with the woman of his fucking dreams.

He held her until her breathing steadied and deepened.

He held her as she slept.

Then finally, on a gratified sigh, he closed his eyes.

Chapter Sixteen

The rare books library in The Archives was empty save for Hyphen and Fellowship, who sat at a large, glossy oak table with ancient texts spread everywhere. They'd been in the library for hours, researching Sylena and her sisters. And while they hadn't found much, Hyphen was more than happy to fill the time thinking about the ten days he and Fellowship had spent together. She only left to get clothes from Pawville; otherwise, she stayed with him. *Stayed.* Having her in his space was effortless. He went running with her; she lifted weights with him. They talked about books and music, history, law, and their childhoods. They had dinner with the twins, and breakfast with Soren. It wasn't perfect, it was real, and he loved it. In fact, he loved her, something that scared him less and less because he was born to love Fellowship Dancy—of that, he was certain.

"You're staring at me," she whispered, her eyes lifted from a leather-bound book.

Returning to reality, he focused. "You wish," he said with a wink. "Find anything?"

"Not yet," she said, returning to the book.

Hyphen tried to read, but concentrating was difficult with her sitting across from him wearing black leggings and one of his chunky sweaters. Eyes on her exposed shoulder, he extended his leg, nudging her foot.

Without looking up, she smiled. "Get to work."

"I can't concentrate."

"Why's that?"

"You know why," he said with heat lacing his words.

She looked up and smiled before biting her lower lip. "We have work, Detective."

"Not when you say it like that."

She leaned forward, resting her elbow on the table and her chin on her palm. "You think Mr. Osmark would notice if I got on my knees and showed you how good you look today?" she asked, looking him up and down like a much-needed snack.

Solneur. Her heat was instant. His dick was so hard he almost forgot his own fucking name. "Fell," he pleaded, realizing he'd made a mistake.

"What?" Her eyes went dark with want as she cocked her head to the side.

"You know what," he mumbled.

"Don't start nothing, won't be nothing," she cooed with a slow, sexy smile.

That's what he got for flirting with the planet's sexiest human. "Fucking pain in the ass," he said, shaking his head.

Laughing, she sat back and resumed reading. "You know you like it."

She was right. He did. He liked every fucking thing about her. Sighing, he returned to the book. Turning a couple of musty pages, he didn't see anything noteworthy. Flipping some more, he saw a brief history of the *Kumalada*. Scanning the text, he stopped at a description of Trianah's most notorious ancient ceremony.

"Listen to this," he started. "The ancient *Kumalada* Ceremony commemorates the alignment of Sylena, the Moon Goddess, and her sisters, Mylena and Uphraine. Every millennium, planet Nehlahni's moons align, creating a sacred portal of cosmic power. The inhabitants of Nehlahni—Aechaih and humans alike—participate in the ceremony, which consists of sacrifice, worship, and the gifting of enhanced abilities. At the last alignment, Rhoman, Queen Aniyah's human husband, and his followers sought control of the kingdom, killing a significant number of Aechaih, including the Aechaih Queen herself. By Tri-Family decree, the *Kumalada* Ceremony would cease to exist. Despite this, Nehlahni's moons will align in the next millennium and thereafter," he said, looking up. Fellowship was focused on him. "The next alignment is coming up."

"It's been a thousand years?"

"I know, right? It's been erased from our social conscious. No one talks about it."

"You think these moonless nights have something to do with it?"

"Maybe."

"During the last class I taught, we discussed Rhoman and the *Kumalada*," she said. "At first, I thought maybe Manicow, like Rhoman, had gotten his hands on some dark magic, but that would've meant so did Nigh and Rey, which I highly doubt. That's when I came up with the idea that they were being targeted."

"If they were targeted, maybe Rhoman was too."

She blinked. "You mean, what if he wasn't a human gone bad?" she asked. "Think about it. Until then, humans and Aechaih lived peacefully. There were even humans *and* hybrids serving on the Royal Court."

"Someone could've used the massacre to split the species, making it easier to kill hybrids and subjugate humans," he said. "And they would've needed the concentrated power from the alignment to do so."

Her brows knitted together in thought as her gaze drifted away.

"What are you thinking?" he asked.

After a beat, she looked at him. "If that's true, then it wasn't Rhoman's uprising, but someone else's. Rhoman was targeted and used to kill the queen, thus shattering the monarchy, which was replaced by the Tri-Family Council."

Dread congealed in his stomach. Before his brother's death, he would've never suspected Aechaih involvement in something like this, but after Hudson died, he saw what his people would do to maintain power. Now he wondered what they did to *obtain* it.

"But our murders are happening *before* the alignment. In Rhoman's case, the murders happened during it," she added, working through the idea.

"True. Unless, as of right now, they don't need the full power of the *Kumalada*. Maybe they're using basic dark magic."

"Hyphen, if we're actually onto something and not fucking crazy, there's a chance that our suspect was alive during the previous *Kumalada* and is targeting humans again." She leaned forward, resting both elbows on the table. "That doesn't leave a lot of Aechaih suspects."

"No, it doesn't, and it also makes implicating one more difficult. The older the Aechaih, the more power they've amassed over the past millennium."

"And the A.A.R can't help us locate them because it doesn't track dark magic."

"True, but those alive during that time wouldn't be in there anyway."

"Why not?"

"The elders aren't registered."

"How convenient." Sitting back, she sighed. "What I don't understand is why someone is doing this. It's not like we've made massive inroads over the past thousand years."

"Perhaps the goal is complete human annihilation instead of limited rights—finish the job," he said, speaking off the top of his head.

"Completely eliminate Pawville," she whispered.

"I mean—"

"No, it's an idea. A very good one," she said, her eyes darkened in sadness.

He was an insensitive prick. Standing, he walked around the table and sat next to her. Hyphen had no clue what it was like to be human—to be oppressed. Pulling her to him, he rested one arm on the table and the other on the back of her chair, creating a small cocoon. "I shouldn't have said that."

She turned to him. "It's a valid point."

"Suggesting that someone wants to wipe out your species is fucked up."

"I'd rather we think the worst-case scenario than miss it completely because we've underestimated the suspect."

It made sense, but he still felt shitty. She smiled, then leaned over and brushed her lips across his. He kissed her back, cradling her neck to pull her closer.

She parted but remained close. "None of this explains the moonless nights or what we should look for if someone *is* using untraceable dark magic."

"We'll just keep searching—see if we find something else about Sylena. Something that'll tie it all together."

"Okay," she said, her face open and trusting.

He kissed her nose and kept his arm around her as they continued to flip through old books, searching for anything to substantiate their claim.

———

An hour later, Hyphen and Fellowship rode the elevator to the main floor of Trianah City Hall. Upon her suggestion, they made copies of texts they wanted to read later that evening. After exiting and rounding the corner, he had the sudden urge to grab her hand. Since they'd spent the majority of the day in the subbasement, City Hall was busier than when they first arrived. Grabbing her hand wasn't an option, so he threw up his shield instead. After a beat, she looked up at him and smiled—she felt his heat. Snaking around Aechaih, they made their way across the lobby when Hyphen glanced at the staircase and spotted his father and Talon descending the stairs. Horace caught his eye, sending daggers of contempt from across the building. Fucking great. He had taken extra care to ensure they didn't run into him while they had been researching, but obviously, it wasn't enough.

"Shit." He understood why he wanted to grab her hand.

Fellowship stopped and looked at him. "What's wrong?" Before he could answer, she followed his eye-line to the stairs. "Shit, indeed," she whispered.

"Father, Talon," Hyphen said as they approached.

"Hyphen, good to see you," Talon said with a smile, then stepped slightly behind Horace as if he wanted no part of what was about to transpire.

"What are you doing here?" Horace asked.

"Working."

"What could you possibly be working on *here?*"

"It's classified." Horace's spiky magic raked his skin. Used to the discomfort, he pushed his own magic toward him in response.

Horace's eyes turned a cold shade of blue before they slid to Fellowship. He eyed her like a smudge on his suit. "Nice to see Auten's granddaughter's up and about, thanks to *our* healers," he sneered.

Hyphen turned to Fellowship whose face was a slab of marble —unbothered.

Horace's eyes narrowed. "The least you can say is thank you, girl."

"I did—to the healers," she replied. She didn't fidget or cower under his gaze. It was one thing to hold her own with Weeden but quite another to remain composed in front of his father. Horace's eyes went from Fellowship to Hyphen and back before something slithered across his face. Making sure his shield was in place, he sent a quick prayer to the Guardians that Horace didn't sense his bite on her. With no time to get on himself about his carelessness, he only hoped Solneur and Sylena would protect them.

"This *partnership* is a waste of time and resources if you ask me. I don't know why anyone would want a human cop on these cases—it's clear they'll be sympathetic to their own. Hence keeping suspects in their Detainment instead of transferring them to us."

Hyphen felt a wall of heat push at his magic—it wasn't his father's, and obviously, it wasn't Talon's because he was too busy trying to blend into the background. Suffocatingly thick, it rolled around him. He slid his eyes to Fellowship who was so eerily still that the hairs on his neck rose.

He returned his gaze to his father. "For someone who claims not to be interested in my job, you have a lot of opinions on the case," he said.

Horace scoffed. "Disrespecting me doesn't make you a man."

"Then what *would?* Oppressing the vulnerable? Upholding Aechaih superiority?" Fellowship asked in a tone he'd never heard before. It was laced with so much authority that even Talon took a step back. That's when he smelled scorched earth, like they were in the midst of a blazing fire.

Horace whipped his head to her, ferocity twisting his features. "How dare you speak to me like that, *human.* Don't you know who I am?"

"Yes. You're someone who had the guts to disrespect the Guardians by rejecting a rare and beautiful gift. Someone who treated it like an inconvenience. A mistake. A *defect.* Someone who believes that their power, although acquired on a technicality, makes them invincible. Well, I'm here to let you know that you are anything but invincible and that your definition of a *man* needs to be readjusted," she said, lifting her chin in such a way that Hyphen almost fell to his knees in deference. He had to physically keep his wings from exploding from his back. Face white with shock, Horace opened his mouth, but nothing came out. As much as Hyphen wanted to enjoy the rare occasion of his father being set straight by a human, he had to get said human out of there as quickly as possible.

"We need to get back. Talon. *Father.* Always a pleasure," he said, ushering her to the exit. It wasn't until they were in the cool Trianah air that he let out a breath. What the entire fuck was *that?* He knew Fellowship was different, but *that* shit was otherworldly. After his brother died, it took years for him to be able to face his father without Hudson's protection. So, it felt natural to want to protect Fellowship from Horace, but truthfully, he didn't have to. She stood alongside him, facing his father with strength, dignity, and elegance. He knew it was totally inappropriate to be as turned on as he was, but he couldn't help it—she was his equal, his partner, refusing to bend a knee to Horace Haslem.

They remained quiet as he pulled into Seacrest traffic. He didn't know what to say, so he drove home in silence until not hearing her voice became unbearable. "I'm sorry you had to see him," he whispered. She didn't respond, just looked out the window with her tote clutched to her chest. He was fucked—it was one thing to deal with Bronwyn, but his father was a whole other level of Aechaih elitism. Although she stood toe-to-toe with Horace, it didn't mean she wanted to. In fact, no human should have to deal with his father. It was a wonder she didn't tell him to take her home, ending the night completely.

Increasingly anxious, he continued driving. Once they got near his place, he tried again. "Baby?" he asked, stealing glances while navigating traffic. Stopping at a light, he looked at her. "Fell?"

She turned to him, her face unreadable. After a beat, it seemed like she came online. "You say something?" she asked, blinking.

"I just wanted to apologize."

"For what?"

"My father."

"You don't have to apologize for him."

Of course, she'd say that. "Yes I do."

"Your father's exactly who I thought he'd be. I'm not proud of what I did back there," she said, returning to the window.

"Are you crazy? It was fucking brilliant."

She looked at him—no smile in her eyes, just regret. "Still. I should've been more respectful."

"Fellowship, you *were* respectful. You didn't say anything my brother wouldn't have said. You were magnificent."

She looked at him before reaching over and running her hands through his hair. He sighed as the tension in his shoulders melted away.

"I never want to disrespect someone's parent, but I couldn't help myself," she whispered.

"Baby..." He shook his head. There were no words for how he felt about her.

"Who was that guy behind him?" she asked as traffic picked up. "His minion?"

"Basically. It's his advisor, Talon Seram. I don't know how he puts up with him."

"Like attracts like."

"He's more of a yes-man than anything else." Stopping at another light, he turned to her again. "I *am* sorry, though."

"Apology not accepted," she said, smiling.

He leaned over and kissed her before traffic resumed. "I don't deserve you," he said, grabbing her hand.

"I wouldn't say that. Although, I don't think I'll be having dinner at the Haslem estate any time soon," she said, giving his hand a squeeze.

He brought her knuckles to his lips and kissed them. How in the fuck did he land someone like her? Smart, stunning, incapable of bull-shit, with the ability to stand up to his villain of a father? He was fucking blessed.

***

The glow from the city lights filled Hyphen's bedroom; it was quiet save for his deep, steady breathing. Leaning against the headboard, Fellowship lazily combed his hair with her fingers as he slept, draped across her lap. After her run-in with Horace, they made dinner, watched a history documentary then fell into lazy conversation over Zion's Ink as Sylena and her sisters appeared in Trianah's dark sky. Looking down at him, she smoothed his hair as he stirred but didn't wake. It was funny; she never spent the night with men. The idea of waking up next to a hook-up wasn't appealing; besides, she always preferred the bed to herself. But then she met Hyphen, and all of her rules and hesitations flew out the window because the unthinkable had happened: she was in fucking love.

She'd suspected it for some time but was reluctant to accept it as truth because, one, she'd never been in love, and two, it was scary as fuck. But despite her inexperience and fear, she loved Hyphen Honor Haslem. Her long-held assumptions said that he was the last person she was supposed to fall, for but the connection was too significant to ignore. With no rules to protect her heart, she had a choice: be safe and in control, or vulnerable and in love. Right there, with him asleep on her lap, she chose love.

"Everything okay?" he mumbled, interrupting her thoughts.

"Yes," she said, looking down at him with a smile because that's all she did now was fucking smile.

"You sure?"

"Yes, Hyphen."

"I can feel you thinking. What's got you up?"

"Nothing, baby."

He shifted off her lap, moving to his side, yet keeping an arm around her. His eyes were piercing, even in the dark. "What's got you up, Fell?"

"Nothing bad, go back to sleep," she said, sinking down to face him.

He pulled her close. "You were thinking about something good?"

"Yes."

"Can you tell me?"

Being in love with him was one thing, but *confessing* that shit was entirely different. What if he didn't feel the same way? He did bite her —that seemed like something. What did the future hold for them with that absurd anti-miscegenation law? Could they really be together beyond the secure world they'd created for themselves? Maybe she wasn't in love, but was sex-satisfied and in her feels. Besides, telling him would only—

"Fell?"

"I love you," she blurted.

Fuck. She buried her head in his chest because looking at him was agony. He was Aechaih-still for what seemed like minutes.

"Hey," he whispered, rubbing her back.

"Hmm?"

"Are you going to look at me?"

"Do I have to?"

"I'd like you to."

Sighing, she pulled back to see his face, which was solemn. Her heart paused—was he about to confess that he didn't feel same way? Fuck it—she felt how she felt, so she steadied herself in preparation for the worst.

"You love me?" he asked quietly.

"Yes." As his eyes searched hers, she refused to look away because the least she could do was face her truth head-on. He held her chin between his thumb and forefinger.

"I need you to listen up good."

"Okay," she said, holding her breath.

"Are you listening?"

"Yes."

He raised his eyebrows. "Are you sure?"

"*Yes,* Hyphen," she laughed.

"Okay, good." Then, taking what seemed like a lifetime, he held her gaze. "I love you, too."

"You do?"

"Very much."

If felt like her heart took a flying leap off a cliff, but instead of plummeting, it soared. She'd never grinned so hard in her life. "You love me," she repeated, just to be sure.

"I love you, Fellowship."

And because she knew he wasn't lying, she allowed herself to accept the beautiful truth. Still smiling, she cradled his face just as he kissed her. Even their kiss was different; something about sharing *I love yous* shifted something for them. Of course, there were unknowns and countless what-ifs, but none of that mattered. He rolled on top of her, still kissing. She enjoyed the feel of his skin as she slid her hands down his extremely hot, sinewy back.

Disengaging from their kiss, she frowned. "Are you okay? Your back's burning up."

"It gets like that when I have to hold my wings in," he mumbled into her mouth.

"*Have* to hold them in?"

"When my emotions run high, I have to work to hold them in," he explained casually.

"So, right now, your emotions are high," she clarified.

"The woman I love just told me that she loves me, so yes, I'd say they're pretty high."

"I see," she whispered as he buried his face in her neck. She tried to rub his back again, but it was almost too hot to touch, and the reason why didn't sit well with her. "How about you don't?" she suggested.

"Don't what?"

"Hold them in."

Drawing back, he looked confused. "What are you asking?"

"I'm not asking you anything. I'm saying that if your back is scorched because you're working to hold your wings in, don't." In a blink, his face was unguarded, bright, and shockingly youthful—he looked like the bashful kid she imagined him to be over two centuries ago. The people who convinced him that his wings were a birth defect were pieces of shit. Hyphen was a *winged Aechaih,* and there was no reason for him to hide that part of himself—at least not from her.

"That's never been an option for me," he said.

"Well, it is now." She caressed his face. "You don't have to if you don't want. I'm just saying, for future reference."

"They're intense," he whispered.

"I can handle it."

"You think so, but..." he trailed off.

"I'm not afraid of you, Hyphen." He rested his head on her shoulder for a long, thoughtful beat. Running her fingers through his hair, she thought about how dreadful it must've been to be different.

An outcast. The Aechaih in her arms was a good man. Fuck them for making him feel less than the magnificent person he was. With nothing on but black boxer briefs, he pushed off her and stood in the middle of his bedroom.

"Turn on the light," he said.

Heart in her throat, she moved to the nightstand and clicked the light on its lowest setting, giving the room a sepia glow. Then she sat on the edge of the bed, tucking the hem of his TMPD t-shirt around her thighs. She really tried not to get distracted by his body. All lean muscle, inked, and in boxer briefs? *Guardians.* Hyphen's eyes held hers before they slipped away.

"Hyphen, I love you. No matter what, I want you, always," she assured him. As soon as his eyes rose to hers, she felt a wave of his magic, and then they were there. Her breath caught in her throat.

Solneur spare her—they were fucking spectacular.

Hyphen's wings were matte black and feathered; the tips a little over his head, the bottoms skimming the floor. But beyond their size and color, they actually *shimmered* as if they'd been coated with a thin layer of diamond dust. Never in her life had she seen something so extraordinary. It felt like she'd been gifted an opportunity to witness something carefully created by the Guardians. It was an honor.

"Hyphen, you're so beautiful it feels dangerous looking at you," she whispered, swallowing the lump in her throat. The muscle in his jaw feathered but he didn't respond. Unable to resist, she went to him—only his eyes moved as she walked around. "Can I?" she asked, her voice small and hoarse.

"Yes."

Standing behind him, they were even more striking as they sprang from his muscled back. Lightly, so as not to disturb, she ran her fingers down them. They felt like the richest silk. Immediately, she imagined being tucked under their protection. They shuddered at her touch, softly rustling. "I'm sorry," she said, pulling her hand back.

"It doesn't hurt, baby, it tickles—no one's touched them in over a hundred and fifty years."

Returning from behind him, she frowned, crossing her arms under her breasts. "What?"

He shook his head with a smile. "Don't. I already know what you're going to say."

"What am I going to say? That it's fucking bullshit that you were shamed for this?"

"Something like that."

"Well, it *is* bullshit, Hyphen." His face was half amused, half something else. Swallowing her rage, she relaxed. "I'm sorry."

"I've never had someone be so indignant on my behalf, especially regarding this."

Uncrossing her arms, she stepped closer to him, taking the opportunity to run her hands down his ridiculous abs before circling her arms around his waist. Resting her chin on his chest, she looked at him. "You're so special, Hyphen. So rare. So lovely. So unique."

Arms around her, he held her gaze for a few beats before responding. "Aside from Hudson, no one's ever told me that. Not that I'm a victim or anything," he said. "I'm just saying." His eyes flicked away and didn't return.

Biting the inside of her cheek to keep from crying *and* flying off the handle, she pressed the side of her face against his warm chest, squeezing him tightly. As much as it upset her that people would wound such a sensitive, loving soul, it wasn't the right time to express her rage. Chin on his chest, she admired his chiseled profile through watery eyes. Jaw clenched, face red, he wouldn't look at her, so she eased into his mind.

Thank you for sharing your wings with me.

He looked down. *You don't have to thank me.*

Yes, I do. I know I bitch and moan about how you were shamed as a child, and while it frustrates me that people would make you feel less than, I would've easily understood if you chose not to share this part of yourself with me.

He furrowed his brow, tenderly caressing her face with one hand. *I was afraid you'd be put off by them. But when you saw them—saw me, you didn't shrink back or cringe. Instead of fear or disgust, your face was a mix of admiration and wonder. It was remarkable. Humans have every right to be afraid of Aechaih, especially one like me. But you're not.*

There's nothing to be afraid of.

But—

Hyphen, if I'm afraid of anything, it's of how much I love you.

Mouth shut, he searched her eyes as his thumb brushed her cheek. *Fell...* He paused like finding the right words was of the utmost importance. *It's scary loving you as much as I do.*

She offered him a wide smile. *See, we're both scared.*

He smiled. Then, as quickly as they appeared, his beautiful wings were gone.

She frowned. *What are you doing?*

I'm not keeping them out.

Why?

Shrugging, he diverted his eyes. *I'm, I—*

"They're a part of you, Hyphen, and I want to be with you—all of you," she declared, raising on her tiptoes. Hand still cupping her face, he slid his green eyes back to hers—all trust and vulnerability. Without thinking, she let go—of what, she wasn't sure. But if she asked for all of him, then he deserved all of her.

"I'm happy I saw you that day," he confessed.

"Me, too. Being shot and almost dying was totally worth it," she deadpanned.

He laughed before she felt his magic and heard his wings materialize. He gave her a feathery kiss. Pulling away, his eyes held hers. "I'm yours."

Smiling, she kissed him back. "You better be."

Reaching down, he picked her up—face to face, he arched an eyebrow. "Or what?"

Hands in his hair, she shrugged. "I don't like to share."

"Well, that's sexy as hell," he said. Pressing a firm kiss to her lips, she opened for him before they fell into a smooth, pliant exchange. Fervent. Charged and fluid, she sucked on his tongue before nipping his bottom lip; with a groan, he drew back. Swirling in his heat and scent, she beheld him and almost came. All dark, possessive eyes and angled jaw, Hyphen was perfection. She'd never get used to him. Pussy tightening, she hooked her legs around him as he walked to the bed. Hefting her up, he tipped her just as she let go, landing with a bounce. Bending down, he leaned over her, hands on either side of her head.

"Fell..."

"Yes, baby?" she purred.

She looked at him from under her eyelashes while peeling his t-shirt over her head. Throwing it, she lay there. Dragging his eyes over her body, he cupped a breast, palming the mound, thumb running over the dark nipple. His hand felt so good, so strong, so possessive. Feeling dangerously sexy, she licked her lips and rolled over on all fours. Pushing her ass back, she looked at him from over her shoulder.

Still in his boxer briefs, he rubbed his dick, eyes as black as his wings. Hissing, he shook his head, then gave her a wicked smile. Just seeing his canines tugged on her swollen clit. She was wild for him—ready and willing to do any filthy thing he wanted. Dipping his left hand into the pocket of his boxers, he stroked his dick as she eased her ass out and down. Groaning, he caressed her ass with his free hand before exploring her slick, pink folds with two thick fingers. Air whipped at her exposed pussy, while he pressed and rubbed her clit, stroking his dick to the exact rhythm. Whimpering, she closed her eyes.

"Open your eyes."

She obeyed. Watching her man eye-fuck her was insanely erotic. On a gravelly moan, his eyes landed on hers just as he eased two fingers inside.

"*Hyphen*," she squeaked. Taking his hand off his dick, he steadied her, fingers slipping in and out at an increasing speed.

"This ass...*fuck*," he ground out.

He slowly finger-fucked her until she was sure his high thread count sheets were ruined from her liquid want. Yanking her closer, he pulled his boxer briefs down, then off. Eyes claiming hers, he slowly stroked his dick. Rarely if ever did she pay attention to dick because in the past, it only served one purpose—to make her come. But Hyphen's demanded attention. Not bald, he was neatly manscaped. With impressive length and thickness, it wasn't obnoxious. No, it's perfection came from its creamy, rose-colored shaft—sleek, satiny, and textured for her pleasure.

"Back up," he ordered. Inching to the edge, she spread her knees so that her ass was perched over the bed's edge. "Just like that, baby," he whispered, nodding. With one hand, he grabbed her waist and with the other, he guided his dick to her pussy, rubbing it back and forth, stopping at her clit. Teasing her with his satiny-slick tip, her legs trembled. Groaning, he spread her lips and with a grunt, possessed her pussy. She was so desperate for this man—everything about him tore her to shreds. Filling her, he didn't move—just admired her ass, while sliding his hands up her sides, down her back, then settling on her soft hips. Horny and out her mind, she pressed into him, then eased forward.

Holding her hips so that she couldn't move, he tsked. "Did I tell you to move?"

"*Hyphen...*" she whined.

"Answer me." His voice tweaked her nipples, sending heat to her core.

"No."

"You want this dick?"

"Yes, Hyphen."

"Then take it."

Slowly, she clenched her pussy and pushed back onto his cock, rotating her hips before moving forward.

"Just like that, Fell, *yes*," he clipped out.

Determined to milk his dick, she rocked back and forth again, and again, increasing speed while feeling every crevasse of his cock. Stopping, she wiggled her ass just enough for him to dig his fingers in her hips, releasing a guttural cry. Brows furrowed, he palmed both cheeks as they rippled with movement. Taking control, he held her in place, then pushed. He felt so good, her body shook, chest falling on the bed. Giving him more access to her ass, she clenched two handfuls of his duvet as he went faster, hitting her spot. Every. Fucking. Time. Her moans turned into wails until she pressed her face into the mattress, muffling her own cries. While one hand clutched her waist, the other rubbed and slapped her ass with just enough sting to push her to the edge. A breath away from coming, he pulled out and flipped her over.

Unprepared—that was what she felt looking at him. Breathing heavily, he watched her with predator-like focus. Abs taut, hair mussed, eyes black, and a hand on his dick, Hyphen was gloriously primal, especially with his wings serving as a backdrop.

Falling to his knees, he gathered her under her ass and yanked her forward. "Keep them open," he said.

Obeying, she watched him drag his eyes over her pussy before licking his lips. Dipping his face between her thighs, he slid his tongue along her folds, stopping at her clit to slowly pull, then suck. Hands in his hair, the shock and heat snatched her voice, leaving her mouth open.

Finally able to breathe, she released a cry as he eagerly devoured her. Rocking her hips, she rode his mouth. Moaning, he gripped her above the thighs, holding her in place as he swirled his tongue around her mound, sucking. Pussy clenching, she pulled her hands from his hair to squeeze her breast, pinching her left nipple as she fucked his gorgeous face. His tongue slid down and into her, sucking as her body convulsed, on the verge of exploding. Pressing into her, his strong tongue left a trail of fire everywhere it explored.

Lifting his head, he smiled. "You taste so fucking good."

She sat up and inched toward him just as he stood. Falling to her knees before him, her hands slid up his hamstrings. She looked at him and before he could speak, she took him in her mouth—tip to tonsils. Biting his lip, he shook his head in what looked like pain, but she knew was pleasure. Hissing through his teeth, his head fell back. The tip of his dick pressed against the back of her throat, but she didn't move; instead, she waited until he looked down at her. Once he made eye contact, she pulled on the shaft as the width of her tongue caressed it. Before popping it out, she swirled her tongue around the tip down the underside, to his tight balls. She gently gathered the delicate sack in her mouth and sucked just hard enough.

"Fellowship!" he cried out. The fact that he enjoyed her mouth only made her wetter. Massaging his softness in her mouth, she pressed her tongue along the main nerve, making him jerk and palm her head. "I'm not going to last," he ground out. Releasing his velvety jewels, she slid her tongue back up the shaft. Using her mouth as lubricant, she sucked-stroked him while his fingers dug into her scalp, pulling her forward. Thrusting his hips, he fucked her mouth as she took it. She sucked and squeezed until he tipped his head back, covered his face with his hands and wailed. Increasing her speed, she moaned around his dick, keeping it wet and sloppy. Pulling him out of her mouth, she smiled. He looked at her with a sexually frustrated scowl.

"Up here, *now*," he ordered.

Standing, she tilted her head. "Yes, baby?"

"Don't 'yes baby' me," he said, picking her up. He walked to the wall and pressed her against it.

"Am I too heavy?" she asked, realizing what was happening.

"What the fuck are you talking about?"

She wasn't a skinny girl and although he'd picked her up before, fucking against a wall was different. "I'm just saying, I'm not light—"

Grabbing her mouth, he kissed her, erasing her protests. Lips claiming hers, he balanced her underneath her ass with his right arm, while his left hand palmed his dick. Ending their kiss, he pinned her underneath his stare. "Fellowship, I'm strong enough to handle you in more ways than one, okay?" The confidence in his voice made her pussy clench as she tightened her legs around him.

"Yes, Hyphen."

"Good." Guiding his dick inside, he grabbed her ass with his other hand. Sliding her arms around his neck, she buried her face in the crook. Slowly, he pushed into her without straining. Resting her head on his shoulder, he increased his rhythm, stretching her pussy walls. "I've got you, baby."

For so long, Fellowship had embodied strength on top of a calculating ambition that facilitated her rise to detective in a male-dominated field. While successful, she forgot what it meant to be soft and cared for. Adored. She forgot that she didn't have to always be so damn strong. Always have it together. She forgot that it was okay to surrender and let someone else carry the burden.

Instinctively, she scraped his neck with her teeth as he tensed, sucking in a breath. Squeezing her, he pumped faster. Love, desire, and need crept through her veins as a rush of extreme heat erupted from her abdomen. Running her tongue over his tattooed neck, the sweet taste of his skin triggered an unknown craving. Kissing his neck turned into slow sucking, then pulling. Blind with primal yearning, she licked him again. Then, without hesitation or consideration of consequences, she bit him *hard*.

"*Fellowship*," he choked out.

Swirling her tongue around the mark, something inside of her *snapped*, and she *knew* that she'd be with him for the rest of her days. That no matter what happened, she was forever connected to him —*bonded* to him from the depths of her soul. Lifting her head, she pushed his sweaty hair off his forehead. The trust and vulnerability in his green eyes shot straight to her heart—she loved him so fucking much. Orgasm threatening to consume her, he pushed harder, slicker, faster.

"Hyphen," she whimpered, wrapping her arms around him. Tongue on her bite mark, she swirled and sucked.

"*Fell*," he whispered.

He didn't have to say more because she already knew—his love for her was palpable. It followed her wherever she went; clung to her skin like his seacoast and lavender scent. Clenching her pussy, she dug her fingers into his shoulders and surrendered to their deep, one-of-a-kind connection, coming on his dick. As her pussy spasmed, Hyphen shook and came on her name. Trembling, he buried his face in her neck; his wings softly rustled with each shiver. Neither moved. Savoring the feel of him inside of her as he rested, she ran her fingers through his damp hair. After a few beats, she cradled his face, holding his gaze.

"I love you, so fucking much," he confessed, his voice barely audible. He nuzzled her, planting faint kisses on her face.

"I love you, too."

Love was such a funny thing. Fellowship hadn't planned for it—hell, she wasn't sure how it really worked. All she knew was that she loved him, and the rest would come. Without effort, he carried her to the bed. Leaning down, she let go and slid partway underneath the covers with him climbing in next to her. Wrapping her in his arms, she snuggled in his nook as his wings stretched over her, tickling her shoulder. Drowsy, she closed her eyes as he lazily rubbed her back. Before she surrendered to sleep, she found him looking at her.

"I must've died and gone to the Salveigh Mist to find someone this perfect," he said.

Giving him a slow smile, she kissed his lips. "You're not dead."

"Are you sure?"

"I'm positive, baby."

"So, this is real?"

"Yes."

"*You're* real?"

Kissing his forehead, her eyes landed on his. "I'm very real. And I love you very much. I never expected this. Expected *you,* but here you are," she said, as it became increasingly difficult to fight off sleep. But she had to make sure he knew how much he meant to her. That everything about him mattered.

His eyes remained on hers—intentional. Focused. "Fell, living over two hundred years may seem amazing to humans, but it can be unbearable if you're alone like I was. Each year, each decade, each century lacked nuance, color, and dimension. Then, on a random day, at a random moment, everything changed. Suddenly, all two hundred and ten of my years on this planet had purpose."

Hyphen's words were as soft and delicate as his feathers, yet as powerful as the sea itself. Face warming, she tried to restrain her tears, but being in love meant she'd have to deal with some big fucking feelings—feelings she'd spent a large portion of her life avoiding. So, instead of resisting, she blinked them free. As soon as he saw them, he pressed his lips to hers and wiped them away. He didn't ask why she cried or whether something was wrong. Instead, he held and kissed her again and again until she succumbed to sleep in the arms of the man she loved.

Chapter Seventeen

Hyphen woke to Fellowship's soft snores. As he focused, he noticed that they were both naked under his pile of blankets. She was curled up, back to him, and too far away, he decided. Reaching over, he realized his wings were out. Taking a second to figure out why, he remembered that she told him not to hide them—at least not from her. Gathering her into his arms, he rolled her back into his nook. Settling down, her breathing resumed its rhythm. Although he was excited for her to wake, he enjoyed watching her sleep. Her lips were slightly parted, with black, curly lashes against her decadent brown skin. Her short black hair was coiled on top. Her narrow shoulders rose and fell with each breath. She was warm, soft, lush, and perfect—so fucking perfect.

Don't worry, Hyphen, you'll find your person—out of nowhere, she'll appear and change your life forever. His mind drifted to a memory of his brother—one he had long forgotten. In the Itchan Forest, he sat with Hudson who had taken him to their special place because he was having a difficult time getting over his first love. He couldn't remember the girl, save for the horrified look on her face when his wings exploded from his shoulder blades after he told her that he loved her. She made up an excuse to leave and ignored his letters until he finally got the hint. Devastated and depressed, he spent weeks in his room brooding until Hudson coaxed him out and into some fresh air. Their spot was tucked away in a lush part of the forest—a clearing with wildflowers, rocks, and a clear, gurgling creek. Sitting on his favorite rock, he threw pebbles into the water as Hudson munched on ciambe fruit. Hyphen couldn't remember how old he was—must've been around the twins' age. Either way, he was convinced he'd be alone forever—that his wings had doomed him to a life of solitude.

"You won't be alone forever," Hudson declared, shaking his head.

"Yes, I will," he pouted. Hyphen had wished he looked like his brother—tall, blond, and blue-eyed like their father.

"No, you won't."

"How do you know?" he spat, his eyes narrowed in frustration.

Hudson shrugged. "Because I do. You have so much life to live, baby brother, so much to experience and learn."

"What's to learn? I've read every book in our library and then some," he retorted, flicking another stone along the stream. He watched it skitter an impressive distance before disappearing into the water.

"I'm not talking about books, I'm talking about life," Hudson said confidently.

"I guess."

"Trust me. Your person will love you—wings included."

"I'll never show my wings to anyone," Hyphen snarled.

"Yes, you will. To the right woman."

Hyphen was so mad, he could have ripped the trees from their roots and tossed them in the clearing. What did his brother know? He didn't have wings. He didn't have to live with the daily reminder that he was different—a freak. He wanted to cut them off, but he read somewhere that if he did, they'd only grow back. Hudson offered him a piece of sticky fruit. Taking it, he chewed in silence.

"Don't worry, Hyphen, you'll find your person—out of nowhere, she'll appear and your life forever." At the time, it was difficult to believe him because the pain of rejection was so raw. But despite that, there was a small part of him that trusted his brother, even if he resented his wisdom at the time.

Fellowship stirred but didn't wake. Hudson was right—this woman appeared out of nowhere and changed his life. He thought back to the clearing in the forest. Hudson took him there because it was the only place he felt safe, the only place he could spread his wings without someone noticing, sneering, or shrinking away. Now that he thought about it, the peace he felt in the clearing was the same he felt with Fellowship. From the moment he knelt beside her and pressed her bloody wound, he was free. Fellowship was his clearing—his secluded, safe space. Tears prickled behind his eyelids. It was overwhelming to think that after losing his brother, he'd been gifted another person who accepted him for who he was.

He rubbed Fellowship's cheek with his thumb. *I love you, Fell.*

A faded smile appeared on her lips. "I love you, too, Hyphen," she sighed, still asleep.

He kissed her, his fingertips leaving a trail down her back. She shifted and moaned, then slowly opened her eyes—they locked with his.

"Hi," she said, her voice heavy.

"Good morning, baby. Sorry for waking you."

"It's a good way to wake up," she said, giving him a barely-there kiss. It was difficult for him to remember life without her. She ran her finger along his neck where she sank her teeth in him. Triggering the pleasure it elicited, he shivered. If he didn't know any better, he would think she had claimed him, too. "I got carried away," she said, eyes wide in remorse.

"No, you didn't."

"It's hard to explain—I *had* to do it. Like something would be missing if I didn't."

"I know that feeling."

"I don't think humans are supposed to feel like that," she said, as worry settled in her eyes.

He propped up on his elbow. "Babe, we've already established you're different. You're going to have to be okay with it."

"That's fair."

"Besides... I've never come so hard in my life."

Her eyes snapped to his before a grin materialized. "What?"

"I almost passed out."

Cackling with laughter, she pushed him. "Hyphen..."

"I'm telling you."

"No one's ever done that to you before?"

"No, I'd never let someone bite me."

"Why?"

Without thinking, he answered. "Because Aechaih mate through our bite." She stilled as he realized what he'd done. Fuck him and his big, fat fucking mouth.

Eyes blinking, she frowned. "*Mate?* That sounds more significant than just boyfriend and girlfriend."

Shamefaced, he held her gaze. "It is, and I should've been clear about that when I asked you."

"What does it really mean?"

"It means that I'll love you for all my days. It means you're my person. It's deeper than a traditional commitment. Our bite is forever. By not telling you the whole truth, I took away your choice, and I'm sorry."

She searched his face. He was worried that she was trying to formulate a polite way of telling him that what he did was fucked up.

"Your bite means you chose me?"

"I chose you long before that," he said. "Biting only solidified it. It showed the Guardians how serious I am about you."

She shrugged. "Well, I can say the same thing. As soon as it happened, it was forever for me too," she said.

Closing his eyes in relief, he sighed in gratitude for her magnificence.

"Although my lifespan is shorter than yours," she added softly.

It wasn't like he hadn't thought about it, but in the end, there was only one answer. "I know, and I don't care."

"But—"

"I'd rather have you for a short period of time than not at all," he said, holding her gaze.

Adoration flashed across her face before she leaned in and gave him a slow, thoughtful kiss. Drawing back, she knitted her eyebrows. "Do you know of anyone who's bonded with a human before?"

He shrugged. "Queen Aniyah?"

She gave him a playful frown. "Someone born in the last millennium?"

"No," he said. "Honestly, babe, I can't figure us out. The only thing I can come up with is maybe helping you that day created a unique space for us—some rift in space and time where we were able to form a deep, meaningful connection."

Hands in his hair, she gave him a cute little frown. "You seem remarkably calm for having bonded with a human."

"I could give a shit that you're human. I'm just happy I found you."

"I'm happy I found you, too."

Pressing his lips to hers, he gave her a squeeze before sliding his hand down her back to her ample ass. Palming it, he pulled her close as she looked up at him through her eyelashes.

"No," she warned.

"A little?"

"No, Hyphen—we've got work," she replied, smiling.

"That smile is telling me something different," he said, wiggling his eyebrows.

She laughed, tipping her head back and exposing her neck. Instinctively, he bent down and ran his tongue along it before he licked and sucked his own bite mark.

"*Hyphen*," she moaned as her arms found their way around his neck. "Work—we have work," she whimpered. "*And* running."

Lifting his head up, his eyes latched onto hers. "How about we burn some calories in the shower instead?"

She licked her lips and smiled. "There's an idea." The timbre of her voice made his dick flinch.

"Let's go before I take you right here."

Before he realized it, she pressed her lips to his for a thought-deleting kiss. Pulling back, she smiled. "If you do that, then you won't be able to get me all wet and soapy in the shower," she whispered, dragging her finger down his jawline.

"It's obscene how much I fucking love you," he said before he could stop himself. She smiled, kissed him, and climbed out of bed. His eyes dropped to her perfect ass before he hopped out and followed her because truthfully, he'd follower her anywhere.

"Hey, Lieutenant."

"I finally got your search warrant. Haslem was right, they put up a fight, but Weeden made them comply."

"That's great news," Fellowship said, as she wiped steam off the bathroom mirror.

"I'm hoping you two can get over there today."

"Absolutely. Hey, can you transfer me to Lemin?"

"What do you want with him?"

"I want his ability to manipulate anything with ones and zeros," she explained.

"What are you looking for him to hack?"

"Their server data. There's no way they're going to hand over incriminating evidence or anything that can lead us to the killer."

"The warrant doesn't cover a server search, so I'll pretend you didn't say that."

Fellowship laughed. "Fair. Hey, I have a question, and tell me if we're off on this—do you think our suspects could've been targeted by a powerful Aechaih?" she asked, wrapping a luxurious bath towel around herself.

It took Ceager a few beats to reply. "Why do you ask?"

"Because I want your opinion."

Ceager groaned. She imagined him leaning back in his chair and rubbing his head. "By *targeted,* you mean using magic to pin a series of murders on them?"

"Yes."

"The thought's crossed my mind. I think it would be hell to prove."

"Again, that's why I need Lemin to see if he can figure out how the killer uses *FBDn* or any identifying markers."

"Did you run this theory by your *Aechaih* partner?"

"Yes."

"And?"

"He agrees."

"I assume he's the only Aechaih who will."

"What does Pope think?"

"He's on the fence—there's a part of him that believes constant oppression has caused us to reach a breaking point."

"It has, but how in Guardians' name can we manufacture enough strength to kill Aechaih?"

"We can't, but it's difficult to prove otherwise."

"Which gives them an incentive to further limit our rights," she concluded.

"Yes."

"And if our hunch is wrong, we're fucked."

"Yes."

"All right, boss," she sighed. "Thanks for the feedback."

"Sure. Be careful out there, Dancy."

"I will, sir."

"Hold on for Lemin," he said, clicking off the line.

Their hunch made sense in theory, but in a world run by Aechaih, proving Nigh and Rey's innocence without substantial evidence would be next to impossible. Not only would they be sent to Containment, but she suspected the murders would continue until Pawville was completely eradicated from Trianah.

"Hey, Dancy, what's up?" Lemin asked brightly.

"Hey, do you have time today to go with Detective Haslem and me to Cygma Tech?"

"Woah, what's going on over there?"

"We have a search warrant for consumer data. I'd like to see what's on their servers."

"And you don't have a search warrant for that," Lemin added.

"Nope."

"Fuck, yes. I'd love to get into their system."

"I was hoping you'd say that. Give me an hour or two. I'll text when we're headed over and bring the warrant when you come."

"Perfect. See you then," he said, ending the call.

Fellowship grabbed her phone and walked out of the bathroom, through Hyphen's bedroom, and into the hallway. The closer she got to the kitchen, the more she smelled breakfast. With her stomach growling, she rounded the corner to find Hyphen frying eggs. His joggers were slung low, allowing her to savor his muscled back that dipped to his perfect ass. Bless Solneur for this man's workout routine.

Licking her lips, she leaned against the counter. "Hey."

"Hungry?" he asked, without turning around.

"Mmm, hmm," she moaned.

Facing her, he smiled. "I meant for breakfast," he said, shaking his head.

Her eyes lingered below his waist, taking him in.

"Excuse me, my eyes are up here," he said playfully.

"My bad," she said, looking at him with a sly grin. "I was distracted."

"I'm more than a piece of meat, you know," he said with a dramatic huff. She laughed as he plated their breakfast. He crossed the kitchen and placed her plate and coffee on the counter. He kissed her cheek, then shoulder. "Why are you in that towel?" he asked, nuzzling her neck.

"Because you don't believe in curtains."

"That's the point of having a penthouse—no one can see us up here."

"Never underestimate rich rationale," she said, shaking her head.

Smacking her ass, he laughed before grabbing his food and coffee. Although he sat next to her on the other barstool, he faced her. "Did I hear you on the phone in there?" he asked around a mouthful of food.

"Yeah, it was my boy toy's morning check in."

"Watch it," he said, yanking her chair closer between his legs.

"It was Ceager," she said, laughing. "We have our search warrant."

"Perfect. You want to go over there today?"

"Yes. I asked Lemin to join us."

"The one who recovered the Manicow footage?"

She looked at him, surprised. "Yes. You remember?"

He nodded as he chewed. "I remember everything you say."

See, it was shit like that that made her get doe-eyed and gooey over him.

"We need to stop by the office first. Ified wants to see me," he continued.

"What for?"

He shrugged. "A check-in, I assume." Polishing off his breakfast, he stood. "I'm going to get dressed."

She looked at her plate, then his. "I've barely touched my food."

He kissed her cheek before walking to the sink. "You want me to sit with you while you finish?"

She smiled. "No, baby. Thank you for breakfast."

"You're welcome," he said. He kissed her again, then headed to his bedroom. She leaned back just enough to enjoy the view of him walking away.

"Stop checking out my ass!" he yelled as he rounded the corner.

Blushing, she laughed. "You wish!"

Chapter Eighteen

Fellowship and Hyphen walked across the Aechaih precinct's bustling lobby. Because they drew attention, it was difficult for passing Aechaih to keep their eyes off them. Fellowship would be lying if she said the attention didn't make her strut more than usual. Hyphen wore a black suit with a stiff, white shirt, open at the collar, showcasing his ink. She wore high-waisted black dress pants, purple-bottom heels, a pink silk blouse, and heavy black overcoat. They were a gorgeous couple, even though they weren't supposed to be one. Sliding a hand into his pants pocket, he motioned for her to enter the elevator before he followed. Alone, they stood face-to-face as the doors whooshed closed.

"You're lucky there's a camera in here," he said.

"Or what?" she asked, arching an eyebrow.

"You know what," he said, pressing his magic around her. Immediately, her pussy spasmed as his heat licked at her skin.

Nipples hardening, she shook her head. "Savage."

"Just a gentle reminder of what's to come when we get home." *Home*—the word rolled off his tongue with such ease that she gladly accepted the fact that his home had become hers.

Biting her lower lip, she looked up at him. "Good thing I'm not wearing panties, or they'd be ruined," she purred. With dark eyes, he clenched his jaw so hard she thought he'd break it. The elevator opened just in time for her to throw a smile over her shoulder and exit. The doors almost closed before Hyphen jumped out, shaking his head.

"And *I'm* savage?" he asked, opening the door for her.

She laughed as they entered the Criminal Investigation Unit. Walking past the bullpen, she followed Hyphen to Lieutenant Ified's glass office. He opened the door for her; she walked in with him close behind. As soon as Ified looked up, she knew something was wrong.

"Lieutenant," Hyphen nodded, unbuttoning his suit jacket before taking a seat in one of the chairs. Fellowship did the same. Ified's eyes moved from Hyphen to her and back again. She could senes his anxiety. Crossing her legs, she sat back and waited for the shoe to drop.

"Glad you could make it in, Haslem," Ified said, clearing his throat. Clasping his hands in front of him, he looked down. "There's been a recent development in the case," he said, looking up.

"What?"

"You've been removed."

"Excuse me?"

"The order's come down from Weeden to replace you with Monroe," Ified said, his eyes darting back and forth.

A lump of dread thudded in Fellowship's stomach; she dug her nails into her hand to keep from losing her temper.

"Why?" Hyphen asked coolly.

"Um—well," Ified, began. "Captain Weeden asked me not to divulge—"

"Please, save me the trouble of asking him myself."

"It was requested that you be removed," Ified said, holding Hyphen's gaze.

The muscle in Hyphen's jaw tightened. "You mean my father told Weeden to take me off the case, or the Aechaih Division would lose half its budget that's provided by the Council," Hyphen corrected.

Ified's face blanched. "Yes. I tried to intervene—"

"I'm sure you did."

Fellowship hummed with anger. Clearly, Horace had a problem with his son working with a human—with *her*. Now, more than ever, she wanted to nail an Aechaih's ass to the wall for these murders—that would shut Horace Haslem up. But Hyphen was the only one who shared her hunch. How the fuck was she supposed to work with this Monroe guy?

"Is Monroe here?" Hyphen asked.

"Yes. He's in his office."

Hyphen stood and looked at her. If she was upset, then he was livid. "Dancy," he bit out before stalking to the door.

Standing, she pinned Ified with her stare. At least he had the decency to look shamefaced. While she felt like flipping his desk and telling him off, she knew he was only a pawn. Turning on her heel, she followed Hyphen out and down the carpeted hallway to his office. He immediately took off his suit jacket, tossed it on the sofa, and sat at his desk.

"I'm sorry," he said, looking at her.

"You don't have anything to be sorry for. I didn't help matters by getting under his skin," she said before setting her tote on the coffee table and taking off her coat. After she draped it on the sofa, she went to him. Hearing a click, she turned around to see that his glass office was frosted for privacy. "Fancy," she said with a smile.

He sighed. "Horace is doing this shit out of spite."

Fellowship perched on his desk just as he reached out and positioned her in front of him so he could rest his head on her stomach. As much as she wanted to be pissed at his father's asshole move, anger wouldn't do them any good. Instead, she ran her fingers through his hair.

"He's a dick, and I hate to say that about someone's dad."

He looked up. "You're right, though. He *is* a dick."

"Not to make this about me, but I don't want to work with Monroe. I don't do well with strangers."

Hyphen smiled. Although he sat up, he kept his hands on her hips as he rolled his chair closer. "Monroe's a good guy," he said. "He's the only person here I trust."

"But does he think humans are being targeted?"

"Probably not, but that doesn't mean he's not a good cop."

"Good cops consider all the evidence."

"Which means we must get the evidence we need."

"We?" she asked, arching an eyebrow.

"You don't think I'm going to drop this case, do you?"

She shrugged. Truthfully, she didn't know what he was going to do, which was why her heart accelerated at the thought of him defying his father's passive-aggressive maneuver.

"Horace doesn't control me—never has," he said, giving her hips a squeeze. "You go to Cygma Tech with Monroe and Lemin, and I'll keep researching Sylena and the upcoming alignment."

Whatever anxiety she had melted away. "Okay."

"Then after that, we can work from home," he whispered. His hands slid to her ass, palming both cheeks before he squeezed. Still smiling like a crazy person, she cradled his face. Yes, he was beautiful, but the man underneath the strong jaw, perfect hair, and green eyes was more than she could ever hope for.

"Okay."

"You wanna meet Monroe?" he asked, still worshipping her ass.

"Yes."

"Good, because I'm a heartbeat away from fucking you on this desk."

"I mean, you *did* just get kicked off our case, so if you wanna take that frustration out on me—"

"Let's go, woman," he said, standing. She laughed as he grabbed her hand and led her to the sofa, where she picked up her stuff before they set off to find Monroe.

———

Cygma Technologies, a publicly traded tech giant, was also located in downtown Seacrest, not too far from the precinct. Founded and run by the Tarnicons, the other family on the Council, the company spearheaded Trianah's push into the future, creating tech advancements that no citizen could live without. After Hyphen's quick introduction, she and Monroe drove to Cygma in silence. After parking, they stood in front of the ornate building, waiting for Lemin and the search warrant. Monroe was tall, with short dark hair and striking gray eyes. He was the most unassuming Aechaih she'd ever seen. Without his pointed ears and elongated canines, she would've thought he was human. He had a rugged handsomeness, as if he'd broken his nose a few times and let it heal naturally. Lacking the usual Aechaih smoothness, he definitely didn't use lusion. Dressed in a plain shirt and brown slacks, he looked like an average guy.

"How long have you and Haslem been partners?" she finally asked.

He looked up from his phone. "We're not officially, but over the past ten years, we've found ourselves working cases together," he said with a curt nod. "I joined the force after him. When I made detective, he was known for being impossible to work with. We got along. The rest is history."

"What earned him the reputation of being difficult?"

"Back then, he had a chip on his shoulder. As a Haslem, most people thought he got the job because of his name. On top of that, he didn't engage in office politics and was known as a truculent perfectionist and certified workaholic."

"And now?"

"Less of a chip on his shoulder. Otherwise, not much has changed," Monroe said with a smile. "He's the realest one-percenter I know. How's it been working with him?"

"It's been okay. Probably because I'm also a truculent perfectionist and certified workaholic," she confessed.

"I like Haslem, so working with a short, human version of him suits me just fine."

She laughed. "I'm glad you think so. Sorry if I came off as cold when he introduced us. I wasn't excited about changing partners."

"I get it," Monroe said. "I would've felt the same."

He gave her a full smile, his face brightening. It was then that she realized ruggedness aside, he was a good-looking Aechaih with aesthetically pleasing features and enviable height. Fellowship could see why Haslem trusted him; he had a solid, reassuring presence.

She eased into Hyphen's mind. *I like Monroe.*

After a beat, she warmed. *What do you mean* like?

She smiled to herself. *He's nice. Unassuming. No-frills. Different than my last partner.*

Is that so?

Yeah, you know me—I'll take substance over style any day.

That's it. No foreplay for you tonight.

That's okay. It doesn't take much to get me wet. Especially when you take off your shirt. Suddenly, she felt a more than his heat travel down the line.

Unfair, Dancy.

What?

You know what.

Looking across the courtyard, she saw Lemin approaching, his messenger bag bouncing as he made his way through a group of pedestrians. He was tall and lanky, with a boyish grin and shaggy brown hair.

Lemin's here, baby. I'll talk to you later.

Be good.

You know me.

"Sorry I'm late," he said to Fellowship. Digging through his bag, he produced the search warrant.

She took it, put it in her tote, then smiled. "We haven't been here long. Monroe, this is Officer Mike Lemin. Lemin, this is Detective Gabe Monroe," she said, motioning to both men.

"Nice to meet you, Monroe," Lemin said brightly.

"Same here," Monroe replied with a nod.

"Before we go in, I'd like to downplay the search. I'm sure they're defensive."

"Is there something in particular you're looking for?" Lemin asked.

"Anything and everything you can find."

"No problem," he said with a smile.

"What's going on?" Monroe asked.

"I've asked Lemin to snoop around their server data. I'm interested in what they don't want to share with us."

"You mean bypass the warrant to find something interesting?"

"Yes," Fellowship said, suddenly worried that Monroe wouldn't be on board with breaking the law.

Monroe looked from Fellowship to a smiling Lemin. After a beat, he nodded. "I see why Haslem likes you," he said.

Relieved, she smiled. "Would you like to take the lead so that they aren't annoyed with having to deal with humans?"

"My pleasure," Monroe said.

Inside, Cygma Tech was an open-concept office with concrete walls and flooring. The exposed ceilings and black, matte trim gave it a modern feel. After checking in with reception, the three were ushered to a conference room where they waited for COO Layne Tarnicon.

"I'm going to need time to upload my malware," Lemin said.

"How long?" she asked.

"Five, ten minutes, tops."

"You're launching malware, and I didn't even know *FBDn* existed until the first murder," Monroe said, shaking his head.

"You had never heard of *FBDn?*" Fellowship asked.

"Do I look like I use hook-up apps?" he asked, raising an eyebrow.

Fellowship squinted at him, then smiled. "You're the least preten-tious Aechaih I've ever come across."

"Meet a lot of Aechaih, Dancy?" Monroe asked with a smile.

"No," she said sheepishly.

"I get what you mean; I'm just giving you a hard time. I grew up in West Seacrest," he said. "That's why I don't look or act like the one-percenters."

Fellowship shrugged. She wasn't quite sure what that meant. She looked at Lemin who shrugged as well.

Monroe smiled. "Neither of you know what that means, do you?"

"I'm sorry," Fellowship said, shaking her head.

"West Seacrest--close to the Pawville boarder. It's where low-income Aechaih live."

"Ah, right," Lemin said, nodding.

"I forget that not all of you are rich," she said.

"No, not by a long shot," he said just as Layne Tarnicon entered.

All three looked up as the female Aechaih eased onto the chair at the head of the table. Obviously, Fellowship couldn't pinpoint the woman's age—for all she knew, she could be seven hundred years old. Layne wore gray dress pants and a red silk blouse. Her ebony hair was cut into a severe bob with one side tucked behind her pointed ear. With strong, angular features and violet eyes, she was beautiful. But it was clear that her beauty had no bearing on her power—that seemed to come from somewhere else. Crossing her legs, she pinned them with an icy stare.

"Detective Monroe, Detective Dancy, and Officer Lemin, welcome to Cygma Tech. How can I be of service to you?"

Monroe cleared his throat and leaned forward. "We don't want to take up much of your time. We found that our perps and victims used *FBDn* to conduct their business. We would like to match up locations and timelines, if that's possible?"

"Absolutely. We were saddened by the news of these horrendous murders. Thankfully, when users download our application, they sign a terms and conditions clause that allows us to mine their data in case something like this happens," she said. "Do you mind showing me your search warrant?"

Fellowship pulled the single piece of paper out of her tote and handed it to Layne, who scanned it quickly, then gave a tight smile.

"We've pulled the requested documents for you to search at your leisure." Suddenly, as if scripted, two employees scuttled into the conference room with six black binders. After setting them on the table and leaving, Layne motioned to the documents. "Here are the data records for the three victims and perpetrators. Feel free to take these with you," she said.

"We truly appreciate your cooperation. This is a great help," Monroe said with more diplomacy than Fellowship could ever hope for. "Do you mind if we flip through these real fast to make sure we don't need anything else?" he asked with a twinkle in his eye. Damn, he was good.

Layne gave them a curt nod and rose from her chair. "If you need anything, let my assistant know. I'll send her in shortly," she said before exiting.

"Okay, kid, you've got a good four minutes before her assistant gets here," Monroe said to Lemin.

"On it," Lemin said, whipping out his laptop. He flipped it open, his fingers flying over the keyboard.

"You were great," Fellowship said to Monroe.

"The only way to deal with one-percenters is to kiss their ass," he said gruffly. Nodding to the binders, he frowned. "I doubt there's anything in there that'll blow the case open."

"I agree," she said, eyeing the neatly stacked piles. "They seem highly protective of their public image."

"Money hides all manner of sins," Monroe said. Fellowship liked him more and more.

"Whose idea was it to get a search warrant?" Monroe asked.

"Haslem. We asked my lieutenant so that, in case they balked, Weeden would have to back him."

"Good thinking."

"Let's go," Lemin said quickly. Fellowship and Monroe looked at him as he stood, snapped his laptop shut, and shoved it in his bag. "Now," he said, walking to the door.

Heart pounding, Fellowship stood and grabbed three binders. Not waiting, Monroe did the same. They left the conference room at a slow enough pace not to alarm anyone, but quick enough to get the hell out of there.

As Hyphen looked through the readings he and Fellowship had copied from The Archives, it took him a minute to look up when someone opened his office door and entered. Once he did, he stilled. Then, after a beat, he tossed the reading on his desk and leaned back in his chair.

"Father?"

Horace Haslem entered, his gray suit pressed to perfection. Hand in his pocket, he stopped at the sofa. "I came to deliver the news," he said with an arrogant smile, his blue eyes sparkling.

"I'm at my desk, so obviously, I've already been told," he said.

"Oh, that," Horace said with a wave of his hand. "That's nothing. I have *more* news," he said, casually strolling to Hyphen's wet bar. Pouring himself a drink, Horace looked at him with a tight, sinister smile. "Want one?"

"No, thank you," he ground out.

"You'll have one," Horace said, pouring another. Sipping his, he moaned. "At least you have good taste in whiskey," he said. "Too bad I can't say the same for your taste in women."

And there was Hyphen's headache, right on fucking time. Rage rumbled from the soles of his feet to the crown of his head. Biting his tongue, he stood and approached his father, who had helped himself to a seat on the chair. Grabbing the tumbler, he sat on the sofa. Resting his right ankle on his left knee, he draped his arm on the back of the sofa and took a sip.

"What do you want?"

Taking a sip, Horace crossed his long legs. "I find it funny that you tried to hide the fact that you've broken the law by bonding with a human," he said, daring Hyphen to challenge him.

Fear took root in his gut. Revealing nothing on his face, he blinked. "And?"

Horace smiled, causing the hairs on Hyphen's neck to stand. "*And* you don't know what you've done. Why bonding with them is illegal."

"*Why* it's illegal? You mean there's a reason besides bigotry?"

Horace scoffed. "You're such a child. The bond extends human life. Their lifespans slow to match that of their mate's. How do you think it worked long ago?"

Hyphen paused. Was his father right? Was that why Fellowship said she felt differently? No one spoke about *how* humans and Aechaih mated, as if it had been erased from history.

"Didn't know *that,* did you?" Horace asked smugly.

"Get to the point, Father. I have work." He just wanted Horace gone so he could fucking think.

Something flashed across Horace's face before he smiled. "End it with the human."

"*That's* why you came here? I could've saved you the trip."

"Both of you will be brought before the Council, where we'll convict her and send her to Containment for her now, thanks to you, longer life. But before she goes, she'll watch as we don't convict you. She'll watch you walk away as a free man, a *voting* member of the Tri-Family Council, and Horace Haslem's second-born son and heir. Then, you can live out your remaining years in Trianah, knowing that she will *die* in Containment because of you and your selfish behavior. No matter how hard you try, you can't outrun your responsibilities to your family, Hyphen. In the end, you will not disgrace the Haslem name by being with a human."

Hyphen tasted blood in his mouth from biting his tongue. Swallowing, he took a sip of whiskey, letting it burn on the way down. Horace refused to look away—it was a showdown, and Hyphen was losing.

"Is that all?" he asked, playing bored.

Horace smiled, knocked back his drink, slammed it on the coffee table, and stood. "Try me. I *dare* you," he said before exiting.

Finishing his drink, Hyphen stood, walked to the wet bar, and poured another. He took a gulp and stared out the window. His father was right. He *was* selfish—selfish for loving Fellowship so much, for thinking they could actually have a life together, for thinking his father didn't sense his bite on her, for believing that love was for him, and for thinking he could finally be with someone who loved him as he was.

Selfish. He was selfish and naive—naive to believe he could have someone so beautiful, rare, loving, and smart.

Was it true that his bite impacted her lifespan? As villainous as his father was, he wasn't known to be a liar. All these centuries later, the truth finally came out. Fuck Rhoman's Massacre; the anti-miscegenation law was put in place to kill love. Swallowing the lump in his throat, he finished his drink. What he knew for sure was that he wouldn't let her go to Containment. It wasn't an option. Even if they continued seeing each other, it would only be a matter of time before his father sanctioned their arrest and ensured her sentencing. He *knew* it—knew Horace would do whatever it took to get his way with no regard for who he hurt in the process. He knew it as deeply as he knew his love for her.

Chapter Nineteen

Hyphen stared out of his office window. He felt Fellowship's presence as soon as she walked down the hall. Closing his eyes, he heard his door open, then shush close.

"Hey, handsome," she said brightly.

Turning to her, he felt his heart physically crack open as soon as he saw her face. As she walked to him, she stopped and looked around.

"What's wrong?" she asked. The light had disappeared from her voice. Her eyebrows knitted together in worry. Dropping her tote on the ground, she lifted her chin. "What's wrong, Hyphen? Tell me," she demanded.

Stopping a few feet before reaching her, he cleared his throat. "My father came by," he said, his voice low and hoarse.

She let out a breath as her shoulders dropped. "*Fuck*, babe. I thought—*fuck*," she said, closing the distance between them. As her scent wrapped around him, it took all of his power not to fucking cry. Resting her hands on his waist, she smiled. "I'm sorry you had to deal with him. Did he want to gloat about getting you kicked off the case?" she asked, looking up at him with beautiful, trusting eyes. He rubbed her arms, then pulled her in for a hug. She hugged him back with all of her love. He felt it—felt her give him all that she was. Pulling away, she rested her chin on his chest. "You wanna get out of here?"

"I can't," he whispered.

"Okay. You want to hear about how stealthy we were at Cygma? It was like a spy thriller," she said with a smile.

He was a piece of shit—a selfish, naive, piece of shit. "No, baby. My father came by because he sensed my bite on you at City Hall."

Her eyes widened. "Oh, no," she breathed. "I didn't realize he could, well, I guess," she said, shaking her head. "What did he say?"

Hyphen swallowed and kept his arms around her. "He said that if we didn't end it, he'd bring us before the Council, convict you, and clear me of any wrongdoing." Watching her process his words was worse than seeing her almost die on the sidewalk.

She frowned. "I'd go to Containment, and out of spite, he'd make sure you didn't."

"Yes."

"Fuck him. We'll fight back. I didn't go to law school for nothing," she said, tenacity lighting her eyes.

Holding her, he didn't reply. Instead, he *selfishly* absorbed as much of her as he could.

"Hyphen?"

Eyes not leaving hers, he saw when understood—when she realized that he was the asshole breaking her heart in his *Solneur-damned office.*

Stepping out of his arms, she frowned. "Hyphen," she said, more firmly than before. Then, like a switch, she flipped cold—colder than he had ever felt her before. "You've already made the decision to end it, to leave at the slightest inconvenience," she said, taking another step away from him.

"It's not an inconvenience, Fell. My father's serious. I won't let you go to Containment."

"*You* won't let me go. So, what? I have no say in this?"

"There is no say; it's Containment. It's not an option."

"That's *my* decision, Hyphen, and you don't get to make it for me. That's not how this works," she said, her eyes narrowed.

He knew her fight would be an issue—her stunning determination. But he had to be strong. He couldn't let her take another bullet for someone. "No, Fell," he said, holding her fiery gaze.

"So, that's it? None of this matters," she said motioning to them. "It's out the window. Never happened."

"Of course not, I love you. Everything I've said to you is real. I'm *bonded* to you. I'll never love another person for as long as I'm on this planet. I *love* you, Fellowship, but you're not going to Containment, not for me," he said, straining to contain his raw emotion.

Scanning her face, he felt his breath catch. Her nose was red, her eyes glassy. All of her heat rushed around him. A silent plea. A silent fight. The lump in his throat wouldn't go down, no matter how hard he tried.

"I thought you said he doesn't control you?" she asked, her voice cracking.

"He controls the Council, the very entity that would put you away forever. I can't, Fell," he said. "I can't lose you like that."

"But you can lose me like *this*? Love isn't easy, Hyphen. It's not something we can pick up and put down whenever we want. I love you. I love you so fucking much. You think I can put this shit down?"

With watery eyes, he looked down, unable able to face her. "No."

"You're fucking right, *no*. And I know you can't put it down either. Why would we surrender to a bully like Horace?"

"You don't know him, Fellowship. Not like I do. There's no winning against him or the Council. They take what they want, do what they want, and leave the rest of us to suffer," he said, meeting her gaze once more.

She was crying. She was fucking crying and he felt like nothing. He never wanted to be the reason she cried, not ever.

"Fell, I love you."

She raised her chin and fixed him with a heated glare. "You love me, but you won't fight for our love *with* me?"

"*Fellowship*," he breathed as tears finally made their way down his face. Tears that hadn't flowed for a long fucking time. Tears he kept contained. Suppressed. Tears that hadn't been allowed to fall since losing his brother.

She grabbed her tote, shouldered it, and wiped her eyes. Then, he watched as she erected her protective wall.

"Fine. Got it."

"Fellowship," he pleaded, stepping to her.

Stepping back, she met his gaze with a cold stare. There was no dazzling smile or biting her lip, no tipping her head back in laughter or playfully rolling her eyes. Her face held none of the expressions he'd grown to love. She was gone, and all that remained was heartbreak.

"You made this decision, Hyphen. *You* did, not me. Remember that," she said before turning around and walking out.

Hyphen used to imagine cutting off his wings. It was an imagined pain he was willing to endure in order to be like everyone else. Then, he lost his brother and the imagined pain became real, but watching Fellowship walk out of his life paled in comparison. If his life was shattered when Hudson died, then it was just decimated at the loss of his mate. But he couldn't let her be sent to Containment. He would rather have her hate him and be safe than love him and be in danger. At least that's what he told himself before sitting down in defeat.

Chapter Twenty

Fellowship's trainers slapped on the wet asphalt as she pushed toward her apartment building. Music blaring, lungs on fire, she pressed further, harder, and faster. Since the incident with Hyphen, her runs had become more frequent and considerably longer. With no desire to go near the sea, she ran thoughtless circles around Pawville, passing shabby stores and homes, with the goal of not thinking about Hyphen, the breakup, or anything else that reminded her that she was foolish enough to believe love was for her.

As the elevator doors whooshed open, she wiped her face with her sleeve and stepped off. Rounding the corner, she stopped to find Rayna sitting by her apartment door, legs crossed at the ankles. Looking up from her phone, she smiled. Still breathing heavily, Fellowship returned it, approaching as Rayna stood.

"Hey, everything okay? You're never up this early," she said, shoving her key into the lock and twisting it open.

Rayna shrugged as she followed Fellowship in. "I wanted to see how you were doing before you headed to Seacrest."

Throwing her keys on the table, Fellowship walked to the kitchen, opened her refrigerator, and grabbed a bottle of water. Opening it, she tipped it back, keeping her eye on Rayna who hopped on her counter, boots swinging back and forth.

"I'm fine," Fellowship said over a swallow.

"I know you're *fine*, but, you know, how *are* you?" she asked, her voice soft with worry. Fellowship knew why she was there. It was Rayna she went to after she left Hyphen that day. It was Rayna who held her as she cried over a fucking *man*. It was Rayna who let her stay the night, who rubbed her back as she slept off and on, waking up mid-sob. And it was Rayna who let her stay for days until she could finally go home.

Leaning on the counter, she looked at her friend. "It's whatever, you know," she said with a shrug.

Rayna considered her for a moment. "Have you seen him?"

"No," she said, wiping her mouth. "Lemin texted last night saying he found a shit-ton of stuff hidden in Cygma's network, so we'll dig through that today." Walking past Rayna, she tapped her knee, telling her to follow. Hopping down, Rayna entered her bedroom, sitting on the plush chair in the corner. Fellowship sat on the edge of her bed and kicked off her running shoes. "What's up with you?" she asked as she peeled off her jacket.

"Nothing much, my sister has a new boyfriend. I don't like him," she said.

"Why?"

"Meh, something about him. He's nice and all. Responsible. Kind."

Fellowship chuckled. "What's the problem?"

"Nothing except that Baeleigh *deserves* more. She deserves fucking passion. Fire. Something that lights her up from the inside," Rayna said, shaking her head.

Hmph. Fellowship didn't have a response to that. Maybe because she had, if only for the briefest of moments, so much fire with Hyphen that she could barely contain the light. Swallowing down the lump of sadness in her throat, she nodded in understanding.

"Anyway," Rayna continued with a shrug. "I want to show you something, but there's a part of me that doesn't."

"What is it?"

"Something I saw online."

"What?"

"I hate-follow Bronwyn," she admitted. "I saw Hyphen."

Hearing his name made her flinch. Part of her didn't want to know, while another, darker part of her *had* to know. "She posted him?"

"It was a fundraiser or something. A Casino Night, I think. Anyway, yeah," Rayna said, her eyes worried.

"Let me see."

Shaking her head, Rayna backpedaled. "I shouldn't have said anything. I just didn't want you to be blindsided if she pulled up to the precinct or something."

Fellowship stood and walked over to her. "Give me the phone, Ray," she instructed calmly.

"Fell..."

"Fine, I'll look it up myself," she said, turning away.

"*Okay*," Rayna sighed as she leaned over and pulled her phone out of her back pocket. Opening it, she scrolled, then handed it over.

Fellowship took it, steeled herself, and then looked. There they were: the prince and princess of Seacrest. At a glossy bar, Hyphen stood in a black tux, holding a tumbler of whiskey, with Bronwyn next to him, posing in a slinky red dress.

Handing the phone back to Rayna, she forced a smile. "Thank you for showing me. I needed to know. I'm going to hop in the shower. Help yourself to some coffee, I'll be out in a bit."

"Fell," Rayna breathed, her eyes wide with remorse.

Smiling, she shrugged. "It's okay. *I'm* okay, I promise. Go get some coffee." Before Rayna could answer, she went into the bathroom, shut the door, and leaned against it.

She was *not* okay.

After a moment, she turned the shower on hot and undressed. As steam wafted above, she stepped in, letting the water pound her skin. Head tilted back, she felt a sob creep up from her gut, through her chest, and then out her mouth, which she covered to stifle the sound.

Closing her eyes, tears pushed forward as her shoulders shook. This was why she didn't open her heart. Why she didn't fall in love. Why she kept people, especially men, at bay. The last thing she wanted was to be where she was: standing in the fucking shower, crying over a motherfucking man.

Hyphen had changed her world, and for a brief moment, she was confident that no matter what happened, he'd be there. A strong, solid presence. Steady. Reliable. She let her guard down and believed in him, in their connection, in the otherworldly way that he showed up and disrupted her existence. As much as she didn't want to, she still felt their *bond*. The line of communication that connected them was still alive. Even if she refused to use it, he was at the other end. Sniffing, she held her face under the hot water as the picture of him and Bronwyn manifested behind her closed eyes.

Horace threatened to throw her in Containment because being human wasn't good enough for his son. Regardless of Hyphen's relationship with his father, he was still a Haslem. Instead of fighting for their love, he cut her loose and appeared on social media with the woman who *was* acceptable. She allowed the water to wash away her tears. She wouldn't allow them to make her feel inferior. Taking a deep, steamy breath, she locked her shit up just as cold, focused determination eased through her veins. Despite the pain, the heartbreak, and the tears, she was still *that* bitch. Still Fellowship Fucking Dancy, and for all she cared, Hyphen, Horace, *and* Bronwyn could kiss her glorious, black ass.

In a shitty mood, Hyphen sat at his cluttered desk, highlighting a copied reading from The Archives. It wasn't case-breaking, but it was definitely significant. Without much sleep, he'd managed to read a decent amount to get a better understanding of the moonless nights. He learned that the Guardians protected the inhabitants of planet Nehlahni—Solneur during the day and Sylena during the night. If there was cloud cover, it could be an indication that evil was at work, essentially hiding the people from the Guardians' protection. Basically, cloud cover acted as a warning system. If Rey and Nigh didn't see Sylena, then some dark shit must've been happening in Trianah.

Running his hand through his hair, he sat back and sighed before scratching at his scruff. He'd adopted a new routine since losing Fell: work, home, workout, drink, pass out. The passing out was essential—if he didn't, then he'd men-com her, begging for forgiveness. Nevertheless, the routine allowed for the bare minimum in his grooming, which meant shaving was out the window, along with dressing for success. Instead of suits, he wore jeans, a vintage t-shirt, and a thick cardigan. He looked like a heartbroken man whose life had taken an unfortunate turn, leaving him without the woman he adored. Standing, he grabbed the papers and went to see Monroe.

Monroe's office was smaller than Hyphen's, with very little decoration save for a picture or two. When he entered, Monroe looked up from his desk and smiled.

"Hey, stranger."

"Hey," Hyphen replied. Sitting on the sofa, he tossed the papers on the coffee table. "I found some shit about Sylena that might help the case."

Monroe stood and approached, sitting across from him on the chair. Picking up the papers, he scanned them quickly, nodding. "Dancy told me both suspects reported moonless nights," he said, looking up.

"Yeah, we thought it meant something, so went poking around The Archives."

Monroe continued reading, eyes widening. "Damn, I didn't know this, did you?" he asked. "If we can't see Sylena and her sisters, something's amiss?"

"No, because we don't talk about dark magic," Hyphen said. "But if Rey and Nigh didn't see Sylena, then there's a good chance someone was using it."

"I never would've considered that," Monroe said, shaking his head. "You two were really thinking outside the box."

"Yeah, something like that," he mumbled, ready to leave. Monroe's office smelled like Fellowship. In fact, every fucking thing smelled like her. His SUV, his home, his bedroom, and his pillows. She haunted him. Every time he smelled warm shea butter, he wanted to cry.

"Thanks," Monroe said, leaning back. "How are things?"

"Great," Hyphen said flatly.

"Uh," Monroe started, tilting his head, "not to be a dick, but you don't look great."

Hyphen shrugged, then stood. "Yeah. Well, there you go," he said, motioning to the papers.

He started to leave but stopped dead in his Solneur-damned tracks as Fellowship opened the door and strode in. Sucking in an inaudible breath, he didn't move as she clocked him, then looked at Monroe, flashing her signature smile. She wore a black, skin-tight sheath dress that clung to her dangerous curves, hitting just below the knee. On the back, which he tried not to stare at, was a gold zipper running from the top down the middle of her ass to the bottom. She wore the purple-bottom pumps that made her legs look delectable, along with her gold watch and a thick gold necklace. Her hair was freshly cut and gleaming. She looked like life without him was perfectly fine.

Heart pounding in his ears, his stomach churned up acid and whatever little food he'd had over the past few days. Meanwhile, her ass in that dress should've been illegal. With the scent of shea butter all around him, he swallowed as his body twitched with muscle memory, desperate to touch her. Hold her. Kiss her. She and Monroe were talking about something, but he couldn't hear shit. Unable to move because his brain had effectively shut down, he just stood there like a heartsick asshole.

"I've stowed Lemin away in my office, if you want to come down," she said to Monroe. "He's brought a bunch of files for us to go through."

Monroe smiled. "Absolutely. Um, so," he started, looking at the papers in his hand, "Haslem brought us some compelling information about the moonless nights."

Holding his breath, he watched as she scanned him from head to toe and back again. Then, to his surprise, her eyes stayed on his for a millisecond before she arched an eyebrow and lifted her chin as if to say: *Yeah, motherfucker, you're the asshole who let this go.* It was a well-deserved punch in the gut.

Returning to Monroe, she smiled. "Great, bring it along and we'll get it on the board," she said brightly. "I'm stopping by the grocery store you all call a break room. Want something?"

"No, I'm good," Monroe said, laughing.

"Okay, see you in a bit," she replied, sauntering past Hyphen in all her regal glory. She was unfazed, unbothered, and uninterested in his existence. His brand was still on her and hers on him. Their bond was a daily reminder that when shit got tough, he abandoned her. He took the easy road, wiggling himself off the hook. Because deep down, before his father showed up with his bullshit, he realized that he loved her so much, he was deathly afraid of losing her. That one day, he'd wake up and she'd be gone. So, instead of living with the anxiety of her inevitable abandonment, he capitalized on his father's tyranny and walked away from the love of his life like a fucking coward.

"Um," Monroe said, voice low. "What was *that?*"

Dragging his eyes to him, he shrugged. "I was kicked off the case so," he said, unable to continue the lie.

Frowning, Monroe stood and walked over to him. "That's not what I'm talking about."

"Doesn't matter." Sighing, he looked upwards. Maybe the Guardians would take pity and end his life.

Monroe continued, oblivious to his pain or ignoring it. "What's interesting is that when you first introduced us, my hair almost blew back from energy you two produced. I mean *damn.*"

Hyphen looked at him. "What?"

"Yeah," Monroe said on a knowing nod. "It was remarkable. Not gonna lie, I was a little envious. Just a little, though."

Hyphen frowned. "You're an intuit and empath, of course you felt something."

Monroe eyed him. "You know I don't use that shit, so if you two were powerful enough to get past my defenses, then it was significant."

Hyphen didn't know if that made him feel better or worse. "Well, don't worry, there's nothing more to envy."

"I gather that."

Hyphen nodded, then left his office. Rounding the corner, his phone buzzed. Pulling it out his pocket, he sighed: it was Haze. He didn't have the energy to appear like everything was okay, but he answered anyway because it was his baby sister, and he'd always answer her calls.

Swiping to accept, he pulled open his office door and entered. "What's up, baby sister?"

"What in Guardians' name is going on, Hy?" Haze snapped.

Sitting at his desk, he frowned. "What are you talking about?"

"I'm talking about this picture of you and Bronwyn on *Vizable*. I thought you were Mom's date to the Casino Night."

Leaning back in his chair, he closed his eyes. "I was. Bronwyn approached me, and the photographers got a shot."

"And she *posted* it? *Really?*"

He could care less what Bronwyn did. "So, what? She always posts shit."

"She scrubbed you from her social media, Hyphen. Posting a picture of you *says* something."

"What could it possibly say, Haze?"

"I don't know—that you're back together?"

"Haze..." Hyphen sighed.

"What if Fellowship sees?" Haze asked. The panic in her voice made him open his eyes and sit up.

"Why are you so worried?"

"I'm *worried* because she's your *person*, Hyphen. Don't tell me you don't know that. I would've thought you'd have claimed her by now."

What the fuck? Clearly it was time for him to stop underestimating the women in his life. "Haze—"

"I *love* her, Hyphen. I really do, and not just because she's good for you but because she's *everything*," his sister whined. Biting the inside of his cheek, Hyphen closed his eyes to keep from coming undone. Leg shaking, he rubbed his temple. How could he tell his sister that, yes, he claimed Fellowship, but as soon as he did, he let her go?

"Fellowship isn't on social media, Haze. Besides, she knows that Bronwyn and I are over."

"Does she know you love her?"

Fuck. He had to get off the phone. "Hazy, I have a meeting, darling. Can we continue this discussion later?"

After a beat, he heard her sigh. "Fine."

"I love you."

"I love you, too," she said as some of the ire in her voice dissipated.

Ending the call, Hyphen rested his head in his hands. He wasn't sure how he'd gotten here—between seeing Fell, Monroe picking up on their attraction, and Haze in near-tears at the thought of him not being with her—was too fucking much. Standing, he shoved his phone in his pocket and eyed the piles of work on his desk. That shit would have to wait because it was time for him to go home, get drunk, and pass the fuck out.

Chapter Twenty-One

"There she is," Auten said. He wore a navy cardigan, a thick white t-shirt, and soft gray pants. Leading the way down a narrow hall, his home was cozy and thoughtfully decorated. Following him into the kitchen, she sat at the glossy table for two. Auten moved around his kitchen, placing a kettle on the fire.

"How are you?" he asked, pulling two mugs out of the cabinet and plopping tea bags into each one.

"I'm okay," she said.

Crossing her legs, she wore leggings, trainers, and one of Hyphen's sweaters because as pissed off as she was, she still couldn't get enough of his smell. Did it make her a miserable masochist? Yes. Did she care? No. After a few days of combing through Cygma's hidden data, she was grateful for the break. Although they couldn't decipher who had access to *FBDn*'s live user feed, they did stumble upon a bunch of ancient Trianah records—stuff that blew her historian mind. Stuff she would've shared with her history nerd boyfriend had he not dumped her.

Auten turned around and frowned. "Just okay?"

"Yep, been working." Taking a beat, Auten considered her. Shifting underneath his gaze, she cast her eyes downward.

"What's wrong?" he asked.

Clearly, her attempt at pretending everything was okay had failed. She shrugged. "It's been hard."

"Working with Haslem? Or the case in general?" he asked, leaning against the counter.

"Both." She didn't want to go into her thing with Hyphen, but Auten's eyes coaxed the truth out of her, and before she could stop herself, she confessed. "Horace pulled Hyphen off the case."

"What?" he said, shaking his head. "I *knew* he'd butt his nose in."

"Maybe, but I believe he did it because I met him at City Hall and it didn't go well," she admitted, fiddling with the hem of the sweater. Auten remained silent until the kettle boiled, then whistled. With smooth, efficient movements, he poured their tea. Handing her a mug, he sat across from her.

"Tell me what happened."

There was a part of her that didn't want to share the grimy details, but again, her grandfather's eyes worked their magic. "We were at The Archives, researching and when we left, Horace and his advisor saw us and well, you know Horace."

Auten sipped his tea, then clenched his jaw, his ease and levity slowly giving way to contempt. "Yes, I do. So, it's been hard for you with Hyphen off the case?"

Biting her lip, she blew on her tea, then took a sip. "Yeah."

Auten took her in and without saying a word, his wise-grandpa-ness forced her to open up even more.

"Hyphen and I were more than partners," she confessed.

To her surprise, Auten's eyes shed their anger, instantly lighting up. "Oh, *Fell*," he sighed. "If you were to fall for anyone, I could only dream it would be Hyphen Haslem."

"Wait, what?"

"He's a good man. How long has this been going on?"

"For some time but—"

"Oh, I get it. It's been difficult for you because you two can't officially work together. But I would assume he contributes when you see each other after hours."

Biting her lip, she looked down. "We don't see each other."

"I don't understand."

"When Horace saw us, he *sensed* that we were together. After getting Hyphen removed from the case, he told him that if we continued seeing each other, he'd have me brought before the Council and charged with breaking the law, but that he wouldn't charge Hyphen. I guess to punish him even more or something," she said with a shrug. Sliding her eyes to her grandfather, Auten looked equal parts livid and devastated.

"Hyphen ended it because he didn't want you to get hurt," he said on a nod.

She gave him a feeble shrug. "You know me, I wanted to fight, to find a way but..." Staring at her mug, she bit the inside of her jaw to keep from crying, then gave her grandpa a faint smile. "So, that's that. Been working through files we retrieved from Cygma's database. Today, I saw something interesting that I wanted to ask you about," she said, hoping he'd let her change the subject. Thankfully, he did.

Eyes blinking, he took a breath and gave her his all-knowing smile that assured her that he loved her no matter what. "What did you see?"

"We found copies of ancient records. Stuff that's not in the rare books library, although it should be. I saw a registry for the palace; it looked like names of people who worked there. More than likely Aechaih. One of the names was a healer named Daelyn," she said. "Clearly, that stood out as it's my middle name. You think it's just coincidence or—I don't know. Could I have been named after an Aechaih healer? That'd be weird, right?"

Auten opened his mouth, but nothing came out. After a beat, his shoulders sank. Rubbing his face, he let out a ragged sigh. "Okay," he whispered more to himself.

Fellowship frowned. "Okay, what?"

Auten stood and went to the cabinet; after a beat, he turned around with a bottle of Zion's Ink. Suddenly, dread expanded through her tightened chest. Sitting, he opened the bottle and poured a little into both of their mugs. Capping the bottle, he took a healthy sip. As soon as he looked at her, the hairs on the back of her neck stood.

"Grandpa?"

"How much of your childhood do you remember?"

She shrugged. "I remember our first apartment in Pawville, meeting Daize, school, you working in the mines. Stuff like that."

"Fell, you were ten when we moved here. What do you remember before that?"

Taking a sip, she searched her memories for anything prior to Pawville but came up empty. "Not much. I remember the Itchan Forest a little, but that's it."

Auten nodded. "I figured as much. Do you remember why we came to Pawville? Why the rest of our family wasn't with us?"

Taking a moment, she searched her memories, then shrugged. "I know our family died, but I can't remember how," she said, feeling around the black curtain that separated her from the past. In her twenties, she used to push at it, desperate to see more, remember more, but after a while, she stopped.

"It's okay," he whispered. "I'm going to lay it all out for you, and when I'm done, I'll answer all the questions you have."

"Okayyy..."

Taking another sip, he let out a breath and began. "Before you were born, generation after generation of our ancestors lived in the forest in small human communities. By the time you were born, things started to shift. Something was in the air, a sinister energy that infiltrated our world. The togetherness we once possessed began to fall away as self-ishness took hold. So, when you were a baby, we moved deeper into the forest, isolating ourselves. It was a wise decision as we, more impor-tantly, *you* thrived. Around three, you began to walk and talk. Around four, you demonstrated magical abilities."

Cue the record scratch. "Sorry to interrupt, you said *magical* abili-ties?" Auten nodded.

Reaching over, she grabbed the bottle of Zion's Ink and poured a healthy portion into her mug. Taking a gulp, she steeled herself for the impending shit show, then nodded for him to continue.

"You were such a bright, lovely soul—the center of our joy. Your mother and grandmother, both magical themselves, worked to help you cultivate your own magic."

What in the entire fuck was happening? She opened her mouth, but Auten held up his hand. Taking another sip, she leaned back, keeping the mug close to her lips.

"By the time you were ten, we knew you could manipulate fire and water. One day, on our way home from the clearing, you suddenly grew quiet. As we approached the cabin, your tiny hand grabbed my arm. I turned around and saw fear in your wide eyes. 'Don't go in there, Grandpa, it's bad,' you said, but nothing seemed out of place. You were so afraid. I told you to stay in the front yard while I went inside," Auten said as his nose turned red. He sniffed, then clenched his jaw.

Suddenly, inexplicable fear and panic spread through her chest. As her heart rate increased, she held her breath. It *was* bad. She knew it —*felt* it.

Auten cleared his throat. "When I walked in," he paused and closed his eyes, "it was unimaginable. I wailed, but realizing you'd hear me, I tried to quiet myself. When I turned around, there you were, standing in the doorway." Auten opened his eyes, releasing his tears.

Fellowship reached across the table and grabbed his warm hand. Then, like fucking magic, the black curtain lifted and she *saw* her childhood home. There was blood everywhere, open, vacant eyes, scattered furniture, and overturned tables. Her family lay dead, all piled like trash. Fear, grief, and anxiety melded into an inconceivable pain. Squeezing Auten's hand, she struggled to breathe—it was real. So very real.

"They were murdered," she whispered.

She smelled the thick, woody forest, wildflowers, and the metallic tang of blood. Her family—her heart—had been butchered. Fellowship's soul had unlocked, freeing memories of a past that suddenly fell into place. Wet, soggy dirt. Cloths for wrapping the dead. Shovels for burying. Bags packed. Night. Tears. Walking. So much walking. Sneaking across the border into Pawville. As the spotlight illuminated her past, an exceptionally painful part of her identity was shoved into place. Its edges were sharp and jagged as her psyche made room for abandoned memories that had been left out in the rain, now swollen and misshapen. It didn't matter whether or not they fit, they were a part of her. She opened her mouth to release the sorrow, but nothing came out. Auten squeezed her hand in support. Finally, she drew in a shuddered breath and looked at her grandpa.

"I forgot. Forgot that we worked all night to bury them. Forgot everything about who I was—who I am. *Magical?* I'm magical. How could you let me forget?"

Auten's eyes were red, tears falling onto the table. She didn't want to make him cry or accuse him of wrongdoing—she just needed answers.

Nodding as if he had prepared for this particular line of questioning, he held her gaze. "From leaving our home in the forest, to sneaking across the border, you hadn't spoken a word. In fact, I didn't hear your voice for a year. You attended school, slept, read, and practiced your magic. I couldn't let anyone in Pawville see your ability, so...I told you to stop. It was the only way to keep you safe. When I tried to talk about our family, you would retreat to your room. Your fire, your light seemed to vanish. It was unbearable to see my vivacious grandbaby become a mere shell—a *ghost*. As afraid as I was, I remained patient and tried not to push. I gave you time and space to cope, to heal. When you turned eleven, you thanked me for buying you the doll you wanted. After that, you started speaking more and more. Then you met Daize, and you finally came back to life—back to me."

"I met Daize when I was twelve."

"Yes," Auten smiled. "Suddenly, you were chatty and bright and okay. All I ever wanted was for you to be okay. And because your light had returned, I was afraid to mention our family, afraid that you'd disappear again, so I didn't." He shook his head, worry clouding his eyes. "I don't know if it was the right thing to do, but I couldn't bear to lose you again."

It made sense why Auten would protect her from the past. Life in the forest seemed like a dream until it wasn't. In retrospect, she could only imagine what it was like for *him*. Finding his wife, daughter, and son-by-law slaughtered. How it felt to raise his only granddaughter by himself. And to think, she had stopped talking to him over some bullshit, essentially leaving him alone in the world.

"I just can't believe it... I'm forty-two, Grandpa. How could I forget so much of my past?" she asked more to herself than to him.

"Sweetheart, no ten-year-old should've witnessed what you did. Your poor little heart was shattered, and I believe you locked those memories away to keep yourself safe."

She nodded and released his hand. "Do we know who killed them and why? Or was it a random act of violence?"

He paused, as if reluctant to answer. After a moment, he finally said, "The Tri-Family Council sanctioned their deaths."

"What?!" she shrieked in horror.

"Some humans stumbled onto our land and saw your mother performing magic. In exchange for food and money, they reported what they saw to someone who relayed it all the way to the Council—the very Council that was certain no more hybrid humans existed. And because you insisted on going to the clearing every day, we weren't there when they came for us. Had we been..." he said, his voice trailing off.

Of course Aechaih would fear hybrids, and of course hungry humans would betray others for survival. With a heavy heart, she shook her head. "I wouldn't be surprised if it was Horace Haslem who put the hit out on our family," she mumbled into her mug.

"He did," Auten said, as if it were the most obvious thing in the world.

Fellowship opened her mouth, but no words came out.

"Hyphen never served on the Council, but his brother—his name escapes me." Auten said, frowning in thought.

Heart racing, Fellowship's skin prickled. "Hudson," she said.

Auten's eyes snapped up. "Yes! Hudson Haslem voted against it. From what I've gathered over the years, Horace took his time to gather enough votes to sanction the murders, and the deed was done. People have said it broke his heart."

"Broke *Hudson's* heart?" she asked, her voice small.

"Yes. I'm sure Hyphen shared with you how he lost his brother?"

Although they talked about Hudson, she never got the courage to ask him how he died. "No, I don't know."

"Oh," Auten sighed. "I don't—do you want to know?"

Truthfully, she did and didn't. But, on an impulse, she nodded and closed her eyes.

After a beat, Auten answered. "He ended his life two years after the vote."

If felt like someone squeezed the air out of her lungs as tears burned behind her eyelids. Hudson was everything to Hyphen—*everything*. Yes, losing her family was traumatic and unbearably awful, but the same could be said for Hyphen losing his brother and father figure. On a ragged breath, she opened her eyes, letting the tears fall. She couldn't help holding both Hyphen and Hudson in her heart—two gentle souls. As she wiped her face, a deep understanding dawned on her: why he had ended things. Reliving the moment in his office, she recognized the fear in his eyes. It was the same fear she had seen when they first met—when he thought she was going to die.

"You think," she started, twisting her fingers in her lap. "You think that's why he ended it? Why he didn't challenge Horace?"

"I'm confident that's why. He and his brother were close, right?"

"Hudson raised him," she said, lowering her head.

Auten released a heavy breath. "Fell, if Horace threatened to put you in Containment, there's no way Hyphen wouldn't believe him. He'd already lost someone he loved to Horace..."

She felt sick. Yes, Hyphen was back with Bronwyn, but that didn't diminish what he had done for her or the fear he felt when Horace confronted him. Nothing was as simple as black or white. They lived in the murky waters of the in-between, trying to make the best out of shitty situations. And this was the shittiest of all.

"This is a lot, Grandpa," she said, rubbing her temples.

"I know, sweetheart."

"So, our ancestors were hybrids? That's why we're magical? Why I'm...an *element manipulator*?" she asked, though the question sounded ridiculous even to her own ears.

"In a way, yes, but only the women are magical," he clarified. Auten's face grew solemn. He closed his eyes for a long moment before opening them again. "Do you remember the bedtime story Granny Reathe used to tell you about a beautiful Aechaih queen who loved her people dearly? So much that when evil threatened the kingdom, she sacrificed her own life to save her baby girl, who would one day become the next Queen of Trianah."

Auten might as well have been speaking a foreign language—she had no recollection of that bedtime story. "No. I don't remember, but it sounds precious."

"It was, but your mother urged her to stop."

"Why?"

"She didn't think it was time."

"Time for what?"

"*Solneur*—I've been trying to figure out how to tell you," Auten said, more to himself than to her. "Then you had the accident. Once you were okay, I was afraid to bring it up because you'd already been through so much. I...forgive me, Fellowship. I've been a coward," he said, tears welling in his eyes.

"Grandpa," she said calmly. "Whatever it is, just tell me."

He nodded and gathered himself. "You're right. That particular bedtime story was about Queen Aniyah. *She* was the Aechaih queen who sacrificed her life for her baby and future heiresses."

"Oh, like an alternate reality," she said with a smile. "That's sweet."

"It wasn't an alternate reality. It really happened."

She frowned. "Rhoman murdered Queen Aniyah and their unborn baby."

"No. The truth is, she escaped to the Itchan Forest and found Daelyn, a royal healer who had served in the palace when she was a girl. Daelyn delivered the baby and swore to keep her safe. Queen Aniyah knew that to protect her child and future heiresses, she'd have to return to the palace and die. In gratitude for her sacrifice, Sylena the Moon Goddess ensured that all of the queen's power would be hidden in the baby's bloodline and passed on to the next Aechaih queen."

There wasn't enough Zion's Ink in the world to help her comprehend what the fuck her grandfather was talking about. "Wait," she said, shaking her head, "so, who killed her?"

"No one knows. All we know was that it *wasn't* Rhoman."

"How could you possibly you know that? Who kept this information safe for a thousand years?" she asked, sounding skeptical.

"Lazlo Lysine helped her escape to the forest and later assisted in returning her to the palace after the baby was born. In the midst of chaos, as he sneaked her in, they found Rhoman dead, lying among a heap of humans. That's when she made Lazlo promise to leave the palace and return to the forest to protect the baby. He reluctantly agreed and spent his days safeguarding Queen Aniyah's heirs," Auten said.

Head spinning, she closed her eyes to process her grandfather's story. "Okay, so let me get this straight: it's the *Kumalada,* and everyone's celebrating until Rhoman and his followers start slaughtering Aechaih to gain control of the kingdom."

"Yes."

"Everyone was led to believe that Rhoman killed the queen, which led to the creation of the Tri-Family Council."

"Yes."

"But according to Lazlo Lysine, Rhoman *didn't* kill her, and no one knows who did. We can only assume it was someone from her court."

"Yes."

"Therefore, it wasn't Rhoman's coup—it was the Tri-Family Council's."

"Yes."

Fuck! She and Hyphen weren't crazy, they were right! Rhoman was targeted just like Manicow, Nigh, and Rey. Because Rhoman was already dead, the killer couldn't use him to murder the queen, so they probably did it themselves.

"Why overthrow the queen? I thought life in Trianah was peaceful during her reign," she asked.

"As peaceful as it was, some Aechaih weren't happy with humans having equal rights, especially with the increasing population of hybrids. She was murdered because she refused to treat humans as less than Aechaih."

Their hunch was right and the killer was out to finish the job. But before she could get into *that* shit, there was something else she needed to clarify. "Your story alleges that Queen Aniyah's heir survived."

"It's not alleged, it's true."

"Fine," she said, rolling her eyes. "And the queen's power was hidden in the baby's bloodline to be gifted to the next Aechaih queen."

"Yes."

"When will that be?"

Auten took a beat. Then another. Then another.

"When. Will. That. Be. Grandpa?"

"The next *Kumalada*."

"Grandpa, please," she said, slumping back in her chair. "You're claiming the new Aechaih queen is supposed to ascend the throne during the next *Kumalada*? C'mon," she said, clearly unconvinced.

Auten didn't waiver; instead, he lifted his chin. "The Aechaih queen's heir survived and had a daughter, who had a daughter, all the way down to a baby girl born forty-two years ago," he said, his eyes suggesting more than she was ready to accept.

Her hands itching with heat, Fellowship swallowed hard. Her mind raced, sifting through memories, books, essays, academic journals —*anything* to make sense of what she was hearing. Nothing. *Forty-two,* wait. She sat up so quickly that the room began to spin. Holding her head, she closed her eyes.

"Forty-two years ago? The heir's supposed to be forty-two?"

"Yes, Fell. She's forty-two..."

Fellowship opened one eye and looked at her grandfather, laughing softly. "You're not saying *I'm* Queen Aniyah's heir, are you? And that's why I'm a hybrid?" she asked, still laughing.

Auten grabbed his chair and dragged it closer to her. Taking her hand in his, he maintained eye contact. The whole scene was eerie— eerie, dramatic, and...*impossible.*

Auten held her gaze. "You're Queen Aniyah's heir and an *Aechaih* with all of her power—the power that Sylena the Moon Goddess bestowed upon her over two thousand years ago."

Guardians, help her. Keeping her hand in his, she leaned forward. "Grandpa, I'm not Aechaih—look at me," she said over a giggle.

"Yes, you present as human, but that's for a reason."

Laughter still tickling her, she leaned back. "What reason is that? Please, enlighten me."

Undeterred, Auten continued. "When Sylena hid Queen Aniyah's power in her bloodline, she ensured that the heir would be Aechaih rather than a hybrid. The human form was meant to protect the baby while also ensuring she understood the human experience. It was a gift, sweetheart."

The joke had gone too far. She was exhausted—all she wanted was to go home, take a shower, and sleep for the next six months. She didn't want to hear her grandfather ramble on about some outlandish, unbelievable nonsense. "Grandpa, I'm not Queen Aniyah's heir," she sighed. "Clearly, I'm not Aechaih. Yes, I might've had magical abilities back in the day, but I assume it's because I'm a descendant of someone who survived the massacre."

"Exactly. You're the descendant of Queen Aniyah's heir who *survived the massacre.*"

"No, Grandpa," she said sternly. She had no interest in playing this game anymore.

Auten didn't respond. Instead, he pursed his lips and held her gaze —the very gaze she'd known since she was a girl. In that gaze, she saw her childhood and the smiling faces of her mother, grandmother, and father. She felt their love and sensed their pride. She felt her grandfather's love—a love that would *never* lie to her. The truth made her stomach churn. Letting go of his hand, she rubbed her palms on her leggings and cleared her throat. Her body felt different—misaligned.

Shaking her head, she frowned. "It doesn't make sense. Mom and Granny Reathe were what? Aechaih. Human. Hybrid?" she asked, frowning through her headache.

"Essentially, they were hybrids."

She sucked her teeth. "And why didn't the generations prior to me take the throne? If they were all heirs, why wait until now? This *Kumalada*. This alignment?"

"It's divine purpose. When you were born, we prepared you for ten years. You were gifted, Fell—an El-man and intuitive, at the very least. Then everything changed. We lost our family, and we were alone. You lived a normal human life with Queen Aniyah's dormant power inside of you."

Fellowship stood and stumbled to the sink, bracing her hands on the cool counter. Her mouth watered as acidic vomit surged up and splashed into the basin. Stomach cramping, another wave erupted as Auten rushed over to rub her back. Eyes watering, she clutched the counter while her stomach expelled breakfast, lunch, and Zion's Ink. Jagged and disoriented, she gasped for air as another wave pushed through her and into the sink. Auten turned on the water, wet a cloth, and laid it on her neck, flicking water around the sink until the vomit swirled down the drain. Coughing and dry heaving, she remained hunched over the sink until she was sure nothing else would come up. Taking the towel from her neck, Auten gently wiped her forehead.

"I'm sorry, honey. I'm so, so sorry. I waited and waited and..." he trailed off, patting her forehead.

Standing, she turned and leaned against the counter. Taking the towel, she unfolded it and pressed it to her face, savoring the coolness. Deep breaths—in and out—were techniques she used to calm herself after a nightmare. Clearly, this had to be a nightmare. One of her vivid dreams; all she had to do was wake up. The knowing, the sensing, the healing, the ability to men-com—it all slid into place. A sob erupted from within as she realized it wasn't a dream. Opening her mouth, a wail tore from her throat as Auten rubbed her back. Shoulders shaking, she sobbed uncontrollably. The violence of memory split her open, leaving nothing hidden—everything she was had been exposed. An *Aechaih?* She was a Solneur-damned Aechaih? What the fuck? Wiping her tears with the towel, she looked at her grandfather.

"What's happening?" she hiccupped through her sobs. "*Why* is this happening?"

"It's who you are. Who you've always been."

Blinking back tears, Auten quickly moved around her, grabbing a glass. He filled it with water and handed it to her. Taking a tentative sip, she crossed her arms and shook her head as tears reappeared, blurring her vision.

"This isn't real," she whispered.

Her stomach sore, she took another sip of water. It couldn't be true. Rhoman, a pawn in a fucking uprising. Queen Aniyah delivering her baby and then returning to the palace to be killed by *someone* in her own court. Lazlo, the gallant captain of the queen's guard.

"I hope," Auten started. "I hope you can forgive me," he whispered.

Looking at him, she frowned. "Forgive you for what?"

Dejected, he leaned against the refrigerator. "For withholding the truth. For telling you to stop practicing your abilities. For not keeping our family's memory alive," he said, bowing his head.

Setting down her glass, she wrapped her arms around him. He squeezed her tightly, letting out a muffled cry. They hugged for their shared loss, for misguided notions and misunderstandings, for misplaced anger, fear, and doubt.

"It's okay, Grandpa. To be fair, I spent a portion of my life not talking to you. All of that lost time," she said, resting her head on his shoulder. "For that *I'm* sorry."

Drawing back, he smiled through his tears. "No apology."

"Yes, apology." Giving him another hug, she took a deep breath, inhaling Auten's familiar scent. Funny, he still smelled like the forest.

Pulling away, she grabbed her water and sat down. "You realize there's no throne for me to take, right?" she said, looking up at him.

"Yes, there is."

"The Tri-Family Council—"

"Built their power on a lie. Sylena knew what she was doing when she hid Queen Aniyah's power in her bloodline. It's going to take all of that power to reclaim the throne, Fellowship," Auten said. "You see what's going on here. You have a heart for the people. This is the only way you're going to be able to help them. Regardless of Trianah Metropolitan, it's still the *Kingdom* of Trianah, and you're the heir to the throne. Only you can restore human rights. Only you can bring peace to this land."

Was he serious? A manic laugh bubbled up and out of her. Stomach still sore, she laughed and laughed as tears crept down her face. She laughed and laughed and laughed because it was ridiculous. So. Fucking. Ridiculous. Wiping her eyes, she looked at Auten who was less than amused.

"Grandpa..."

With a face set in seriousness, he held up his hand and left the kitchen. Suppressing her leftover giggles, she sipped her water. When Auten returned, he sat down and handed her a scuffed wooden ring box. His face held no trace of glee. Taking a deep breath, she opened it. Setting the lid on the table, she peered inside. There, resting on a tuft of cream satin, was a gold leaf band ring. She drew in a sharp breath, recognizing its ancient significance and its original owner. Tears welled in her eyes as she looked up at Auten whose face had softened.

"Is this...?" she whispered, unable to complete the sentence. How? How could something so rare end up in her hands?

"After the queen's baby was born, she had only a brief time with her. She left her royal ring with Daelyn, instructing her to ensure that it passed down through each generation, so that when the time came, her heiress would wear it."

Wiping her eyes, Fellowship let out a tiny sob before gently touching the ring. It was exquisite, and it belonged to her and those who came before. Her head felt too heavy for her body; it was all *too* much.

"We moved to the city because the forest was no longer safe. I was confident that the Council assumed there wasn't an heir, but I needed to keep an eye on things. That's why I became Human Ambassador—"

"*That's* why you became Human Ambassador? I thought—"

"I made connections and built relationships. When the time was right, I proposed to the Council that an ambassador was what Trianah needed to bridge the gap between humans and Aechaih. Given the rise in human tensions, they agreed."

Letting out a breath, Fellowship rubbed her face and then looked at him. Despite her confusion and frustration, she was certain he was telling the truth; after all, she was holding Queen Aniyah's fucking *ring*. It was impossible for her to grasp everything at that moment or to process what she'd learned. While it made sense, it all seemed improbable. She needed time to work through it, but something told her that time was a luxury she didn't have.

Chapter Twenty-Two

"You wanna get up, take a shower, and eat?"

Pulled out of sleep, Hyphen's eyes opened. The room was dark and his head was spinning. He rolled over, clicked on the light, and blinked until things came into focus. He saw Soren leaning in the doorway. With a chalky mouth, he rubbed his face.

"What are you doing here?"

"Wellness check. Get up and take a fucking shower. I brought food," he said, disappearing down the hall.

Hyphen didn't want to get up; he preferred being a sad-sack. But knew his friend wouldn't take no for an answer. Sitting up, he groaned—he felt like shit. Sighing, he dragged his sad ass to the bathroom.

Hair wet and headache subsiding, Hyphen padded to the kitchen where he found Soren sitting on a stool, scrolling through his phone. Looking up, Soren gave him a satisfied nod before standing and entering the kitchen. Hyphen slid onto a stool and rested his head in his hands as the smell of food made his stomach growl. He couldn't remember the last time he had a real meal instead of a handful of chips washed down with whiskey. Soren slid a plate in front of him, along with a fork, and then sat down to dig into his own dinner.

"Thanks," Hyphen mumbled, shoving a mound of food into his mouth.

"The twins called me, worried because they haven't heard from you. What's going on?"

"Horace kicked me off the case and said that that if I didn't end it with Fell, he'd send her to Containment for breaking the law."

"Containment? Why? What happened?"

"I bit her. We saw Horace a week later, and he sensed it."

Soren's eyes went wide. "You *mated* with her?"

"Yeah."

"What—what was it like?"

Hyphen looked up. His friend was serious. "No words."

"*Fuck*. Then you ended it?"

"I had to, didn't I?"

"I know you can't underestimate Horace, so yeah."

"Exactly," he said, shoveling more food into his mouth.

"And Fellowship? She understood?"

She understood plenty: that he abandoned her, didn't fight for their love, and ended things with her in his office. But instead of saying that, he grumbled something inaudible. Still, Soren understood.

"Fair," Soren said with a nod. "Mom said she saw you at the Casino Night. Was that before or after?"

"After. I'd already agreed to take my mom," he said, thinking about how shitty he felt that night. Drinking his feelings had kept him from finding an empty stall in the restroom to cry. "Bronwyn was there," he added.

"Yikes."

"She came up to me at the bar, spewed some of her venom, and made sure one of the photographers got a shot of us. Who does that?"

"A certified bitch."

Hyphen huffed a laugh. "I've been to work and here ever since."

"If you're off the case, who's working with Fellowship?"

"Monroe," he said, gulping down some water. Letting out a sigh, he actually felt less like death.

"That's not bad. At least you trust him," Soren mused. "Have you seen her since?"

Closing his eyes, all he could see was her in that black dress. "Yeah."

"That bad?"

Hyphen looked at his friend. "Worse and who can blame her? I broke her fucking heart. Saw the exact moment it happened. It's on repeat in my head."

"Your heart's broken, too," Soren said gently.

"I deserve it."

"Why? Your father's a sociopath. You *had* to end it. It was the right thing to do."

"Was it? She wanted to fight..." What was the point of explaining? Running his hands through his hair, he stood, grabbed his plate, and took it to the kitchen. Barely able to look at his friend, he leaned against the counter.

"What?" Soren asked, his blue hair falling over his forehead.

"I'm a coward for obeying my father. I'm an asshole for hurting her. I'm trash for thinking it was easier to let her go than to lose her."

"Easier to let her go? I don't get it," Soren said with a frown.

"How long would she have stayed with me? I mean...she would've left me, right?"

Soren frowned, then after a moment, it clicked. "Like Hudson," he whispered.

Flinching, Hyphen stalked out of the kitchen and through his living area. Standing at the window, he shoved his hands into his jogger pockets. He heard Soren sit on the sofa.

"You might not want to hear this, but Fellowship's in love with you. You wouldn't have lost her."

"How can you be so sure?" Hyphen mumbled, turning to face his friend.

"She let you bite her. Fellowship Dancy isn't a stupid woman, Hyphen. She *chose* to let you, an *Aechaih*, claim her."

"Full disclosure—I didn't tell her how serious it was until later."

"Was she pissed?"

"No. She was just concerned about her shorter lifespan but..." he trailed off.

"But what?"

"But Horace told me that the main reason for the anti-miscegenation law is that if an Aechaih bonds with a human, the human's aging slows to match that of their partner."

"Wait...is that true?"

"My father's an asshole, but he's not a liar."

"Therefore the threat of putting Fellowship in Containment becomes even worse. Bro, your *dad...*" Soren said, shaking his head.

"Fell wanted to fight him. Fight for us."

"Does that sound like a woman who was going to eventually leave you?"

"That's the problem," he said. "She would've been sent to Containment for me, and I couldn't let that happen."

"I understand, but it sounds like you don't think you're worth fighting for—worth the sacrifice. At least that's the vibe I'm getting."

"I'm not."

"That's fucking bullshit, Has, and you know it," Soren snapped.

Hyphen blinked at the shock of his friend's pushback.

"You're not the piece of shit you think you are. You're a loyal fucking friend, an amazing brother, good son, and a good cop. You show up for people, even when you don't show up for yourself. How the fuck can you walk around here thinking you're not worth anything?"

Swallowing, Hyphen looked down. He was so used to thinking the worst of himself that it felt uncomfortable hearing someone else's perspective of him. Letting go of the part of himself that had been shunned, cast aside, laughed at, and abandoned was difficult.

Soren continued. "I get it. The way you were treated when you were young was fucked up. But despite that, you were loved. Your brother *loved* you. He did everything for you—"

"He fucking left me!" Hyphen yelled.

The outburst surprised both Soren and himself. Taking a step back, he bumped into the glass. Trapped and embarrassed, he looked around for an escape. He slid his eyes to Soren, who sat on the edge of the sofa, elbows on his thighs, head down.

"I didn't mean to—I'm sorry, Syx," he mumbled. What a fucking dick. First, he abandoned Fellowship, and now he snarled at his friend. Dejected and exhausted, Hyphen flopped on a chair.

After a few moments, Soren looked at him, his face was solemn and his eyes almost glowing blue. He sighed. "There's nothing to apologize for. You're right—Hudson left. He did. But that doesn't mean he didn't love you."

Hyphen nodded unable to find the right words. It was hard to deny Hudson's love for him, but it was equally hard not to feel abandoned— just as he had abandoned Fellowship.

"You're not a piece of shit, Has," Soren added. "And pushing Fellowship away in order to avoid some imagined future doesn't solve anything. I believe you were protecting her, but don't sell yourself some lie that you're unlovable and that in the end, she would've left you because that's bullshit."

Looking at his friend, he nodded. He may never get her back or figure out how to best his father, but Soren was right. Although he felt like a piece of shit, he wasn't. Although he sometimes felt unlovable, he was very much loved. Not only by the girls, but his brother, best friend, and Fellowship Dancy.

Fellowship can't contain her excitement as she and her grandpa wander through the forest. The sodden ground squishes beneath her tiny bare feet as she brushes past every leaf and flower. The forest air is wild, natural, and sweet, like ciambe fruit. Her grandfather glances back at her with a loving smile, his eyes bright. Fireflies flit around her, some landing in her thick, black hair. Looking up, she glimpses Solneur through the canopy of lush, green trees and waves at him before continuing to follow her grandpa. They finally reach a clearing dotted with large boulders, velvety grass, and a clear, gurgling creek.

"Well, girl, show me what you've got," her grandfather says, leaning against a tree. Biting her lip, she sits cross-legged on the ground, moisture damping her thin pants.

"Watch this," she says, eyeing Auten. He nods and smiles as she takes a deep breath. Closing her eyes, she focuses her attention on the sounds of the forest. Its symphonic melody bounces along her ears. Resting her hands palms up on her thighs, she continues breathing until the sounds disappear. Immediately, her hands warm just as she lifts them off her thighs, centering them in front of her—left palm hovering over the right. The heat intensifies until she can feel the softness of fire take form between her small, brown hands. After a moment, she opens her eyes and looks at her grandfather. His face is slack with shock.

"You did it!" he exclaims.

Nodding in concentration, Fellowship gathers the orb of flame, centering it in her right hand. Standing, she carefully walks to her grandpa who meets her halfway.

"Look at you, girl," he says, looking at the flickering ball of fire.

"Watch this," she says. She turns toward the creek and launches the orb; it disappears, in a puff of steam. Then, stepping to the edge of the water, she stretches out her thin arms in front of her, palms down. After a moment, thin ribbons of water rise up to meet her; swirling her arms, she expands them over her head, hands reaching toward the sky. Droplets of water shoot up then fall around them. Turning around, she grins at her grandfather whose face looks different—worried.

"What's wrong?" she asks, walking toward him.

"Where did you—I thought you could only manipulate flame."

"I did, too," she squeaks, bouncing on her feet. "But the other night, I got a funny feeling that I could manipulate fire, water, land, and air. So, I've been practicing and now I can move fire and water."

"Solneur," her grandfather breathes.

She wraps her arms around him, squeezing him as tightly as she can. "I love you, Grandpa," she says, her voice muffled.

He squeezes her back. "I love you, too, so very much—"

The bright forest darkens, turning ominous and foreboding. Suddenly, she's running; her heart struggles to keep up with her pace. She feels the ground dig into her bare feet. Fear has taken root as she scrambles for what to do. As stems slash at her face, she continues to run. She'll never make it. Figure it out. All is lost. The agony of defeat chases her down as she stumbles onto the sodden ground. Grabbing her stomach, she wails in pain—

Fellowship woke with a labored breath. Disoriented, she looked around until her eyes focused on her bedroom rather than the forest. She was safe and, more importantly, not in pain—at least not physical. Wiping sweat from her forehead and neck, she sat up and leaned against her headboard. After a few more calming breaths and finished it in a few gulps.

She was magical.

She was Aechaih.

She was the heir to the throne of Trianah.

She was scared.

Her eyes landed on the scuffed ring box, resting on her nightstand. How in Guardians' name was she supposed to process this shit? Nigh and Rey were still detained. The case had stalled, yet something told her that darkness lurked on the horizon, biding its time. Throwing back the duvet, she stood and went to the window. Looking out over Trianah, she saw the darkness of the sea in the distance.

She missed Hyphen.

More than anything, she wanted to step into his arms so he could hug her and tell her that everything would be okay. It was one thing to discover her past and another to discover it alone, separated from the person she loved. His bite on her neck pulsed, like a GPS desperate to reach home. The dull ache in her chest, persistent since she'd left his office, refused to fade. Her love for him was all-consuming, ingrained so deeply in her bones that she couldn't—nor did she want to—remove him from her system.

According to her grandfather, she was Aechaih. Besides taking a non-existent throne, she and Hyphen could be together legally. As much as she wanted that, wanted *him*, she was terrified. Did she really want to give her all to him only to be let down again? It didn't matter since he was with Bronwyn and she had a lot of ancestral-heiress-to-the-throne shit to deal with. Her stomach growled as she glanced at the clock on her nightstand: 1:30 AM, the perfect time for a late-night snack.

Fellowship's mouth watered as she entered Santander's. She hadn't eaten anything since losing her breakfast and lunch at her grandfather's the day before. Approaching the counter, Mrs. Santander appeared from the kitchen with a smile.

"Detective, how are you?" she asked, wiping her hands on a stained apron. Face red from working in the kitchen, Mrs. Santander had the kind of warm, welcoming face that Fellowship needed to see in the middle of the night.

"I'm doing well, what are you doing working the night shift?"

The old woman shrugged. "I don't mind. Don't need much sleep anymore these days. Your usual?"

"Yes, ma'am, I'd appreciate it," Fellowship said, pulling a wad of bills from her jacket pocket.

Mrs. Santander frowned. "Detective, you know your money's no good here," she said, swatting Fellowship's hand. They'd been doing the same song and dance since Fellowship became a regular after joining the force. Mrs. Santander disappeared around the back, giving her enough time to stuff a bunch of bills into the tip jar. Turning around, she paused and smiled. There was Sylve tucked away in the alcove by the window.

Approaching, Fellowship shook her head. "What are you doing out so late?"

"Detective! Guardians, it's good to see you," she said, smiling. "Oh, I like to pop over to get a midnight snack when I can. Care to join?"

Taking off her jacket, Fellowship hooked it on the back of the chair and sat down. "Thank you," she said, setting her keys and phone on the table. Bright-eyed, Sylve nodded and resumed eating.

"Here you are," Mrs. Santander said, setting Fellowship's bowl down in front of her.

"This looks great, thank you."

With a pat on the shoulder, Mrs. Santander shuffled away. Picking up the spoon, she dipped into her broth and took a moment to moan over the warmth spreading through her chest.

"Delicious, isn't it?" Sylve asked with a smirk.

"Unbeatable. How are you?"

"Oh, Detective, I can't complain. The Guardians are good to me," she said, wiping her soft, wrinkled hands on a napkin. Her halo of hair seemed to glow under the restaurant's lights.

"I'm happy to hear that."

"How's your case coming along?"

Fellowship sat back and wiped her mouth. "A little harder than I thought it would be, but I'm hoping for a breakthrough."

Sylve nodded. "If anyone can figure it out, it's you."

There was something special about an older person's belief system. Their wisdom always offered a higher perspective. If she didn't know any better, she'd say that Sylve was one of her biggest supporters. "I appreciate your vote of confidence."

"Absolutely. Now, tell me," Sylve said, setting down her spoon and leaning forward. "How's that beautiful Aechaih of yours?" she asked, eyes dazzling.

Fellowship didn't realize she could flinch and flutter at the thought of someone, but she did. "Detective Haslem's no longer on the case," she said quickly, returning to her soup.

Sylve's blue eyes narrowed. "Oh, no. What happened?"

She shrugged. "Politics."

"I hate to hear that. You two are still friends, right? From what I can tell, he likes you," Sylve said with an encouraging nod. Her cheer scraped at Fellowship's open wound of sadness.

"Um." She wasn't sure how to proceed, so she continued eating. There was no way she'd expose her love life to Sylve, even if the woman had an uncanny ability to make her feel safe.

"Oh, I see," Sylve said with an omniscient nod.

"Pardon?"

Sylve's face melted into a smile. "I see that you like him, too, but something happened," she said.

Okay, so more than an ability to make her comfortable, she could also read minds.

"Tell me what happened with you and your Aechaih, Detective."

Setting her spoon down because trying to eat was futile, she held the woman's gaze. Immediately, hurt, disappointment, and confusion pressed at her until she looked away in a pathetic attempt to hide her tears.

"Oh, Detective," Sylve breathed, sliding her a napkin.

Taking it, Fellowship dried her eyes, utterly embarrassed.

"Humor an old woman and tell me what happened," Sylve pressed. Sylve's care, wisdom, and attention snapped Fellowship's resolve in two. Tears flowing at a steady pace, she sniffed, wiping her eyes.

"I'm sorry," she mumbled.

"Don't you *dare* apologize. It's clear you're hurting. Tell me why."

Swallowing down a lump of heartbreak, she twisted the napkin in her hands. "You were right. We liked each other and grew very close. As you know, his family serves on the Tri-Family Council. One of his family members discovered our relationship and threatened him, saying that if he didn't end it, I'd be prosecuted for breaking the law."

"*Guardians,*" Sylve breathed. "I assume the family member you're referring to is Horace Haslem?"

Fellowship nodded.

"Did he threaten to put his son in Containment as well?"

"No, ma'am."

Sylve scoffed, clearly indignant. "What a despicable thing to do to young love," she said, shaking her head. "If you're sitting here in this much pain, that means he ended things. Am I right?"

"Yes. You know me, Miss Sylve. I don't back down from a fight."

Eyes bright with agreement, Sylve smiled. "Absolutely not. It's why some of us in Pawville have managed to hold on as long as we can.

Because of people like you," she said, then returned to her noodles. Smacking, she munched away. Fellowship returned to hers, grateful for the abrupt pause in conversation. After finishing her noodles, Sylve tipped her bowl, dipped her spoon in, and took a long slurp before setting it down and wiping her mouth. Then, she fixed her gaze on Fellowship.

"Do you love Detective Haslem?"

Fellowship looked up and frowned. "That's beside the point. I get why he did it, why he walked away, but the pain—"

"Yes or no, Detective?" Sylve responded with a smile.

Fellowship's mouth snapped shut as she set down her spoon. Sylve's eyes remained warm and open even if she had just come for Fellowship's soul. Biting her lip, she twisted the napkin in her hand.

"Yes, ma'am."

"I thought so. Can I share something with you? I only ask because sometimes young folks don't want to hear what us old folks have to say —they think they know it all."

Guilty as charged. Leaning in, she nodded. "Please."

"I've found that loving is hard and painful—not love itself, but how we choose to engage with it. I've learned that when we choose to love, we choose to accept someone for who they are," Sylve said, clasping her hands on the table.

"I did choose to accept him," Fellowship countered. She did nothing but accept Hyphen for who he was. But when it came time for him to accept the fight within her, he walked away.

Sylve nodded and smiled. "Did you continue accepting him after he hurt you? After he *chose* to do what he thought was right?"

Although the question was simple, its meaning detonated inside of her heart, releasing a mushroom cloud of perspective, quickly followed by guilt. As soon as Hyphen made a decision she didn't agree with, she shut down. There was no conversation or seeking to understand and there definitely wasn't acceptance. Wiping her eyes, she looked at the woman.

"No, ma'am."

"I know, honey. Choices are difficult because they come from various places within us. Your Aechaih was afraid, so he chose to end things with you in order to keep you safe. You were hurt, so you chose to take his choice at face value instead of accepting him and his fear. And now you're choosing to be upset with him, but I don't think you're upset as much as you're afraid of what it all means."

Blinking through her tears, Fellowship shrugged. "What does it mean?"

Sylve smiled. "It means you love him, Detective."

Dropping her head, Fellowship's shoulders shook as Sylve's words exposed the raw, aching truth.

"Oh, honey. It's okay," Sylve said, sliding her another napkin. "I think it's safe to say that no one's hurt you as much as your Aechaih. *That's* what scares you, but you still have a choice."

"I don't—I don't know what choice to make."

"Sure, you do. Love is a choice, Detective. Love is choosing to accept someone without stipulating that they never hurt you. Never make mistakes. Never be afraid and make a choice out of that fear. When we love, we choose to accept. We choose to trust. We choose to be vulnerable, open, and exposed. We choose it even if we're afraid."

Leg shaking under the table, Fellowship sniffed. Through her tear-filled eyes, she could barely make out the woman's smile. Sylve took Fellowship's hand and, with an incredibly soft and warm touch, gently rubbed the back of it with her thumb.

"It's okay. Situations like this arise when it's time to leave our comfort zone. And the most effective way to do that is through love."

Wiping her eyes with a tattered napkin, Fellowship nodded. "Facts," she choked out.

Sylve laughed. "My Kahleb says that all the time," she said, handing Fellowship another napkin. "Now, answer me again, do you love your Aechaih?"

Sylve wasn't asking whether she loved the idea of Hyphen, but did she love the man. Did she love him without conditions or fine print? As her heart searched for the answer she already knew, she saw him: his green eyes and bashful, sexy smile. His intellect and care. Thoughtfulness and support. Her number one fan. His hugs when she was sad. His listening ear. His melodic laughter. There wasn't anything he wouldn't do for her. Fellowship didn't require these things from him—she didn't have to. He offered them freely because it was the kind of man he was. Yes, he made a choice. Agree with it or not, who was she to withhold her love—withhold her acceptance? Who was she to attach a price to something so priceless? It felt natural to love Hyphen, to be in his space, and share his world. And of course, the little old woman who prayed to the Guardians that she lived was right. Love was a choice. It was acceptance. As she accepted herself and some of the choices she'd made, it became evident that she needed to do the same for Hyphen.

Fellowship looked at Sylve and smiled through her tears. She was grateful for the little old woman. Until then, she had no fucking clue what love was. Sure, she had the feelings—the tingles. She had the daydreams and bold declarations, but Sylve offered her the truth about love—the truth she needed to hear. The truth that saw past the surface level down to the core of who she was: a woman who had been through some shit, but finally understood the nuances and complexities that came with love. With choices. Her heart ached for Hyphen. She could care less about Bronwyn or Horace. She was heir to the fucking hypothetical throne of Trianah and she needed her winged Aechaih and all of his lovely, thoughtful, protective love.

Chapter Twenty-Three

Hyphen finished his last set, placed the barbells on the rack, grabbed a towel, and sat on the bench. Out of breath, he looked around for his water. *Fuck.* He'd forgotten it. Rolling his eyes, he wiped his face, then looked at himself in the mirror. Since his conversation with Soren, he got rid of his beard-of-despair and put some effort into his appearance at work, but that was the extent of it. He was still heartbroken. Not being with Fellowship was like losing a vital organ and while he knew it sounded dramatic, the shit was true. Every time he got in his vehicle, he'd get an overwhelming sense of panic like he'd forgotten something. In the middle of the night, he'd roll over, reaching out for her only to find empty air. After remembering that they were no longer together because he was a fuck-up, he'd press her pillow to his face, inhaling what was left of her scent, then fall asleep with it in his arms. His phone buzzed. Picking it up, he groaned in disgust.

Horace: Your mother and I are coming over tonight. Be home.

Under no circumstances did he want to see him. That fucking piece of shit had done enough damage. If he wasn't bringing his mother, he'd tell him to fuck off but instead, he gave a curt reply.

Hyphen: Fine.

Sighing, he put his head in his hands. Fellowship Dancy had changed everything. Because of her, he wanted to live—to wake up every morning and see her stunning face, hear her infectious laugh, and feel her hands in his hair. Because of her, he had a renewed sense of enjoyment at his job. Researching, brainstorming, and finding suspects went from tedious to exciting because she was with him. Since losing her, days at the office were barely tolerable; in fact, the vibrance Fellowship brought to his life had been erased, leaving his existence drab and gray. Lost, he didn't know how to fix his mistake. Did he show up at her place and apologize for being a coward? Or better yet, men-com so that she could *feel* his regret? What combination of words would heal her heart?

You made this decision, Hyphen. You did, not me. Remember that.

How could he forget? He relived the moment all day, every day. Standing, he suppressed his grief and walked out of his gym. Heading to the kitchen, he got an overwhelming whiff of warm shea butter and perfume. Up his nose, it swirled around his brain, triggering an intense flood of memories. Stopping, he looked upward—were the Guardians trying to kill him? If so, the least they could do was speed up the process. Rounding the corner, he stopped as the two pieces of his broken heart shot to his throat.

There she was, standing by his elevator. She wore one of his sweaters with leggings and trainers. Her diamond studs glinted in the light, illuminating her face. What was happening? Was this real? Nothing was out of place, so he wasn't dreaming. Was she there to pick up what little stuff she'd left behind? Feet nailed to the floor, towel in his hand, and a sweaty mess, he just stared—stared at her like a fucking idiot. Tugging on the sleeves, she bit her lip—that's when he realized something was off. Something beyond what was going on between them.

"Fell, what's wrong?" he asked, frowning.

Her shoulders sagged as tears streamed down her face. Approaching him, she hiccupped on uneven breaths but remained silent. When she met him halfway, she threw herself into him with such force that he had to steady himself to avoid falling. With her arms around him and her face pressed into his t-shirt, she cried—her sobs raw and uncontrollable, tearing at his insides. He held her close, resting his chin on top of her head, and took a deep, steadying breath. These tears weren't solely about him; whoever had her crying like this would face his wrath once he got his hands on them. For now, he had to keep his wings in, stay calm, and find out what was going on.

"Baby, tell me what's wrong," he whispered. Trembling, she sobbed but gave no answer. Rubbing her back, he tried again. "Fell, I can't help until you tell me what's wrong." Finally, pulling back, but still clutching his shirt, she looked up at him with puffy, bloodshot eyes that almost ended him.

"Everything's fucked up and I couldn't tell you because we weren't talking and then I talked to Sylve and realized and I came over to tell you but then I saw you and..." she said on one breath, hugging him again.

Okay. From what he could tell, something was fucked up, but he wasn't sure what. And maybe something happened to Miss Sylve? Drawing back, he took his towel and dabbed her tears. Watery eyes on him, she offered the saddest, cutest smile he'd ever seen.

"Did something happen to Miss Sylve?"

"No."

"Is Nigh and Rey okay?"

"I think they are. It's just *too much,* Hyphen, I can't," she cried, burying her face back into his chest.

What the entire fuck was going on? He had two choices: find out who hurt her (besides him, of course) and kill them or get her to talk. He hated to do it, but he had to; otherwise, he couldn't help her.

"*Fellowship,*" he snapped, grabbing her arms. "What. The. Fuck. Is. Going. On? Who do I have to kill for making you cry like this?"

Eyes wide, she sniffed back a sob. "No one, Hyphen. You don't have to kill anyone."

"Then *please* tell me what happened," he begged.

Blinking rapidly, she nodded as tears continued to fall. She looked so small, so vulnerable. The only thing he could think to do was care for her until she was ready to talk. Hands on her arms, he bent down and draped them around his neck before lifting her up. Face to face, she wasn't *actively* crying, but tears still tracked down her cheeks. With a tender, soul-crushing sigh, she rested her head on his shoulder, hiccupping through sporadic sniffles. Solneur, he loved her so damn much—even if she wasn't there to take him back, holding her in his arms was enough to piece his broken heart back together.

He walked to his bedroom, stopping at the bed. "I'm going to put you down and get you some tea and tissues, okay?"

Without lifting her head, she nodded. He laid her down, then she crawled to the headboard and curled around his pillow. Before leaving, he removed her shoes and draped the cashmere throw over her.

Clenching his jaw, he went to the kitchen. Hands shaking, he put the kettle on, pulled out a mug, and dropped in a teabag. Grabbing a bottle of water, he took a quick swig. Like him, Fellowship had managed to project an icy-cold exterior of togetherness—steady, solid, unbothered. But, like him, the facade could only last so long before cracking under pressure. He assumed that's what had happened, but he didn't know what caused her to break. It must have been significant if she came to him—the person who broke her heart. After the kettle whistled, he made her tea, sliced a lemon, and dropped it in. Snatching a box of tissues from his coffee table, he walked back to his bedroom. She was still curled around his pillow; he sat beside her on the edge of the bed.

"Hey," he whispered. Opening her eyes, she smiled. It was enough to make him cry in relief. Sitting up, she leaned against the headboard and took the mug.

"Thank you," she said, blowing it before taking a tentative sip. Setting the box of tissues on his nightstand, he rubbed her legs.

"You want to tell me what's going on?"

Nodding, she held her mug with two hands in front of her mouth, so all he could see were her red, puffy eyes.

"I'm sorry for the drama," she said, her voice hoarse.

He squeezed her calf. "What's got you so upset? Let's start with the facts."

"Just the facts?"

"Yes."

"I love you."

Startled, his breath hitched in his throat. After a moment, he blinked away the shock. "I love you, too."

"And I've missed you."

Fuck. Now *he* was going to cry. "I've missed you, too, Fell. So fucking much."

Her chin quivering, she fought to suppress a whimper and blinked away more tears. Reaching for a tissue, he leaned in and gently dabbed her face.

"Are there any more facts you'd like to share?" he asked softly.

Nodding, she rested the mug in her lap. "I'm sorry, Hyphen. I'm sorry that I didn't really hear what you were saying when you ended things. I should've asked questions, dug deeper, but I didn't. I made it all about my hurt."

Hyphen was fully aware of how emotionally intelligent she was, but this was another level. Stunned silent, he stared at her. "I'm not sure if you should be sorry, Fell," he said.

"I should be and I am. I never had the courage to ask how you lost Hudson; I didn't know how to approach it, so I didn't. But when I spoke to my grandpa about us, he told me about your brother. I'm so sorry— for everything. For how you lost him and why. It shouldn't have taken discovering that for me to understand and accept the choice you made about us, but once I did..." Shaking her head, she bit her lip as tears snaked down her face.

He was already emotionally fucked-up *before* she showed up a wreck. What was he supposed to do now that *she* was apologizing to *him*? And not only did she apologize but she backed it up with life context that he didn't disclose the last time they talked. Biting down to keep from losing his shit, he tried to focus on the facts.

"Auten knows?"

"Yes. It's just all so fucked up, Hyphen. I—"

"You keep saying that, baby. *What's* fucked up?"

"It was my family that was killed in the forest all those years ago."

Perhaps her words didn't make it to his mind for processing because nothing made sense. The family in the forest—the one his father sanctioned to die—was magical. When she told the twins that she'd lived in the forest and he wondered what had happened to the rest of her family, he never thought—shaking his head, he looked at her for more information.

"I know," she said, nodding. Setting her tea on the nightstand, she rested her hands in her lap. "My grandfather and I talked about a lot of stuff, but one of the things that came up was my past. My family. After essentially reliving what happened to them, I asked him why and he told me that the Council sanctioned our deaths."

The report said they saw an older human woman performing magic. Those were the words his brother had told him after he returned home from a Council meeting. The blood drained from Hyphen's face. Dropped into the memory, he drifted away.

"My father called for the family to be executed but Hudson refused to vote in favor of it. He said that they were a harmless magical family and had every right to continue their life in the forest. Some members agreed with him, so he was outvoted. But that didn't stop him—he campaigned, making ridiculous claims that if the family lived, at some point, Trianah would have another human uprising. After a few weeks, he gathered enough votes, and the Council sanctioned the murders. My brother immediately stopped serving on the Council. He fell into an even deeper depression because, well, not only was he disillusioned, but he also felt like there was blood on his hands. Then two years later, he..." Blinking, Hyphen refocused on the present. Looking at her, he frowned. "I don't understand, how did you and Auten survive?" More like what kind of twist of fate had brought her into his life? Who in Guardians' name would connect them in such a deeply satisfying yet painful way?

She grabbed his hand and laced her fingers through his. "We happened to be on one of our adventures and when we returned..." she said, trailing off.

His eyes slid to hers and there he could see *all* of her. The depth and nuance of her lived experience was unearthed. She was so remarkable, it was breathtaking.

"A harmless magical family in the woods," he said more to himself than to her. "That's what Hudson called you."

"I'm sorry about your brother. The fear you have of your father is obviously legitimate, and if I were you, I would've done the exact same thing to protect the person I loved."

Clamping down on tears, he squeezed her hand. "I couldn't see you hurt. But the more I sat with my choice, the more I realized there was a part of me that felt like I wasn't worthy of your love," he said, looking at their hands. "That I'd lose you eventually."

After a moment, she gave his hand the gentlest tug. "Hey." Looking up, she was leaning forward, eyes on his. "Did you really think that? That you weren't worth it?"

"Yes. I just—it was shit I carried from the past, you know?"

"Baggage."

"Yeah, exactly. I, um..." He wasn't sure if he should tell her, but seeing her open, loving face and her bright, though red, eyes reminded him that she was his best friend—that he could tell her anything. "I was a mess when Hudson died," he started. "I knew he struggled, but until that horrible day, I never understood that his pain was deeper, darker. Weeks at a time, I'd be twisted up on the inside because as much as I missed him, I was so angry that he had left me. He was the only person I trusted—who I felt loved me no matter what. Who didn't make me feel like shit for being who I was. And he was gone. For five years, I spiraled. It wasn't until I went to my family's estate and the twins cornered me with tears in their eyes that I realized I was slowly killing myself. I cleaned up and joined the force. And although life got better, I was never close to anyone again...until you," he paused and swallowed. "What I felt—what I *feel* for you is so powerful, so all-consuming that I convinced myself I wasn't worth it and that one day you'd leave me. Letting you go seemed like the logical choice," he admitted.

Instead of a response, she tugged on him some more until he realized she was pulling him to her. Making room, she moved over on the bed as he took her place, resting against the headboard. Then climbing on top, she straddled him before wrapping her arms around his neck. Arms around her, he squeezed all of his love into her.

After a few beats, she pulled back and searched his eyes. "I'm sure it was torture for Hudson to leave you, but we both know how deep the darkness goes. We've both been at the place were death seemed easier than life. But somehow, we made it and to each other at that. In a way, Hyphen, you're a beautiful, loving reward for fighting to see another day." Giving him a soft kiss, she looked at him with the force of her boldness and tenacity. "I love you, Hyphen. No matter what. Even if you're back with Bronwyn, it doesn't matter because I love you."

Recoiling, he shook his head. "Who in Guardians' name said I was back with *her?*"

Confused, she frowned. "I thought... I mean, we saw you on *Vizable* at a Casino Night or something," she said with a feeble shrug.

Solneur, she thought he was back with that *snake.* "Baby, no. No. No," he said, shaking his head. "I was my mom's date for the fundraiser and Bronwyn saw me at the bar. She came over talking shit and a photographer took our picture. I'm so sorry you thought that," he said, rubbing her cheek with his thumb.

Biting her lip, she looked at him from under her lashes. Unable to help himself, he pulled her to him for a kiss. Opening her mouth for him, he savored her like never before. She even tasted differently, sweeter, and more pronounced. Or maybe that was what love tasted like? Moaning, she cupped his face, then ran her fingers through his hair, causing his body to relax in gratitude.

Drawing back, he held her gaze. "Fellowship, there's no one on this planet for me but you, okay?"

She nodded. "Okay."

"Solneur, I can't believe you thought—*fuck.*"

Hands up her back and down, they settled on her ass. Then she gave him that smile. The one that made him feel invincible. The one that had become his drug of choice—not only did it chase away his darkness, but it buoyed him to a stratospheric realm of euphoria. *Guardians*, it was like getting a shot of sunshine right to his heart.

"I'm so sorry for all of this shit—for my fucked-up family. For the loss of yours, *because* of my fucked-up family. Sometimes, I hate being a Haslem," he complained.

"There's more to the Haslem name than hurt and pain," she said. "There's Hudson, a brave lone voice who tried to save a human family he didn't even know. There's Haze, thoughtful and confident; Harleigh, charismatic and insightful. And then there's Hyphen, tender and loving. Protective and loyal. You should be proud to be part of such a wonderful group of people."

Guardians, this woman. "I don't know what to say," he whispered, then it hit him. "Wait, Fell, you're a *hybrid?*" he asked, snatched from the sadness of their past.

Letting out a sigh, she rested her head on his shoulder as he rubbed her back. "That's a shitshow of a story, babe."

"What happened?" Instead of a response, she groaned in protest. "Tell me," he said over a laugh. Another groan, then a whimper. Shaking his head, he gently pushed her off him so he could see her face. She was actually pouting. Stifling a laugh, he kissed her nose. "It can't be *that* bad."

"It is."

"As bad as my father sanctioning the death of your family?"

"Worse."

"Bullshit."

"Oh, yeah?" she asked, shoulders sagging. "I went to my grandfather's because, in the shit Lemin retrieved from Cygma's network, I found a palace registry that mentioned a healer named Daelyn. I asked him about it, which led me to rediscover my family history and how they were killed by the Council. His revelation about my past also showed me that I'm magical—a fire and water El-man, intuit, and possibly more. Then, he proceeded to tell me that me that I'm not a hybrid but a full *Aechaih* and, as it turns out, the heir to the fucking throne of Trianah."

Mouth opened, he blinked because *what the fuck?*

"Yeah."

"Uh."

"I know. You wanna know more?"

He wasn't sure, but he nodded because what the hell?

She continued. "As you can imagine, I tell my grandfather that his story is bullshit because we all know that Queen Aniyah was murdered by Rhoman during the massacre. Well, and you'll enjoy this, she wasn't. Turns out, Lazlo helped her escape to the forest where she found Daelyn who delivered her baby and vowed to keep her safe. Sylena hid the queen's power in the baby's bloodline to remain dormant for a thousand years until the next fucking *Kumalada*. Lazlo sneaked the queen back into the palace—with no one the wiser that she delivered her baby. As they moved through the chaos, they saw Rhoman who was already *dead*. It was then that the queen forced Lazlo to return to the woods and protect her heiress until the end of his days. He left and she was killed—presumably by the same person on her court who not only targeted Manicow, Rey, and Nigh but who orchestrated a whole-ass uprising a thousand years ago." Letting out a sigh, she slid her arms around him, then returned her head to his shoulder. "See what I mean?"

Okay, so he had no words. The best he could do was hug her while he sorted through his thoughts and turned them into a coherent response. Maybe working through it point by point would help.

"We were right about Rhoman being targeted."

She bolted upright. "Can you believe it? Totally fucking right!"

"And you're Queen Aniyah's living descendant."

She sank back down onto him. "I guess," she said, her voice muffled.

"To be honest, it doesn't seem far-fetched." For some reason, he wasn't surprised. If anything, it felt like it was something he already knew.

"And supposedly I'm *Aechaih*. For all I know I could wake up one day with pointed ears and elongated canines or some shit."

"And you'd still be beautiful," he said, squeezing her waist.

Sitting up, she looked at him with a cute little pout. "You'd still love me if I presented as an Aechaih?" she asked, her voice small.

"Baby, you could wake up a hamster and I'd still love you," he clarified.

She laughed, the sound bouncing along his skin. "I can't with you," she said, shaking her head.

"As much as you love history, I'd think you'd be psyched. Think about it—Lazlo helped Queen Aniyah escape and because of that, she was able to protect her bloodline. And because she protected her bloodline, we now have you," he said, giving her a nod and smile. It wasn't all that complicated. In fact, it was probably one of the reasons he felt so damn drawn to her. There was no one else in Trianah like her, and now he knew why. "It's not as outlandish as you think."

"It's not?"

"We've always known that Queen Aniyah was powerful and one of a kind—now we know why, and that she's passed that same power to you."

Fellowship blinked away tears and hugged him, burying her face in his neck. "I love you." Squeezing her tightly, he heard her sniff as he gently rubbed her back.

"I love you, too, Fell, so fucking much. I can only imagine how you must feel. I mean it *is* kinda crazy—all that we know to be true is a lie. For example, I discovered that humans age slower if they mate with an Aechaih."

She sat up frowning. "What?"

"Yeah, Horace told me that was the main reason for the anti-miscegenation law."

It took her a moment, but then she got it. "*That's* how humans and

Aechaih were able to mate," she said. Then her eyes widened. "Oh...I see..." she said, *really* understanding Horace's threat.

"It's a lot to take in," he said with a knowing nod.

"It's overwhelming."

"I know, baby," he said, running his hands up and down her sides.

"What do I do now? Grandpa made it seem like I *have* to claim the throne—like all of Trianah depends on it."

"Well, in a way it does, right? We can't go on like this—the human population is suffering because of archaic rules imposed by a group of people with illegitimate power."

"The Tri-Family Council has very legitimate power, Hyphen."

"Not anymore. Not with an heiress who's alive and well. Fuck, I was prepared to burn the Council down to the ground to be with you, but now I don't have to because you've already done it."

"I haven't done anything."

"You will," he said proudly.

"Ugh, you're so fucking charming, it's ridiculous," she said, rolling her eyes. "What am I going to do with you?"

"I mean, I'm sure you have ideas."

Suddenly, her laugh turned into a smolder. "I've missed you," she whispered.

Fuck, he was already hard. "I missed you, too," he breathed. Before he could say anything else, her mouth was on his. Clawing at him, she rocked on his dick. Moaning into her mouth, he drew back, breathless. Cradling her face, he looked into her heavy-lidded eyes. "Fellowship, Aechaih or not, heiress or not—I love you with all that I am." It'd taken him centuries to find her, and he wasn't letting her go. Not again. Not ever.

Eyes watering, her chin trembled. Blinking down tears, she smiled. "I know I have Queen Aniyah's power or whatever and that I've been doing a lot of shit on my own, but I need you, Hyphen. Not because I'm weak or incapable, but because you're my best friend. There's no Queen Aniyah without Lazlo and believe me, there's no Queen Dancy without Hyphen *Fucking* Haslem."

All efforts he made to contain his bubbling emotions had been rendered useless. The love he felt for her expanded throughout his chest, easing up his throat to form a lump of tears. Unable to swallow it down, his eyes burned.

"Well played, Dancy. Now you've got *me* fucking crying. I was trying to be all tough and supportive for you."

"You don't have to be all tough around me. And remember, I'm here to support you, too."

That's when it felt like all of his past shit collided with his present shit and smashed into him. Grabbing a tissue, she dabbed his eyes, then leaned forward and pressed her lips against his. Slow and methodical, her kiss was a salve on old wounds that had finally surfaced to be healed. Hands up his—*her* sweater, he unhooked her bra and slid his hand around, cupping both of her breasts. As warm and soft as butter, he moaned into her mouth as she ran her fingers through his hair, nipping his bottom lip.

Pulling back, he looked at her. "You caught me after a workout, should I shower?"

She frowned. "What the fuck are you talking about?"

"I'm just saying—"

"Hyphen, if you don't fuck me, I swear to Solneur."

"Okay, Your Majesty," he said with a wink.

All of her heat receded to a simmer. Cupping his face, she smiled, then wrapped her arms around him as he tipped them over on his bed.

Chapter Twenty-Four

Of all the things Fellowship loved about Hyphen, she couldn't get enough of his slow, intentional kisses and his strong hands on her ass. He pressed further into her mouth with unbearable heat as she clung to his shoulders. Freshly scrubbed and still damp from their shower, he smelled like the beach after a summer rain. They spent the day having incredible make-up sex, drifting to sleep, waking in each other's arms only to do it again. Something about breaking up and getting back together secured their bond. An unbreakable thread that connected them beyond space and time. Hyphen was a part of her; his presence was a fixture in her life, complementing her individuality as she did his. Drawing back, she could barely see him for the love haze over her eyes. Cupping her face, he kissed her nose, then her lips.

"I love you," he whispered, his green eyes intense.

"I love you, too," she said, sliding her arms around his midsection, pressing her face to his bare chest. "Tell me again why your parents are visiting you."

"Who knows, baby," he groaned. "I have no desire to see Horace.

It's going to take everything within me not to snap his neck and pull his soul from his ancient body."

Drawing back, she looked at him with shock and amusement. "Damn, babe."

The muscle in his jaw feathered as his rage receded, smoothing out his features. "I know," he sighed.

"Not that it's not hot. I mean, *should* your rage be hot? I don't know, but it is." She slid her hands down his back, moving under the waistband of his joggers. "Hopefully it won't be bad."

"Thankfully, Honey's coming. She's the only one who can keep him under control. What are you about to do?"

"I don't know, I feel like the case has stalled. There hasn't been so much as a peep from our killer. That worries me."

"At least Sylena and her sisters are visible *and* aligning," he offered.

"True. By the way, thank you for getting us that research on the moonless nights. I appreciated it even if I didn't say so," she said, thinking back to how fucking sad he looked when she ran into him in Monroe's office. As pissed as she was, she still couldn't stand seeing him so dejected.

"Of course. Oh, and can we talk about that dress? *Fuck*," he said, shaking his head. "Almost brought me to my knees."

"Oh, yeah?"

"I was fucking sick."

"Aw," she said with a playful pout before sighing. "Yeah, a dress like that serves one of two purposes: to show a man what he's lost, or to flaunt what he has."

"I like the second one."

"Me, too."

"I want you to wear it on our official first date," he said with that effortless confidence that made her swoon like a dickmatized mess.

"Yes. And you'll wear your black suit, black shirt, and one of those beautiful watches."

He arched an eyebrow. "Tie or no tie?"

"No tie—open at the collar. I want them to see your ink, so they know what I get to run my tongue over every night." His eyes darkened, as his magic pushed at her, making her pussy throb. Jaw clenched, he shook his head. "What?" she asked innocently.

"You know what." Hand on her ass, he jerked her to him so that she could feel his length harden.

Running her tongue along her teeth, she looked him up and down. "You better watch it. I'd hate for Honey and Horace to come in here and catch me riding their son's face," she purred.

Squeezing her ass, he closed his eyes. "You're nothing but fucking trouble," he ground out.

"I guess I better get out of here," she said brightly.

Opening his eyes, he pinned her underneath his intoxicating, alpha-gaze. "I hate the sound of that, but okay." Kissing her, they slow-walked to the elevator where he pushed the button without removing her lips from his. Doors opening, she pulled away and smiled as she stepped on. Seeing him standing there, shirtless with wet hair and joggers slung low, she could only thank the Guardians for blessing her with such an extraordinary man.

"I love you, Fellowship."

"I love you, Hyphen," she said as the doors closed.

Still in Seacrest, Fellowship sat at a red light, daydreaming about her gorgeous Aechaih boyfriend—who hadn't reconciled with his awful ex and who held her in his arms all day. Her gaze drifted up to Trianah's dark sky, illuminated by Sylena in mid-alignment with her sisters. While she was relieved there hadn't been another murder, she couldn't help but wonder what power this alignment might offer someone who knew how to harness it. As her phone rang, she pressed the button on her steering wheel to answer just as the light turned green.

"Hey, Monroe."

"Dancy," Monroe's voice said through her stereo.

Immediately, her blood chilled. "What's wrong?"

His voice was low, like he was whispering. "It's bad."

Heart pounding in her ears, she pulled over and parked in front of a line of Seacrest boutiques. "There's been another murder," she said.

"Not quite, I'm here now. Stepped out for privacy. Dancy," Monroe sighed. "Layne Tarnicon was attacked and left for dead. When we got here, one of the healers felt a faint pulse. She's being worked on at Septain as we speak."

Fuck. Going after a member of the Tri-Family Council was a power play designed with one thing in mind—permanently destroy Aechaih-human relations. "Let me guess, the perp is human," she said as her head began to ache. There was no way Layne Tarnicon was on *FBDn*—that shit was unlikely as hell, even if her company did design it.

"Yes, but not just any human."

"Who?" As Monroe took a beat, a *knowing* punched through her consciousness, settling into her stomach. "No," she whispered. "*No.*"

"He's on multiple security cameras. His prints are all over her apartment."

Although she heard Monroe, a part of her had floated above and looked on as her fists itched with heat. "*Monroe...*please," she pleaded.

"I'm so fucking sorry, Dancy. Auten has signed in and out of her apartment multiple times over the past year," he explained.

"The past year?!"

"According to the doorman, he's a regular."

She felt vomit rise up. "*What the fuck...*"

"Look, they're still processing the scene, but Weeden's already sent someone to make the arrest. The Seacrest-Pawville borders are about to close, and Cormac and Rygle are headed to Aechaih holding. All three will be sentenced tomorrow, as per Weeden's orders. It's moving so fast that I doubt anyone at the human precinct will know until the transfer van arrives for the detainees."

It was just a dream—another one of her dark, vivid nightmares. As soon as she found the strength to wake up and call her grandfather, he'd answer and reassure her that everything was okay.

"Dancy?" Monroe asked, interrupting her thoughts.

"I'm here."

I'm calling because something about this doesn't sit right with me. I'm not sure what it is, but after talking to the doorman, it seems impossible that Auten would attack Layne. He mentioned that they appeared serious and that she had worked hard to protect their privacy.

"I'm going to Aechaih holding," she announced. She wasn't sure where the idea came from, but as soon as she said it, it felt *right*.

"What are you going to do?"

"Besides checking on my grandfather, I don't know," she said, flicking on her siren and pulling into traffic.

Monroe took a beat. "Okay. Holding's down in the basement. There should be at least one patrol cop manning the desk."

"Okay," she said as her car powered through Seacrest. "Monroe?"

"Yeah?"

"Can you call Hyphen for me? Tell him what's going on."

"Of course."

"Thanks."

"Be careful, Dancy," he said before ending the call.

Be careful. Fuck being careful. Zipping in and out of traffic, Fellowship's hands gripped the steering wheel tightly. With no idea who was behind this, her mind raced through ideas and scenarios, desperately trying to connect the dots. Nothing made sense. While Cygma had extensive archives, they couldn't pinpoint who had access to FBDn to monitor its users. Even with her grandfather as her top priority, she knew only that whoever had the power to manipulate humans into killing Aechaih was the same entity behind the rebellion in the Kingdom of Trianah and the murder of Queen Aniyah. That kind of power would only grow during the alignment. Switching lanes, she took a hard right, tires screeching. Arriving at the Aechaih precinct, she skidded to a stop, parked, grabbed her 9mm and holster from the glove box, and sprinted to the entrance.

Aechaih holding was essentially the same as the human precinct, except with more space and newer equipment. Bright lighting and white walls made the processing desk appear twice as large as the one in Pawville. The only difference was that no one was there. Everything seemed undisturbed—perhaps too undisturbed. She hoisted herself onto the desk to see behind it. Bingo. An Aechaih patrol cop lay crumpled on the floor. Pulling herself up, she swung her legs around and hopped down. Pale, with a trickle of blood coming from his ears, she pressed her fingers to his neck and waited. There it was: a pulse.

Stepping around him, she pulled out her gun and pushed through the large metal door toward the holding cells. The hall smelled of disinfectant. Gun pointed, she checked each empty cell as she walked by. *What the fuck?* Nothing about this situation seemed—

"Oh, good, you came. I hoped you would," someone said.

Whipping around, her gun was pointed at... Talon Seram? The tall, thin man stood there dressed as he had been at City Hall. At first glance, he looked young, but closer inspection revealed thin lines around his eyes and a downturned mouth. His pale, paper-thin skin stretched over his face, showing blue veins along his neck and forehead.

Gun still pointed, her eyes flicked around but they were alone. "Talon?"

With a little bow, he smiled. "At your service."

"I don't understand," she said as her body surged with adrenaline. "Do you know where they're holding my grandfather?"

"Oh, yes, I do," he said brightly. His voice may have sounded jovial, but the darkness in his eyes suggested otherwise. Nothing about him felt right; the air around him smelled ancient and musty.

"Can you tell me where he is?"

"I can do you one better and take you." Waving his hand, her gun flew out of her hands and clattered to the floor. Then, with another flick, searing pain ripped through her body, as if being gutted from the base of her spine up to her head. A piercing wail erupted from her mouth. Talon's eyes were black and glassy, devoid of any whites. He was pure evil unlike anything she'd ever encountered. Fear struck her hard as she realized the true orchestrator and puppet master behind all this shit was Horace Haslem's right-hand man.

Darkness.

Chapter Twenty-Five

Was it possible to die from happiness? If so, then Hyphen was dead and on his way to the Salveigh Mist. As soon as the elevator doors closed on Fellowship, he got dressed and devoured a sandwich, practically giddy. It wasn't just because she was Aechaih and they could legally be together, or that she was the heir to the throne, or even that the Tri-Family Council would soon be dissolved. He was giddy because she loved him. Their brief breakup had forced him to confront his past and release the dark pain that had held him captive for most of his life. He had come to a profound realization that he was worthy of love, especially *her* love—a love that seized his heart the moment he saw her at Queen Aniyah's Temple. It was a love that made him sprint across the street and fly her to the hospital, a love that held her hand while she slept, and a love that saw her face every time he closed his eyes. As he set his plate in the sink, the elevator dinged. His mood shifted from being in love to defensive as he rounded the corner, ready to face his parents. But it wasn't his parents standing by the elevator.

It was Horace.

Solneur. Adrenaline shot through him as he fought the urge to kill his father. Sliding his hand into the pocket of his flat-front pants, he arched an eyebrow. The wall of magic emanating from his pores made it clear that his father was not to take another step into his safe space.

"What the fuck could you possibly want *now?*"

"That's no way to great your father," Horace said, stepping forward but stopping just short of encroaching on Hyphen's personal space. Dressed in his usual suit, vest, and tie, his thick blond hair was neatly combed back. "I came to tell you that you don't have to worry about ending it with your human," Horace sang, uncharacteristically mirthful. "Now that we know she's a hybrid, she'll be sentenced to death."

Hyphen stilled. How in Solneur's name did he know? *Fuck.* The only way to find out was to keep him talking, which was something Horace loved to do when he thought he had the upper hand.

"What makes you think she's magical?" Hyphen asked in a you-bore-me-tone.

Annoyance flitted across Horace's face before he finally confessed. "The ambassador's home may or may not be tapped."

Of course, he'd tap Auten's residence. Although Hyphen's insides were molten lava, he kept his face impassively cool. "Why would you wiretap Auten Dancy? He has no power."

"Because he's a human and humans can't be trusted."

Hyphen continued to push without revealing his hand. "Did you actually *hear* Auten claim she was magical or is this a desperate attempt to throw her in Containment because she's my mate?"

Horace took the bait—his blue eyes darkening with self-importance. "I don't have time to listen to the comings and goings of a human. Talon reviewed the recording and reported back to me," he said with a wave of his hand.

Hyphen's mind went into overdrive. If Horace knew Fellowship was Queen Aniyah's full-Aechaih heir, he wouldn't be in his penthouse gloating like a basic bitch. It meant he didn't know shit, and he didn't know because Talon hadn't told him. Hyphen needed to figure out why —*fast.*

"That's it? She's a hybrid?" he asked, words dripping with disdain.

He felt his father's spiky magic scrape against him. He was pissed. *Perfect.*

"What do you mean *that's it?*" Horace spat. "It's obvious, she's the human we've been looking for. Somehow she's managed to empower humans to kill Aechaih. She even used her own grandfather to murder Layne Tarnicon. No one believed me, but here we are again—just like Rhoman."

Just like Rhoman. The hairs on Hyphen's neck stood as his stomach rolled in fear. Talon Seram was alive during the last alignment. What if he was responsible for targeting Rhoman and staging an uprising to only copycat himself a thousand years later? If any of that were true, then Talon wanted to get his hands on Fellowship, which would explain why he'd target Auten.

"Where's Talon now?"

Horace rolled his eyes. "Handling business, why?"

"Where's Fellowship?"

"By now, I assume she's in Containment with her grandfather." The darkness residing in his father had been stoked for over a thousand years by his piece of shit advisor. All this time, Horace thought Talon was serving him, when in fact it was the opposite. Shaking with rage, Hyphen stepped to his father as his wings threatened to be released. He didn't have much time, but before he searched for Fellowship, Horace needed to know the truth.

Horace blinked but didn't budge. "What are you going to do, boy? *Kill me?*"

"It was Fellowship's family that you had killed all those years ago."

Horace flinched but recovered quickly. "Pity she survived."

"She did survive. Just like Queen Aniyah's heir."

Recoiling in disbelief, Horace waved his hand. "You don't know what you're talking about."

"No? Then ask your faithful advisor why he failed to mention Fellowship's true lineage."

Horace winced again. "That's preposterous. You'd do anything for that human of yours."

"You mean I'd do anything for my full-blooded Aechaih *mate*."

The color drained from Horace's face, and Hyphen seized the moment to press on. "During the massacre, Queen Aniyah fled to the forest and found an old palace healer named Daelyn to deliver her baby. She returned to the palace, knowing she'd be killed by someone in her court—*not* her husband. I'd bet my inheritance that the bastard who murdered her was Talon Seram."

Horace blinked rapidly before backing away. *"Daelyn?* How?" he sputtered. It was obvious Hyphen had hit a nerve—Horace knew exactly who she was.

"Doesn't matter. As Talon filled your head with poisonous lies, he manufactured Rhoman's Massacre to justify the genocide of humans and hybrids. Meanwhile, Queen Aniyah's court created the Tri-Family Council where you all sit around oppressing humans while shitting on her legacy of peace. So much for loyalty."

Blustering, Horace stammered. It was the first time Hyphen saw his father without his normal shield of self-assurance. "I *was* loyal to her, but her human husband—"

"Did you witness the murder of Queen Aniyah?"

Horace's eyes were wide with fear. Taking another step back, he finally looked all twelve hundred of his years. "It's not true," he whispered more to himself than to Hyphen.

"Did. You. See. Rhoman. Kill. The. Queen?"

Shaking his head like it would delete the conversation, his father finally looked at him. "No. Talon. Talon told us that he witnessed it."

"I'm sure he did, seeing as he's the fucking murderer."

"No, no, no," Horace repeated to himself. "It's impossible. Rhoman. Murders."

Hyphen's body shook with rage. "If it's impossible, then go ask Fellowship *Daelyn* Dancy how she got her middle name. Ask her why she can men-com, why she can intuit and why she can manipulate fire *and* water."

Horace continued to shake his head, his blue eyes lost and confused.

Unable to restrain his fury, Hyphen stepped to him. "Fellowship's family died because of you. Hudson died because of you. There's so much blood on your hands, there isn't enough soap in Trianah to clean them. And for what? Humans didn't hurt Trianah—you and your *advisor* did. And now you've unleashed him on my *mate*?" Wings ripped through his shirt, tearing from his back. Heat surged through his body as he faced Horace—wings spread wide, canines bared.

"I didn't know," Horace stammered, stepping back as his eyes widened at the sight of Hyphen's wings—wings he hadn't seen in over a century. "Hyphen, I didn't—

"Get out. And if you go running to the Council in some pathetic attempt at blocking Fellowship's claim to the throne or if something happens to her, to my *queen*, I will kill you. Try me. I *dare* you," he said through clenched teeth.

Horace's mouth opened, then closed before he backed to the elevator, pushed the button, and stumbled on.

Turning on his heel, Hyphen's wings snapped in. He patted his pants—where the fuck was his phone? Hands shaking, he tried to mencom Fellowship.

Fellowship, where are you? Can you hear me?

Nothing. He heard nothing and felt nothing. *Guardians, please.* Swallowing his fear, he stalked past the kitchen to his bedroom where he found his phone on the bed. Pressing it, he saw a dozen missed calls from Monroe. Dialing him, he put it on speaker as he tore off his shirt, walking into his closet.

"Where the fuck have you been?" Monroe barked.

"You don't want to know. Have you heard from Fell?" he asked, setting his phone down.

"Yeah, she told me to call you. They picked up Auten."

Hyphen pulled out one of the many tailor-made sweaters created to accommodate his wings. Pulling it over his head, he picked up the phone. "For killing Layne Tarnicon. I know," he said, striding out of his bedroom.

"She didn't die," Monroe clarified. She's at Septain. Look, Haslem,

Dancy went to our precinct to find her grandfather. I told her something didn't feel right. Between Auten and the swiftness of Weeden getting the humans transferred over. Closing the borders. None of it makes sense."

She was at the precinct. Walking to his sliding glass window, he opened it as a gust of wind smacked him in the face, tousling his hair. "You're right. Talon Seram is our suspect. He's been playing multiple games at once."

"*Seram.* Your dad's puny advisor?"

"If you call being over twelve hundred years old and a master of dark magic puny, then yes," he said, closing the sliding door behind him.

"Fuck," Monroe hissed.

"Talon used Auten as bait," Hyphen said, walking out to the edge of the building.

"Why would he want Dancy?"

"She's Queen Aniyah's heir. I wish I had time to explain."

"Um. *Okay.* That's fair."

"Meet me at the precinct, I'm leaving now."

"On my way," Monroe said, ending the call.

Wings bursting from his back, Hyphen didn't have a moment to savor the freedom before shooting into the dark Trianah sky. With every beat, he prayed to the Guardians, desperately hoping he'd reach her in time. He couldn't bear the thought of finding her lifeless on the ground, her light fading away. He prayed they'd protect his best friend, his love, his queen.

Chapter Twenty-Six

Fellowship felt brand new. Was this death? She blinked until the blurry image of Itchan Forest began to take shape, though it never quite came into clear focus. Surrounded by velvet greenery and towering ancient trees, the scent of sweet soil reminded her of life before Pawville.

She was neither asleep nor fully awake. Though she was standing, her feet didn't touch the ground. Amidst the canopy of trees, a golden, shimmering mist drifted on a nonexistent breeze, settling around her. The forest seemed to clear, making space as her childhood home materialized. A quaint cabin with three steps leading to a porch appeared before her. Floating closer, she stopped at the steps. The house was nestled in a small clearing, surrounded by thick foliage. The vision obscured whether she was clothed or naked, leading her to believe she had arrived at the Salveigh Mist, home to her ancestors.

The heavy black door of the home creaked open, revealing Limber Dancy, Fellowship's mother. With her rich mahogany skin and short, coiled hair, Limber descended the steps with her chin lifted. She wore an ornate, off-the-shoulder gown that fell gracefully past her bare feet—green and brown overlaying a gauzy silk. Whether in the Salveigh Mist or not, seeing her mother smoothed the rough edges of Fellowship's traumatic past, erasing the memory of Limber lying dead. As dreamlike as it seemed, there was a palpable realness to the experience, stirring deep-rooted emotions in Fellowship's heart.

Walking to her mother, Limber opened her arms and embraced her daughter. The sensation was strange—warmth mingling with a tingling coolness that swirled through her body. As she clung to her mother, a wave of emotion escaped in a breath that turned into a sob. The release was unlike anything she'd ever known, as her consciousness unraveled from long-held tension: stress, worry, trauma, loss. Limber gently rubbed her back, rocking her back and forth. Fellowship cried without feeling tears and wailed without opening her mouth. In her mother's arms, she felt light, as if floating on water. Drawing back, she looked at her mother's regal face. Limber smiled, her straight, white teeth gleaming, her dark eyes shining with love.

Fellowship. Look at you, Limber said, her hands resting on Fellowship's arms.

Fellowship remembered gazing up at her mother with complete adoration as a girl. She could feel Limber's hands in her hair, washing, detangling, and twisting it. Holding her brown, makeshift dolly, little Fellowship would sit on the hardwood floor while her mother tended to her with gentle care. Whether it was reality, a dream, a memory, or death, none of it mattered—she was home.

You're so beautiful, Fellowship said.

I'm beautiful? You're beautiful, Limber said on a smile as she squeezed Fellowship's arms. *My beautiful baby girl.*

I've missed you, Fellowship confessed. *So much.* It was hard to remember life without her mom—the fearful nights, anxiety-ridden days, moments of insecurity and doubt, heartbreak, and embarrassment. A range of life experiences, though unavoidable, would have been different with her mother's support.

I've missed you, too, Limber said, her smile lines spilling from the corners of her eyes.

Fellowship looked around. *The Salveigh Mist is beautiful.*

Darling, this isn't the Salveigh Mist.

Fellowship frowned as gold dust sparkled around her.

Rubbing her arms, Limber smiled. *We're between here and there.* It was vague, but Fellowship understood—sort of. *We've come for you.*

To escort me to the Salveigh Mist?

Limber shook her head. *No, baby. You're not joining us there. Not yet.*

On an unction, Fellowship turned back to her childhood home. Standing in the doorway was Granny Reathe, shorter than Limber and wearing a similar nature-made gown. Instead of joining them, Reathe watched from the threshold. It felt as though multiple eyes were upon them. Although unseen, a circle of warmth and strength seemed to envelop her and her mother.

Mom, I don't understand.

We wanted so badly to be there as you grew. As you evolved into this fiery woman. We wanted to guide and support you as you learned your true heritage. Even though we weren't there, look at you. You're magnificent.

Suddenly embarrassed, Fellowship often wondered what her mother would think of her. Would she be proud of her accomplishments? Now that she stood with her, she felt underprepared, like perhaps she could've done more with the time she had.

You're magnificent, Limber reiterated, holding Fellowship's gaze. Clearly wherever they were, her mother was still able to sense what she was thinking. *I wish we had more time,* Limber said, nodding behind her.

Turning toward a wall of forest, Fellowship watched as a shimmering fog danced along the ground, covering it like a sparkling blanket. From the depths of the mist emerged Queen Aniyah. *What in Solneur's name?* Limber shifted, standing beside her as the queen approached with a wide, glowing smile and elongated canines. Save for the canines, it was the same smile as Fellowship's, the same as her mother's. A seemingly innocuous trait had been inherited from the most remarkable woman in Trianah's history.

Finally able to look down at herself, Fellowship saw she was wearing a sparkling cream gown, reminiscent of the one she'd worn to the gala fundraiser. But this one flowed to the ground in layers of sheer, gold-dusted fabric. Standing before her was the last Aechaih queen—her idol, her heroine. Taller than Fellowship, the queen's long, thick black hair cascaded in soft curls down her back, pinned up on the sides to reveal elegantly pointed ears. Like Fellowship, she wore a cream gown sparkling with the same gold dust that surrounded them. A gold, jewel-encrusted tiara perched on her head, catching the light. She was luminous, with rich brown skin, expressive eyes, and Fellowship's own defined jaw.

It's such an honor to meet you, Fellowship, Queen Aniyah said, smiling broadly. Fellowship wanted to speak, but all she managed was a squeak and a nervous curtsy. Laughing, Queen Aniyah extended her arm, inviting her to walk with her. As soon as Fellowship took a step, the scenery shifted like a page turning in a book, revealing a clearing beside a dazzling creek. *It might be easier to talk here. A lot has happened to you, Fellowship. I'm sure you have questions.*

Did she ever! Taking what she considered a deep breath, Fellowship turned to Queen Aniyah. *Why me?* Guardians—she really wanted to be more articulate, but the words escaped before she could process them.

All of my descendants are remarkable, Queen Aniyah began. *They've all made good use of their time on Nehlahni and in Trianah, including you. But as you know, the Kingdom of Trianah has lost its way. A millennium of Aechaih wealth and human oppression has reached a breaking point. The Kingdom wasn't founded on the value system that's currently in place. If it's to survive, it must evolve—not just in terms of currency and technological advances, but beyond selfish ideals.*

You want me to right a thousand years of wrongs?

Queen Aniyah smiled. *Never. I'm asking that you create space for growth. Trianah must change or it will die.*

I've always wondered why humans and Aechaih walked planet

Nehlahni together. It feels like humans were made to suffer. We're not magical. We don't live for centuries. I don't understand, Fellowship said.

The queen nodded in consideration. *The Guardians created both humans and Aechaih because they need each other. Aechaih, with their long lives and perceived power, can become consumed by their own importance. They take much for granted, living under the assumption that time is endless. In contrast, humans are acutely aware of time's preciousness and love with all their hearts despite its brevity. This love has kept Trianah in balance. Humans may not manipulate elements or foresee the future, but their extraordinary ability to create community, support one another, and love deeply is invaluable. By restoring balance to Trianah, Aechaih and humans can begin to integrate and bond once more. Through this renewed connection, any human who chooses to bond with an Aechaih is gifted with a longer lifespan.*

Horace was telling the truth. Fellowship continued. *Did you know that Talon Seram was behind it all—Rhoman's Massacre and the uprising?*

Smiling, Queen Aniyah nodded. *Yes, but not until it was too late. Fellowship, power drives people crazy. Talon wanted power so badly that he was willing to sacrifice anything or anyone to get it, including myself. At first, I thought Horace Haslem would be good for him. Provide him with perspective. Smooth out the angry, entitled edges, but the opposite happened. Horace fell victim to Talon's ire and well, you know the rest.*

Wait, what? Fellowship didn't want to follow up, but she had to because who else would she get this information from? *You're telling me that Horace Haslem hasn't always been a villain?*

The queen tipped her head back and laughed, her voice creating a symphonic explosion in the forest. Fireflies, drawn to the melody, danced around, flitting and chasing the echoes of her laughter. *No, he was a good man. He fell in love with Honey Lysine and found his stride in my court. He doesn't know the truth of how I died. He believes it was Rhoman and that assumption has fueled his wrath against humans.*

Fellowship's historic brain hummed. Desperate to not come off like a ridiculous nerd, she steadied herself. *Honey Haslem's related to Lazlo Lysine? Did people know that?*

Yes, of course.

That's why her son was born with wings.

That's exactly why.

Then why was he ostracized for having them? Why didn't they tell him that he's Lazlo's descendant? Fellowship asked.

Fellowship, Lazlo was the most powerful Aechaih in our kingdom. His power was both respected and feared. When I instructed him to leave and protect my heiresses, he was forgotten. Over the centuries, no one had seen a winged Aechaih until Hyphen Haslem was born. In their desperation to modernize and create an Aechaih-first society, it was easier to shun the baby, as he reminded them of a past they wished to erase.

Fellowship couldn't stop the questions from coming. *Please tell me if I'm being rude, but I read somewhere that you were deeply bonded to Lazlo. Is that a myth?*

For the first time, the queen looked into the distance. After a moment, she returned. *No, it's not a myth. Lazlo and I were mates. We were bonded, and my love for him ran deep. But duty called, and for the sake of Trianah, I married a human—a kind, gentle soul whom I also loved dearly. Lazlo stayed by my side until the end, serving as captain of my guard. With him, Trianah was formidable, a true force to be reckoned with. I believe this is why Hyphen Haslem endured such an upbringing. For the Council, it was easier to erase the past than to embrace it. A winged Aechaih like Hyphen would serve as a stark reminder of an era they wanted to forget. He is not just a physical embodiment of a powerful warrior but a testament to a man who fiercely protected Trianah and me. A man who was both honorable and fierce.*

Fellowship felt a blaze erupt in her chest, spreading like wildfire through her entire being. Those assholes mistreated Hyphen because they *knew* he was special and rare—a beautiful, gentle soul. If she could, she'd line them up and cuss them the fuck out for being selfish cowards. Queen Aniyah's laughter rang out again, and Fellowship's gaze dropped, her shame mingling with her anger.

I'm sorry.

There's nothing to be sorry for. What you feel for him is real and very powerful.

Fellowship shook her head, fist clenched. *I get so angry about how he was treated. And to know that you loved Lazlo, but couldn't be with him...*

Oh, don't be sad for us. We're together in the Mist.

You are?!

Queen Aniyah chuckled. *We are. Death can't break a bond like that. And yours with Hyphen is even more powerful. I'm sure you've noticed how exceptionally deep your connection is.*

Fellowship's eyes widened. *It was his pain that I felt in some of my nightmares. It felt familiar, but I wasn't sure what I was feeling was real. I'm not sure what to say...*

Queen Aniyah smiled. *Sometimes there are no words. I'll say this: the transformative love between you and Hyphen has ushered you into your power and has done the same for him. See for yourself,* the queen said with a nod.

With expectant eyes, Fellowship scanned the forest, half-expecting someone else to appear. When no one did, she turned her gaze to her hands, then up her arms. Intricate, golden lines had woven their way across her skin, forming stunning, ornate patterns. Like delicate veins, they traced up her arms and, she assumed, continued across the rest of her body.

Ancient markings. They've always been there, Queen Aniyah explained. *An indication that your time of expansion has arrived. These golden veins tracing your skin represent root systems stretching beneath your feet—a symbol of where you come from and who you're connected to. We are made of earth, soil, rock, and sludge. It has taken many, many years to shape you, Fellowship. This unique design affirms that you're never alone.*

Fellowship's eyes traced the lines as they glimmered like Solneur at noon. *Your Majesty...*she just didn't have the words to express her gratitude.

I wish we had more time, Fellowship, but you must get back.

Panicked, Fellowship retreated, shaking her head. *What am I supposed to do? I don't know how to govern a kingdom or a city. Meanwhile, I don't have my gun; I haven't performed magic in years. How do I defeat Talon?*

With kindness in her eyes, Queen Aniyah extended her hand toward Fellowship. After a hesitant glance at the hand, then up at the queen, Fellowship reached out. The moment their hands met, a wave of warmth surged through her, quickly intensifying into a searing heat that ricocheted through her entire body. The power from her markings erupted in a brilliant burst of light. It should've been painful, but instead, it was exhilarating. As the light flowed through her, Queen Aniyah gently released her hand.

Fellowship, magic isn't some mystical force—it's a natural part of who you are. You've inherited the same power that Sylena, the Moon Goddess, once gifted to me. My blood flows through your veins. Trust in your own knowing. You don't need to learn how to be a queen because you already are one. You're ready for this. I promise, the queen said, turning toward the wall of forest. *You carry my essence and my royal ring. If you need further reassurance, behind my throne is a loose slab of marble where my sword and tiara are hidden. Reveal the truth about what happened to me. The Council will understand. Even if they resist giving up their power, their responsibility is to remain loyal to the Queen of Trianah. And lastly, since it's the Kumalada, as my gift to you, you will always have access to me and your ancestors,* she added with a nod.

Fellowship glanced around and noticed figures of light among the trees surrounding them. Across the creek, she saw her mother and grandmother, standing proudly. Though she thought she understood what the queen meant, she wanted to clarify. *You're saying I can mencom with my ancestors or anyone else in the Salveigh Mist?*

Queen Aniyah nodded.

Fellowship glanced at her mother and grandmother again, taking them deep into her heart. Fuck it—she was the heiress to the throne, she loved Lazlo's descendant, and Talon was a piece of shit. If she wanted to help those she cared about, if she wanted to save Trianah, she had to embrace who she was. Queen Aniyah's blood flowed through her, just like Limber's and Granny Reathe's. She wasn't alone. So, lifting her chin, she gave her queen a nod of acceptance.

Darkness.

Fellowship heard the steady drip of water and smelled mildew, as if she were in some subterranean space. Though her body was free of pain, she could tell she was lying on something hard. Opening her eyes, she saw only darkness. As she blinked, trying to bring her surroundings into focus, she made out misshapen old beams and blankets of cobwebs. If she didn't know any better, she'd say she was in a dungeon—ominous as hell. As her eyesight adjusted to the dark, she noticed a small window at the top of the right wall. Moonlight streamed through it, mere inches from where she lay. With no clue where Talon was, she moved slowly. She heard a quiet shuffling of feet against what sounded like a filthy, grainy concrete floor. She froze.

"Please, Guardians, please," she heard Auten whisper.

Adrenaline pumped through her veins—not only was he alive, but he was locked in a cell, perhaps?

"Please, Guardians, please," he whispered again as the shuffling continued.

Fellowship felt his energy, his distress. She realized that adrenaline-fueled fighting wouldn't help anyone, so she steadied her racing heart. Carefully moving her arm to check if she was tied down, she discovered that she was free. Sitting up, Fellowship heard a gasp. She quickly turned around and saw her grandfather, Nigh, along with Rey and Lemin, crowded into a dark, dirty cell with rusted, moldy bars. She was perched on what seemed like a table or bench, her feet dangling. Nigh's disheveled hair fell over her face as she covered her mouth. Rey's eyes were wide with shock. Both looked pale but otherwise unharmed. Auten was crying, as usual, and Lemin looked at her as if witnessing a miracle. Bracing herself, Fellowship slid down onto the wet concrete and wiped her hands on her pants. Still wearing her motorcycle jacket, she approached the cell. Auten grabbed the bars, tears streaming down his handsome face.

"Hi," she whispered.

"Talon," he said, voice hoarse. "I should've known. I'm so sorry."

Fellowship grabbed his cold hands. "Fuck Talon."

Auten's head snapped up. "What?"

"Fuck him," she said. She looked at his cellmates. "Are you guys okay?"

Nigh held out her dirty, pale hand—it was frail and ice-cold. "Professor, look at you. You're...you're beautiful," she said, her eyes red-rimmed.

"I'm happy you're safe. You, too, Rey," she said, nodding to him.

"Fell, what happened to you?" Auten asked.

"He knocked me out," she said, releasing Nigh's hand.

"No..." Auten said.

"I don't know what you mean. We don't have time—"

"You're an Aechaih!" Nigh said, her excitement barely contained as she kept her voice low.

Fellowship frowned and examined her hands and arms. The thin gold markings were faint but still visible. Aside from a lack of pain, she didn't feel much different, though everything seemed clearer than before, and her hearing was heightened—she could even make out faint footsteps. Running her fingers along her ears, she discovered they were *pointed.* Quickly, she pulled them down and rubbed her tongue over her *elongated canines,* looking around at everyone, almost too stunned to speak.

After a moment, she sighed. "Okay, guys, looks like I've changed a bit, but I'm still me."

"You look like a fucking badass," Rey said.

"Thanks?" With no time to waste, she looked at the cell. Maybe her

newfound Aechaih-ness could help her free her people. "I've gotta get you out of here."

"I don't think so," Talon drawled from behind her. There he was, she knew she heard something.

Whipping around, she pressed her back against the cell bars.

"Good to see you up and about," he said, emerging from the darkness like a true creep. Hand in his vest pocket, he tilted his head as he beheld her. "I see you've been upgraded."

"I have," she said. Clocking her surroundings, she saw a large marble bench in the middle of a hexagon with waxy candles sporadically placed. Was this motherfucker about to sacrifice her? Eyes flicking upward, she saw that Sylena's light was getting closer to the bench. "What the fuck do you want, Talon?"

"That's no way for a future queen to talk to her elder," he tsked.

Slowly, she edged away from the cell, moving left as Talon mirrored her, shifting to his right. After a careful, measured approach, they found themselves face to face with the hexagon-shaped bench in the center.

"How did you discover I was Queen Aniyah's heiress?" It was a stall tactic, but it was all she had until an idea formed. Her hands itched with heat, but she wasn't sure if it was enough to challenge an ancient, dark Aechaih. But like Queen Aniyah said—magic wasn't all woo-woo, right?

He shrugged and flicked a piece of lint off his arm. "I have my ways."

"Spare me the bullshit. How'd you know?"

Eyes flashing with inhumane darkness, he tilted his head. "I've known about you for some time. I had suspected Queen Aniyah was hiding something when I slaughtered her," he said, motioning to the bench. "Killing someone as powerful as her during the alignment meant I'd inherit everything Sylena gifted her. But," he said, shaking his head, "upon taking her last breath, I didn't sense a surge in power. After everyone viewed her body and left, I gutted her and found her womb empty."

Fellowship's stomach churned as her eyes fell to the marble slab in the middle of the hexagon where he had defiled her queen's body.

He continued. "After years of searching, I couldn't find the baby, so I waited," he said with a disgusting, distorted smile. "I was overjoyed to hear of a magical family living in the forest. I just *knew* it was her, but when I walked into the shabby home, I realized those women—though descendants—weren't the *true* heir. Slitting their throats and killing the human man who was with them, I thought I had been outdone. Then an informant told me that a little girl and her father crossed border control into Trianah Metro's city limits. Keeping an eye on her, I waited until she was of age before finding and seducing her. When I realized she had no power, I disposed of her, too. After stuffing her in a garbage bag behind her apartment building, like the trash she was, I was sure I'd never find Aniyah's descendant. That is, until one of my colleagues at Septain Memorial told me that Hyphen Haslem had brought in a human gunshot victim with extraordinary power. They said that by the time the healers got to her, she had begun healing *herself*. Imagine my surprise when Horace told me that the victim was Auten Dancy's granddaughter. That's when I ensured his home was wiretapped."

The. Motherfucker. Killed. *Daize?* Daize and her father had moved from the forest to Pawville about a year after she did. The difference was, Daize and her father had lived among other humans and had no fear crossing into the city, whereas Auten *knew* they had to sneak over in case someone was watching. Hands shaking, it was impossible to keep her thoughts from seeing Daize's face, dead and frozen in fear, her family's eyes wide and vacant, and Queen Aniyah's body gutted and destroyed. Until she knew what to do next, she relied on her police training. Eying the Aechaih, she realized Talon was a typical serial killer. Although perfectly content doing his dirty deeds in secret, in the end, he couldn't find true happiness until he received the credit he felt he deserved. This was Talon's time. He had hid behind Horace Haslem for too long, now he wanted everyone, or at least her, to know what he'd been up to.

"If you were after the heir, why kill Aechaih and blame humans?"

Narrowing his eyes, Talon smiled and tilted his head. "How did you know that was me?"

"Who else would have the wherewithal to pull it off, especially with your access to *FBDn*." She wasn't sure if he had access, but it felt plausible.

"Oh, and you discovered my means of communication," he said like the slimy motherfucker he was. "Too bad all humans aren't like you—able to recognize genius," he sighed. "To answer your question, I did it because humans are a *blight* on Trianah. I figured it was time to permanently edge them out, and framing them for murder was the easiest, most efficient way. *FBDn* gave me the perfect cover seeing that I'm a silent partner with Cygma Tech. When I discovered that someone had been snooping around their network, I realized that my trail had been picked up. That's why I grabbed *him*," he said, nodding to Lemin.

"When did you know for sure that I was Queen Aniyah's heir?" As sick as it was, she wanted to know what he knew and how.

With a wave of his bony hand, he smiled. "When I saw you in City Hall. The power you channeled to put Horace Haslem in his place was nothing short of brilliant. I immediately recognized Aniyah's energy—her *essence* emanated from you. With *Kumalada* rapidly approaching, everything had aligned for me to not only destroy Trianah's monarchy for good, but also rid it of its pest problem. Your conversation with Auten sealed the deal and here we are," he said, looking up to Sylena's light pouring from the window. "It's finally time for me to come into my true power."

"Actually," she started, "you'd be coming into *Queen Aniyah's* power so...yeah. But I understand what you mean."

"I don't care who it comes from, once your blood fills this space," he said, nodding to the bench and hexagon, "it's mine."

"Too bad you've been consumed by envy."

"Who could I possibly be envious of?"

"Queen Aniyah. You hated that she had the love of both humans *and* Aechaih. Your villain origin story is predictable: poor Talon, all alone in the shadows, mad that everyone loves the beautiful Aechaih queen instead of him. Playing second to Aniyah *and* Horace has taken its toll," she said, nodding like she was a fucking psychoanalyst. If she were, then she'd know not to provoke a sociopath with delusions of grandeur, but poking him felt *right*. That is until his eyes went other-worldly dark. With a flick of his wrist, pain exploded in her body. It felt like her skin was peeling off in ribbons. Worse than being shot, her muscles seized as she cried out, her throat raw.

"You have a mouth on you, girl," he said. "Perhaps I'll break you before gutting you like I did your ancestor," Talon mused.

Closing her eyes, she transmuted the pain, turning it into the heat she felt when she took Queen Aniyah's hand. That's when she heard Talon gasp. Opening her eyes, she arched her eyebrow and smiled at him, then tilted her head.

"I understand your desire for power, but your reign of terror is over."

"What are you talking about?" he spat. "After killing you, I will possess this land. This is *my* kingdom."

"Talon, do you hear yourself? This type of super-villain grand-standing might've worked a thousand years ago, but now?" she said, shaking her head. Raising her hands in the air like every monologuing villain she'd seen on TV, she mocked him. "Argh, everything will be mine! I will rule it alllllll!" she said in an exaggerated version of him. Putting her hands down, she sucked her teeth and sighed. "Soooo over-played if you ask me."

Facing twisting in rage, he lifted his hands. Summonsing broken slabs of rock, he hurtled them at her. On instinct, she manipulated energy so that a gust of wind sent the stones crashing into the wall. Unbothered, she understood what Queen Aniyah meant. Magic wasn't some amorphous thing; it was a skill, like being a teacher or a cop.

"I'll get what's *mine*," he spat, sending a surge of energy toward her. Stepping to her left, it collided with the wall, causing the space to shake, sending rocks scattering.

"No!" Talon screamed.

Lifting his arms above his head, he rounded them, then pushed them toward her. She felt his magic scrape at her skin, but after a moment, it was gone. Lifting her hands in front of her chest, her left palm hovered over her right. Closing her eyes, she felt like *little Fellowship* in the clearing. Then, a cool heaviness formed between her hands. Opening her eyes, she saw an orb of flame materialize, licking at her palms. Fireballs, huh? Not bad. Hands rotating in a circular motion, the orb spun, then, on instinct, she hurtled it toward Talon, who stood watching, dumbfounded. Moving just in time, it crashed into the wall behind him and disappeared.

As Sylena's light inched perilously close to the slab, Talon's face melted into a hideously distorted snarl. Mouth and eyes black, he was monstrous. She heard Nigh yip in fear. His skin looked like melted plastic as he stalked toward her. Before she knew it, he pushed his hands in her direction. A gush of heat knocked the breath out of her, sending her slamming into the cold, hard wall. Stars behind her eyes, she landed on the ground, knocking her head as blood filled her mouth.

Dizzy, she lifted her head, moving onto all fours. Finally pushing up, he hit her with another wave of heat. It smelled like rotten food as he pushed her back into the wall. Hitting her head again, she was sure it had cracked opened. Landing on the wet concrete, she lay there, face pressed against the cool stone. In the distance, she could hear Talon's snarling laugh over his prisoners' screams. Darkness nipped at her consciousness. She'd been here before—facing the inevitable. The dark unknown. Cold and weak, she lay crumpled on the filthy, slimy floor.

FELL?! she heard Hyphen scream in her head. *Fellowship, focus on my voice. Where are you?* His warmth filled her as she took ragged breaths, each one more painful than the next. She wanted so badly to talk to him, to answer, but she couldn't. It felt like all of her confidence and power from Queen Aniyah had slipped away. She was nothing but a weak human, unable to defeat a dark Aechaih. *Fellowship, listen to me,* she heard him say. *I love you with all that I am. Your power astounds me. Your beauty inspires me. Your love strengthens me. You are not alone, Fellowship Dancy!*

Alone. She wasn't alone. Eyes closed, she saw figures of light in the forest: her mother and grandmother, her queen. She saw everyone she loved. Then, she saw Hyphen—her friend, her mate. She wasn't alone. She was enveloped by acceptance, power, and love. She had to rise—had to push through the pain and fight. As soon as she stirred, she felt Hyphen's warmth pressing into her. Without hesitation, she rolled over and stood. Blinking the world into focus, she spit out a glob of blood.

"You want *more?!*" Talon screamed. "I don't have time for this!"

Wobbling on weak legs, head pounding, she braced her hands on her thighs before standing upright. Talon, face frozen in desperate evil, flicked his eyes to the cell. If this motherfucker thought she was about to let him hurt her family, he was more fucked up than she thought. Before he flicked his wrist, she extended her arms to her sides, palms up, then down. She felt energetic tension obey her movements. Bringing her hands back up, she sensed its weight. Before she could overthink, she pushed it to him. It forced him back onto his ass. Shaking his head, he stood again and moved toward her family.

"No," she said, her voice calm and steady.

Talon snarled and pushed his arms toward them. Before anything hit them, she darted in front of the cell with Aechaih speed and knocked the energy back, throwing him into the stone wall, his body landing with a thud. Turning around, she made sure they were safe. Wide-eyed, they smiled at her before Auten's face melted into fear. She felt Talon before he made a move. In the millisecond before she faced him, she knew what was needed to end this whole fucking nightmare. Turning around, she saw Sylena's light on the empty slab of marble which meant he had already failed. He saw it too, which unleashed an otherworldly rage; it was so insidious and evil that it made her insides churn. Black eyes narrowed, he snarled and launched himself at her.

Using his own energy as a tether, she manipulated it with her hands, palms up. Suspended in the air, his face went slack with shock. With a power she had never felt before, she held him there as he thrashed and snarled like a wild animal. She then floated him over to the marble slab.

"Aechaih *bitch!*" he spat as his sweat-covered face shimmered under Sylena's light. "You'll never govern Trianah, you hear me? Not another Aechaih bitch will rule—"

Tired of his mouth, she crossed her arms in front of her chest, then twisted her wrists. In a second, she heard his body snap, then land on the slab. Neck broken with limbs at unnatural angles, he lay sprawled on the same place he slaughtered her queen. His hair was caked with dirt as black liquid pooled in his mouth, dribbling down his chin. Then there was a soft hiss as his body crumbled into ash and blew away. Nothing of Talon Seram was left save his clothes.

Well fuck. She hadn't expected that. Turning to face her family, she shook her head and waved her hands in front of the bars, which then vanished. None of them moved. Nigh and Rey's jumpsuits were filthy, Lemin's hair was disheveled, and her grandfather had smudges on his face. She glanced around before turning back to them.

"Did it not work? Or...?" she asked.

Nigh took off at full speed toward her. Before Fellowship could brace herself, the girl slammed into her, wrapping her thin arms around her neck. "Professor," she choked out over shuddering sobs. Hugging Nigh, she rubbed her back until her sobs settled into hiccups. Slowly, her grandfather and the others eased out of the cell.

Drawing back, she looked at her student. "I'm sorry you lost your friend, Nigh," she said.

Nodding, Nigh sniffed back tears. Her eyes and nose red, she leapt back into Fellowship's arms. Finally, she pulled away and walked over to Rey, who draped his arm around her neck. Auten stood in front of her. Though he looked tired, his eyes were bright.

"Look at you," he said, shaking his head.

It was her turn for comfort—without hesitation, she stepped into his arms. Relishing in his hug, she let out a deep sigh of relief.

Auten shook with tears as he rubbed her back. "I love you," he whispered.

"I love you, too," she said into his shoulder. Pulling back, she smiled, then arched an eyebrow. "Oh, by the way, Layne Tarnicon survived."

His eyes widened, his mouth open. After a few beats of stunned silence, he finally blinked and whispered, "*Guardians.*"

"She's at Septain."

"Once I came to, I saw... It was so awful. I..." Auten's face crumbled into a silent sob as he hugged her again. He drew back, then shoved his hand into his pocket and produced a wrinkled handkerchief. She laughed on a breath as he dabbed his eyes. Ever the gentleman, her grandpa.

Fellowship smiled. It had to feel good for him to know that his ladylove was okay. "Meanwhile, you're going to have to answer for keeping secrets," she tsked playfully. "I mean Layne Tarnicon—damn, Grandpa. I would've never thought."

Auten choked on a laugh. "We couldn't tell, I mean..."

"Oh, I get it," she said, thinking about her *own* love. "Meanwhile, I have to get to Hyphen before he tears this city apart. Does anyone know how to get out of here?"

Chapter Twenty-Seven

Hyphen felt powerless as he gazed out over Trianah. With no idea where Fellowship was, he had no choice but to wait. After flying to the precinct, he and Monroe had scoured the entire building searching for her. The only thing they found was her gun, down in holding. Despite multiple attempts to reach her via men-com, he was on the verge of taking to the skies to search the city when Monroe stopped him.

"Where are you going to go?" he asked as Hyphen paced back and forth in front of the precinct.

"I don't know. I can't just sit here," he snapped.

Monroe nodded. "Or, you and I can go up to your office and wait to hear from her," he suggested.

"But—"

"Haslem, you're no help to Dancy or anyone else if you're flying around Trianah in a fucking panic."

Annoyed that he was right, he snapped his wings in. "Fine."

Monroe stayed silent as Hyphen paced his office, his hands shoved into his pockets. He'd walk a few steps, then stop to stare out over Trianah, repeating the pattern. When the office door opened, he turned and frowned at his boss. Without a word, he returned to the window, pointedly ignoring him.

"Have you heard?" Ified asked.

"What?" Monroe replied.

"Neither suspect was transferred to holding and Ambassador Dancy is missing. No one knows what's going on, where they are, or what happened. Weeden thinks that they've escaped."

"Weeden's a dick," Hyphen said, turning around.

Ified's mouth opened, but nothing came out.

Looking from Ified, then back to Hyphen, Monroe intervened. "What did the human precinct say?"

"They reported that a TMPD van arrived and picked up the suspects, but the van didn't return here."

"And the Ambassador?" Monroe asked.

Ified shrugged. "They checked his house, office—nothing," Ified said.

"How much you wanna bet Talon Seram has them," Hyphen said.

"Seram? I don't understand. Why would he—"

"It's a long story, boss," Monroe interrupted. "From what we can tell, no one ever arrived to holding except for Detective Dancy looking for the ambassador."

Ified's eyes widened. "Solneur," he breathed. "Nothing about this seems right," he said, shaking his head. "I can't put my finger on it."

"Same," Monroe said, nodding.

With no desire to share anything about Fellowship with Ified, Hyphen continued to stare out the window. Searching for their connection for what felt like the millionth time, he came up empty. It was like when she was in Septain—their link seemed severed, and he was sick to death over it.

"Did you get an update on Tarnicon?" Monroe asked Ified.

"She's stable. I'm going to have someone review the garage footage to see who checked out the van. Maybe there's something there," he said.

"If you need me, I'll be in here," Monroe replied.

"Sounds good," Ified said. Hyphen continued to watch him in the reflection. Ified stared back, then on a nod, he left.

"He's an idiot, but he's not malicious," Monroe said to Hyphen's back.

"I know."

After that, they continued to wait until Hyphen sent a reluctant Monroe home. Frosting his office for privacy, he sat in his desk chair, head in his hands. That's when he felt her—faint but distinct enough to make him sit up and call for her. Though there was no response, he sensed her presence. The connection was weak; she was weak and losing hope. His heart pounded in his ears as he struggled to determine her location and her situation. The best he could do was urge her to hold on, to tell her how much he loved her and that she was more than capable. Sending his love, heat, and magic down the line, he felt the connection strengthen before she was gone again. Flopping back in his chair, he sucked in a breath. She couldn't be dead. He couldn't lose her.

Unable to go home, he sat at his desk, staring at nothing. He felt empty, lost, and hopeless. Sick to his stomach, he couldn't stop seeing her on the ground in front of Queen Aniyah's Temple, her blood-soaked sweater, and her gaze locked onto him. He couldn't stop hearing her call him *Aechaih*. The depth of his despair rivaled the void he felt after Hudson's death, but now it was even colder and darker. How could the Guardians have given him someone as remarkable as Fellowship Dancy and then taken her away? How could he endure without her by his side? Fellowship wasn't just a woman he was dating or a fling; she was his mate. He was created to love her, and if she was truly gone, he wondered what life could possibly hold for him.

Then, as if seeing her smile, he felt her unique warmth hum through his body. Sitting up, he looked around, wiping his face as he stood. Had he deceived himself into believing she was alive when she wasn't? Before he could send anything down their line, there she was:

Hey, handsome.

In his two hundred and ten years, Hyphen had known moments of relief. Haze, as a baby, sick with fever—he stayed up all night until it broke. Relief. Finding a purpose beyond mourning Hudson. Relief. Seeing Fellowship stable after she was shot. Relief. Ending things with Bronwyn. Relief. Seeing Fellowship waiting at his elevator after their breakup. Relief. And now, feeling her loving warmth down the line, strong and potent as ever. Fucking relief. He flopped down in his desk chair and let out a ragged breath.

Baby?

Who else would it be? she asked because even after enduring whatever the hell she had just endured, she still had a smart fucking mouth.

Laughing, he ran his hands through his hair. *Just checking. Where are you?*

Even after all of this time, you still can't ping me. Tsk. Tsk.

How are you a pain in the ass after all of this? He felt her laugh.

I'm at Queen Aniyah's Temple.

He frowned. *How'd you get there?*

Turns out, there's a nifty dungeon underneath where, from the looks of the setup, Talon was preparing to sacrifice me.

Standing, he shoved his keys and phone into his pockets and walked out of his office. *I'm so sorry you had to go through that alone. Is everyone okay?*

Yes. I lost my phone, but Lemin had enough juice to call Rayna once we were up here. I had her come and get them.

Walking across the precinct's lobby, Hyphen stepped out into the Trianah night air. *He grabbed Lemin, too? What the fuck?*

I know, right?

Outside, Hyphen materialized his wings and shot into the air. *I'm on my way.*

Oh, good, because I miss you.

I miss you, too, Fell.

Flying across the city to reach her was better than the perfect Zion's Ink or Santander's noodles. With the wind whipping at his face, he hovered over the temple, circling until he spotted her sitting at Queen Aniyah's fountain.

Landing, he walked over to her. She sat with her jacket in her lap, staring off into the distance. As she sensed his presence, she turned and smiled. Despite her visible fatigue, her smile was still luminous, radiating warmth. He stopped short, taking in the sight of her—his love, his heart. She stood, walked toward him, and then ran into his arms. Closing his eyes, he held her as tightly as he could, resting his chin on the top of her head. She felt so good—so soft and so alive. Her arms tightened around him, a bit stronger than he was used to.

"I'm so happy to see you," she said, her voice muffled.

Swallowing the lump in his throat, he squeezed her until he was confident that his voice wouldn't sound weepy. Because, to be clear, he was weepy as fuck. "I'm happy to see you, too."

She pulled back enough to look up at him.

Solneur. Sylena. Solneur and Sylena. Fuck! He wanted to say something. *Should've* said something. Why didn't he say anything? Fellowship Dancy was incandescently beautiful—breathtakingly beautiful, heart-stoppingly beautiful. Everything about her was different and yet the same: pointed ears, elongated canines, and faint gold markings on her face. She was Aechaih—a Solneur-damned Aechaih.

"You..." It was all he could manage as he continued to gape at her.

"I hope you meant what you said about loving me if I presented as Aechaih because, yeah..." she said with a sassy smile.

Guardians. When they discussed her lineage, he wasn't surprised to learn she descended from Queen Aniyah, but seeing that heritage manifest was a shock. Fellowship was a stunning human and an even more radiant Aechaih—not just because of her pointed ears and elongated canines, but because of the newfound confidence and power. The vitality. The *royalty.* She was still shorter than him, still soft and rounded. Still Fellowship. Still his love.

Then, like the seductress she was, she ran her tongue along one of her canines. "These are new, too. Down to let me try them out?"

"I love you," he blurted.

Smiling broadly, the gold lines in her face glowed in prominence. "I love you, too," she said, sliding her arms around his neck and lifting up to kiss him.

Mouth on hers, he grabbed her ass, pulling her closer. Hands in his hair, her kiss reached down to the depths of his soul and yanked it up. Instantly hard, he tried to pull away, but she wouldn't let go. She grabbed at his sweater as her kiss swallowed him whole. The heat was so fucking intense that it clawed at his primitive instincts. His fingers dug into her softness as he moaned into her mouth. Then, to kill him, she nipped him with a canine.

"Fuck," he ground out, pulling away. Her eyes were dark, glassy, and full of heat for him.

Cocking her head to the side, she looked around. "Would it be indecent to fuck right here?"

He barked out a laugh before he cupped her face, kissing her nose. "You're perfection. So fucking beautiful."

She smiled—oh, her smile. How could something stop his world? Change his life? Alter his chromosomes?

"Your voice in my head," she whispered, smile fading. "I was so cocky at first, then he hit me with so much magic, I was sure I was going to die. Then you were there."

"It was the scariest moment of my life and when I met you, you were half dead."

"Thank you for loving me, Hyphen."

"Fell." It was all he could get out. Shutting his eyes, tears squeezed through, zigzagging down his face.

"There's something I want to give you. I thought I could wait, but I can't."

Opening his eyes, the rest of his tears fell. Still cupping her face, he smiled. "What could you possibly give me? You being alive is enough."

"It's two things, really," she said, grabbing his hand. She led him back to the fountain where they sat next to the gurgling water.

His eyes landed on the two boxes next to her. "What are those?" he asked, nodding.

She followed his eyeline. "Oh, that's Queen Aniyah's sword and tiara."

"Oh."

"I know," she said. "When Talon knocked me out at the precinct, I slipped into another realm—somewhere between the Salveigh Mist and here. I saw my mom and grandmother, and I saw Queen Aniyah."

The hairs on the back of his neck stood as she inched closer to him. Threading her fingers through his, she looked at him.

"Did you know that your mom is related to Lazlo Lysine?"

"Uh..." He was ashamed to admit that he didn't even know his mother's maiden name.

"Everything I'm about to say might sound crazy, so just roll with it," she said, taking a breath. "Queen Aniyah told me that Horace was actually a good guy at first. She had hoped he'd help smooth out Talon's rough edges. She mentioned that he married Honey Lysine, Lazlo's cousin, and was doing well in her court. She admitted that Talon's darkness had influenced Horace, and you know," she said, nodding. "But she also said that Horace didn't know the full truth; he genuinely believed it was Rhoman."

"Oh," he breathed.

"What?"

"I told him about you and..."

"He was surprised, wasn't he?"

He nodded. Although he wasn't sure whether it would heal their relationship, there was a part of him that was relieved to know father hadn't always been a self-serving, power-hungry asshole.

"I asked her if your wings came from your mother's lineage, and she confirmed it. Despite your tough upbringing, you're the descendant of a great warrior—a man who protected her *and* Trianah."

He was overwhelmed. How could Fellowship find audience with Queen Aniyah and ask about *him?* Chest swelling with pride, he smiled at his love. "Fellowship..."

"It's a lot," she said, nodding. "But she knows how much I love you. It wouldn't surprise me if she *knew* what I'd ask."

Kissing her cheek, he bit back his tears. "That's a wonderful gift, baby," he said around the lump in his throat. Knowing he was the descendant of his favorite winged Aechaih was deeply powerful and transformative.

"The queen gave me another gift," she added. "She told me that I can talk to her whenever."

He cocked his head to the side. "Like..."

She nodded. "I can *men-com* my ancestors."

"Now, that's something I definitely read about when I was younger. That's an old-ass ability—a *connector*," he said, eyes wide. "That's remarkable, Fell. *You're* remarkable."

"I want to give you something, Hyphen," she said as the lines on her face began to shimmer alive.

"Finding out about my lineage is enough..." Besides, he wasn't how much more he could take.

"Please, let me," she whispered. Inching even closer, her thigh pressed against his. She squeezed his hand and closed her eyes. After a few beats, she smiled as a tear escaped the corner of her eye. Finally, she opened them and looked at him. He felt a shiver work its way down his spine. "You ready?"

"For what?"

"I found Hudson," she whispered.

Clearly, he had heard her wrong, so he leaned forward. "I'm sorry, what?"

"I told him that I'm your mate and here with you now."

It was one thing to show up with pointed ears and new teeth, but another to fuck around like this. Heart rumbling in his chest, he frowned. "Fellowship," he said, trying to retreat. Holding onto his hand, she didn't respond; instead, her magic engulfed him like a strong, loving hug. Exactly like the hugs he received from his brother. *No. No. Fuck no. It was impossible.* "Fell..." he choked out, eyes wide in worry. It didn't make sense. How could he feel something he hadn't felt in thirty years? How could he feel *him*? What the fuck was going on? He felt in and out of his skin at the same time.

She used her free hand to push his hair off his forehead. "Do you trust me?"

The panic and worry that bubbled up faded into nothing. He nodded because in the end, he loved *and* trusted her.

"Okay, baby," she whispered.

The warmth was otherworldly. At first, he felt Fellowship's energy —humming, warm, and vibrant. Then, after a moment, he sensed Hudson's calm, cool presence, an energy he thought he'd never experience again. Breath catching in his throat, he closed his eyes. Despite the doubts his mind harbored, his heart believed. Fellowship squeezed his hand and rested her head on his shoulder. Hudson's presence grew so strong it felt as though he was right there with them by the fountain. Overwhelmed, the bashful, awkward version of himself resurfaced, longing desperately for his big brother.

Hyphen?

Hyphen nodded, tears escaping his eyes. *I'm here.*

I see your love found you. Hyphen felt Hudson's smile along the line—his bright, charming smile.

She did.

I told you she would.

I've missed you so fucking much. Part of me can't believe this is happening. Then there's another part that's totally okay with it, he said on one long thought.

I've missed you, too. I'm glad she found me because I've been wanting so badly to apologize to you. He felt Hudson's smile fade into sorrow and guilt.

What do you have to be sorry for? he asked. He felt his brother pause. Suddenly, he could imagine sitting across from him in their family library. Hudson was always slow to respond. Contemplative. Careful. He felt his brother search for the right words.

I'm sorry I left you.

Hyphen took a shuddered breath as Fellowship held his hand. Feeling Hudson's energy again, all the anger and resentment he had felt melted away. Yet, Hudson knew that an apology was still necessary. *It's okay.*

No, it's not. I let the darkness consume me—so much so that I couldn't see beyond my own pain. It felt like it would never get better and—

You don't have to explain—

Yes, I do. It's important to me that I do. Hyphen, I need you to know that before it happened, I saw your face. I saw it small and red—the day I brought you home from the hospital. I saw it light up with excitement when you took your first steps. I saw it whenever you smiled at me when I walked into the room. I saw it when you were older and pissed off at being so special. I saw you, Hyphen. I saw you and, in that moment, I convinced myself that you'd be okay. That our time together was enough. That you'd be better off without me or my darkness. Hyphen, I love you beyond words...beyond anything in your world or mine.

Dropping his head, Hyphen let out a choked sob. He kept his mouth closed, holding back the cry until he felt Fellowship's gentle squeeze—a small, reassuring sign that he wasn't alone. As the sobs grew stronger, he opened his mouth, letting the emotions spill out. His shoulders shook as he clung to her hand, the pain of losing his brother pouring out in waves of raw hurt. There was no shame, no worry, no embarrassment—just the comfort of her presence as the walls he'd built around himself crumbled.

Hudson continued. *We can sense the energy of our loved ones here in the Mist. For a long time, I couldn't feel yours. I searched for you whenever I could, but there was nothing. It hit me then how much my actions had affected you—more than I realized. I was so afraid, fearing you'd show up beside me here, but when you didn't, I thought the worst had happened—you were alive in body but dead in soul.*

Then, out of the blue, I felt you. Faint, frail, but unmistakably you. I was relieved, yet still concerned because it wasn't the full version of you I knew. Despite that, I was grateful to the Guardians for the steady presence of your energy. It grew stronger, so much so that I thought I was imagining it. The energy was excited, then hesitant and unsure. It was hopeful, then worried, as if you wanted something deeply but didn't know how to reach it.

Gradually, it became stronger, warmer, and more confident. It faltered but then stabilized, growing bigger and brighter. Before I knew it, I felt you, baby brother—the you I know, alive in body and soul. That's when I realized—you had found her, and she had found you.

Growing up in Trianah, everyone knew about the Salveigh Mist —the realm where their loved ones and ancestors resided after leaving the physical world. But he had no idea they could still feel the presence of those left behind. That they could sense their concern, worry, happiness, or sadness. What Hudson had described was Hyphen's life without him, from joining the force to finally finding Fellowship.

She saved me, he told his brother.

Funny, she told me that you saved her.

Hyphen laughed. *That sounds like her. How about we saved each other?*

That sounds right. What's she like?

Hud, she's fucking spectacular. Smart and thoughtful. Caring and unique. This woman...this woman changed my life.

You fell in love with the Aechaih queen.

Yes, I guess I did.

She told me that you've spread your wings.

For her, I did.

She sees you and loves you so much. When her energy arrived over here, I felt her power. It was like she burst through the door screaming, "Where's Hudson Haslem?!" Hyphen felt his brother's amusement dance along the line. Opening his eyes, he looked down. Fellowship was asleep, hand still clutching his.

I love her so fucking much. I love you, too.

I love you, Hyphen. And I'm so happy you're okay—it's all I ever wanted for you.

I am. It's...it's a miracle.

It's a miracle for me, too. How are the twins? I always feel them, snapping and crackling.

That's exactly how they are. They've been my saving grace, aside from Fell.

And Mom? She keeps a steady energy, but it's been a spiky lately. Don't know what's going on there.

She's okay. I'm not sure what's going on either, but I made the commitment to tend to our relationship more.

That's good. And...Father?

Hyphen took a deep breath. *As of right now, he's no better than he was thirty-two years ago.*

I'm sorry to hear that. I hope...I hope it gets better. That he finds his way...

We'll see...

That's fair. I feel that your queen is asleep. Get her home.

I will. I love you.

I love you, too, Hyphen. I'm so proud of the man you've become. Don't forget to check in and tell me how you and the queen are doing in Trianah.

I will. I promise. I love you, Hudson.

I love you, Hyphen.

And then he was gone. Hudson's energy gradually faded, but not completely. It was as if he had left the door ajar, allowing Hyphen to always find him. Looking down, he saw that Fellowship was out. He owed the Guardians an apology for doubting their ability to keep her safe. Not only had they protected her, but they had ensured she made her way back to him. What a fucking gift. Kissing her forehead, she stirred, then moaned.

"Come on, my queen."

Blinking open her eyes, she smiled. "Everything okay?" she asked, her voice hoarse.

"Yes, baby. It's perfect."

"Good."

Grabbing her chin between his thumb and forefinger, he kissed her softly. "I love you, Fellowship."

"I love you, Hyphen."

"Let's go home."

Helping her up, she groggily stumbled, getting her balance. He helped her into her jacket before she bent down and picked up her sword and tiara. Clutching them to her chest, she looked up at him and smiled.

"I don't want you to freak out but I'm going to fly us home, okay?"

Eyes lighting up, she unleashed her light, surrounding him with her heat. "Fly? If you say so," she whispered, looking up at him with a Multayvien Sea's worth of adoration.

"I say so, Fellowship."

Chapter Twenty-Eight

Fellowship dropped fresh ice cubes into several tumblers, using her water manipulation—a skill she'd been honing alongside her fire magic and other new abilities that had emerged over the past few weeks. With Talon dealt with, life had finally calmed enough for her to schedule a meeting with the Tri-Families to discuss the future of Trianah Metro. The details of her lineage, her confrontation with Talon, and her connections with Rhoman and Queen Aniyah were all public knowledge. Her grandfather had even told her that Horace, of all people, had confirmed her status and advised the Council against challenging her power. Where the hell that came from was beyond her. Truthfully, she had no clear idea of what the future held, but she was confident it would unfold as it should. And if not, she'd men-com Queen Aniyah.

Her body hummed as the scents of seacoast and lavender drifted by. Moments later, Hyphen rounded the corner, his hand in his pants pocket. He looked stunning in a black suit and shirt, the collar casually unbuttoned. Flashing her a smile, he entered the kitchen and hugged her from behind.

"Hey, handsome."

"Did I mention how good you look in that dress?"

Facing him, she slid her arms around his waist, then looked down at her black, sheath dress. "This old thing?" Hands on her ass, he kissed her neck, giving it a swipe with his tongue. Biting her lip with a canine, she moaned. "You better watch it, Haslem."

"Or what?"

"You know what," she said, pressing her heavy, magical heat around him.

Eyes dark, he gave her a little growl—the one that never failed to get her wet. "Savage," he said, licking his lips.

"Remind me again why we have company?" she asked, regretting that she couldn't drag his ass to the bedroom.

Laughing, he kissed her neck and turned her back around to face their guests. "Because we love them," he said, chin resting on her shoulder, arms around her waist.

She looked outside at their family. Haze and Nigh were deep in conversation on the sofa, while Rey, Harleigh, and Zaphine relaxed on the other side. Her grandfather and Layne Tarnicon chatted warmly, sharing loving smiles. Monroe and Lemin conversed on another sofa, while Soren and Rayna had drifted to a dim corner, completely engrossed in each other.

"You see that?" she asked, nodding to their best friends.

"Solneur help us," he groaned.

"What'd you think would happen if they got together?"

"I'd assume something resembling Rhoman's Massacre."

"Hyphen!" she admonished, facing him.

"I'm serious," he said, shaking his head.

"First, it's *Talon's Uprising*."

"Either fucking way, if *they* become a thing, I'm escaping to the forest," he deadpanned.

"What about me?" she asked, laughing.

"You can come, too."

"Well, thank you," she said, giving him a playful shove. "Can I have a kiss?"

"You can always have a kiss," he said, pressing her against the counter before giving her one of those toe-curling kisses that ruined her panties. Arms around his neck, she ran her fingers through his hair, as the combination of their heat tweaked her nipples.

"I like kissing you," she whispered into his mouth.

"I like kissing you, too. Now that you've adjusted to those," he said, nodding to her canines.

"I only nicked you a couple of times," she said, arching an eyebrow.

Kissing her nose, he gave her that hot, lazy smile. "So, I wanted to ask you something and let me know if it's too soon or whatever."

"Okay..."

"Would you like to move in with me? I have so much room here and..." he trailed off just as his face turned the cutest shade of pink.

She cocked her head to the side. "Are you blushing, Detective?"

"Pain in the ass," he said flatly.

She laughed, then looked around his penthouse. "You realized I came for the twins' interview and never left, right?"

He shrugged. "I wanted to make it official."

"Oh, yeah?"

"Yeah," he said, his voice low.

"I didn't realize you were *into* official."

It took him a moment, but once he understood, he sucked his teeth. "Fucking Monroe," Hyphen said, rolling his eyes. "We don't have to be *official* partners. We just partners."

She laughed. "I like that you wanna be official with me because I wanna be official with you," she said, sliding her arms around his waist.

He eased into her mind. *I love you.*

I love you, too, she said, pulling him down for a kiss.

So, you'll stay with me?

Where am I gonna go, Aechaih?

He smiled broadly, his eyes a crisp, clear green reminiscent of the forest. Leaning down, he kissed her so deeply she was sure her dress had melted off. Clawing at his shoulders, she felt the steady hum of his magic crack around them—he had released his wings. Countless unknowns lay ahead. Would she stay at TMPD? Continue teaching? How would she govern Trianah Metro or support the human population? There were no clear answers, no concrete plans. But one thing was certain: she loved her family. Becoming who she was meant to be had been worth every tear and heartbreak, every moment of doubt, loss, and pain. Worth bleeding out on the sidewalk and facing death. For it was through the darkness that she had found the light—found him: her best friend, her mate, her winged Aechaih, and loving protector.

Epilogue

One Year Later

Fellowship bolted upright in bed, a whimper escaping her lips. The only sound cutting through the ringing in her ears was the frantic pounding of her heart. After a moment, she felt a familiar, reassuring hand settle on the small of her back.

Hyphen.

As her eyes adjusted to the dim light of their bedroom, she could make out the sharp lines of his jaw and the furrow in his brow, etched with concern. The Trianah rain pelted against their penthouse windows, its rhythmic drumming soothing her almost as much as the sound of Hyphen's voice.

"What was it?" he asked, softly. His dark, heavy hair was tousled with sleep, but his seafoam green eyes were alert—focused.

"Darkness," she croaked out before reaching for the glass of water on her nightstand. After a sip, she leaned back against the cushioned headboard. Hyphen joined her, the duvet falling from his bare, tattooed chest. On instinct, she curled into his warmth, hand still clutching her glass. His long arms wrapped around her like a shield. "Darkness from the Salveigh Mist, coasting along the sea. Like a black fog creeping toward the city."

"Hmph," he said as he squeezed her tighter.

"I know. Ominous as fuck."

"And where were you when all of this was happening?"

"We were standing on the pier, watching. Waiting."

"I was with you, good," he whispered more to himself than to her.

"Does it sound cliché to suggest something bad is coming?"

"Is it how you feel?"

She didn't want to answer him because, in the end, there was no lying to her mate, her person. After she knocked back her water, Hyphen took the glass and set it on her nightstand. Then, gathering her in his arms, he pulled her close and wrapped them in the duvet.

"Not answering me, is an answer," he said, his face close to hers.

"I know," she whispered.

"I feel your fear," he said, rubbing her back.

I don't want to say it out loud, she relayed mentally.

Then tell me here.

Something's coming, and I don't know when or what it is, or whether we have the capability to stop it. Whatever it is, Has, it's coming for all of us—for Trianah.

We'll figure it out, baby. I promise. You're not alone.

Okay.

"I love you, Fell."

"I love you, Has."

She smiled, a deep sense of reassurance washing over her. It felt as if the Guardians had a grand design when they gifted her with Hyphen. Whatever lay ahead for Trianah, she knew she would need her mate by her side—her protector, her winged Aechaih. With him, she was ready to face anything that came their way.

About the Author

With a deep-rooted belief that love transcends boundaries, Chantell Monique crafts sexy, sophisticated love stories that delve into the complexities of human connection. When she's not weaving tales of passion and adventure, you'll find her immersed in a good book or indulging in her latest TV obsession. A passionate advocate for mental health and self-love, Chantell resides in the Midwest with her lovable pooch, Beans.

For more information and updates:
www.chantellmonique.com

instagram.com/chantellmoniqueromance

tiktok.com/chantellmoniqueromance

pinterest.com/chantellmoniqueromance

Bonus Chapter Introduction

To My Elite Readership:

Thank you for diving into the revised version of *A Unique Space for Us*. I hope you have fallen in love with it just as much as I have. Chapter 15.5 takes you through the days following Fellowship and Hyphen's deepening connection, right before they visit The Archives in Chapter 16. These scenes, though not advancing the main plot, are a heartfelt glimpse into their lives after finding each other and before the next wave of story events. They hold special significance for me, offering a window into their journey. I hope you enjoy this intimate exploration. Thank you for being a part of this adventure.

Chapter 15.5

Fellowship hauled two overnight duffels and a garment bag into Hyphen's private elevator. Clearly, she was crazy because not only did she sleep with her Aechaih partner, but she was essentially moving in with him a little over twelve hours later. Everything that transpired after the twins left was a surprise. Their shared truths, the way he coaxed her to orgasm on the kitchen island, held her as she slept, then sank his teeth into her, causing her to come harder than she'd ever come in her fucking *life*. His presence had erased every start-stop, bullshit relationship she had in the past. There was only him. And while that shit was overwhelming, there she was, claiming her space in his life. Leaning against the elevator wall, she sniffed the chunky, cashmere sweater she swiped from his impossibly large closet. It smelled like seacoast and lavender—*him*.

I'll always want you here.

She hoped he meant that shit because she had never wanted to be with someone more. Hyphen's energy flowed with her, not against. With him, she was at home. At peace. She was seen and protected—drawn into his warm, magical force field of adoration, and Sylena help her, she couldn't get enough of it.

The elevator doors to his darkened penthouse slid open. Desperate not to wake him, she quietly set her things down and slipped off her trainers. As she peeled off her jacket, her body began to warm, just as the hallway light flicked on. She turned to find a tousled-haired Hyphen standing there, clad only in gym shorts, his face a mix of panic and relief—he'd feared she'd left him. She knew it before he even spoke. Walking over, she craned her neck up to meet his half-hurt, half-relieved gaze.

"Hey," she whispered.

"You were gone," he whispered more to himself than to her.

"I went to Pawville. I didn't want to wake you."

"I thought..." He gave a small shake of his head.

Fellowship wrapped her arms around his waist, pressing her face to his warm chest. As she poured her apology into him, he let out a sigh and hugged her back.

"I thought I could get there and back without you noticing," she said.

He remained still for a moment, then grabbed her chin so that his green eyes were on hers. "I noticed."

"Why didn't you men-com?"

He looked away. "I just—I figured..."

Solneur. His tenderness seized her heart. On her tiptoes, she covered his mouth with hers, gently prying open his lips so that she could taste him. After a beat, he settled into the kiss, clutching her ass before sliding his hands under her sweater.

"No bra," he whispered, looking at her.

"Of course not, my intention was to crawl back in bed with you," she said. Finally, he gave her a half smile before burying his face in her neck.

"I don't mean to come off as needy or whatever," he said, his voice muffled.

"*Needy?* I'm the one who showed up with half her apartment in three bags. I even brought my favorite coffee mug," she said.

His body reverberated with a chuckle.

She rubbed his back as he continued to hold her. "I hope you meant what you said about wanting me here because I'd hate to lug this shit back to Pawville."

He stood, his jaw set in earnestness. "I'll always want you here."

"Always?" she asked with a smile.

"Always, Fell."

Her smile widened as she lifted her arms. On instinct, he reached down, picked her up, and slapped the hallway light off before walking to the sofa. The city lights cast a blue hue across his living area. Lowering her down, he dropped to his knees and slid his hands up her thighs.

"I like your sweater," he's said.

"This old thing? I picked it up in that shop you call a closet."

"It's not *that* big," he said, squeezing her thighs.

"Hyphen, it's a department store. It took me twenty minutes to find this."

He smiled, settled in between her legs, then gave her a slow I-missed-you-kiss. She returned it, hands in his hair. Whatever fear she felt about staying with him had been replaced with certainty. Hyphen dipped his fingers under the waistband of her leggings and peeled them off, then spread her legs so that he could appreciate her.

"Fell," he whispered before leaning forward and swiping her pussy with the width of his tongue. Her body immediately reacted to him—to his heat and magic. On a soft moan, she rested her hands on his head as he gently licked, then sucked at her clit with intentional pulls and nibbles. After a moment, he raised his head and sat back. A beat passed, then another as his eyes roamed over her in the darkness.

"What?" she whispered as his hands caressed her thighs.

He shook his head. "Nothing."

"It's something," she said with a smile.

It was definitely something, but he didn't want to say. That was okay because she had no trouble reading his face. She inched to the edge of the sofa, wrapped her arms around his neck, legs around his waist, and planted her lips on his. His hands slipped up her sweater before hugging her tightly. Their kiss felt like a dream—otherworldly and fluid. Mirrored movements of tongues and lips. He pulled away and in one swift move, sat on the sofa, pulling her onto his lap. Straddling him, she cupped his face and took a minute to admire his beauty —he was shadowed yet open. His seafoam green eyes almost glowed. He was breathtaking with his wild hair and slightly swollen lips.

"What?" he whispered.

"You're beautiful," she said.

He remained silent, as if she'd stolen his reply. After a moment, he leaned forward and gave her the softest, most delicate kiss. Then, with impressive speed, he pushed his shorts down to release his dick before he set her on top of him. "*Oh,*" was all she could get out as his cock touched a place in her that no one had ever reached. *Ever.*

Eyes dark, mouth plush, and eyebrows furrowed, he clutched her ass. "Fuck me," he commanded, voice so low she could barely hear.

At some point, she needed to make an altar to properly thank the Guardians for their creation. Hyphen had infiltrated her bloodstream, commandeered her thoughts, and hijacked her emotions. She was so fucking gone for him. Hands braced on the back of the sofa, she rocked on his dick. Filled to the brim, heat swelled in her core.

"Fellowship," he moaned. "You're *everything.*"

She kissed him, pressing her tongue into his open mouth. Pulling on his thick lips, she let him move her ass on his cock with increasing speed. Waves of molten lava crawled through her body until she disengaged, burying her face in his neck.

"You feel so good," he whispered in her ear. One hand up her sweater and one on her ass, they rocked themselves to the brink. Dazed, she looked at him—his jaw was clenched as his eyes held hers with unmitigated devotion.

"*Hyphen.*"

It was on the tip of her tongue, but she couldn't say it. How could such words demand to be spoken in so little time? She wrapped both arms around his neck and squeezed in an effort to communicate her feelings. He did the same as they tumbled into the deep unknown.

Accelerating, she rested her hands on his shoulders, pressing her forehead to his. Left hand bracing the small of her back, his right slid up her sweater to cup her breast, tweaking her nipple. Stars behind her eyes, she whimpered on each breath as an orgasm stormed her body. Hyphen palmed her ass, thrusting. Opening her eyes, she took him in—his face was flush with adoration. Adoration that squeezed her heart, causing her to jerk and wail on his dick. Moments later, he followed, moaning through his climax. Eyes on each other, they reached their peaks, then descended. There was no denying what she felt for him—it was as clear as the Trianah blue sky. She relaxed, resting her head on his shoulder. After a beat, he rubbed her back.

She looked at him. "Hi."

"Hey," he whispered with a sex-satisfied smile.

Leaning in, she took his mouth with an exhausted hunger; cupping her face, he matched her energy. Then she moved off of him, crawling to the end of the sofa, resting against the arm.

"Come here."

Smiling, he slid up his shorts and eased to her, laying on her chest. Fingering his hair, she kissed the top of his head and closed her eyes just as he burrowed into her, doing the same.

Hyphen heard his elevator door whoosh open. Opening his eyes, he sat up and looked at Fellowship, who was asleep with her mouth slightly open. Then, looking toward the elevator, he saw Soren standing with a self-satisfied smirk. Shaking his head, he eased up and walked to his friend.

"Am I interrupting something?" Soren whispered.

Sliding onto a barstool, Hyphen ran his fingers through his hair, then cast a quick glance at Fellowship as Soren took a seat next to him. "What's up?" he asked his best friend.

Soren, still smiling, rested his chin on the heel of his palm. "It's a wellness check. You weren't picking up your phone."

"It's in the bedroom."

"Oh, it's okay," he sang, then with a dramatic sigh added, "so, what did I miss?"

His best friend was a child. "Fuck off," Hyphen admonished with a smile.

"How long has she been here?"

"The twins interviewed her for their project yesterday and... she stayed."

"She stayed, huh," Soren replied, crossing his legs.

"I know," he said, looking at his friend whose eyes were on something behind him. Frowning, he turned around to see Fellowship standing by the sofa, horrified. "It's okay, baby. It's just Soren."

She tugged on his sweater in an attempt to cover her luscious thighs. "Um. Hi, Soren... I'm just going to..." she said, snatching up her leggings before doing a side shuffle toward his bedroom.

"Hi, Miss Dancy," Soren purred.

Hyphen turned back to Soren and frowned. Soren's ice-blue eyes were focused on him; he was so still, it seemed like he wasn't breathing.

"What the fuck's wrong with you?"

"You're in fucking *love*," he whispered.

"Is that a question?" Hyphen whispered back.

"It's an astute observation. Look at you," Soren said with a nod. "You're glowing even more than when you admitted to liking her."

"Whatever."

"You make me wanna find a cute human for myself."

"Shut up."

"You think I'm fucking around, but I'm not."

"Okay, Syx."

"Ask her if she has any friends interested in a tall, charming, blue-haired El-man who loves fine dining and exclusive parties."

"I will not."

"That's okay, I'll ask her myself," he said just as Fellowship rounded the corner. Smiling, she approached him, leaning her hip against the counter.

"What are you two whispering about?" she asked.

Putting his arm around her, he pulled her close. "Nothing. Soren's just being, Soren."

"How are you, Soren? It's a pleasure to meet you."

"Oh, Fellowship, I couldn't be better. And the pleasure's all mine," Soren replied with an extra helping of charm.

"I'm happy to hear it. Was there something you wanted to ask me?" she asked, raising an eyebrow.

Soren's eyes sparkled. "You heard that?" he asked, cocking his head to the side.

"I heard you say you were going to ask me yourself. Ask me what?"

"Nothing, baby," Hyphen interjected. Soren narrowed his eyes at him, then hissed.

Fellowship laughed. "Don't worry about him. You can ask me."

"Thank you, Fellowship," Soren said with a huff. "I wanted to know if you had any cute human friends you could hook me up with."

"Oh," she said, eyes wide. "I only have one female friend, so..."

"That's okay. Tell me about her."

"She's smart, sexually fluid, and doesn't believe in monogamy."

"I love her already," Soren gushed. Fellowship laughed as Hyphen pulled her close. Half standing, half on his lap, she rested her arms on the counter as he rubbed her back.

"Are you staying for breakfast?" she asked just as Hyphen grabbed Soren's eyes and shook his head *no*.

"I'd *love* to," Soren sang.

"Oh, good." Then, turning to him, she smiled. "Will you make us breakfast?"

Obviously, he couldn't tell her no, so he kissed her on the nose and smiled. "Of course." Standing, he walked into the kitchen as Soren watched with pure glee. Shooting his friend a death stare, he started breakfast.

"Hyphen said you've been friends forever."

"We have. How many years, Has?"

Hyphen turned around to see his two favorite people staring back at him. Fellowship was luminous, and his friend looked completely relaxed around her, which was an added bonus. "Around one seventy-five—give or take."

She shook her head. "I'll never get used to hearing numbers like that. What was he like back then?"

"Pretty much the same as he is now save for the muscles and tattoos," Soren mused.

"He said he was tall and skinny."

"He was, but to be fair, it was years before he grew into his height. Did he tell you about the summer I took him under my proverbial wing?"

"Yes, which was very sweet of you by the way."

"Thank you. Did he mention that was the summer of his growth spurt?"

Asshole. Hyphen whipped around, shooting daggers at his best friend, who ignored him.

"No," she said, looking at him, then back to Soren.

"So—"

"Don't you fucking dare," Hyphen threatened. Soren looked at him with his impish grin, giving extra imp.

"Tell me," Fellowship said, practically bouncing on her seat. Catching his eye, she smiled. *I wanna know.*

It's fucking embarrassing—

"Don't burn our breakfast," Soren playfully chastised.

Turning around, he tended to their eggs and sausage as Soren began his tale.

"I invited him to the end-of-summer bonfire. He'd grown significantly taller since we started hanging out earlier that year. When we met up, I froze. Not fully aware of how much he'd grown—since Aechaih don't experience growing pains—he wore a pair of his regular pants, made for five-foot-ten Hyphen, not six-foot-three Hyphen."

"No," she laughed.

Fuck his life. Hyphen plated their food and turned around. He snarled, practically throwing Soren's plate at him. Then, with a smile, he placed Fellowship's plate down in front of her. He grabbed three glasses and filled them with juice.

"My sad, little awkward friend's pants were well above his ankles," Soren said, shoveling food into his mouth. "Not to mention his wrinkled shirt was *tucked in*."

"I bet he was so cute," Fellowship sang, her voice soothings his embarrassment.

"He was. Obviously, he got it together as he bulked up and found some style," Soren admitted.

"He said something else happened after he bulked up," she replied.

Soren looked at Hyphen, raising an eyebrow. Hyphen shrugged in response. The truth was, he'd never told anyone about their antics when they were young, so the fact that she knew meant something.

"We had a few run-ins, no big deal," Soren said offhandedly.

Hyphen handed them their glasses of juice, took his breakfast, and sat down, sandwiching Fellowship between himself and his best friend.

"A two-person gang sounds like a big deal to me," she said with that sassy tone he loved.

Soren choked and grabbed his juice to wash it down, his face turning red. "Well, we—"

"Tell her the truth, Syx," Hyphen said around a mouthful of food. "Otherwise, she'll use her *occupational superpower* on you." Fellowship turned to him and beamed; he responded with a wink.

"Okay, I'll admit that we sought revenge on our bullies," Soren said. "But we weren't wild and reckless with it; we took a strategic approach."

"Meaning?"

"We handled business away from prying eyes," Soren explained.

"In the shadows," Hyphen added.

She looked back and forth between the two of them. Then, after a beat, she nodded. "I see."

"After we established power, Hudson had to sit us down and tell us to knock it off," Soren said laughing.

"He was like, what the fuck is wrong with you two? The bullied are now the bullies? What the fuck?" Hyphen said in a parental tone followed by a laugh. "He was grateful that I'd found a friend, but he was also worried that we'd turn into crime lords or something."

"To be fair, we were on our way," Soren agreed.

"Is Syx your gang nickname?" she asked.

"No, it's a family nickname."

Hyphen could tell his friend was weighing whether or not to divulge the backstory of his nickname.

After a few beats, he continued. "My mom had five miscarriages before I was born."

Fellowship sucked in a breath and placed her hand on Soren's arm. "Oh, no."

Soren looked at her and smiled. "When she was pregnant with me, she didn't tell my dad for the first month or so. Instead, she talked to me all day and night, making it a point to celebrate every day she carried me. When I was born, I was their lucky number six," he said.

"Oh, that's. Wow. Your mom sounds like a wonderful woman. Thank you for sharing that with me, Soren," she said softly.

"Thank you for listening."

"Syx and Has," she said, lightening the mood. "A two-man gang of adorable trouble."

"Has is the brother I never had," Soren said.

The admission warmed Hyphen's heart. They *were* brothers. Always had been. Always will be.

"Since you're an enthusiastic audience, Fellowship," Soren continued. "I'll admit that I was the first to know he was totally gone for you," he declared, nodding to Hyphen.

Hyphen's fork stopped mid-air. "What are you talking about?"

Fellowship smiled at him, then returned to Soren. "How'd you know?"

"Well," Soren said, wiping his mouth with a napkin, "he flew you to Septain."

Hyphen relaxed. That was an obvious tell. He thought his friend had *real* dirt.

"Then there was the Sylena Lunar Ball."

Hyphen froze.

"I didn't realize you were there," she said.

"I saw him talking to you and Ambassador Dancy. He looked like he was about to be sick. That's when I realized he was smitten."

This motherfucker never told him that he saw them talking, let alone that he looked *smitten.*

"Smitten?" she asked, turning to him with the biggest smile.

He rolled his eyes at Soren, then looked at Fellowship. "Soren's kidding, baby. I don't *smit.*"

Something flashed across her face before she gently placed her hand on his knee. Arching an eyebrow, she tilted her head in that I-know-you're-fucking-lying way of hers. "You don't?"

His lower body was on fire. He could *not* get a hard-on in front of his Solneur-damned best friend. "Fell..." he warned.

Looking at him from under her lashes, she threw him that sexy smolder before sliding her hand higher. She licked her lips. *Guardians.* This woman would be the end of him.

"Okay, I was *fucking smitten,*" he admitted over Soren's laugh.

"I love that you noticed, Soren."

"How could I not? I'd never seen him like that before," he said, tone suddenly serious.

"Oh," she breathed.

"I know most guys say something like that to their best friend's girl, but I'm not bullshitting you," Soren said, nodding.

Fellowship turned to Hyphen and stole his breath. If he didn't know any better, he'd say her eyes were wide with *love.* Without a word, she leaned forward and kissed him. Pulling away, she gave him a mega-watt smile that melted his insides.

"I like you, Soren," she said, returning to his friend.

"I like you too, Fellowship," he replied. "I'm glad we found you."

"*We?*" she asked, amused.

"He's a package deal: two for the price of one," Soren said with a confident nod.

"Don't forget the twins," Hyphen added.

"Right! *Four* for the price of one," Soren corrected.

"I'd have it no other way, Syon."

Hyphen glanced at Soren, who gave him an acknowledging nod. His heart swelled so big that if he didn't hold onto something, he'd float away on affection for his girlfriend and deep gratitude for his best friend.

Hyphen stepped into the elevator to his penthouse, feeling the weight of a long workday compounded by Weeden's last-minute meeting. Just before leaving, Fellowship had sneaked a kiss on his cheek and told him she'd see him at home. *Home.* It was the first time she'd used that word in the five days she'd been staying at his place, and it had been enough to get him through the meeting and Seacrest traffic.

Their time together flowed as seamlessly as it was sexy. They fell into an easy rhythm, as if they'd always lived together. He knew she was smart, but their uninterrupted conversations on various topics kept his mind buzzing and his dick hard. Every morning, they worked out—running, lifting weights, or sometimes both. Afterward, they showered together, and seeing her wet and soapy became one of the many highlights of his day. He'd cook breakfast while she read the newspaper aloud, and then they'd eat and clean the kitchen together. With her products in his bathroom and clothes in his closet, she had brought such warmth to his life that he wondered how he'd ever lived so long without her.

The elevator door opened, and he was met with the smell of dinner and animated chatter. He stopped short as soon as he rounded the corner. There she was—no, there *they* were—all piled in his kitchen, moving around like they'd done it a million times before. Fellowship, Haze, and Harleigh were making dinner. Fellowship had changed into one of his sweaters and her black leggings. She was sipping a glass of wine and stirring something on the stove. Haze had her back to him, chopping, while Harleigh sat on the counter, legs swinging. The sight was more than his heart could take—

"Brother!" Harleigh yelled, hopping down. Fellowship turned around and smiled just as Harleigh accosted him with one of her bony hugs. She kept her arms around his neck as he entered the kitchen.

"Hey, Brother," Haze said over her shoulder.

Fellowship turned down the stove and grabbed his eyes. *Hope this is okay*, she said, easing into his mind.

It's better than okay. It's perfect.

She smiled and gave him a kiss on the cheek. It was intimate yet appropriate, given that it was their first display of affection in front of his sisters. The twins watched with smiles as bright as Sylena on a clear Trianah night.

"C'mon, let's set the table," Haze said to Harleigh, shoving a stack of plates into her hands. As they meandered to the dining area, he loosened his tie and wrapped his arms around Fellowship who had returned to the stove.

"They called as soon as I left the precinct, asking if I wanted to have dinner. I told them that I was heading to your place, and they immediately suggested we cook for you."

His face was buried in her neck. "I'm so happy you're here. All of you," he said.

She turned around, dark chocolate eyes on his. Her face was scrubbed clean, diamond studs sparkling. She looked young, bright, and happy.

"Me too," she said.

He couldn't help himself. Leaning down, he pressed his lips to hers. Instantly, her arms wrapped around his neck, and all his remaining stress melted away in her embrace.

"How was the meeting?" she asked after pulling away.

"Could've been an email," he replied, grabbing her wine and taking a sip.

She laughed. "I'm glad you're home."

At that moment, he nearly confessed his love but instead, knocked back her wine. "Me too, baby," he said, once he was sure he wouldn't reveal his heart.

"Hyphen, tell Harleigh that I walked before she did," Haze demanded from the dining area.

Both he and Fellowship turned their attention to the twins. He had no idea what prompted this discussion, but he was happy to intervene. "You walked first," he confirmed.

"See!" Haze said over Harleigh's frown.

"That doesn't mean anything. There are plenty of things I've done before you," Harleigh said with a haughty tilt of her head.

"Like *what?*" Hyphen asked, suddenly interested in their spat. Both looked at him, blue eyes wide with guilt.

"I mean..." Harleigh sputtered.

"Nothing crazy, like..." Haze added, trying to save her twin.

"I'm sure she meant learning to ride a bike or wearing makeup first," Fellowship said, casually bailing them out. The girls looked at her in admiration, then back at him, sheepish.

"Humph," he grunted. Fellowship laughed as he refreshed her wine. "Better be," he mumbled.

She slipped in his mind. *They grow up fast.*

Too fast, he responded. *I can't imagine them dating. Or...* He couldn't finish the sentence.

Fellowship gave him a soft-lipped kiss. *Go get changed. Dinner's almost done.*

He planted another kiss on her cheek and watched the twins with a sense of awe before heading to his bedroom. Seeing them in his space was a new and cherished experience. They never spent time with Bronwyn; their visits had always been limited to when she wasn't around. But now, with breakfast alongside Soren the other morning and dinner with the girls, it was impossible not to feel the profound shift that Fellowship had brought into his life. Her presence had woven a thread of togetherness he'd never known before, and it was impossible to ignore how deeply it touched him.

Fellowship never imagined she'd stay with a man, yet here she was, washing her face in Hyphen's enormous bathroom before bed. The change in her life was almost surreal. After their delightful dinner with the twins, they'd strolled through his neighborhood, stopped for ice cream, and then spent hours talking at home. Living and working together had turned out to be easier than she'd expected. True, they still drove separate cars to the precinct and maintained a professional distance in front of co-workers, but when they were alone, their bond was undeniable. They finished each other's sentences and flowed seamlessly in and out of men-com like seasoned pros. Truth be told, it was becoming increasingly difficult to remember a time when Hyphen wasn't a part of her life.

Once out of the bathroom, she stopped short. There he was in bed, hair mussed, shirtless, and *reading*. If that wasn't the sexiest shit she'd ever seen, she didn't know what was.

After a beat, he looked up. "What?"

"You know what," she said, walking across the room. She slid under the covers next to him as he snapped his book shut and placed it on the nightstand. She couldn't help snuggling close—she was addicted to his heat and smell. Arms around him, she buried her face in his neck, inhaling like a crazy person. "You smell so *good*, Solneur," she said, her voice muffled. His strong hands stroked her back, sliding up her t-shirt. She took another whiff. "You don't even have to wear cologne."

He laughed. "I'm glad you like it."

She lifted her head. "But really, I understand the seacoast. I assume the Haslem estate is by the sea, right?"

"Yes."

"What about the lavender? Is this a gift from the Guardians, or is there a reason for it?"

He smiled. "There's a reason."

"Tell me."

He paused, a mixture of emotions dancing across his face. "When I was a baby, I couldn't sleep at night. Hudson tried everything, but I'd just scream and scream. One night, he took me to our garden and walked around with me as I cried. Finally, he sat by our row of lavender, and after a few minutes, I stopped crying and fell asleep. He thought it was a fluke, so he took me to the same spot the next night, and it worked. From then on, he made sure lavender was always in my room. I never had trouble sleeping again."

It wasn't what she had expected. The story was so sweet, all she could do was press her lips to his. The more he shared about his life, his past, the more she adored him.

She shook her head. "You never cease to surprise me, Haslem."

"What do you mean?"

"All my life, I thought Aechaih were shallow, privileged snobs. Then I met the most grounded and sincere Aechaih ever. You're this beautiful being—physically beautiful," she said as he blushed. "With so much hidden deep within, such kindness and care. I bet people don't know how wonderful you truly are."

He shrugged. "No, but that's because I don't let them in."

"Why'd you let me in?" she asked, her voice barely above a whisper.

"I didn't have a choice. As soon as I saw you, I wanted to be next to you."

"*Hyphen*," she sighed.

"I can't lie to you, Fellowship. You know that."

Yes, she knew. "It'll do your heart good to know that I can't lie to you either."

"No?" he asked with a twinkle in his eye. "Then why'd you give *me* a chance?"

She bit her lower lip. It was a culmination of things, but she wasn't sure how to articulate it.

"You don't have to answer," he said, squeezing her hip.

After a moment, she gathered her thoughts. "The fact that you're Aechaih takes a backseat to how I feel when I'm with you. I've never felt so...*connected* to another person. I feel your energy before you walk into a room. I feel your eyes on me. Even if we don't men-com, I feel like I know what you're thinking. It's such a unique experience, and because I have nothing to compare it to, I figure it must be real."

"It's definitely real," he said softly.

"You think?"

"I know."

"How are you so sure?"

He took a moment to think as his large hand slid up her side. "Everything's better when you're around."

The man was singular in his honesty. Heart racing, she kissed him. It was open-mouthed and intentional, energized yet languid. She was falling—falling, falling, falling in love with a beautiful Aechaih.

"Thank you for having dinner with the twins," he said.

"Thank you for having *me*. Period. The way you've let me in your life," she stopped as a lump took shape in her throat. Tears burned behind her eyelids. She'd spent so much of her life alone—isolated, with work as her only companion. Then, out of nowhere, she reconnected with her grandfather and became part of the Haslem family. "You know what I mean," she said, recovering.

"Fell, having you here is the easiest thing I've ever done. It's where you belong."

She didn't know what to say, let alone how to express it. Instead, she gently explored his face with her fingers—tracing his soft eyebrows, smooth skin with its hint of stubble, and his plush lips and strong jawline. Hyphen closed his eyes as she memorized every detail of his face, her touch conveying a depth of feeling that words couldn't capture.